"ARE YOU SPYING ON US?"

At the sound of the boy's voice Rachel was gripped by a chilling paralysis. She had often read of blood freezing in the veins; now she was experiencing this phenomenon for herself. She had been found out, revealed as that worst of creatures—a sneak, a peeping Tom. The shame of it was unendurable. She felt quite sick, unable to breathe or move. She wanted to die—quickly, that minute, no hanging about.

She had immediately recognised the voice that had challenged her. It belonged to the younger boy, the one they called Barney, which wasn't quite as bad as if she had been discovered by his sister Diana, or Gavin, the big boy; but even so it was something she had dreaded ever since finding the loose brick in the wall that, once removed, had provided such an enchanting window on life next door. Perhaps, she thought, if she kept very, very still . . .

CHARMED CIRCLE

BARBARA WHITNELL

St. Martin's Paperbacks

First published in Great Britain by Hodder and Stoughton Ltd.

CHARMED CIRCLE

Library of Congress Catalog Card Number: 93-33527

ISBN: 0-312-96512-5

Printed in the United States of America

St. Martin's Press hardcover edition / January 1994
St. Martin's Paperbacks edition / September 1998

St. Martin's Paperbacks are published by St. Martin's Press, 175 Fifth Avenue, New York, NY 10010.

10 9 8 7 6 5 4 3 2 1

To Brenda
best of sisters, best of friends

Introduction by
Rosamunde Pilcher

This is a book about wartime in Britain, but also a sort of Cinderella story, which invariably holds much charm. As well, it depicts a glamorous, Bohemian but self-absorbed family, the Rossiters. They accept the humble Rachel into their home, and yet never totally make her one of their charmed circle.

Which is, perhaps, just as well, for theirs is hidden and unguessed-at darkness lying beneath the shining surface of their enviable life-style.

Despite their influence upon her, Rachel finds her own strengths, and as the story unfolds, so her own personality develops. So that by the end, we find her very much her own person, capable of dealing with her own problems, and forging, without the Rossiters, the framework of her own life, and her eventual happiness.

If you like to remember, and to be taken back in time, then this is the book for you.

Rosamunde Pilcher

ONE

Suppose Barney had come on any other day? Suppose it had been one of those awful days when a teething Tess had kept her up all night and her head felt as if it were stuffed with cotton wool, not an original idea in sight? Could she then have presented him with quite such a brave and independent front?

Probably not, Rachel thought; but it so happened she was walking on air that day, despite the fact that it had proved one of those maddening mornings that had, for once, begun with the promise of real summer, only to collapse limply under a blanket of cloud, like some pathetic convalescent testing his strength too far.

Ignoring all warning signs, she had spurned Nancy's prudent urging towards cardigans and umbrellas, and had left home in her one decent dress of navy-blue linen with a red and white dotted silk scarf at the neck, the knotting of which had caused her considerable time and trouble. For once she had felt pleased with the overall effect. It was a day, she told Nancy, for ermine and pearls. And bathing in ass's milk. What it was emphatically *not* was a cardigan sort of day.

"You'll be sor-ry," Nancy had sung out as she left home; but though she was undeniably cold, she wasn't sorry. Nothing could spoil this marvellous day—not the weather, or the crowds, or even the drabness of the London streets, still showing signs of wartime austerity even though the war itself had been over for more than a year.

Better times were coming—for her, for the country. Never mind the goose pimples, she said to herself as she strode up Piccadilly towards Green Park tube station with her head up, biting her lip to hide the exultant grin she was powerless to subdue altogether. Never mind the fact that a casual glimpse at her reflection in a shop window had shown her that the scarf had taken on a life of its own and was now sticking up in two points like rabbits' ears in a wholly unsuitable position somewhere below her left ear. She was above such petty considerations. Indomitable, that's what she was. Capable. Self-sufficient.

Had one small success really achieved all this? One swallow doesn't make a summer, she warned herself, rather as Grandma might have done—Grandma who could never bring herself to forswear the pleasure of pricking her bubble of happiness. Or anyone else's, for that matter.

Oh, *pooh* to Grandma! She had a right to exult. This, after all, was the day when all her childhood dreams had become reality. This was the day when she had signed the contract that had turned her into a real, live author. No frog, transformed by a kiss into a handsome prince, could possibly have felt more elated.

There had, after all, been disappointments in plenty. Times when, sunk in despondency, she had been quite certain that she had no talent at all, no fresh ideas, nothing to offer; days, in short, when the future was too frightening to contemplate. No doubt there would be more, but at this moment she was undismayed by the thought of them. This was the day that hope was born; no, not hope. Certainty. They would be all right, she and Tess. As people said with irritating frequency during the war, they could take it.

Thus it was in buoyant mood that she hurried along, oblivious of the rain that, having threatened for the past few hours, was now beginning in earnest. What did getting wet matter? Or being jostled by the milling throng in the station? She had intended to come home earlier, but had found much to talk about with Graham, her newly appointed agent, and now had struck the beginning of the rush hour.

Anxiously she looked at her watch. Tess was all right with Nancy, she knew that, and there was a bottle made up for her, but she had promised to be back for the six o'clock feed. The last thing she wanted was to appear to be taking Nancy's good nature for granted; heaven alone knew she did enough! She paid an acceptable amount of rent for her room, but because she worked odd hours at the BBC was often free and always willing to look after Tess in an emergency. In addition, she nearly always cooked the evening meal. She enjoyed cooking, she said, and it was more satisfying to cook for two than for one—not to mention the advantage gained by having two lots of rations to play with. And because she had a talent for making a little go an appetisingly long way, Rachel could see the force of her argument. Nevertheless, she was aware of the need to tread carefully.

It was still drizzling when she left the train at Hammersmith, but fortunately Inverness Street was no more than a five minutes' dash from the station. Number 14, which Rachel had bought with the money left to her by her grandmother, was in the middle of a yellow-brick terrace, bay windows to the ground and first floors. Identical houses stretched to the right and left, as far as the eye could see, except for a gap towards the end of the street caused by a doodlebug. You could still see the remains of pink nursery paper on an exposed wall and the place where a staircase was once fixed to it.

Rachel never walked past that gap unless she couldn't possibly avoid it. Bomb damage was still everywhere in London, grown over for the most part with rosebay willowherb. She had learned not to notice it, but somehow this was different; perhaps it was the wallpaper, and the fact that it was so near home.

As she opened the door the savoury smell from the kitchen wafted towards her and her stomach churned with hunger. There was no sound from Tess; no sound, even, from Nancy, which was unusual. She was given to singing about the house: opera, music-hall ditties, the latest hits—anything. But now there was only silence.

"Hallo, I'm home," Rachel called, as she squeezed past the pram that occupied most of the hall space. "And you were absolutely right about the weather. I'm freezing!"

She followed the smell through to the kitchen. Nancy was stirring something on the stove. She turned as Rachel came in, and at once it became clear that something unusual and of great import had occurred. Nancy had one of those sort of faces. Her joys were more joyful; her tragedies soul-searing; her laughter the very essence of amusement. Now she was registering suppressed excitement and an all-consuming curiosity, her small, sallow-skinned face positively vibrating with the momentousness of the situation.

She cut short Rachel's apology for her late arrival with a wave of the cooking spoon.

"There's someone to see you," she hissed. "A man!"

"Man?" Rachel was startled, almost as if Nancy had mentioned a hitherto unknown species. She glanced down the hall towards the front room, to where her visitor presumably sat in cheerless isolation. "Who, for heaven's sake?"

Nancy opened her dark eyes wide and sucked in her cheeks. "Guess!" she said.

"*Who?*"

At the sight of her face, Nancy relented. "Barney Rossiter," she mouthed, in an exaggerated, lip-stretching way. "I didn't know what to do with him," she went on, only slightly more audibly. "I didn't want to bring him in here because of all the nappies drying. He might have guessed—"

"What do you suppose he thought when he saw the pram in the hall?" For a moment Rachel looked panic-stricken; then she shrugged her shoulders. "Oh, who cares! Let him think what he likes, he's getting nothing out of me. Where is Tess, anyway?"

"Still asleep. I thought it better to leave her. The later the last feed, the longer she'll sleep tonight and the more peace you'll have. I'll see to her when she wakes up. Go on," Nancy added, making a shooing motion with the cooking spoon as Rachel still clung to the doorpost as if in need of support.

Barney. Here.

The best of the bunch, certainly. But she hadn't wanted to see him again. What should she say? How should she handle it? She wasn't ready. She needed more time.

"At least you've got some good news to tell him," Nancy added, turning back to the pan on the stove.

Yes, of course. The book! She had good news. You're strong, she reminded herself. Successful. Indomitable. She stood a little straighter.

There was no mirror downstairs. Well, it didn't matter. She didn't care what Barney thought, did she? Still, she fluffed out her hair with her fingers, smoothed her skirt and tugged at the scarf before taking a deep breath and making for the front room.

He was not, after all, sitting. He stood by the bookcase, studying the titles on the shelves, his back towards the door. The sound of her entrance was masked by that of a car revving up in the street outside. She looked at him silently for a moment, gathering her resources. It was going to be even more difficult than she had imagined.

The best of the lot, she thought again. There had always been a bond between them. She'd even fooled herself into believing that she could love him once, a long time ago. Perhaps she could have done. Perhaps she might yet. Seeing his familiar blond head, the way the hair grew on the nape of his neck, she was conscious of a deep well of affection for him. They might have been happy. If only—

But he'd *known*! Remembrance and pain and common sense came rushing in like shock troops to save her from vain regrets. He'd known—or at least suspected—and said nothing! How could she ever forget that, or forget where his loyalties would lie if ever there was another show-down? Besides, there was Tess. If ever anyone was off limits, then Barney Rossiter was the one.

But when, sensing her presence, he swung round to look at her and she caught the full force of those blazing blue eyes, she reached out blindly to hold the back of a chair, so desperately did she need something to cling to.

"Hallo, Rachel," he said softly. His small, fine-boned face with the high-bridged nose and thin mouth was just as she remembered, but his smile seemed more tentative. "Should I have thrown my hat in first?" he went on as she continued to stare at him blankly.

With an effort she pulled herself together.

"Barney! What a surprise! It's wonderful to see you."

"You're sure?"

"Of course. Why shouldn't it be?"

He gave a brief, incredulous laugh. "I don't need to tell you—"

"It wasn't really your fault."

"You've forgiven me, then?"

Suddenly the awkwardness was gone and there was only delight. She crossed the room towards him, hands outstretched. "Oh Barney, of course I have! You were on my side. I knew that, really, and it's so good to see you—it's been ages—''

"And whose fault is that? I thought you were lost and gone for ever. Sunk without trace! No one's heard a word from you since—since heaven knows when. How are you, Rachel?''

"Fine! And you? Are you out of the Army?''

"Oh, for three months now.''

They stood with hands joined, smiling at each other. Was he as conscious as she of the overwhelming weight of all that had happened, she wondered? What could she say? Where did they begin?

She turned from him, struck suddenly by the unwelcoming atmosphere of the largely unused room. It never caught the sun at the best of times. Now, with the rain pattering against the windowpane it seemed utterly cheerless.

"August!'' she said bitterly. "Summers used not to be like this—''

"When you were a gel?'' Barney laughed. "You sound like Ma. She says it's the bomb that's upset the weather.''

"Maybe she's right.'' Awkwardness again. Rachel hugged herself against the cold. "To hell with austerity, I'm going to light the fire,'' she said. "Dammit, no matches—'' Without a word he proffered his cigarette lighter, an amused twist to his mouth as if such unpreparedness was no more than he might have expected. As if it brought back memories.

"What are you doing with a lighter, anyway?'' she said as she crouched down. "You used not to smoke.''

"Well, I do now.''

He would have changed in other ways as well. Foolish to think that he wouldn't.

"There, that's better,'' she said, standing up straight and smiling at him once again. "Do sit down, Barney. I ought to get you something. Tea? I'd offer something stronger if I had it—''

"Do shut up,'' he said, not sitting down. Rachel was aware suddenly of the pounding of her heart. He looked at her, those startling eyes unreadable. "Are you really glad to see me?'' he asked her.

"Of course!'' She reached out towards him once more and suddenly was in his arms and they were hugging each other just as if nothing had happened and there were no shadows between them. Just as if there were no Tess, no Gavin, no Diana.

But that was an illusion, Rachel reminded herself. There were shadows in plenty. And Tess was more than a shadow. Tess was a three-dimensional reality, and the most important thing in her life. Gently she extricated herself from Barney's embrace. The danger signals in her head were flashing too insistently to be ignored.

"You might as well sit," she said.

He settled himself into the chair she indicated and crossed his knees, still regarding her thoughtfully. By the time she had arranged herself in the chair opposite, she had achieved a degree of calmness. Friendly but uninvolved delight was the order of the day, she warned herself.

"Now tell me how you tracked me down," she said.

"Your aunt told me," he said. "Mrs. Courtney, isn't it? Sylvia Courtney. She came to Warnfield last week."

"Why would she do that? She hardly ever came when Grandma was alive. Oh, of course—I remember now. She asked your mother to keep some things from The Laurels for her, didn't she?"

"That's right. She wrote to Ma when The Laurels was sold and asked us to keep those blue ceramic pots for her, the ones that were in the porch, and a couple of prints. She said she'd collect them later. That's why she came last week. She stayed for tea and told us about you."

"Dear Sylvia!"

"She said she only found out herself that you were in London a couple of weeks back."

"I know. I ran into her in Jermyn Street outside the cheese shop. I was on my way to the London Library."

"*Why*, Rachel?"

"I wanted to check some facts about Women's Suffrage—"

"Don't be an idiot! I mean why the secrecy?"

As if on cue, Tess began to cry—great, whooping yells which meant that she had woken, she was hungry, and furthermore thoroughly outraged that six o'clock was upon her and not a bottle in sight.

Rachel was fully aware that having a baby who slept from three to six most days seemed, to most people, not only eccentric but possibly immoral as well; but it was a routine that suited

her way of life perfectly—and since it was Tess herself who
had imposed it, she could only assume it suited her, too. It meant
that she would be awake and lively until Rachel went to bed,
when she would then—teething apart—sleep soundly all night
until well after eight in the morning. As Rachel had little social
life and worked as much as possible during the day, the evenings
she spent with her small daughter were precious to her, and
unbroken nights equally so.

There was a loud and reassuring cry from Nancy and the
thump of footsteps running up the stairs.

"Coming, my darling. Hush, my sweetheart—"

"Who is that woman?" Barney asked.

"That's Nancy. A friend. She rents a room upstairs."

He pulled a face. "Bit of a bind, surely, having a tenant with
a kid? Odd-looking woman. She's awfully dark, isn't she?
Touch of the tarbrush, I imagine."

Rachel welcomed the spurt of anger this caused. She didn't
want to remember the good things about him—would rather
think of his arrogance. It proved he was still a Rossiter, still felt
superior to the rest of the world, still judged people by crude,
Rossiter standards.

"I've always considered that such an offensive figure of
speech," she said coldly.

"Sorry!" He lifted his hands as if in supplication and raised
his eyes to heaven. "I didn't mean anything derogatory."

And if you believe that, Rachel thought silently, you'll believe
anything.

"Nancy's a friend in a million," she said.

She didn't elaborate. How could she begin to describe the
times that Nancy had been her rock and anchor and guiding
star? She it was who had comforted her in bad times and re-
joiced in the good. She had visited her in the maternity ward at
Tess's birth, and taken her share of walking the floor in those
early days when feeding problems had reduced Rachel to a
worn-out wreck. Together they had laughed and cried; but
mostly they had laughed, for Nancy was blissfully, delightfully,
irrepressibly funny.

"Is there a husband?" Barney asked. "Oh dear," he went
on, as Rachel shook her head. "A Fallen Woman! Ma was very
involved in Fallen Women at one time, when we were very

small. Lannie and I used to imagine them littering the High Street.''

Rachel's smile was barely discernible, and Barney grimaced once more.

"Sorry," he said. "There I go, putting my big foot in it again. But don't you mind having a yelling kid in the house? She's damn lucky to find someone so amenable.''

"I don't mind. She doesn't yell much." Rachel looked away from him and smiled vaguely in the direction of the popping fire.

She had told no one from her old life about Tess, and she was certainly not going to begin with Barney Rossiter. Only Nancy knew all the facts. She hadn't told Sylvia, her father's only sister, when she had run into her in Jermyn Street. She hadn't even told her parents who were far away in Africa, where they had been throughout the entire war.

They would have to know one day, of course. They would be home on leave before too long, as soon as passages became available, but until then it had seemed utterly pointless to agitate them by announcing the arrival of an illegitimate grandchild, or run the risk of their total rejection.

Undoubtedly, had they been in the country, they would have urged adoption—but now, by the time they knew of the matter, Tess would be far too old for there to be any question of such a thing. And if, in fact, they did reject her—

No. She still didn't want to think about that.

So she had kept her secret, and bought the house. Nancy and she had been good friends during the war, on a bleak RAF station in Scotland. It had seemed heaven-sent when Nancy was offered a translator's job by the BBC, and let it be known that she was looking for accommodation in London. Barney's guess had been right, even though she had disliked his turn of phrase. Nancy's maternal grandfather originated from Ceylon and had made sure that she spoke Tamil, even though she had lived in England all her life.

Freelance writing had kept the wolf from Rachel's door. She had attended a local clinic, pretending not to notice the sneering glances at her ringless fingers, and had written chatty, superficial letters to her mother and father; and not once had she mentioned Tess.

"Barney, you'll never guess—such a wonderful thing has happened to me." She turned to him now, full of eagerness. "I've written a novel and it's been accepted. There! What do you think of that? I signed the contract this very day—not a bad advance, either. It'll keep me until I finish the next one. Isn't it terrific? Didn't I always say I would?"

She leaned forward, vivacious and beguiling, reminding herself of nothing more than the bird who trails a broken wing to distract the predator away from her brood. She was trailing her excitement, her small success, and it had the desired result. The baby upstairs was forgotten.

"Rachel, that's *wonderful*!" He looked genuinely delighted on her behalf. His smile, the way his face lit up, was as appealing as ever and she was surprised by a sudden pang of longing. She had been lonely, it seemed in that moment, for a long, long time. It would be so easy to turn to him, to capitulate. But she mustn't—she mustn't!

He reached for her hands and held them tightly in his.

"I knew you'd make it! This calls for a celebration. You'll have dinner with me, won't you?"

Rachel withdrew her hands and smiled at him nervously.

"I can't, Barney."

"Why on earth not?"

"I have to work."

"Oh, come on, now—"

"Besides, Nancy's cooked supper and she'd die if it went to waste. I'd ask you to stay, but—"

"I wouldn't dream of it."

He was hurt; and who could blame him? Somehow she and Nancy could have made the meal go round, if the will had been there. Fleetingly she remembered the lavish, casual hospitality of the Rossiters before the war and wondered if rationing had affected them in the same way as everyone else. It was hard to imagine, somehow.

Barney didn't argue any more, but looked at her, faintly puzzled.

"Tell me about you," she said hastily. "What are you doing with yourself?"

He gave a small, self-deprecating laugh.

"Not very much," he said. "Casting around, mostly."

"Are you going back to Art School?"

He laughed again.

"No, I'm not. You know damned well I was never any good. I only went because Ma wanted it so much. Somehow she managed to convince me I had some talent, but it was wishful thinking, nothing more. She was so desperate for one of us to take after her."

— "You did some good things. I loved that picture you painted for me. I've still got it somewhere."

"Kid's stuff! No, I never had what it takes."

"So what are you going to do?"

He sighed. "Remember Guy Seamark? He's really keen on antiques. His house was always stuffed with them—I suppose he grew up knowing a fake Chippendale or Hepplewhite or whatever from the genuine article. Anyway, he wants to open a shop—"

"In Warnfield?"

"No, no. In Yorkshire. He got married during the war to a girl from Huddersfield. A nice kid, really. She was a Wren. Very pretty. But—well, his parents didn't go for it at all. I suppose you can understand it. Her accent's pretty ghastly. They gave him an ultimatum—her or them. He chose her, so they've sort of cut him off."

Rachel stared at him, disbelieving.

"Go on," she said.

"Well, Guy wants me to go in with him. I mean, I may not be much of an artist but I know a bit about painters—"

"It sounds as if it might be fun, Barney."

He sighed again.

"Ma's dead agin it. She says Guy's unreliable—"

"Unreliable? What about all those years of dogged devotion to Diana?"

"Yes, well, that's different, I suppose. She says his judgment can't be relied on—I mean, marrying a girl like that."

"With a Yorkshire accent? Is that really all they've got against her?"

"She simply isn't their sort, Rachel. Her father's a platelayer on the railway and her mother works in a textile factory. She left school at fourteen. Honestly, the war's got a lot to answer for."

"D'you know," Rachel said, after a short pause. "I didn't vote Labour at the last election because I was so pro-Churchill; but you make me feel I wish I had."

"Oh, God!" Barney laughed and ran his fingers through his hair. "Don't get on your political high horse again. You know what sort of trouble that gets us into."

There was a second's pause as they both remembered.

"Anyway," Barney said, hurrying on to cover the awkward moment, "whatever the rights or wrongs of it, Guy's living up in a place called Holmfirth which he says is lovely, and he wants me to go up there too and put my little bit of gratuity in with his. Neither of us have got much. His people won't lift a finger, even though they could, and mine have never had a lot to spare. Of course," he went on, "it's the going so far away that Ma doesn't like, just as much as the precariousness of the whole thing. She's got me an interview with a shipping firm in the city. That's why I'm here. I've been there today."

"And?" she prompted.

"Well, I think the job is mine if I want it. It's not wildly exciting, but it's got good prospects. And of course, I could live at home until I'm able to afford something else."

"Lovely," Rachel said ironically. "You could wear a bowler hat and striped trousers and catch the 8:15 from Warnfield with all the other zombies. My grandfather did it for years."

"Well, it's a living. A good one, actually. We can't all be creative, you know."

"Talking of which," Rachel said. "How's Alannah?"

"Fine. She's finished her stint with ENSA, and she's at home at the moment. Resting, they call it. Actually, she's not resting at all, but dashing around the place trying to get a job in some new scheme for taking theatre to the masses. Diana's getting married in a couple of months. A doctor. A brilliant chap, a wonderful GP. Ma saw him first and kind of homed in on him."

"He can't have stood a chance."

"He didn't need much encouragement, once he saw Di. He dotes on her."

"How nice."

"Oh, come *on*, Rachel," he said awkwardly. "Forgive and forget. He's asked me to be his best man and Alannah's to be bridesmaid. You must come—well, perhaps not," he finished, seeing her expression.

"Thanks for the thought, at least, but I don't think so, do you? What about your love life?" Rachel asked recklessly, "Are you married or engaged or anything?"

"No, not anything. At least—" His smile was tentative, his eyes watchful. He leaned towards her. "Rachel—"

"I've just remembered," she interrupted, jumping to her feet. "We do have about two inches of sherry left in the kitchen. We really ought to drink a toast."

To what? she asked herself as she bustled out to the kitchen for bottle and glasses. Nancy raised questioning eyebrows almost to her hairline, giving every evidence of a curiosity beyond bearing, but Rachel merely wrinkled her nose teasingly and kissed Tess's cheek in passing.

What kind of a toast would be appropriate? To the past? To the future? But there was no future. No Barney-and-Rachel future, anyway, though judging from the look in Barney's eyes, he still cherished hopes. Unbelievably.

"You ought to find a nice girl," she said on her return to the front room, dividing the sherry between the two glasses.

"Don't be so bloody patronising!"

"Nothing like the love of a good woman to steady a man." Relentlessly jolly, she held out the two glasses towards him. "There—I pour, you choose." It was an echo of childish days—days of ginger pop and lemonade and Tizer. He grinned in recognition of it.

"Rachel—" he began again.

"Cheers!" She lifted her glass towards him. "Here's to my future as a bestselling author and yours as a successful entrepreneur, and may we both prosper mightily. Tell me, what happened to Daphne? Daphne Baker?"

"Daphne?" He looked a little taken aback. "She's still around. As a matter of fact—" he paused, embarrassed.

"As a matter of fact what?"

"I'm taking her to some Municipal dance thing next Saturday. Ma's throwing a sort of party first, so there'll be a crowd of us going."

"Well, that's good." Rachel smiled at him widely. "You

could do a lot worse than Daphne Baker. She always had a soft spot for you, you know.''

''Dammit, I'm only taking her to a dance!''

''She's a nice girl. Pretty, too. Do you remember that time when she and Alannah—''

''Rachel, forgive me, but I didn't come here to talk about Daphne Baker. I couldn't give a damn about Daphne Baker. I wanted to see you, to find out how you are and what you're doing with yourself and to ask you out to dinner. If you won't come out with me tonight, we can surely make a date for some other time, can't we? Warnfield isn't so far away. And if I do take this shipping job, I'll be here every day. Hey—I've just had an idea! You could chuck out the Fallen Woman and let her room to me.''

''You've got a hope! She's a marvellous cook.''

''Well, OK, forget that bit—but please, I really would like to see you again.''

''Oh, I don't know, Barney. I don't think so.'' Rachel looked down into her drink. Some rather strange foreign bodies were drifting about down at the bottom and she tried hard to fish them out, pretending that this concern was the only thing on her mind. ''I say, have you got these black things in your sherry, too?''

He didn't answer her and when she looked up she found his eyes on her, his lip caught between his teeth.

''Rachel, I know how hurt you were—how we hurt you,'' he said softly. ''I couldn't regret it more. It was a rotten, lousy business, but it's all in the past now. I've always felt—you bloody know how I've always felt! About you, I mean. I've often thought about those few weeks at the beginning of the war, and Shawcross Street, and how happy we were. How happy I was, anyway. Remember that day on Box Hill?''

Too well, Rachel thought regretfully. Barney had seemed then much as he seemed now: the best and most attractive option open to her. Which wasn't fair on either of them. She abandoned the foreign bodies and put the glass down on the table beside her.

''Barney—'' she began, and fell silent as she saw the intensity of his blue, blue gaze.

Just one word, she thought. That's all it would take. One

word, one gesture of encouragement, and he would leap at the chance to take her back into the world she had vowed never to enter again.

Never mind the past. Never mind Daphne, or any other girl Barney might take home to be charmed by his father, baffled by his mother and condescended to by his sisters. Never mind the fact that she had long consigned the entire Rossiter family to perdition. Barney was, after all, the best of the lot, the one who had first shown her friendship, the one who had always been on her side. Well, almost always.

She wasn't in love with him; had never been in love with him. Yet affection was there and—amazingly—a touch of magic. Rossiter magic. Surely, surely, she wasn't still in thrall? Impatient with herself, she got up and went to the window, fidgeting with the catch as if unsure whether to open it.

One word, and her loneliness and insecurity would be a thing of the past. Barney loved her. She'd always known it. He might even love her enough to accept Tess; and even though there was no passion on her part, there was affection. There were, surely, worse grounds for a marriage?

But it was out of the question. No matter in what direction she turned, she could see nothing but danger and the certainty of grief. Even if Mrs. Rossiter did another of her amazing U-turns, and welcomed her back into the fold—as she might do, Rachel recognised, if it meant that by so doing she would keep Barney in Warnfield—the whole idea was impossible.

She had danced too often to the Rossiters' tune and she would have no more of it—not now, not with success within her grasp, and certainly not now that she had Tess.

The lock of fair hair had fallen over Barney's brow, just as it had always done. It gave him a vulnerable look, at odds with the arrogance in those deep blue eyes.

"Go in with Guy, Barney," she said suddenly. "Do what feels right to you."

He pushed the lock of hair away in the gesture she remembered so well.

"I don't know," he said. "Ma's right, really. Guy's a bit of a scatterbrain—"

"He could have grown up."

As Barney hadn't, she realised suddenly. There was a fatal

weakness in his character, perhaps more apparent now than it had been before. Dunkirk, Tobruk, years in the Eighth Army. Promotion, certainly. Medals, perhaps. Who knew what had happened to him during all that time?

Whatever it was, it hadn't changed him significantly. He still toed the family line. He was a Rossiter, through and through.

"It's been so good to see you, Barney," she said, a note of finality in her voice. "Do remember me to everyone."

"Is that it, then? Aren't we going to meet again?"

"Oh, of course! Why shouldn't we? I can't say exactly when, I'm afraid. I may be going away. My plans are very uncertain."

"Well, let me know."

"I will, I will!"

"You'd better tell me the name of your book."

"It's called *With This Ring*—"

"A love story?"

"Well—" she hesitated. "Sort of. Love and hate. Life, you might say. It's supposed to be quite funny."

"*With This Ring.*" He took a notebook from an inside pocket and repeated the title slowly as he wrote it down. It suddenly sounded, Rachel thought, as silly a title as she had ever heard, but he said that everyone would be thrilled to hear about it, especially Alannah. She would be the most thrilled of all and would certainly want to get in touch now that Rachel was found again. And Rachel nodded and smiled and assented to everything, certain that he would be proved wrong.

He left, finally, walking out into a blue and gold evening that suddenly seemed to have remembered, after all, the morning's promise. Rachel closed the door behind him and leant against the wall in the passage for a moment.

Illogically, she felt bereft. Had she done the right thing? It might have been all right . . .

Fool, fool, fool, she berated herself. Of course it wouldn't have been all right. Never, never was Tess going to be subjected to the Rossiters. It was madness to have let the thought even cross her mind, and equally crazy to think that she could find happiness within a hundred miles of them, taking into account all that had happened.

It was then that it dawned on her that neither she nor Barney had actually mentioned Gavin by name, and she knew then that she hadn't been wrong. The past was something she had to put behind her.

"He's gone," she said to Nancy, who was sitting in the old wheel-back chair Rachel had found in a junk shop in the Gold-hawk Road, giving Tess her bottle.

Rachel crouched down beside them, looking at her daughter with love, all her ambivalent feelings for Barney receding. Tess relinquished the teat for a moment to give her mother a wide, milky grin before suddenly coming to her senses, realising she was wasting good feeding time and sucking with renewed earnestness and concentration.

Nothing else matters, Rachel thought. Only Tess.

"Shall I take her?" she asked Nancy.

"OK. I'll see to the vegetables." To the accompaniment of rumbles of discontent from Tess, Rachel took Nancy's place in the chair, placating her hungry child by making all the foolish sounds and grimaces that mothers make, until once more the teat was in place and the contented sucking could continue. "I just hope you know what you're doing," Nancy said, pursuing the subject as with great vigour she mashed the potatoes. "That family have got off altogether too lightly."

"Maybe. I only know I must keep away from them if I want to save my sanity."

"I have to admit that he was rather charming, though, your Barney Rossiter."

"They're all rather charming. Always were, every man jack of them."

They had certainly charmed her. They had caught her young, put their mark on her, and Barney's visit had only proved that it was there still. They were stamped all through her, she thought, like the letters in seaside rock.

With the bottle finished, she stood up and sat Tess in her high chair.

"It's a beautiful evening," she said. "Why don't we take her out for a stroll to the park after supper?"

Nancy was instantly agreeable.

"Good idea. Supper's ready now."

"I could push the boat out and stand you a half of shandy at the Green Man by way of celebration. We could sit outside."

"Why not?"

Nancy, putting plates on the table, turned to smile at her, but there was something in Rachel's face that caused the smile to fade a little.

"Put it all behind you, Rachel," she said softly. "You don't need them. Forget them."

"I'm going to," Rachel said. "I have already." But she sighed as she spoke, and hearing it, Nancy gave a small, sceptical laugh.

"That'll be the day," she said.

⇥ TWO ⇤

"Are you spying on us?"

At the sound of the boy's voice Rachel was gripped by a chilling paralysis. She had often read of blood freezing in the veins; now she was experiencing this phenomenon for herself. She had been found out, revealed as that worst of creatures—a sneak, a peeping Tom. The shame of it was unendurable. She felt quite sick, unable to breathe or move. She wanted to die—quickly, that minute, no hanging about.

She had immediately recognised the voice that had challenged her. It belonged to the younger boy, the one they called Barney, which wasn't quite as bad as if she had been discovered by his sister Diana, or Gavin, the big boy; but even so it was something she had dreaded ever since finding the loose brick in the wall that, once removed, had provided such an enchanting window on life next door. Perhaps, she thought, if she kept very, very still . . .

"I say, *you*! You in the spotty dress. Don't think I can't see you. You'd better come out and explain yourself. We Rossiters don't like being spied on."

Rachel's cheeks were burning as after a few more minutes of immobility she wriggled out backwards from the shrubbery where the lilac tree cascaded over the wall from the adjoining garden. Ineffectually she tried to pull the twigs and leaves out of her hair, at the same time tugging at the skirt of her outgrown cotton dress which Grandma considered quite good enough for playing in the garden. Bad enough to be caught redhanded in her shameful activity without giving this arrogant, accusatory male a glimpse of navy-blue school knickers.

He was sitting on the wall that divided the two gardens, subjecting her to an unfriendly stare. Even his nose seemed intimidating, being bony and high-bridged, and as for his eyes, she felt as if they must be able to look right through her. She had never seen anything like their colour or their clarity. His grey flannel shorts were dirty in a long-standing way and his shirt was torn. His socks were wrinkled and shoe-laces flopped, untied, from disreputable plimsolls; yet, in spite of all, he looked, well—*posh*! There was no other way to describe it; not, at least, one that sprang readily to Rachel's twelve-year-old mind despite her insatiable appetite for the written word.

She felt at a considerable disadvantage, having to look up to meet that gaze.

"I—I wasn't exactly spying," she said miserably, rubbing at the side of her face where a twig had scratched her. He remained implacably hostile.

"What would you call it, then?"

Helplessly she searched for the words that would exonerate her, scuffing the gravel on the path with her sandal in a way that would have earned a sharp rebuke from Grandma.

"Well?" He was as stern and inflexible as any schoolmaster facing an errant pupil.

"It's just that—" nervously she hesitated. What on earth could she say? "Just that watching you is like watching a play?" "Just that life over the wall at Kimberley Lodge is a hundred, thousand times more fun than life at The Laurels"?

"Just that there's no one here but me," she said at last.

Nervousness made her voice quaver, and even in her own ears the explanation sounded pathetically weak. She forced herself to meet those extraordinary eyes and saw that Barney was subjecting her to an unwavering scrutiny, biting the inside of his cheek as if in thought. His blond hair hung carelessly over his brow and stuck up in a tuft at the back of his head. If it were not for the eyes, she told herself, he would look quite ordinary—not like the other boy. Gavin. No one would ever consider him ordinary.

He frowned and nodded slowly once or twice as if he had considered the crime, weighed the evidence, and found that, after all, there might just possibly be a few mitigating circumstances.

"Well." He paused, as if unsure what to say next, then seemed to make up his mind. "Have a humbug?" he offered, pulling a crumpled paper bag from his pocket.

The clutch of fear Rachel had felt at the first sound of his voice loosened its hold a little, and she accepted this substitute for an olive branch with humble gratitude.

"I say, thanks. I—I don't think I can reach it, though."

"Can you catch?"

Not very well, would have been the honest answer. She had no eye for a ball—a lack which had served her ill at St. Ursula's, the boarding school to which her parents had despatched her from Uganda. St. Ursula's was the kind of school where an inability to put balls into nets was rated as only slightly less heinous than compulsive arson.

It would not, therefore, have surprised her in the least if the humbug had evaded her inept grasp and landed on the gravel at her feet, but by some miracle she managed to hang on to it.

"Thanks," she said again. She put it in her mouth and licked the palm where it had left a residue of stickiness. Still regarding her thoughtfully, the boy put a sweet into his own mouth and for a few moments conversation languished.

"What's your name?" he asked at last.

"Rachel." The reply was indistinct, hampered by the humbug. "Rachel Bond."

"I'm Barney Rossiter."

"I know."

"Yes, I suppose you would." He appeared to retreat a little from his former tentative friendliness. "I suppose there's not much about us you *don't* know."

"I don't know all that much," Rachel said defensively, as if by minimising the extent of her knowledge she would make the crime that much less.

She knew a great deal, though. She knew that the Rossiters seemed to laugh a lot and that their quarrels, heated though they could be, were soon over. She knew that Mrs. Rossiter painted pictures and worked tapestries, and was blonde and smiling and serene, making nothing of misdemeanours that would have sent Grandma into hysterics and would even have raised objections from her own mother—things like eating buns out of a bag or pouring milk direct from a bottle into a teacup. They seemed, in some indefinable way, above such things as doileys and paper napkins. The fine summer weather had meant that the family seemed almost to live in the garden, and Rachel had therefore experienced ample opportunity to observe their eating habits.

She knew that they had a big, buxom, slow-moving maid they called Pommy, whose name was really Mrs. Pomeroy, so Doreen said. She came in daily and could be seen walking to and from Kimberley Lodge night and morning with a curious rolling gait, a shopping bag made of oilcloth banging against her ample thighs.

She knew, too, that the children went to local schools—the boys to King Edward's College and the girls to Brookfield House—and had friends who came and went in a casual manner. She knew that Mr. Rossiter laughed every bit as much as his children, teasing them and being teased in return. She knew that they were all keen on games and caught and threw balls with enviable grace and expertise. She knew that Diana played the piano and that Gavin was as handsome as any film star and that Barney liked to go off on solitary, unexplained exploits of his own, which often annoyed Alannah. Only that day Rachel had heard her complaining to her mother on the subject.

"Don't whine, dear," Mrs. Rossiter had said equably. "It's frightfully unattractive as well as unproductive."

Her voice was melodious and measured, matched by the way her needle went in and out of the canvas in an unbroken, hypnotic rhythm.

No matter how Alannah complained, no matter how any of them argued and plotted, Rachel knew that they were an entity, a corporate force, united against all outsiders. As she watched through the wall, envious of the fun and the jokes and the easygoing camaraderie, even of the sudden squalls, it was this unity that struck her more than anything else.

"I don't know anything at all, really," she said now, hoping Barney would believe her.

He remained silent for a moment, sucking his sweet reflectively. Then, quite carelessly, as if they were of little importance, he said the magic words she had sometimes dreamed of hearing without ever believing the dream would come true.

"Do you want to come over? As you're on your own."

She almost choked on the humbug.

"I'll have to ask my grandmother," she said.

"Tell you what." He had swung his legs back to his side of the wall and was speaking to her over his shoulder. "I'll get Ma to come round and issue an official invitation if you like. Your grandmother can't refuse that, can she?"

"Would your mother really do that?" It seemed too miraculous to be true.

"She will if I ask her."

He sounded sure of himself, but as he prepared to leap down from the wall and out of her sight Rachel felt a sudden shaft of fear that such a marvellous thing would never—*could* never—come to pass.

"When?" she asked urgently.

Barney looked back at her, frowning.

"Well, *now* of course."

What a hope, she thought as he disappeared. Surely he must know that grown-ups didn't behave in that way. They were always busy and required notice, and they had to make up their faces and put on their hats and gloves before paying calls. "Presently," Rachel's mother always said, not meaning it in its literal sense at all, but rather "tomorrow" or "next week" or "some unspecified time when I'm in the mood."

But perhaps Mrs. Rossiter was different in this, as well as in other ways. Rachel's sightings of her had, naturally, been subject to certain limitations, but she had seen her in the garden often enough to know that she was as unlike her own mother as it was possible for anyone to be. Her mother was called Kitty, and Rachel had always thought it an exceptionally suitable name. She was sleek and beautiful and very slim, with long, mysterious green eyes that were much admired by the young Colonial officers in Entebbe. No one could believe that she was old enough to have a daughter of Rachel's age. When the mood took her she could be lively and skittish, the best of companions. In those moods, Rachel adored her, and even she could see that she was very young, both in looks and ways, to be a mother. She guarded her complexion jealously against the hot sun of Uganda and it was pale and smooth as a lily—whereas Mrs. Rossiter bloomed and billowed rather like one of the peonies that flamed in Kimberley Lodge's wild and magical garden.

Would Grandma let her go to Kimberley Lodge? Oh, she had

to—she *had* to! Rachel bit her thumbnail in agitation, unable to guess what reaction Grandma would have to the invitation. She had already divined that, when it came to the family next door, her grandmother found herself in something of a dilemma.

The Rossiters were well thought of in the town. Although this summer holiday was Rachel's first experience of Warnfield and she had been at The Laurels no more than two weeks, she had learned that much from Grandma's conversation with her cronies over the teacups. Mr. Rossiter was an architect—*the* municipal architect, employed by the Town Council, and had been responsible for the design of the new Town Hall, generally agreed to add a great deal of distinction to an otherwise lacklustre High Street. And Mrs. Rossiter was a well-known local artist whose paintings were often exhibited at the library. Gavin and Diana, for their part, were the leading lights of the Tennis Club, and had distinguished themselves by winning the Mixed Doubles two years in succession.

Set against this was the undeniable fact that they played loud music and entertained visitors who banged car doors late at night. And the grass verge in front of their house remained unmown, a lush island of untrammelled growth in a sea of green velvet. The Rossiters were, Mrs. Bond said, a law unto themselves, caring nothing for the opinion or the convenience of their neighbours. It was some time before Rachel cottoned on to the fact that they felt themselves superior to such things, and many years before she fully appreciated the seriousness of this charge in her grandmother's eyes. She, Rachel was later to realise, dedicated her entire life to the pursuit of genteel conventionality.

"But what can you expect," she had heard Grandma demand of Grandpa, "of a mother as *arty* as Mrs. Rossiter? If you can call those pictures she paints 'art'! I certainly can't! They're nothing but great splodges of colour simply flung at the canvas! And as for her clothes—why, there are times when she looks like a gypsy."

Mr. Rossiter was no better. An architect was, after all, a professional man and it was surely up to him to dress the part, not wear those dreadful hairy tweeds and—would you believe it?—*golf* stockings to work. What was wrong, Grandma would like to know and frequently demanded, with black coat and striped trousers, wing collar and bowler hat, as worn by every other decent man in civilised society? She thanked God that she had no trouble of that kind with Grandpa, a senior bank manager of subdued and amenable disposition who saw to it that the garden was neat and the verge mown, and was often heard to say that he had nothing left to strive for now and was content to "bat quietly until retirement."

But then again—oh, poor Mrs. Bond! It really was a dilemma of immense proportions—Kimberley Lodge was bigger and more imposing than The Laurels. And Lady Garfield-Ponsonby, herself a pillar of the Art Society, as well as being a respected member of St. Ethelburga's where Mrs. Bond herself worshipped Sunday by Sunday, was a frequent visitor.

The house stood on the corner of Ranelagh Gardens and Parkside Avenue and had a turret and two huge bay windows, no less impressive for being half-hidden behind a tangled shrubbery. As well as painting, Mrs. Rossiter sat on committees (in company with Lady Garfield-Ponsonby, yet again, as well as other crowned heads of Warnfield) and was a leading light in the Women's Institute, giving talks and judging competitions. Such things, after all, carried weight.

When would Mrs. Rossiter come? Rachel didn't for one moment expect the sort of instant response that Barney appeared to think possible, but still a burning hope took her into the house and upstairs to her narrow little room that was over the front hall, its window giving an excellent view of the front gate.

She peered out cautiously, ever mindful of Grandma's dictum that it was vulgar to be seen peeping from behind the curtains. A Council road-sweeper was at work on the pavement of Ranelagh Gardens, just outside the gate, and across the road a Waring & Gillows van was delivering some small item of furniture to Mrs. Minns-Faulkner at Magnolia House. Rachel saw Mollie come to the door in answer to the delivery man's ring and watched with interest as he exchanged some bantering words with her, finally throwing back his head to laugh unrestrainedly.

In spite of her distractions, Rachel smiled in sympathy. She liked Mollie. She was Mrs. Minns-Faulkner's house-parlourmaid and sometimes came over to visit Doreen, who worked for Rachel's grandmother. She was full of jokes and laughter and the kitchen always seemed a brighter place when she was in it, though Mrs. Bond never cared for her. She cherished an irrational, unexplained prejudice against the Irish—or perhaps Catholics. Mollie was both.

A movement nearer home caught Rachel's eye, and through the bushes that bordered the road she saw a flash of colour. The road-sweeper touched his cap, and there—oh joy, oh rapture—was Mrs. Rossiter, actually opening the gate and coming towards the house.

She had actually come! Rachel couldn't believe it. Oh, what a simply *marvellous* sort of mother to have—one that simply dropped everything and did what you asked her. And what if she did wear the kind of colours that Grandma would criticise as being *outré* (one of her favourite words, especially where the Rossiters were concerned)? Rachel thought she looked absolutely splendid in the loose jacket that was splashed with pink and mauve flowers, worn over a voluminous crimson skirt which appeared to be made of hessian and was decorated with several rows of braid. Her hat was of plain straw, wide-brimmed and weighed down with poppies and cornflowers.

Barney wasn't with her—which perhaps was as well, Rachel thought, bearing in mind the informal nature of his clothing when she had last seen him. Grandma set a great deal of store by neatness—the apparent lack of it was, in fact, one of her main objections to the Rossiters—and had ways of making her disapproval felt without a word being spoken.

Mrs. Rossiter disappeared from view into the stone porch at the front of the house. Rachel heard the doorbell ring and the sound of Doreen's footsteps as she went to answer it. She spent a good deal of time with Doreen in the kitchen reading her copies of *Peg's Paper* and other assorted magazines which gave details of the lives of film stars, and was on good terms with her. She was a kindly creature, but Rachel had long since recognised that she was hardly the brightest thing on two legs. She hoped devoutly that Doreen wouldn't goggle and gawp at Mrs. Rossiter and keep her standing on the step, but would show her inside as she had been taught. It wasn't something anyone could bank on.

She crept to the top of the stairs. She could hear Mrs. Rossiter asking to see Mrs. Bond, and to her relief she heard Doreen, in reply, inviting her into the hall. Out of sight, around the bend in the staircase, Rachel sat on the topmost stair hugging her knees, her eyes squeezed shut. There was nothing she could do now but pray.

The silence seemed to go on for ever. What on earth could they be talking about? Surely the question of whether Rachel did or did not go to play at Kimberley Lodge hardly warranted a protracted debate? At last she heard the distant sound of a bell, and she knew that Doreen was being summoned from the kitchen, either to go in search of her or to show Mrs. Rossiter from the house. Her prayers took on an added fervour. This latter alternative was too horrible to contemplate.

In the hope that for once Grandma and she would be in agreement and that Doreen was about to come looking for her, Rachel stood up and smoothed her dress and her straight brown hair, scowling with annoyance when she realised that she still had remnants of the shrubbery entangled in it. What a fool she was! Why hadn't she used this waiting time to smarten herself up? Grandma would be furious!

There was no time now; Doreen was already halfway up the stairs—had turned the corner and had seen her.

"Yer granny wants yer, love," she said. " 'Ere—guess what! She's got Lady Paint Pot with her."

This was Mollie's name for Mrs. Rossiter, but much as Rachel liked Mollie, she wouldn't—*couldn't* smile. Under the circumstances it would have seemed like an act of betrayal.

"Thank you, Doreen," she said, with all the dignity she could muster. She swallowed nervously as she braced herself to walk downstairs, where, in the drawing room, she found Mrs. Rossiter and her grandmother sitting in silence. Mrs. Rossiter appeared to be gazing with wrapt attention at the picture of highland cattle which hung over the fireplace and was smiling faintly, her chin resting on her hand. The wide sleeve of her jacket had fallen back to reveal a plump arm, creamy and smooth. By contrast, Grandma reminded Rachel more than ever of a plucked chicken. She was fingering her pearls, which was always a bad sign, indicative of some inner turmoil; but she too was smiling, even if the smile was only a small and half-hearted effort.

"Ah, Rachel," she said as her granddaughter entered the room. "I don't believe you have met Mrs. Rossiter who lives at Kimberley Lodge next door. Say 'how do you do,' nicely."

One day, Rachel thought—*one day*—she would say "how-do-you-do-nicely" just to *show* Grandma, but this wasn't the day to make any such gesture of defiance.

"How do you do, Mrs. Rossiter," she said, and bobbed a little curtsey, as insisted upon at school when greeting the headmistress or any important visitor.

"My, my—such pretty manners!" Mrs. Rossiter beamed at her. "It's to be hoped you have a civilising effect upon my gang of ruffians." Later Rachel was to become aware that the deprecatory way Mrs. Rossiter referred to her family was no more than an affectation; at that moment, however, she was conscious of a twinge of apprehension. Surely they weren't really ruffians? How would they treat her? What would Grandma think? "You will come and play with them, won't you?" Mrs. Rossiter continued. "They're simply longing to meet you."

Rachel knew perfectly well that this was untrue. Barney had taken pity on her, nothing more. They were so self-sufficient as a family that the others probably knew nothing of her existence. Well, they'd know about her now, all right. Barney no doubt had told them about the circumstances in which he had discovered her, and she felt she would be lucky if they even spoke to her, never mind "longing" to meet her. Still, it was kind of Mrs. Rossiter to be so polite.

"I'd love to," she said breathlessly.

"Then run along and make yourself tidy," Grandma said. "Your hair is a disgrace. Give it a good brush."

Mrs. Rossiter laughed.

"Oh really, there's no need," she said. "Compared to my brood, Rachel is already tidiness itself."

She might as well have saved her breath. Grandma didn't stop smiling, but the smile seemed to tighten and harden and her eyes took on the kind of determined glint that Rachel had early learned not to disobey. There was an added edge to her voice when she spoke.

"Run along, dear."

Rachel did not hesitate but turned and ran from the room. Grandma had a sort of fixation about hair; nothing angered her more than seeing it falling over her granddaughter's face. Her own hair was shingled at the back, but on either side of her face were rigid iron-grey waves, protected at night with a salmon-pink net which she tied under her chin. She wore plain dresses in muddy colours which she considered suitable for her age, her only adornment the single string of pearls and a modesty vest edged with lace which filled in the V-necks favoured by her dressmaker.

Rachel was back in a few moments, breathless with haste and excitement. Mrs. Rossiter and Grandma rose to their feet immediately, as if thankful that their meeting need not be prolonged any further.

"We lunch at twelve thirty," Grandma said.

"I shall see she is back in good time."

"It's very kind of you—"

"Not at all. The children will be delighted."

On a flood of polite phrases Mrs. Rossiter wafted out of The Laurels. She smiled at Rachel in a kindly way as they progressed side by side down the path and out of the gate. Anxiously Rachel smiled back, worried about her reception next door, the word "ruffians" returning to haunt her. Would the girls hate her? She couldn't see any reason why not.

She was so nervous that it was hard to concentrate on Mrs. Rossiter's questions, still less answer them, and was thankful that the lack seemed to pass unnoticed since Mrs. Rossiter mostly supplied the answers herself.

"Do you enjoy boarding school?" she asked. (*Enjoy* boarding school! How could anyone do that?) "Yes, of course you do! Such fun to have your friends with you all the time. And do they feed you well? For we are what we eat, my dear, no one can deny it. Nutrition is of such importance. The mind *is* the body."

Rachel was silent as she contemplated the heavy puddings, the lumpy custard, the thick shiny gravy that was the daily lot at St. Ursula's. There seemed no way to express adequately their repellent nature, but she was saved the necessity of trying to do so as Mrs. Rossiter continued her monologue.

"We thought of it for the boys," she went on. "My husband was anxious for them to go to his old school, but I couldn't bear the thought of parting with them. Perhaps I was selfish—"

"Oh, *no*," Rachel assured her, as her voice appeared to trail away uncertainly. "It's much better at home."

Mrs. Rossiter smiled faintly, but said nothing. Nor did Rachel, for they were already entering the gate of Kimberley Lodge and the panic which swamped her drove everything else from her mind. She found herself wishing suddenly that she had never left The Laurels, where little was expected of her except to be quiet and tidy and make no trouble. It might be boring, but it was at least safe. It was, however, too late to change her mind now. Here she was, on the other side of the wall, in the area of garden that was so familiar to her.

There was no sign of the big one—Gavin. She was thankful for that, for it was quite unnerving enough meeting the girls. Diana was swinging indolently in a hammock reading a book. She had thick, corn-coloured hair pulled back in a single heavy plait with tendrils escaping to curl around her face. Her mouth was full, rather sulky in repose, but she smiled as she said hallo, and her eyes were amused. She knows, Rachel thought, shame engulfing her again. They all know. I can't bear it. Shall I turn and run?

"Were you really spying on us?" Alannah, the younger one, asked. She had straight, short, slippery fair hair caught back with a tortoiseshell slide that looked as if it was about to fall out. She was wearing a pair of boys' khaki shorts, fastened at the waist by a belt with a snake buckle.

"Shut up, Lannie. I told you not to say anything about that," Barney said severely. "She's all on her own."

Alannah continued to look at Rachel curiously, neither welcoming nor hostile. "How old are you?" she asked, getting down to essentials. "I'm eleven and three-quarters and Barney's thirteen. Diana's fifteen."

"Sixteen next month," Diana corrected her, not lifting her eyes from the page.

"I'm twelve and a half," Rachel said.

"Gosh, you don't look it. Does she, Barney? I'd have said *much* younger." Rachel thought she detected a scornful note. "Are you living next door for ever, or just for the holidays?"

"Just for the holidays. I'm at boarding school."

'Gosh!' The note had subtly changed. Now Alannah sounded intrigued—even admiring. "Is it awful, or is it absolutely super, like in books? Do you have midnight feasts and things, and lots of fun in the dorm after lights out?"

Rachel struggled for honesty, knowing that a denial would diminish her in Alannah's eyes.

"Well," she said at last. "Not very often."

Not ever, if she were to be truthful. An image of the dormitory flashed on her inward eye, cold and austere. Iron bedsteads in two rows, separated by a line of washstands bearing chipped bowls and ewers. She saw the granite face of Miss Simkins, the housemistress, as she stood with one hand on the light-switch, her eyes travelling from one bed to the next as if suspecting all manner of nameless crimes would be perpetrated the moment the room was plunged in darkness. She heard the stifled sobs of Alice Jamieson in the next bed, whose parents were in Singapore and who suffered the pangs of homesickness less stoically than most. Poor Alice lost all control of her emotions once lights were out; as Rachel did herself, were she to be honest. The only difference between her and Alice Jamieson was that she made no sound, but lay with the tears trickling silently across her cheeks and into her ears, longing painfully for everything that she had left behind in Africa.

Resolutely she turned her thoughts away from St. Ursula's. There were still six weeks of the holiday left, and they seemed to stretch all the way to infinity.

"I always thought school stories were daft," Alannah said.

"No you did not." Barney crowed with laughter. "Look how you lap up those dopey Dimsie books—"

"Only 'cos they're *hilarious*!"

"Shut up, you two." Diana's voice was weary. "Rachel didn't come here to listen to you arguing. You'll make her wish she'd stayed on her side of the wall."

"Are the girls nice? Have you got lots of friends?"

"Well—" again Rachel hesitated. "Not lots," she said at last. "Just one or two."

There was Alice, of course, who regarded her as an ally. And Julia Dodd, who slept in the bed on the other side of her. She was the daughter of a country clergyman—a dreamy, peaceful girl who read as avidly as Rachel herself and was equally useless at games. She had attained St. Ursula's on the strength of a scholarship awarded to promising offspring of the clergy, which made her the object of wariness and some distrust on the part of the other girls, who tended to despise her clothes and her possessions and her general lack of push. Recognising each other as misfits, the two girls had gravitated together, finding, much to the relief of each, great affinity.

"Why are you at boarding school, anyway?" Alannah asked. "And why are you staying with the old—with Mrs. Bond?"

"She's my grandmother. My parents are in Africa—Uganda, actually. That's where I was born."

"Gosh, *Africa*!" No doubt about it Rachel thought, cheering up a little, she had succeeded in impressing Alannah. "Do you live in the jungle, in a mud hut?"

Rachel laughed at that.

"Heavens, no! My father works for the Government and we live in Entebbe. That's a township by Lake Victoria. And our house is made of stone."

"Sounds as if you might just as well live in Warnfield. Are there any wild animals?"

"Crocodiles in the lake, and hippos too. They come at night and eat the vegetables in the garden."

"What about savages?"

Rachel thought of Melika, the warm, comforting, uncritical presence who stayed with her at nights when her parents were at the Club or out to dinner with friends. Who, with whispers and giggles, got her up and gave her breakfast the next morning, very quietly so that Mummy shouldn't be disturbed. Daddy was always off at the crack of dawn, no matter how late he had been up the night before.

"We have black servants," she said. "But they're not exactly savages."

"Aren't you afraid of ending up in a cooking pot?"

"Oh, *do* shut up, Lannie." Barney sounded disgusted by his sister's ignorance. "You really do talk utter rubbish."

"You shut up. I want to find out about Rachel." She turned to her again. "Were your parents sad when you had to leave? Ours would be *devastated*!"

"They'd pay to get rid of you," Diana murmured into her book. No one took any notice of her.

"Of course they were sad," Barney said, more irritated than ever. "*Honestly*, Lannie! You're such an idiot. Come on, let's do something. Let's play cricket. You can bat first, Rachel. Diana, move yourself—come and make up the side."

"Not on your life." Unmoving, Diana continued to read.

Rachel prayed that she wouldn't weaken and that Barney would abandon his idea. One ball, and the small amount of status she had acquired in Alannah's eyes would melt away and they would all realise how utterly unworthy she was to receive their friendship. But Barney, grumbling, was already fetching the equipment from a shed and hammering stumps into place.

"Don't be a spoilsport, Di," he urged as he laboured. "We can't have much of a game with three of us. You'll ruin everything if you don't play."

"Too bad." Diana's voice was a study in indifference.

A new voice made itself heard.

"Do you want me to make up the side? I'll bowl if you like."

Gavin. The big one. Rachel's humiliation, then, was to be total.

She turned to see him leaning casually against the open french window, tall and elegant, a striped silk scarf knotted at the open neck of his shirt. She knew she had never seen anyone more beautiful in her whole life. His hair was a reddish gold and seemed to gleam in the sun and his eyes were as blue as Barney's; bluer, if anything. His smile revealed perfect teeth. With a movement of his shoulders he pushed himself away from the window and sauntered across the grass, setting Diana's hammock in motion as he passed.

"Whom have we here?" he asked, smiling in Rachel's direction.

"This is Rachel—Rachel Bond from next door. Mrs. Bond's granddaughter."

This last piece of information was heavy with meaning. Rachel could tell at once that Grandma was a joke with the Rossiters and that Barney was warning Gavin to watch his words.

"She comes from *Africa* and goes to *boarding school*." When Alannah spoke you could almost see the italics.

"Well, well—such grandeur! Welcome, Rachel-Bond-from-next-door."

Rachel was too overwhelmed to reply. He was still smiling at her, but all she could manage in reply was a small, apologetic smirk, and when he actually proffered his hand, her taking of it was no more than a reflex action.

"Cold little paw," he remarked loftily. "Well, Barney-me-lad, what about this game of cricket, then? I have to be in town by eleven thirty, but if you want me on the team until then, I'm your man. Who's in first?"

"Rachel," Barney said.

She thought briefly of fainting dead away. It seemed the only way out.

"I've changed my mind," Diana said, tipping herself out of the hammock. "Bags I bat first."

"But I promised Rachel—"

"I don't mind a bit," Rachel said quickly. "I'll field if you like."

"OK. You're a good sport, Rachel. Go over by the apple tree. A bit further. *There*, that's fine." Barney was as authoritative as if he were captaining England. "Look, you and Gavin better be against the rest of us because he's so good. Everyone ready?"

Gavin, tossing the ball from one hand to the other with his back to Rachel, turned and smiled at her over his shoulder.

"We'll show them, won't we?" he said.

Her heart seemed to turn a somersault and suddenly it was difficult to breathe. She felt hollow inside, as if she really were going to faint, and at once she knew the reason for it. Hadn't she read about such feelings a dozen times in Doreen's magazines?

She, Rachel Bond aged twelve and a half, had, on the twenty-seventh day of July, 1933, fallen hopelessly, irredeemably in love. There could be no doubt of it.

"You must ask your new friends to tea," Grandma said, after Rachel had been paying daily visits to Kimberley Lodge for over a week. "One must return hospitality." However distasteful such a duty might be, she could have added, if the expression on her face was anything to go by. The fact that her granddaughter had apparently been welcomed next door did not, it seemed, go any way towards crystallising her ambivalent feelings towards the Rossiters.

The whole idea of issuing such an invitation filled Rachel with horror. Teatime was an informal affair at the Rossiters. If there was cake, then they ate cake, with no nonsense about the need to eat bread and butter first, and during this spell of warm weather they helped themselves in the kitchen and brought a laden plate out into the garden, tea or lemonade slopping from thick mugs.

Rachel knew from experience that tea at The Laurels would be a very different affair, with fish-paste sandwiches and egg-shell china, and Grandma presiding behind the silver teapot, questioning the Rossiters about their lives and their parents' activities in that relentless, probing way of hers, pretending she was doing nothing more than making polite conversation. They would be on to her in a flash, Rachel knew, and she wouldn't put it past Diana to make up shocking stories of life next door out of sheer devilment. Rachel had learned quickly that Diana liked to shock, and instinct told her that if by so doing she could make life difficult for the newcomer to the family circle, then she would find it all the more amusing.

Diana, while not positively unfriendly, wasn't an easy person to know. She was pleased with herself—well, hadn't she the right to be, looking the way she did? Rachel couldn't blame her. And she seemed to be good at everything. She'd won a special prize at school, Alannah told her, for French, and was the only girl *ever* to have got a hundred per cent for Maths. In addition, she moved with easy, athletic grace, and had won cups for hockey and the high jump, as well as tennis.

"It's simply frightful for me! She's absolutely always top," Alannah complained—but proudly. She liked to bathe in her sister's reflected glory, even though it irritated her when teachers at school held her up as an example. "It just isn't fair! And it'll be worse next year when she's in the Sixth Form. I bet she's made a Prefect right away."

Rachel couldn't argue with that. Diana was one of life's natural prefects. She didn't know how she could bear it, sitting at tea, attempting to toy with a sandwich, knowing that this glittering, superior creature was shrieking with laughter behind what would undoubtedly appear to be a demure exterior.

At least she didn't have to worry about Gavin because she was perfectly certain he wouldn't come even if invited—in itself unlikely since it was Gavin that Grandma objected to most of all. It was his friends who banged car doors late at night, calling out over-enthusiastic goodnights and last-minute witticisms. And it was Gavin (or so Grandma believed) who was responsible for playing "that dreadful jazz" which could sometimes be heard floating from an open window. Rachel had not seen fit to tell her that Mr. Rossiter was equally responsible, for her opinion of him stood low enough without adding anything so damning. "Negro music" she called it, considering it both infantile and decadent. That any responsible adult could actually enjoy it was simply beyond belief.

No, Gavin wouldn't come, Rachel felt sure. He lived a life apart—a life which only Diana was privileged to share, except for occasions such as that first day in the garden when he had deigned to bestow the honour of his presence, briefly but with such devastating results. Rachel continued to worship him humbly from afar. Shy and unsure of herself with all of them, the very sight of Gavin was sufficient to turn her into a blushing imbecile, incapable of speech, with all such moments lived and relived with increasing embarrassment once she was on her own again.

His particular friend was called Guy Seagrave, the son of a wealthy businessman who resided in Warnfield but owned a string of small department stores to the north of London.

Guy had the unbelievable distinction of owning a sports car, and together, bathed in glamour, he and Gavin dashed here and there, playing tennis in the park, drinking coffee at the Moo Cow Milk Bar, sauntering through the High Street in their striped blazers and straw boaters like two young princes.

Perhaps, Rachel thought, if she ignored Grandma's suggestion for long enough the whole thing would be forgotten. She should have known better than that. Grandma was like a dog worrying at a bone when an idea took root in her head. Usually it was Grandpa who suffered; he was always being badgered about fixing the days for their holiday (one week in a rather superior private hotel in Hove), or having the house painted, or mowing the verge. Now it was Rachel's turn.

"I think Thursday," Grandma said reflectively at breakfast one day. "I shall send round a written invitation—"

"Oh, you don't have to do that," Rachel said hastily, worried that after all Grandma might invite Gavin by name and that he might feel obliged to accept. "I can quite easily ask them."

"I trust I know how to behave." Grandma's voice was icy and her thin nostrils dilated gently.

In the event, and much to Rachel's relief, only Alannah came. By great good fortune, Grandma had picked a time when Barney was away spending a few nights with a friend who lived on a farm outside Warnfield. He was due back that very day, but Mrs. Rossiter considered his time of arrival too chancy to allow her to accept on his behalf. Diana pleaded a headache at the last moment—best cured, she considered, by exercise and fresh air; i.e. by going to the open-air swimming pool in the park with Gavin and Guy. Rachel happened to see her driving off, perched on the folded-back canvas roof of Guy's car, and felt nothing but relief.

The occasion was as stiff and formal as she had feared, but Alannah—clad unfamiliarly in a pink-and-white checked dress with a smocked yoke—handled it superlatively, carrying on a conversation with Grandma about local matters with aplomb and apparent enjoyment, coping with admirable efficiency with the sandwiches and the Worcester china. Alannah, Rachel knew by this time, liked nothing better than to act a role, adopting different voices and manners with astonishing ease. This afternoon she was Being a Lady Out to Tea, and was being it to considerable effect; though Rachel's appreciation of her performance was diminished by the sure knowledge that it would be enacted all over again for her family's amusement once she was home again.

"The child has good manners, I'll say that for her," Grandma said with some surprise after she had gone.

"They all do, Grandma."

Grandma shook her head in bewilderment, defeated, as always, by the contradictions presented to her by the Rossiters.

"Really, it's quite beyond my comprehension," she said, and declined to explain when Rachel questioned her. Not that any explanations were necessary, for Rachel knew exactly what she meant. Was not her grandmother's reaction precisely the same as her own had been, when, on that first morning, she had discerned Barney's essential poshness despite his disreputable garb?

"It's a great pity," Mrs. Bond said with a sigh—meaning, Rachel presumed, all the noise and the laughter and the flamboyance. "I do hope dear Ivor would approve of my letting you play with them." Her eyes strayed to the photograph on the mantelpiece which showed Rachel's father in his Colonial Officer's uniform, staring straight ahead in a solemn, resolute, responsible kind of way. She sighed. "It's a heavier duty than you appreciate, Rachel, to be a proxy parent, especially at my age. I had thought that your Aunt Sylvia . . ." She neglected to finish her sentence, but she did not need to. Aunt Sylvia couldn't be bothered with her, Rachel knew that. She wasn't sure what her aunt did with herself in London, but she had made it abundantly clear that beyond the occasional meeting of a train and tea at Fullers,' no more could be asked of her. Her life, it seemed, was too much of a social whirl for her to welcome the complication of an unwanted niece.

"I do appreciate it, Grandma, and I'm sure Mummy and Daddy would approve of the Rossiters. They'd want me to enjoy myself."

"Be that as it may . . ." Clearly Mrs. Bond remained unconvinced.

"Mummy would like them, I know." Unwisely Rachel pursued the subject, and Grandma smiled thinly.

"Perhaps Mummy would," she said, faintly ironic. Mummy's standards, her tone implied, left much to be desired. Rachel was not supposed to know how strained the atmosphere was between the two women closest to her father, but she was not that much of a fool. She had once overheard Grandma describing her mother as a "flibbertigibbet," and there were times when she sighed and referred vaguely to "poor Ivor." Rachel said no more, but took up a book that Alannah had lent her—a book that was supposed to portray boarding-school life but to her seemed as far from the truth as some fantasy by Jules Verne.

"I think bath and bed," Grandma said, as eventually the clock on the mantelpiece chimed eight.

Automatically Rachel protested.

"But Grandma, it's not nearly dark yet—and Grandpa's not home. He said we'd have a game of chess."

"My dear child, these Lodge Meetings go on until all hours. I'm not expecting him for a long time, and chess is certainly out of the question. Now off you go, there's a good girl. Goodnight and sleep well."

Resignedly Rachel kissed the cold cheek that was offered to her, thinking that it didn't matter, she could just as easily read in bed—yet vaguely aware that there ought to be something more, that though the sun had faded and the shadows were long it was not yet time to close the door on the day. Upstairs in the bathroom at the back of the house she opened the window and leaned out.

Music and laughter floated towards her on the still evening air. There they all were, all the Rossiters, hidden from her by the shrubbery and the wall and the trees, but clearly audible just the same. She could hear Mr. Rossiter's voice and a shout of laughter from Barney, now home from his visit. Diana was playing the piano, the sound of a Chopin nocturne floating through the open french windows. She would slow down in a minute, maybe play a wrong note or two. It was a hard bit, she said. *There*, that was it.

Gavin was in the garden—she heard Mrs. Rossiter call his name from inside the house, and the sound of it made her feel weak with love for him—for all of them. Rachel longed with every nerve, every pore, every fibre of her being to be with them, not here in this chill, aseptic bathroom with its pungent aroma of Wright's Coal Tar soap.

There, in that moment, she knew a greater loneliness than she had ever experienced in her life before. All warmth, all colour seemed to be concentrated in that garden beyond the wall and she saw herself, small-faced and pale, standing bleakly apart, destined always to be outside the charmed circle.

For a little while she stood there, not seeing the beauty of the summer evening, not seeing anything except the desirable world that was closed to her. Then quietly, matter-of-factly—because what else was there to do?—she closed the window and ran her bath.

⸲ THREE ⸳

It was a week after Barney's visit to Inverness Street that the letter came from Sylvia asking Rachel to lunch with her in Kensington.

"How antisocial of you not to have a telephone," she wrote plaintively. "Still, you can always phone me. If I hear nothing from you I shall assume that you will come on Wednesday at 12:30, when I shall look forward to a really good chat!!"

Rachel's own feelings about a really good chat, particularly of the type that merited two exclamation marks, were definitely mixed. On the one hand, she admitted to herself that she yearned, in the absence of any other relatives to brag to, to tell Sylvia about the book. On the other, was she to come clean about Tess, or continue to conceal her baby's existence?

Until Jermyn Street, she had not seen Sylvia since before the war. They had never been close; in fact the opposite had been the case. She had always known that as far as Sylvia was concerned, she was nothing but a nuisance. The summer of 1936 when, much to the dismay of both of them, she had been forced to spend several weeks under her aunt's roof, was still something she remembered, if not with horror, then with desolation. Certainly the small amount of train-meeting and escort duty that had routinely been required of Sylvia was carried out only under sufferance. Rex Courtney, her husband, was something quite high up in the Civil Service, though Rachel had always been vague about his precise function.

Soon after the outbreak of war he moved to the Foreign Office—an appointment that was greeted with a certain amount of awe in the family. Rex's new job, it was generally believed, was hush-hush and of great national importance. Churchill, Mrs. Bond frequently told her friends, would have been lost without him.

Whatever it was, the job kept him in London throughout the blitz and the buzz bombs and all the quiet period in between; and though, no doubt, it had its stressful moments, there were times when he was able to relax and enjoy himself, as was proved when Rachel happened to see him once at the theatre on one of her rare visits to London during the war. She had pretended not to, however, because he was with a predatory-looking blonde in ATS uniform.

Sylvia evacuated herself to the West Country. Rex's family had come from Cornwall and he had inherited a cottage in the village of St. Bethan, at the mouth of the river Pol, not long before the war. The Courtneys had spent several holidays there prior to 1939 and Rachel had heard much regarding St. Bethan's charms.

"You really must come down," Rachel clearly remembered Sylvia saying with casual insincerity on several occasions.

"I'd love to," she had invariably replied; untruthfully, of course, for after the summer of 1936 she would have preferred to enter a corrective institution rather than submit herself to any further holiday with Sylvia. No definite invitation had ever materialised, however, which came as a great relief.

Her grandmother had made the journey once, just after her husband died in 1942. She had reported that St. Bethan was like a picture on a calendar, but even so she had not liked the place. She had mistrusted the drains, it seemed, and complained that the seagulls shrieked incessantly, making sleep impossible. However, she further told Rachel, Sylvia had found some bridge-playing cronies who lived within reach, and was apparently enjoying herself.

Rachel had been shocked, feeling it immoral that an able-bodied woman in her forties should pass a war playing bridge; and as she held Sylvia's letter in her hands and wondered what she should do, she reflected that it explained why Sylvia, almost alone among the population of London, should look quite unchanged by the past five years. She had always been, if undeniably on the plump side, a stylish woman; beautifully coiffed and well made-up, nails painted and earrings in place. One was,

Rachel thought, more than usually conscious of face powder in her presence, its scent and texture. She was always velvety with it, like a bee dusted with pollen.

Nothing had ever ruffled the surface of her self-satisfaction and certainly five years of war had left no mark. If there were now a few silver threads among the gold, it seemed likely her hairdresser had dealt with them competently—and no doubt expensively—for none were visible. She'd had no son or daughter in the forces to cause her concern; no bombs or fire-watching duties to disturb her rest. Looking at her, one could not imagine she had worried about Rex in London or her parents in Warnfield, or had ever gone short of the little luxuries that everyone else had learned to live without.

Well, good luck to her Rachel thought now, less censorious than she once had been. Who could blame Sylvia for finding a comfortable little niche? At least she had relieved Rex of the necessity of worrying about her while he was getting on with his important job at Churchill's right hand, which perhaps was a more valuable contribution to the war effort than donning a uniform to perform duties that she was, as like as not, totally unsuited for.

Yes, she would go to lunch, Rachel decided, but she wouldn't take Tess. Nancy was at home that day and readily agreed to look after her. She *liked* looking after her, she maintained stoutly. Nothing would be easier than to give her some lunch and put her down for a sleep.

Rachel was suitably grateful. She might, she said, take advantage of the really good chat to confide all to Sylvia—or at least, as much as she intended to confide to anyone.

The flat had suffered some bomb damage, Sylvia had told her when they met, but it was not immediately obvious. It looked to Rachel just as she remembered it—not large, admittedly, but cosily affluent, like a satin-lined casket. The blue ceramic pots from The Laurels were in evidence in the entrance hall, one on each side of the front door, containing spectacular and exotic greenery.

Sylvia greeted her warmly, clasping her to her soft, cashmere-clad, pearl-decked bosom in a way she certainly would not have done when Rachel was a child.

"My dear, it's lovely to see you," she cried. "I'm simply

bursting to tell you my news. Rex has been posted to Washington! Isn't it wonderful? We're off quite soon, and I must say I can hardly *wait*! Just imagine—no rationing and no austerity and no beastly Socialists! Won't it be perfect bliss?''

Rachel was duly congratulatory.

"That's marvellous," she enthused.

"We'll have a sherry to celebrate, and you must tell me all your news," Sylvia went on; following which she reverted, without pause, to the subject of Washington: the house she would be justified in expecting, the entertaining, the clothes. Quite understandable, as Rachel reminded herself, for who would not be excited at such a prospect? "My dear, forgive me," Sylvia said at last. "Now it's your turn. Tell me what you've been up to."

"Well, actually—" Rachel began.

"More sherry, dear? You're sure? The man at the corner shop is such a poppet, he always keeps this brand for me. He's one of the old school, not like most of them. You should have heard them in Peter Jones the other day! Simply take it or leave it! Life is never going to be the same again, you do realise that, of course? These people have us where they want us now, and well they know it." She fell silent, regarding her niece thoughtfully. "Just think!" she mused. "I could have a daughter your age myself if things had been different. It might have been fun, choosing clothes and so on. Well, no use crying over spilt milk. When do you expect Ivor and Kitty to come home?"

"When they can get berths. In the spring, they hope."

Tess would be fourteen months old by March. No one would expect Rachel to give her up, not then. She'd be safe by March. Oh, what a fool she was! She was safe now. She wasn't a child to be ordered to do this or that. She was an adult, a mother, and she'd go to the stake rather than give up Tess.

She took a deep breath.

"Sylvia—"

"Rachel, my dear, you did say when we met in the street that you kept busy with your little stories and articles?"

"That's right. And you'll never guess—"

"They do pay you, these magazines?"

"Yes. And Sylvia—"

"Then, my dear, I hope you'll forgive me for saying it but I do advise a really good haircut. I know just the man. In Grafton Street. Look on it as an investment. It's the same with dress, quality never dates. Remember how pleased you were with my choice of clothes, that time you stayed with me before the war?''

That at least was true, and Rachel opened her mouth to acknowledge the fact; but even in this she was thwarted.

"Ah, here's *dear* Mrs. Morrissey to tell us that lunch is ready," Sylvia said, rising to her feet. "You're quite sure you won't have another sherry? Well, I'll just top up my glass . . ."

She was nothing more than an audience, Rachel realised. Sylvia had no interest in her affairs; how she had passed the war, how she spent her time now. Well, she thought, as she tucked into her steak and onions, mashed potatoes and cauliflower, at least she was getting a damned good feed out of it.

"How is Rex? Is he pleased about this move to Washington?" she asked, when Sylvia drew breath for a moment.

"My dear, of course! It is promotion, after all." Sylvia looked, Rachel thought, like a large contented pussy-cat as smilingly she contemplated her husband's successes. "Oh, I must tell you, Rachel," she went on, changing the subject as yet another random thought occurred to her. "I was up in Warnfield recently and saw Mrs. Rossiter. You hadn't been in touch with any of them, she said. What a funny little person you are! She seemed most concerned about you. The girl was home—the pretty one. Diana. The one that was on all those recruitment posters during the war. She's engaged—getting married fairly soon, I understand. I gave them your address, so I expect you'll get an invitation."

"I doubt it," Rachel said. "I wouldn't accept it, anyway."

"Why on earth—?" Sylvia stopped masticating a moment to stare at Rachel in astonishment, then, quite unabashed, resumed her meal. "Well, I can see it might be embarrassing for you—"

"You could say that."

"Well, whoever was at fault, it's all water under the bridge now. They don't appear to bear a grudge."

"I should think not!" Rachel gasped with amused outrage. "If any grudges are to be borne, then I'm the one to bear them. Not that I do, believe me. I just don't want to have any more to do with them."

"Well, I think you're very foolish. Barney came in while I

was there. He's matured very nicely, *and* it seems he's in the running for a good position with a shipping firm. Of course, it's all who you know these days, isn't it? Mrs. Rossiter managed to get an interview for him through Lady something or other in Warnfield.'' She paused for a moment, glimmering knowingly. ''He's an attractive creature, and *most* interested to hear about you. How old are you now? Twenty-five? Time you settled down and found yourself a nice husband. Don't be surprised if Barney comes looking for you.''

''He already has.''

''There, now—what did I tell you?'' Sylvia looked delighted with her prescience. ''Did he take you out?''

''No.'' Rachel went on cutting up her meat, avoiding her curious gaze. ''He did ask me but I was busy that night.''

Her aunt stared at her.

''You must be out of your mind! Is there someone else? Is that it?''

''No, it's not that,'' Rachel assured her. ''It wouldn't do, Sylvia—you surely must see that! Besides, I have other things on my mind at the moment.''

Perhaps if Sylvia had pursued the subject of just what was on her mind, Rachel thought afterwards, she might have force-fed her the news about the acceptance of the novel; even told her about Tess. But she reverted once more to the joys she might expect to await her in Washington and the moment was gone.

Clearly, Rachel thought, her aunt wasn't interested in her affairs, and it would, under those circumstances, be pointless to parade her little triumph before her, still less to tell her of Tess's existence. With any luck, Sylvia would go to Washington and stay there for a considerable time. Rachel had an idea that Harrods, or possibly Sloane Square in view of the mention of Peter Jones, represented the end of the known world to her, so that even visits home to London would be unlikely to include a side trip to Hammersmith.

This, then, was likely to be the last time she saw Sylvia for a very long time. So she ate her lunch, listened to her aunt with a polite smile on her face, admired her photographs of Cornwall (you had to hand it to her—who but Sylvia would contrive to pass five years of war in such an idyllic situation?) and left at ten to three, thanking her for the lunch, and wishing her good luck in Washington.

Out on the street once more, Rachel was conscious of a feeling of depression. She had wanted to like Sylvia; wanted to be assured that blood was thicker than water and that, after all, they could communicate with each other now that she was an adult and not an importunate child.

It hadn't worked like that. Somehow the meeting had only served to underline the fact that she had no one but herself to depend upon.

She had Nancy, of course—but one could hardly expect her to be around for ever. She'd been seeing a lot of George lately. Whether that meant anything or nothing, Rachel wasn't sure, but it certainly gave her pause for thought.

Gone was the euphoric feeling of self-confidence that she had experienced on the day that Barney had appeared at her door. Now, suddenly, she was worried about the next book. She had managed to write one acceptable novel, but there was no assurance of continued success—no absolute guarantee that she could pull off the same trick a second time.

It was only later, when she was in bed, that she associated this mood with the Rossiters. It seemed as if they were reaching out their hands from the past to denude her of all her confidence, stripping off, piece by piece, the tough outer shell she had grown over the years to reveal the quivering, raw flesh beneath. And even when she slept the fantasy continued, only now she could see their faces quite clearly, all of them except Gavin. Where was he? In her dream she seemed to think he was hiding nearby. She was desperate to tell him about her book, but though she searched for him she couldn't find him. Nevertheless, she knew he was there somewhere, quite close, and to the accompaniment of Rossiter laughter she searched on, ever more frantically.

The dream was confused, the events without logical sequence, but suddenly he was present in the room, and everything was just as it had been once upon a time when Rachel was young and innocent and believed in happy-ever-after. He put his arms around her and she was warmed and comforted, so that it was with a rush of gladness that she woke to the sound of a bird singing in the ornamental cherry outside her bedroom and the little gurgling noises that meant that Tess was greeting the day in her own particular way.

It took a full five seconds before she realised the truth—that there was no happy-ever-after, and that she was alone. A wave of sadness swept over her, followed by one of sheer panic. She closed her eyes and willed herself to overcome it, as she had done so many times before when her loneliness and responsibilities seemed too much to bear. She was strong, she reminded herself. Indomitable. Remember?

"What on earth's the matter with you?" Nancy asked her at breakfast. "You look ghastly!"

"Well, gee, thanks. Nothing like the odd compliment to boost the old ego."

"You're not worrying about you-know-who, are you? I thought you were going to put the past behind you."

"So I am." Rachel sighed gustily. "I had the most ghastly dream, that's all. I can't seem to shake it off."

"Oh, dreams." Nancy shrugged hopelessly. "What can you do about dreams? I don't know which sort are the worst. I dreamed that I was being chased over a Scottish moor by that rather nice redheaded RAF doctor—d'you remember him?"

"Yes," Rachel said dryly. "He was the one who sounded your chest no matter what was wrong with you. Ingrowing toenail, earache—"

"Well, he caught me, and I was just waiting for him to have his wicked way with me when he stuck a thermometer in my mouth."

Rachel, spooning Farex into Tess who sat pink and placid in her high chair, smacking her lips as if she were savouring some gastronomic delight, looked up and grinned.

"Oh, frightfully Freudian," she said, and was grateful. Trust Nancy to put things in perspective, she thought.

"Oh, by the way," Nancy went on, "is it all right if I invite George to supper tonight?"

"Yes, of course. You don't have to ask, you know that. I like him."

"Do you? Honestly? You don't think he's a few bob short of a pound? He has some crazy ideas, you know. My God, is that the time?"

The pips heralding the nine o'clock news had caught her unawares. Without waiting for an answer, she gulped her coffee, grabbed her mackintosh (unlike Rachel, she was constitutionally unable to trust the morning's promises, no matter how cloudless the sky) and rushed from the house.

It was a warm, still day; a day for the country, not London. Rachel dressed Tess in a beautifully embroidered frock of pink lawn that Nancy had made for her, and with much difficulty added a pink and white cotton sunbonnet.

Several old ladies stopped and clucked at Tess during the excursion down the sunlit street. She looked (Rachel thought in her totally unprejudiced way) more than usually fetching with her fair quiff peeping out from her sunbonnet.

"Little love," they said, and, "Bet her Daddy's proud of her," and, as always, "What lovely blue eyes she's got!"

All the better to enslave me, Rachel thought. And all the better to betray my secret. She smiled at them, giving no hint of the chill of fear their words engendered. She was suddenly conscious again of panic—a dark, jagged threat on the horizon of this golden day. She slowed her steps, dawdling towards the park, silent now, all her fears rushing back. She hated the thought that she was once more within the Rossiters' orbit, her whereabouts known. The nightmare was only a sympton. Was she now to be haunted by them?

No, of course not! She sat down on a park bench and idly rocked the pram, lifting her face to the sun, forcing herself to be calm. She had rebuffed Barney. He was hardly likely to seek her out again, whatever he had said at the time and whatever torch he had carried over the years.

But suppose he did? Suppose this time he caught sight of Tess? What then? Oh, *damn* Sylvia! It had been the worst possible luck bumping into her like that just before her visit to Warnfield.

It was impossible to relax, to enjoy the sun and the flowers and the expanse of grass. Restlessly she got up and pushed the pram back the way she had come.

As if catching her mood, Tess began to whimper and rub her nose with her fist—a sure sign that she was tired or bored or wanted a drink. Perhaps all three.

Rachel quickened her steps, anxious now to be home. And not only for Tess's sake, either. The urge to close the door on the outside world was irresistible. Once home, she tried to swamp her unease in a frenzied attack on the household chores. Tess, in high spirits now having had her drink of juice, crowed with delight as she hurled small toys to the floor.

This was a new game. Was she encouraging bad habits, Rachel wondered, as patiently she retrieved them? Was she spoiling Tess?

Maybe, but somehow she doubted it. She found it hard to believe that there could ever be too much kindness displayed towards children. Or warmth, or approval, or understanding.

She remembered too well how she had longed for it—how once she imagined that she could find it in the Rossiter household, how she warmed her hands at their fire.

Though the sun shone that summer of 1933 there was little warmth at The Laurels. After an early supper, Grandma usually settled down to some knitting, while Grandpa would either potter gently in the garden or sit and read *The Times*. Occasionally he would challenge Rachel to a game of chess or Halma, but not often.

No one spoke very much. Mr. Bond distrusted Ramsay MacDonald but on the whole supported the National government, relying on the good sense of Stanley Baldwin to keep the Labour riff-raff in order. These, however, were thoughts he kept to himself. Though he was sometimes inspired to give grunts of approval or snorts of derision as he rustled the pages of his paper, he seldom gave voice to anything that made sense to Rachel.

Not that she minded. The world of politics and governments and foreign affairs was something for adults, something so far outside her experience that though she might, if pressed, have been able to supply the name of the Prime Minister, she knew of no other politician and was happy in her ignorance; until, that is, she entered the Rossiter household.

There, things were very different—though even among the Rossiters, politics was clearly a masculine preserve for it was only Gavin and Mr. Rossiter who chose to speak of them; and not only speak, but argue forcibly, since each took his stance on an opposite side of the fence.

Gavin supported the Labour Party. He was an ardent pacifist and tended to shout his views about the inequity of means test-

ing and the need for class struggle and a new order, while his
father regarded Neville Chamberlain's financial policies with approval, was in favour of free enterprise and assured all who
would listen that the spendthrift policies of the Socialists would
bring the country to its knees.

"Look at Russia," he instructed Gavin several times a week.
"Is that the kind of society you want here?"

"Why not, if we can't get rid of the stinking, rotten cesspit
of capitalism any other way. Who starts wars? The capitalists,
that's who—the fat cats at the top who don't give a damn about
the workers. Our class-ridden society is evil. The game's up,
Dad—"

"*God*, you're a bore, Gavin!" That was Diana, reaching for
something to throw at him. "And such a hypocrite! You love
your comforts and privileges as much as anyone."

"Not at the expense of everyone else. Yes, of course I like
my comforts, but in a perfect world everyone should have them!
There should be a levelling up, not a levelling down—"

"Ha! You mean like Russia? Tell that to the peasants in the
glorious Soviet Union!"

"Children, children!" Mrs. Rossiter was always smiling, pacific, her needle going in and out. She never shouted or became
angry; and though she sometimes shook her head at Gavin's
more extravagant excesses Rachel quite rapidly discerned that
while she was proud of all her children, for Gavin she reserved
a very special pride. And who could blame her? Certainly not
Rachel.

Though he and his father argued constantly, the arguments
sometimes spilling over into exasperation, even rage, there was
little animosity in it. Mr. Rossiter was, in Rachel's eyes, a quite
remarkable father.

He was, for one thing, a great joker. At first Rachel was wary
of him, not knowing how to take him. She was not accustomed
to a father who performed a soft-shoe-shuffle into the dining
room, hat and cane in his hand; or one who delighted in singing
comic songs round the piano with his family.

He loved to play games, and he played to win. Not like
Grandpa when he played chess, always leaving himself open so
that Rachel could take the game—a ploy which annoyed her
more than she could ever express. Mr. Rossiter liked nothing

better than a family game of cricket or rounders; but if wet weather should keep them indoors, then with equal enthusiasm he would join in Racing Demon or charades or—Rachel's absolutely least favourite thing—a game called Adverbs, of which all the Rossiters seemed inordinately fond. It called upon one member of the party to leave the room, returning to guess what word had been chosen in his or her absence by demanding certain actions to be performed "in the manner of the adverb."

Her baptism of fire as far as this game was concerned came quite quickly after her introduction to the Rossiters.

Had they chosen things like "quickly" or "dreamily" or "hesitantly," Rachel thought, going over and over the day as she always did once she was in bed, it wouldn't have been nearly so bad; or simple actions like—well, like setting a table or combing one's hair. She was still smarting, and did for many days, about her failure to act convincingly the catching, killing and plucking of a chicken "perfectly." It had been *awful*! She hadn't known where to start and had just stood there, head bent, pleating her skirt between her fingers.

Only the kindness and the tact of Mr. Rossiter had saved her. Oh, he was such a kind man, she thought. If she wasn't already in love with Gavin, then she might quite easily be in love with him. If he hadn't been so old, of course. He must, surely, be all of forty—but still handsome, for all his great age, with glossy, chestnut-coloured hair and those sparkling blue eyes, and his air of enjoying everything so much.

"It's only a game," Diana had said to her amusedly after the Adverbs debacle. "There really wasn't any need to get upset. You really are a goose, Rachel." She was smiling at her in a lofty, head-girl kind of way.

"No, she's not!" Alannah, in those early days, was always passionate in defence of her, as if Rachel was her particular responsibility. "You shouldn't have given her such a hard thing to do. You know what Mummy said—we've got to be kind to Rachel. We should *pity* her, being so far away from her own home and having to live with old Mrs.—with her grandmother."

"Pity," Diana said, "is only another form of self-indulgence. It's patronising to pity people."

"How can you say that? What about the starving children in India?" Alannah was clearly intent on widening the argument.

"What about the men who pull rickshaws in China?"

"When I see Rachel pulling a rickshaw," Diana said, arranging herself in the hammock, "then I might pity her."

It was a disquieting thought, that the Rossiters were under orders to be nice to her. Rachel had hoped—it was only a little hope, but it had undoubtedly been growing—that she was making a place for herself in the family. She wasn't any good at cricket, or even at Adverbs as she had so obviously demonstrated, but Limericks was another matter altogether. This was a game where she felt she had come into her own, a game where each player supplied the line of a limerick. She was inventive at rhyming, quick-witted when it came to the amusing twist at the end. Her most satisfying moment, the most wonderful moment of her entire life, had been when Gavin had laughed and commended her, just the other day.

And there was another thing. She and Alannah were collaborating on writing a book. It was, naturally, a school story, about which Alannah was far more of an authority than Rachel.

"It'll be the school story to end all school stories," Alannah said. "We'll have a madcap of the fourth, and a school sneak, and a *marvellous* hockey captain called Pamela, and a Head Girl who's *odiously* calm and wise—"

"Helena?" Rachel suggested.

"Perfect! And the sneak will be called Ethel Craddock—gosh, can't you *see* her, all poky and pointy-faced? What'll we call the Madcap of the Fourth?"

"Daphne?" offered Rachel, but Alannah looked unconvinced. "Pauline? Pat?" Still Alannah shook her head. "Dymphna?"

"*Dymphna*! Oh, that's it! Oh, clever you, Rachel! Dymphna it is. Hurrah for Dymphna!"

It became a catch-phrase in the family, a kind of battle cry. Making a catch at cricket, Mr. Rossiter would throw his panama hat in the air and shout it in triumph; or the whole family would roar it in unison when Mrs. Rossiter came from the kitchen bearing a cake for tea.

There were numerous things that they roared in unison. Apparently when Alannah was a little girl, she had asked someone to "do her a flavour." 'Certainly, madam," Gavin had replied smartly. "Chocolate or strawberry?" Nowadays, no one asked

for a "favour," always a "flavour"; and the reply always came
back "chocolate or strawberry." In unison, of course. It was,
Rachel thought, the most enormous fun, and she was proud that
Dymphna had achieved the same status.

"One day," she said dreamily, lying on her back in the grass
one summer's afternoon after a satisfactorily productive writing
session, conscious of the scent of the honeysuckle hedge, feeling
happy and at peace with herself, "I'm going to write a proper
book."

Alannah was beside her, lying on her stomach. She was chewing a pencil, an exercise book open in front of her.

"This *is* a proper book!"

"Oh, you know what I mean. A book that people will buy.
A book that will go in libraries."

Alannah's silence was heavy with doubt.

"Oh well," she said after a moment, obviously making a
great effort to carry out her mother's instructions regarding
kindness towards their less fortunate neighbour and speaking
with a patently false note of encouragement. "Perhaps you can
do it. Anyway, it's good to have ambition."

"I mean it, Lannie." Rachel opened her eyes and looked at
her determinedly. She saw that Alannah was regarding her with
concentrated compassion.

"I know you do, Rachel. It's just that it must be awfully hard
to write a proper book. I wouldn't want you to be disappointed." Her voice was full of concern for her friend. "I mean,
it seems to me that you have to be quite clever to write a book."

"I'm good at English. It's my only thing, really."

Alannah said nothing, but her expression implied doubt.

"I expect Di could do it," she said after a moment. "She's
so clever, she can do anything. No, I wouldn't be a bit surprised
if Di wrote a book one of these days. But I'm not sure about
you, Rachel. You can *try*, of course—"

"I intend to," Rachel said huffily, not at peace any more.

"Oh, don't be offended! Please, please don't be offended!
You're my best friend, you know that, but I have to be honest."

Rachel was offended, in spite of this. I *will* do it, she thought,
gritting her teeth with determination, but saying no more; and
later, before she went to sleep that night, she indulged in a
highly entertaining fantasy wherein she was signing copies of

her books in a huge London store, besieged by a throng of people all anxious to buy, among their number the entire Rossiter family.

She wouldn't let them pay for her book, she decided, but would rise to her feet, and would graciously present them each with a copy, for which they would be suitably thankful.

"We knew Miss Bond before she was famous, you see," Mrs. Rossiter would explain to others in the crowd. "We are so proud of her."

One day, she thought. One day.

The Rossiters had other friends who often dropped in from time to time. Sometimes they stayed for meals, quite without arrangement, and there always seemed enough to go round, no matter how many sat at the table. At first this had astonished Rachel—and even more astonishing was the casual way these friends used the telephone to let their parents know they wouldn't be coming home. It was, she thought, like being in a different world. Just imagine Grandma—well, one couldn't, and it was hopeless even to try. She would have had fifty fits to have her hospitality taken for granted in this way.

Guy Seagrave was a frequent visitor because not only was he Gavin's friend, but he was madly in love with Diana. At the beginning of the summer, when Rachel had first got to know the Rossiters, his devotion had been welcomed by the object of it—even encouraged. He was reasonably nice-looking—not as handsome as Gavin, of course, but just as tall, with black hair and brown eyes, and of course there was the car. Such a possession was enough to increase any young man's sex appeal, even in the eyes of someone as self-sufficient as Diana, and even if he did have spots.

Alannah didn't care for him at all—mainly, Rachel suspected, because he didn't take any notice of her.

"He's so wet," she said to Rachel scornfully. "He doesn't have a word to say for himself when Di's about."

"He must be awfully in love with her." Rachel knew the feeling and was sympathetic.

"Well, I hope no one's ever in love with me, if all it does is make them so soppy. Di says he's the strong and silent sort, and she's not wrong there. He doesn't say a word. He just *gawps!*"

"I expect he's just shy when she's about."

"It won't last you know," Alannah prophesied sagely. "I've seen it all before. She likes boys to fall for her, but once they do, she can't be bothered."

"What about Gavin?" Rachel had longed to ask since that first day, but had been afraid to do so. "Is he in love with anyone?"

Alannah pursed her lips and wrinkled her nose.

"Don't think so. There are lots of girls who like *him*, of course, and he took Polly Roberts out for a while. They were always going to the pictures and dances and things, but he went off her—which didn't surprise me one bit! She's got the most terrible laugh I ever heard, just like a braying donkey."

"You don't think he likes Marjorie Newton?"

Alannah thought for a while before answering, her head on one side, while Rachel went on turning the pages of the *Girls' Own Paper*, trying hard to look as if the question was of no importance. She was distinctly worried about Marjorie, who had started coming to the house with great frequency. She was a friend of Diana's, a thin, rather intense girl with red hair and green eyes who became highly animated the moment Gavin appeared, tossing her spectacular locks and flashing those sparkling eyes. She was clever, Diana said. Rachel thought her prickly and even more unpredictable than Diana herself, but she did have a certain kind of distinction.

"He might," Alannah admitted. "She makes him laugh."

"Who makes who laugh?" Barney asked, joining them without warning. He, alone among the children, spent as much time with friends outside the confines of Kimberley Lodge and its garden as he did within them. No one knew quite what he did with himself. His mother encouraged him to take a sketch-book out into the country with him, but he was always reluctant to show what he had done.

"Marjorie Newton makes Gavin laugh. Rachel wanted to know if I thought he liked her—"

"I was just *asking*!" Embarrassed, Rachel was blushing scarlet.

"I think he does," Barney said. "He's put her photograph on his chest of drawers in the bedroom."

"Well that proves it, then," Alannah agreed. "Di won't think much of it, will she?"

Rachel stared at her.

"Why not? I mean, Marjorie is her friend—"

"Bet she won't be for long. Di doesn't like her friends to fall for Gavin."

It seemed incomprehensible; but then, much of what went on in Diana's and Gavin's world was beyond Rachel's understanding. Brother and sister were very close, and would often remove themselves out of earshot of the others to sit and talk and talk and talk, always very quietly, as if they were exchanging secrets. About what? Marjorie? Guy? Other friends? Politics? Rachel had no idea.

But equally there were other occasions when a quarrel would flare up, and this Rachel hated more than anything. It was always quite different in nature from the brief spats between the other children which were usually about the ownership of certain articles, or the division of labour. There was a frightening intensity about the way the insults flew between Diana and Gavin—a tense, unbearable whiteness, a feeling that nerves were at breaking point and that anything might be said, anything done.

"I hate you, I hate you, I hate you," Diana had screamed one day, a fight erupting out of one of their sotto voce conversations, this time in the corner of the living room. Rachel, alone with them since Alannah had temporarily removed herself to get lemonade from the kitchen and Barney was out on his own concerns, felt her stomach constrict with panic. She watched in horror as Diana flung herself on the carpet and pounded it with her clenched fists. Aghast, Rachel looked on, biting her fingers, close to tears, seeing the end of Rossiter family harmony for all time. "I could kill you, Gavin Rossiter! I wish you were dead!"

"So do I," Gavin spat in return. His face was a greenish white, his lips drawn back in a snarl. No sign now of the debonair charmer whom Rachel had adored on sight. "Because then I'd never have to speak to you again. In fact if I ever *see* you again, that'll be too soon for me."

"Beast, beast!" Diana leapt up from the floor and, like one demented, threw herself on him, flailing at him with her fists. Gavin grabbed hold of them and twisted her arms behind her back until she screamed with pain. Wildly Rachel rushed out to find Alannah.

"It's awful in there," she gasped. "I think they're going to kill each other—"

"Just ignore them," Alannah said calmly, filling two glasses with lemonade from a large jug.

"It's all you can do," Pommy said, shaking her head as she rolled pastry, as if she had long given up any hope of understanding either Gavin or Diana. "It'll all be over in five minutes, mark my words."

"Pommy's right," Alannah assured her. "They'll be back to normal before long. Di's awfully baggy lately because of waiting for her School Cert. results. Mum says we've got to make allowances."

"But she said she hated Gavin! She said she wished he was dead."

"She always says that. She doesn't mean it."

Alannah hadn't seen Diana's face, Rachel thought, disbelieving her. Or Gavin's, come to that. Surely it meant something, all that blanched, furious hatred?

"We'll just leave them alone," Alannah said. "Let's go up to the old nursery."

It was a day of brief spells of sunshine interspersed with prolonged squally rain; just the day for concentrating on the book—*Hurrah for Dymphna*, as it was now officially titled. But somehow Rachel could find little joy in it. She kept thinking of those frightening scenes down below. It was like a fire or a shipwreck, she thought. Even when the shouting was over, the damage would still be there. For once, time seemed to hang heavily, and long before her normal time of departure she made an excuse to go back home.

In the front hall she encountered Diana and Gavin, just emerging from the sitting room, amicably making plans for the afternoon.

"Just off, then?" Gavin remarked to her in his normal pleasant manner.

"Oh Gavin, your talent for stating the obvious almost amounts to genius," Diana said, sounding affectionately amused.

Rachel, shaken by the fierceness of the quarrel, was now equally amazed by the absence of any trace of it. Diana was calm and smiling, more beautiful than ever, as if the rage that had possessed her had been cathartic, leaving a radiant tranquillity in its wake.

That's the Rossiters for you, Rachel thought, as, totally baffled by them, she made her way next door. She'd never understand them. Never.

⊰ FOUR ⊱

Mr. and Mrs. Hugh Rossiter request the pleasure of the company of Miss Rachel Bond at the wedding of their daughter, Diana Marguerite, to Dr. Thomas Penrose, MD, DSO, at 11:30 a.m. on 20th October 1946 at St. Mary's Church—"

Rachel stared at the invitation in disbelief. She had recognised Mrs. Rossiter's bold, flamboyant hand the moment she saw it adorning the square envelope on the mat in the hall, and had guessed what it must contain. That she should even dream of sending such a thing surely demonstrated an insensitivity that beggared belief, Rachel thought, even though she held the irrefutable evidence of it in her two hands.

There was a little note included with the invitation.

"Dear Rachel," it said. "We were so glad to discover where you have been hiding yourself all these years. I do hope you can come to Diana's wedding! You were so much one of the family in the old days and it would be lovely to see you again. I am coming to town shortly to look for something to wear for the occasion. Perhaps we could meet?"

It was signed: "With love, as always, Carina Rossiter."

As always? Rachel couldn't help feeling a touch of sardonic amusement at that, but though she smiled she was conscious of a twist of fear. Her instinct hadn't been at fault, then. The net seemed to be closing. They were moving in on her.

It was a day for Beattie Jenks from next door to look after Tess during the morning. Three times a week she came in, Mondays, Wednesdays and Fridays, from ten o'clock to twelve thirty, and Rachel had developed the habit of being poised for flight the moment she came in through the door. Otherwise she found herself pinned to the kitchen wall while Beattie regaled her with the latest in the long-running saga involving various members of her colourful family and acquaintances.

On this particular Wednesday morning Rachel was caught unawares, the invitation still in her hand. Beattie spotted the unmistakable gold lettering and the wedding bells with entwined ribbons almost before she was inside the door, and was thrilled and excited on her behalf, wondering aloud what Rachel would wear.

"You'll have to buy a new outfit," she said. "When is it? October? Ooh, I love an autumn wedding! It'll be all chrysanths and dahlias. I wonder what the weather will be like? It could be chilly by then. A nice fine tweed suit would be the thing. I can see you in a sort of beigy colour with tan etceteras. Suit you a treat, it would, honest. I'll get you the coupons, easy."

Rachel shook her head, managing at length to break in on Beattie's speculations.

"I'm not going," she said. Beattie's mouth fell open.

"What? Oh, that's a shame, that is! You don't get out much. If it's Tess that's the problem—"

"No, no, nothing like that," Rachel assured her. "Nancy would have her for the day, I'm sure, but I simply don't want to go."

Beattie looked astonished and seemed inclined to debate the point, but Tess provided a welcome diversion by starting to wail and was borne off upstairs for a nappy change.

Rachel took the opportunity to escape into the dining room which doubled as her study. She was working on an article about holidays for children, commissioned by a magazine—the kind of thing that had been her bread and butter for the past eighteen months and as such was not to be despised—but somehow, much to her fury, the words remained elusive. It was all because of the Rossiters, she thought angrily. Foolish though it might be to think it, they had re-entered her life and they posed a threat.

George Collins came to supper that evening. It was impossible, in spite of Nancy's apparent doubts on the matter, not to like George. He had the face of an engaging monkey, boyish and mischievous, as if his sins, cheerfully admitted by him to be many, were no more than lovable idiosyncracies. Rachel doubted if he were capable of fidelity to any woman, yet he was the sort of man that a woman could forgive and forgive and forgive again.

And Nancy loved him. Looking at them across the table that night Rachel was suddenly sure of it, and was guilty of a sinking of the heart. She was only too aware that anyone not blinded by George's charms would realise that marriage to him would be more of a roller-coaster ride than a bed of roses. What she, personally, would do without Nancy to buttress and cheer her, she could hardly bear to think.

He was, she saw as she came back into the kitchen after putting Tess to bed, in a particularly elevated mood.

"Tell Rachel your news," Nancy urged him.

"Sure." He poured more wine, and, his face alive with excitement and confidence and the kind of vitality that made him the man he was, he lifted his glass towards her.

"Pray raise your glass to Collins Air Services. God bless them and all who fly with them. You may well look amazed! I'm in business, Rachel my love! How about that?"

He and an ex-RAF engineer had somehow managed to buy an old Lancaster bomber, he told her, which they were going to convert to fly freight from an airfield in Norfolk. Air freight was the coming thing. Between them they had the know-how, the enthusiasm, the capacity for hard work. They couldn't fail!

"But planes can," Rachel pointed out. "Parts can. You'll need massive capital, George."

"We've raised a loan. We've got enough, believe me." His eyes as he leaned across the table were bright with excitement. "All we need is this little bundle of efficiency here to run the office and do the hustling for freight—" He turned and smiled at Nancy, putting his arm around her shoulders. "Imagine what her contacts on the Indian sub-continent can do for us!"

"George, you know quite well I haven't agreed," Nancy said. But she would, Rachel saw with resignation, wishing she could feel happier about it.

Afterwards, when George had gone, Nancy came slowly back into the kitchen where Rachel had started washing the dishes.

"You don't approve, do you?" she asked. "What we didn't mention, but is rather germane to the entire thing as far as I'm concerned, is that he's asked me to marry him."

"Oh, Nancy—"

"You've got to have faith, Rachel."

"And hope," Rachel admitted. "And love. And the greatest of these is love."

"I hate the thought of leaving you in the lurch."

"You won't be, Nance. You've seen me through the worst. I want you to do whatever makes you happy. Honestly."

It was true, she assured herself. It was, it was! But the panic that seized her once she had gone to bed was purely selfish. She had relied so much on Nancy—her presence, her practical help, her common sense. From the beginning they had fitted in with each other without strain. How could she manage without her? Nancy had been her family these past two years.

She'd have to find a new lodger. Oh, what an awful, awful thought! She didn't want a new lodger; couldn't bear the thought of a stranger in the house. An advertisement in the newspaper might produce anyone, anyone at all—a homicidal maniac, or a child molester. How could you tell?

It was as if, while she slept, her mind had been methodically examining her options, for the moment she opened her eyes in the morning she knew exactly what to do. Later, while on a visit to the shops, she parked the pram outside the telephone kiosk and dialled Sylvia's number.

"It's Rachel," she said, when she heard her aunt's voice. "I've been wondering—the cottage in St. Bethan. Is it occupied at the moment?"

"My dear, *such* a worry," Sylvia replied, maddeningly avoiding a direct answer. "I want to sell the place, but Rex won't hear of it. I had enough of it during the war without wanting to spend any more holidays there, and now there's this Washington posting which means we won't be in a position to use it for ages even if we wanted to, but Rex says—"

"Is it occupied?" Rachel asked again, more urgently. Tess had been sound asleep when left outside the telephone box, but through the glass Rachel could see she had pulled herself up and now sat grasping the sides of the pram, her mouth pulled down into the crying position.

"Well, no. Were you wanting a holiday? The thing is, Rex was thinking of a long let—"

"That's what I want," Rachel said. "A long let."

"Oh!" Sylvia sounded surprised, and a little dismayed. "We'd have to charge rent, you know."

"Well, of course! I'm not asking for any favours. I want to get out of London and thought I might let my own house and rent yours, if it happened to be available."

"But what on earth would you want to do that for? My dear, what an extraordinary idea! What about your work?"

"I could do it better there. Look—can I come and talk to you about it? Say, tomorrow morning?" Beattie would be on duty once again, which meant she could leave Tess for an hour or so.

"Very well." Sylvia still sounded bewildered. "You'd better come at ten. I have a hair appointment at eleven. I can't promise anything, though. I'm not at all sure that Rex—"

"I'd be a good tenant, Sylvia, I swear. There'd be no trouble about the rent, and I'm quite house-trained these days, I promise."

"Rex was thinking more of a family. Someone settled."

"I'm settled! Or at least I can be until you want the house yourself. There might be advantages in having someone known to you, who'll look after your interests, don't you think? Look, Sylvia, I have to dash—" Tess was definitely crying now, unhappy at her abandonment. "I'll see you at ten tomorrow. And you will put in a good word with Rex about me, won't you?"

"I can't make any promises," Sylvia said again. "I believe Rex has already written to a house agent in Truro."

However, the following day when Rachel presented herself at the flat, she was smiling in a conspiratorial way.

"I managed to talk Rex round," she said. "He didn't think much of the idea at first, but I put it to him that blood is thicker than water and that Ivor would want us to help you if we possibly can."

"I'm sure he'd be grateful—"

"We discussed everything last night. All the arrangements. Rent, and so on."

The sum mentioned seemed, to Rachel, exorbitant.

"Of course, for a stranger we'd charge more," Sylvia went on, seeing her shock. "Empty properties are like gold dust at the moment. No doubt you'll be able to get an equal amount for your house."

"My house," Rachel pointed out, "has three good bedrooms and one tiny one, and is five minutes from a tube station. But never mind. If that's the going rate, then I'm happy to pay it. Please thank Rex for his generosity," she added sardonically—and then wished she hadn't. She wanted the cottage no matter what rent was demanded. Alienating the owners was hardly the best way to go about the matter.

She need not have worried, for Sylvia had noticed nothing amiss.

"There's a Mrs. Hoskings who looks after the place," she said. "Let me know when you intend to move and I'll drop her a note and tell her you're coming. I still can't imagine what you think you'll find to do down there! It nearly killed me, I can tell you."

"Well you see, there's this book," Rachel began. "I've written one that's coming out next year, and the publishers want another—"

This glorious fact had, she realised, been obscured by Barney's visit and her ensuing obsession with the Rossiters, plus Nancy's coming departure, now an established fact. Now, suddenly, it was the only thing that mattered. Relief and joy flooded through her and she grinned hugely at her aunt.

"It's rather marvellous, isn't it?" she said.

"Why, my dear, yes, of course. How very exciting! I *do* hope it has a happy ending. I can't abide these nasty modern novels that purport to show life as it is, can you? Not, of course, that I pretend to be much of a reader. However, let me know when it comes out and I'll put it on my list at Harrods. They're awfully good about getting absolutely anything! Well, keep in touch. I must fly now."

Yes, of course—the hair appointment, Rachel reminded herself. She would have to leave. And she *still* hadn't mentioned a word about Tess!

No time now. Anyway, it didn't matter. Rex, apparently, had preferred to let his cottage to a family rather than a single person. Well, she was a family! She hadn't, after all, lied about anything; just neglected to tell the whole truth.

Back in Inverness Street, Beattie reported that Tess had been good as gold the whole morning.

"But not a wink of sleep," she said. "She should go down the minute she's had her din-dins, bless her."

"This," Rachel later said to Tess, spooning strained carrots into her mouth after Beattie had gone, "is *dinner.*"

At which information Tess smiled seraphically, made a grab at the spoon and smeared carrot over bib, face and hair.

"And you are a little monster," smiled her mother, adoringly.

Loving mother though she was, she was pleased when Beattie's prediction came true and Tess went to sleep the moment she was tucked up in her cot. It meant that Rachel could work for an hour or so, and maybe get the article finished.

Meantime the invitation to Diana's wedding lay beside her typewriter, demanding an answer. She wrote a formal refusal— "Miss Rachel Bond regrets—" and hesitated for some time about the necessity of replying to Mrs. Rossiter's letter. In the end, she wrote a few lines saying that she was sure Mrs. Rossiter would understand that she felt unable to attend, though she wished Diana and her fiancé well. She added that she was leaving London shortly so was unlikely to be able to meet her. Anyone normal, she reflected, would get the message; but she had no real conviction that this applied to a monumental ego such as Mrs. Rossiter's.

How sad it was, that things should come to this! It was hardly believable, when one considered how much she had revered them all and longed for their approval.

Now she wanted nothing more than to get as far away from them as possible. She would, she resolved, set about letting the house the very next morning. Nancy might know someone suitable at the BBC.

And then—Cornwall! A new place, a new beginning. It would be a challenge, she thought, not getting on with the article, but instead staring into space. She'd be on her own again. Well, that was nothing new; hadn't she always been on her own when it came down to it? She was happiest that way.

Which was strange, really, when you considered how she had longed, when young, to belong. To be part of a family. One of the Rossiters.

"They sound an awfully jolly crowd," Julia said when she had returned to school after that first summer holiday in Warnfield. "You must have had wonderful hols, Rachel."

"Didn't you, then?" Rachel couldn't miss the touch of wistfulness in Julia's voice. "I thought you were going to Margate."

"Cliftonville, actually. Well, we did go there, but it was a bit dull. It was a special guesthouse, you see, for clergymen and their families, only the trouble was that there was no one of my age there. The other children were just toddlers—quite sweet, most of them, but not what you'd call kindred spirits, exactly."

"Oh, bad luck!"

How unbelievably satisfying it was, Rachel thought smugly, just to be able to say "bad luck" to someone else, when, at the beginning of the holiday, she herself had been so sunk in gloom; and how wonderful it was to have so much to tell Julia and Alice! All about the games and the laughter and the songs around the piano; and the picnic they all had on Chuffington Common when the news came through about Diana's marvellous School Certificate results.

Well, perhaps not quite all. Rachel didn't mention how the thought of Adverbs was enough, still, to engulf her in shame, or how dull it was at Grandma's house, and somehow cold, even on the warmest day. Or how Diana and Gavin had one of their awful rows on Chuffington Common and nearly ruined the whole occasion. She had, in fact, almost forgotten such things herself, so enchanted was she by her retrospective look at the holidays.

"I think Barney sounds nicest," said Alice.

"Barney's all right," she admitted. "So's Alannah. We're writing a book."

Oh, there was so much to tell that it quite overcame the awfulness of going back to school; and in fact, even this wasn't the horror that Rachel had anticipated because although Miss Scrimgeour, the fearsome headmistress, was still in evidence, Miss Simkins had left and her place had been taken by Miss Rayner, who was much younger, with a thin, eager face and an Eton crop. No one knew why and the whole school buzzed with speculation. Milly Danvers-King said she thought Miss Simkins had been taken ill.

"Nothing trivial, I trust," Rachel said, which is what Diana had said when Guy Seagrave had gone down with some stomach complaint just before the end of the holidays, long after she had grown tired of him. This witticism had a gratifying response, raising quite a laugh. Rachel even heard Janet Fanning repeating it to Morag Blunt, who had been out of the room, and it was all she could do to keep the smile of delight from her own face. No one, last term, had taken the smallest notice of anything she said.

"Maybe English lessons will be better from now on," remarked Janet when they were unpacking in the dormitory; and Rachel, only half listening, her mind back in Warnfield with the Rossiters, was suddenly brought back to the present with a rush of joy. For English was her *thing*, as she had said to Alannah, and having Miss Simkins to teach her had removed any pleasure she might have taken in it. Now, surely, it would all be different.

"Don't you hate being back?" Alice Jamieson whispered, her homesickness for Singapore as intense as ever. But Rachel grinned at her, unsympathetic.

"Could be worse," she said. "Cheer up, Alice."

Alice looked betrayed. She had known about Rachel's nocturnal tears, even if they were silent, and had regarded her as an ally. But now it seemed she had no one.

"You've changed," she said accusingly to Rachel.

"Oh, rubbish! Here, have a sweet." They were humbugs, pressed upon her as a leaving present by Barney. He *was* nice, Alice was right—none of the others had given her anything. Nice but, well, ordinary. Not like Gavin. Alice took a sweet, but repeated the accusation.

"You have changed, you know."

Rachel didn't deny it again. Alice, she thought, was probably right. Just *being* with the Rossiters must have had some effect, surely? Maybe some of their Rossiter-ness had rubbed off on her. And if so, then she was jolly glad.

"Dear Mrs. Rossiter," she wrote after a few days back at school. "I hope you and Mr. Rossiter are well and happy. I am writing to thank you for being so kind to me during the school holidays. I enjoyed the times I spent at Kimberley Lodge very much and hope I wasn't a nuisance. It was the best holiday I have ever had.

"I have heard from my parents that they are coming home on six months' leave soon, and will be here by Christmas, so I might not be at Grandma's house next hol-

idays. We may take a flat in London, my mother says, but
it's not decided. Perhaps it won't happen. I hope not, anyway.

"We have a new English mistress who is very nice. Being back at school isn't as bad as I thought.

"Well, that is all the news so I will say goodbye.

"Love from Rachel."

The possibility of the flat in London for the period of her parents' leave—information so lightly dropped in a letter from her
mother—had shaken Rachel to the core. She could see no possible reason for it. There was, after all, plenty of room at The
Laurels.

Maybe it wouldn't happen. Sometimes her mother was inclined to get ideas—expensive ideas—and though her father
didn't actually oppose them openly they somehow failed to
come to anything. The question of the flat seemed, to Rachel,
to be just one of those kind of ideas. How she hoped so! She
couldn't bear to miss Christmas with the Rossiters.

"We always do a pantomime and have a big party, with dancing and everything," Alannah had told her. "Everybody comes.
I expect we'll even ask your grandma and grandpa if you're
here."

"Your grandmother can take the short cut, Rachel," Diana
had said, with mock sweetness. "She can fly over the wall on
her broomstick."

Traitorously, Rachel had smirked at this, but Barney had
kicked Diana under the table and told her to shut up.

Alannah had sworn she would write once Rachel had gone
back to school, and indeed one long letter did arrive early in
the term. It told her that Diana was now a Prefect, just as she
had foretold; and it contained a rambling and totally confusing
account of Alannah being caught writing *Hurrah for Dymphna*
when she ought to have been doing her French prep, and how
she was sent to the Head and had an awful wigging, and how
abso-bally-lutely awful it was to be the sister of a Prefect, constantly asked why she wasn't as clever as Di all the time, as if
she could help it!

"If only I could be sent to St. Ursula's!" Alannah wrote longingly. "I've been *begging* Mummy and Daddy to send me but they won't hear of it. I've told them that if your parents can stand it, then they jolly well ought to be able to, but it isn't any good, they won't listen. If you have a midnight feast or anything please take notes because we may be able to use it for the book. I'm not doing any more of it now because there's so much prep I'm getting writer's cramp and anyway it's not the same without you. I hope your parents decide to stay in Warnfield for the Christmas hols, or what shall we do?"

Rachel was touched and pleased by these last remarks and wrote back at length and at once; but she heard no more from Alannah who, it seemed, had exhausted her writing capacity by this one initial effort. Or perhaps the amount of prep had swamped her altogether. It was left to Mrs. Rossiter, answering Rachel's previous letter, to give her the news from Warnfield.

"Thank you for your charming letter. You were a most welcome visitor during the holidays and I am sure I speak for us all when I say we shall be glad to see you back in Warnfield again, whenever that might be. I happened to see your grandmother in town only yesterday, and she assured me that you and your parents would be spending Christmas at The Laurels and, indeed, that they would be staying there for the period of their leave, so perhaps the latest news is that they have decided against the London flat."

The letter continued with news of Diana's elevation to the position of Prefect, and Gavin's achievements on the Rugby field; of details of a children's art competition in which Barney had won a prize and had several pictures on display in the Public Library ("Such a thrill," Mrs. Rossiter wrote, "that one of my sons is following in my own footsteps. I cannot express to you my emotion as I stood in that room and gazed at them!"); and of the role that Alannah had secured in the school play, Barrie's *Dear Brutus*:

"Because although she is, perhaps, a little young, there is no doubt she is talented above the ordinary. Needless to say, she is quite delighted at the honour—even, perhaps, a little nervous—but I know that she will cover herself with glory and make me very proud of her, as indeed I am of all my children.

"As for you, my dear, I can only wish you an enjoyable and successful term and thank you once again for writing. I may say that, by the time you left us to go back to school, we had grown very accustomed to seeing you on this side of the wall! You were quite one of the family, almost a Rossiter."

Almost a Rossiter! Rachel's heart swelled with pride as she read these words, and she hugged the thought close to her all the day long, and at night, too, until she went to sleep. Alice was right, then, she thought. She *had* changed! She was almost a Rossiter! She wondered if her mother and father would notice it.

"A fire in the bedroom," said Grandma, "is nothing short of extravagance, and downright unhealthy, if you ask my opinion. Except in case of illness, of course."

"You must remember, mother, that we left Uganda in November when it was beginning to get quite hot. Kitty simply isn't used to this climate."

Ivor Bond's voice was the same one he used when settling disputes among the natives: calm, pleasant, utterly reasonable, yet at the same time firm. Keeping the peace between his mother and his wife, he reflected, had much in common with his duties among the litigious Baganda, the only difference being that in Africa he wielded more power. Here in Warnfield no one took a great deal of notice of him, least of all Kitty. And they had been at The Laurels less than a week!

"Then she should wear warmer clothes!" Underwear, Mrs. Bond meant, but she could not demean herself by discussing such a matter with her son. She had been shocked to the core by the sight (in the wash, naturally) of the sketchy garments worn by her daughter-in-law, who surely should be old enough to have enough sense to know that winter in England demanded good, long, winceyette knickers and wool-next-the-skin. Now, *they* would have been a sensible use of poor Ivor's salary, instead of that coat and hat which must have cost a fortune in Bond Street! Kitty must have dragged him to the West End the moment her foot had stepped on dry land! She'd had a good look at the labels and knew quite well where they had been purchased. That was an unnecessary extravagance if ever she saw one, for had not she, personally, kept in mothballs the coat worn by Kitty on her last leave? Good warm velour with still a great deal of wear in it. But not good enough for my lady, oh dear me, no!

At least she'd been able to scotch her daughter-in-law's ridiculous plan to rent a flat in London. What a dreadful waste of money that would have been, when Ivor had a perfectly good home to come to! Not to mention the chaos that would have ensued. Why, Kitty had no more idea of running a home than a child—and Mrs. Bond didn't hesitate to say so on all possible occasions.

"I'm sure I don't know how you'd get on, my dear, having to think of providing meals without the help of servants," she said, as Kitty made a late appearance for lunch. "Good dinners don't cook themselves, you know." And:

"I'm so happy to have you staying here. Flats in London cost a great deal of money. Someone, after all, has to think of poor Ivor's pocket." And:

"What a good thing you have such a large bedroom, my dear, bearing in mind the way your things seem to get scattered about! Flats in town are so small and poky, aren't they? So inconvenient—and, after all, not at all what Ivor is used to."

Kitty said nothing to all of this, but Rachel saw her little, three-cornered, kitten's smile and knew that underneath the surface her mother was boiling with rage. She was conscious, too, of the sound of her mother's voice haranguing her father, once they were alone in their bedroom at night. Grandma and Grandpa couldn't hear the low, insistent whisper because they were at the front of the house; but Rachel, from the adjoining room, could hear it, rising and falling, on and on. She couldn't distinguish words, but didn't need to. Her mother, she knew, was not happy with the situation. Who could be?

Rachel had gone next door to Kimberley Lodge the day after she had arrived back from school. Alannah had greeted her warmly and Barney, too, had grinned at her in a friendly way and asked her if she'd made the First Hockey XI yet, which was his idea of a joke. Neither Gavin nor Diana had been at home. They were out doing their Christmas shopping, Alannah said, and she and Barney were busy doing their lists, and what did Rachel think? Would Gavin like a volume of W. H. Auden's poetry, or a cigarette lighter? A cheap one, she added gratuitously.

"I didn't know Gavin liked poetry," Rachel said, in some surprise.

"Well, he likes Auden—at least, he says he does. Auden's all the thing, isn't he, because he's one of the young intellectual revolutionaries? That's what Di says, anyway. And Gavin does like being all the thing. But on the other hand, he's just started smoking a pipe, so I'm a bit torn. I'm going to buy Di the music of *The Gay Divorcee*. She's mad about it! I say, do you want to be in our pantomime?"

"Can I be?" Rachel's delight lit up her face.

"You could be an ugly sister. We were having to make do with just me, but there really ought to be two. Di's Cinderella, of course, and Gavin's Prince Charming, and Barney is Buttons—"

"Who's the Fairy Godmother?"

"Well, that's *it*, you see. That's the whole joke. We haven't got one, but Dad's going to be Father Christmas instead. He's written it so that he comes down the chimney on Christmas Eve and instead of finding the whole house asleep, he finds Cinders still cleaning up the fire and getting in his way and at first he gets really cross. He's so funny! When we did the read-through, we were laughing so much that we couldn't go on for ages and Mummy banged on the door and said if it was as funny as all that, then she was going to come and listen too, but we wouldn't let her because it would spoil the surprise."

And she, Rachel Bond, was going to be part of it! It was just too marvellous for words. This was going to be the best Christmas ever. Mrs. Rossiter said that of course the whole household from The Laurels must be invited, she was longing to meet Rachel's parents. She would write a little note that very minute, asking them to the pantomime and party on Christmas night.

"What's this?" Grandma said suspiciously, when Rachel handed her Mrs. Rossiter's letter.

"It's an invitation," Rachel explained. "The Rossiters want us all to go over. They're doing a pantomime, and Alannah wants me to be an Ugly Sister—"

"Well, I hope you told her it was out of the question," Grandma said. "We don't go out on Christmas Day. It's a family time, I always think."

"But Grandma, they *need* me! I'm an Ugly Sister! And there's a party afterwards with games and dancing, and lots of people are going. All their friends and neighbours and relations. Mr. Rossiter's parents are staying for Christmas, so you'd have other older people to talk to, and Mrs. Rossiter said particularly how much she wanted to meet Mummy and Daddy—"

"Then surely it would be the height of rudeness to refuse, mother-in-law?" Kitty smiled but her voice reminded Rachel of icicles, cold and clear and hard. "I, for one, should hate to offend your neighbours and Rachel's good friends, so pray don't turn down the invitation on our account."

She left the room without saying any more, but the speaking look she gave her husband as she passed him on her way to the door told him what she expected him to do, and uncomfortably he cleared his throat.

"I think, perhaps, Kitty is right on this occasion, Mother—"

"Well, I can't agree! Christmas is being together with one's family in one's own home—"

"We can be together in our own home on Boxing Day, Grandma," Rachel pointed out.

"It seems typical of the Rossiters to turn the whole thing into a—a *jamboree!* Have they forgotten the meaning of Christmas? Why, the vicar was only saying last Sunday that the forces of commercialism are taking over—"

"The Rossiters aren't going to charge us," Rachel said, in the kind of voice that Diana would have used had she been present. Both her father and grandmother looked at her in astonishment.

"Well! I think we can do without that kind of rudeness, Rachel."

"Please don't use that tone to your grandmother, Rachel," her father said sternly.

"I didn't mean to be rude, Grandma, honestly." Rachel had been as surprised as the others at her own temerity, and hastened to make amends. "It's just that I do want to go so much, and be in the pantomime and everything, and it really will be awfully jolly. I'm sure you and Grandpa will enjoy it just as much as everyone else."

"I doubt that!"

"Mother, I think Rachel has a point." Ivor cleared his throat again, gearing himself up for opposition—never a stance that came easily to him. "It's not as if Sylvia and Rex are going to be here with us to make it a real family gathering, is it?" This matter was a sore point with his mother, and it was bold of him to raise it at this juncture. "We shall no doubt all enjoy it, and Kitty and I are certainly keen to meet Rachel's new friends. Why don't you give me the letter and let me reply on your behalf?"

"Well, I can hardly insist that you stay at home, I suppose, if you are determined not to."

She was, however, far from mollified, and Rachel heard her complaining bitterly, sotto voce, to Grandpa after he came back from the bank, about the lengths that poor dear Ivor would go to just to please Kitty.

"I swear I'd have walked out of the house then and there if she'd insisted on refusing that invitation," Kitty said with unusual frankness when she came into the bedroom for a cosy chat before Rachel went to sleep. "But your father knows I'm just about at the end of my tether! Can you imagine how awful it would be, sitting here looking at each other in dead silence, knowing that a party was raging next door? You're a poor little puss, having to put up with her every holiday."

"It's not so bad, really; not now that I know the Rossiters."

"You're very fond of them, aren't you? Your letters were full of them. I must say I'm dying to meet them, though Mrs. Rossiter sounds—" she broke off, smiling, her lip caught between her teeth. "I'm sure she's really quite charming," she said.

"Oh, she is, Mummy. You'll like her, I promise—and Mr. Rossiter, too. He's awfully nice, and terribly funny."

"And the boys? Are they funny?"

"Yes. Well, sometimes."

"And handsome?"

"Mm. 'Specially Gavin."

"I believe you have a soft spot for him!"

Rachel knew she was blushing and hoped the bedside light was too dim for her mother to see.

"He's got loads of girlfriends."

"And Mr. Rossiter? Is he handsome?"

"Oh, yes. Terribly."

Kitty gave a small crinkly smile indicating complicity, and gently pressed her forefinger on the tip of Rachel's nose.

"I can't wait to meet them all. Now, go to sleep, darling. Tomorrow we'll go shopping and buy presents for them, since they've been so good to you. And for everybody else, too—though what to get Grandma I can't imagine."

"She could do with a new broomstick," Rachel said pertly, quoting Diana but making no acknowledgements, and was delighted to see her mother's eyes brim with laughter.

"Oh, wicked!" she said, not in the least angry. "You're as bad as your naughty mother! Go to sleep and wake up a better girl."

The town was crowded when they went to do their shopping next day. All the shops were decorated and there was a Father Christmas outside Drake's Department Stores.

"This is fun, poppet, isn't it?" Enlivened by the festive atmosphere, Kitty Bond's cheeks and eyes were bright with a sudden access of good spirits. "When we've finished with everyone else, I'm going to buy myself a gorgeous dress. Come on, let's go and spend some of Daddy's hard-earned. What on earth shall we buy for Grandma—seriously, now! No more funny suggestions."

They settled on a handbag, and a pure silk tie for Grandpa. Presents for the Rossiters took a little longer, but at last they decided on a puzzle for Alannah and a hand-painted bracelet for Diana, and a new sketch-book for Barney.

"We could buy a really expensive cigar for Mr. Rossiter," Rachel suggested.

"He smokes cigars, does he? Mmm—I do love the smell of cigars!" Kitty narrowed her eyes as if in ecstasy at the very thought. "Now Gavin! What shall we get for him?"

"I don't know about Gavin," Rachel said.

"And Mrs. Rossiter?"

"I don't know about her, either."

"Soap? Or talcum powder? I haven't met the lady, but I imagine she would like something pretty and flowery and thoroughly wholesome, don't you? Parma violet, perhaps."

Rachel darted a quick glance at her mother. There was something in her voice—but no, she looked serious enough.

"That would be lovely," she said. "Soap, I think."

"Which only leaves Gavin. Any ideas?"

Rachel bit her lip in perplexity. She wanted to get something special—something that would impress him with her thoughtfulness and understanding, that he would want to keep. A book, perhaps? Something other than Auden? Who was the poet that Miss Rayner had recommended so highly?

She browsed in the bookshop while her mother disappeared in search of a dress, and it was there that her eye fell on a book of Stephen Spender's poems. That was it—that was the name!

She picked up the book, and turning the pages found the verses she was looking for, the poem that Miss Rayner had read to them one morning just before the end of term. She had been thinking of dinner at the time, obsessed by hunger, but in no time she had forgotten all such mundane considerations. Now, reading it again, she felt the same strange prickling at the back of her neck, the excitement in the pit of her stomach that she had felt then.

Through corridors of light where the hours are suns
Endless and singing. Whose lovely ambition
Was that their lips, still touched with fire,
Should tell of the Spirit clothed from head to foot in song.

It was wonderful, wonderful! What it meant, she didn't know—but it didn't matter! It was the sound and the shape of it that she loved; and reading further, she came to "streamers of white cloud/And whispers of wind in the listening sky."

How she loved "listening sky"! Oh, there was no doubt about it, this is what she would buy for Gavin, but she would read all the poems in the book before she wrapped it up and would try to make sense of them. And when she got back to school she would tell Miss Rayner how much she liked them. That particular poem, anyway.

When she arrived at the shop, her mother was pirouetting in a black satin dress with a low scooped neckline, no back at all, and a hem that flared in zigzag lines.

"What do you think, darling?" she asked Rachel, peering over her own shoulder to see her back view in the pier glass. "It's rather gorgeous, isn't it? And not all that expensive, really. Grandmama will disapprove, of course, but then she'll do that anyway, and I'm desperately in need of something to wear at the Rossiters'."

"You look lovely," Rachel said, truthfully. "But—"

"But me no buts, darling." Kitty's mind, it seemed, was made up. "Daddy won't grudge me a new dress at Christmas, I'm quite certain."

Rachel smiled and shrugged her thin shoulders. Her mother was probably right, she thought. And it really was a super dress. Everyone would surely admire it. Even the Rossiters.

) FIVE (

Kimberley Lodge seemed to vibrate with music and laughter and winking lights, which were strung not only on the Christmas tree inside the drawing room but in the trees outside the house as well. There were coloured paper chains everywhere and great swags of holly over pictures and mirrors and on top of the grandfather clock.

Rachel had arrived before the rest of her party, as there was to be a last, quick run-through of the pantomime before they changed into their costumes. The rehearsal seemed to go quite well. She didn't have much to say, being very much the junior Ugly Sister. Her contribution was largely confined to shrieks of rage and astonishment, and a brandishing of fists. It was given to Alannah to do most of the clowning, which she did with supreme self-confidence.

The performance was to take place in the hall where rows of chairs had already been arranged, full use being made of the stairs and the half-landing in a way that had been perfected over the years. This was the eighth year in succession that Mr. Rossiter had produced a pantomime. Christmas wouldn't seem the same without it, people said.

The girls changed and made up in Alannah's bedroom, amid much excited mirth—at least on the part of the Ugly Sisters. Diana was a little more contained.

"I'm not sure," she said, combing her hair down over her shoulders for the opening scenes, "that I'm not getting just a bit beyond all this. It's all rather childish, don't you think?"

"Oh, rubbish, Di!" Alannah wasn't having any of that. "If Daddy can do it, then you can."

"Dad's just an infant at heart. Gavin says he feels a real idiot in his tights. *He* says it's positively the last year for him." She peered closer at her face in the mirror, smoothing her eye-shadow with a delicate finger. "Maybe next year we could put on something a little more sophisticated. Noel Coward, or something."

"Rats," muttered Alannah. "Who wants to be sophisticated at Christmas? Besides, we'd have to learn lots of lines if we did that. In a pantomime we can say what we want to, more or less."

"Ad lib," said Diana. "That's what they call it in the real theatre."

"I know!" Alannah tossed her head, already embellished with her Ugly Sister's wig, made with loving care by Mrs. Rossiter. Rachel, a very recent member of the cast, had to make do with a highly improbable and vastly inferior cotton-wool-over-cardboard edifice, but she knew it didn't matter. No one would be taking much notice of her.

"It's a pity about Rachel's wig," Diana said, as if she could divine her thoughts. "I'm afraid it was a bit last-minute. Mummy said she didn't have the time, so I would have to do it. But I didn't have much time either—"

"It's all right," Rachel said. "I'm supposed to look ridiculous."

"There's ridiculous and ridiculous," murmured Diana obscurely.

Rachel's feeling of pleasurable excitement ebbed considerably, its place taken by one of anxiety. She might have guessed that she would look ridiculous in quite the wrong kind of way. Why on earth had she wanted to be in this wretched pantomime anyway? She could have been down below with her mother and father and grandparents—they'd surely have arrived by now—waiting with all the other guests to be entertained; preparing to laugh, preparing to enjoy herself. She was going to make a hash of it, she felt it in her bones. She was going to be nothing but a disgrace to herself and her parents, and no one would ever speak to her again—

"Come on, girls," called Mr. Rossiter, banging on the door. "Are you decent in there? It's time to start."

The show opened with the Ugly Sisters sweeping arrogantly

down the stairs. The audience crammed the hall, some sitting on chairs, some on the floor at the very front, many standing at the back and around the edges. Paper hats were on heads, glasses in hands, and there was laughter and applause as Alannah and Rachel made their entrance.

Rachel felt a little better. She saw her parents at once and couldn't resist grinning at them. Even a quick glance showed that her mother looked outstanding in the new black dress, and that, alone among the company, Grandma, like Queen Victoria, was plainly not amused by the sight of the Ugly Sisters.

It didn't matter. Everyone else was laughing and barracking as, at the entrance of Cinders, the sisters displayed their utter, utter beastliness. Rachel's confidence grew and she found she was beginning to enjoy herself after all. Maybe she wasn't going to make a hash of it. She could see her mother smiling, clapping her hands with delight as Cinderella and Buttons performed their dance. Diana, it had to be admitted, was wooden as an actress when compared with her younger sister, but she moved so gracefully and looked so charming that the delivery of her words was unimportant.

And then came Mr. Rossiter in the guise of a petulant, over-worked Santa Claus, his comic irritability causing much amusement. Oh, but he was *good!* Rachel thought, peeping through the kitchen door which roughly served as the wings. Everyone was enjoying it. She could see her mother joining in the singing of "Ain't it Grand to be Blooming Well Dead" which somehow Mr. Rossiter had contrived to include in the plot, and even her father, who was inclined to remain on his dignity, was smiling and nodding his head in time to the music.

Old hands said afterwards that it was the best pantomime ever.

"Aren't you glad you came, mother-in-law?" Kitty demanded of Mrs. Bond.

"Very clever, most droll," Mrs. Bond said, giving a wintry smile. "Such a pity it all has to be so *noisy!*"

"Mr. Rossiter is to be congratulated," her husband said, with unaccustomed firmness. "And our little Rachel did very well, very well indeed."

"How handsome the elder son is!" remarked Kitty appreciatively.

"Handsome is as handsome does." Mrs. Bond's dour reply was entirely predictable, and Kitty gave a small, suppressed smile.

"Let's mingle," she said, putting her arm through Ivor's. "I believe Mrs. Rossiter is trying to get us all into the drawing room so that the hall can be cleared for dancing."

Ivor responded with alacrity. Having been in Colonial Administration for a considerable number of years, he knew full well that a hostess's every whim must be obeyed—and in any case, he had rather taken to Mrs. Rossiter. She had welcomed them on their arrival with a charming little speech and a kindly smile. She was, he thought, a truly motherly woman. He liked her luscious curves and the old-fashioned modesty of her un-bobbed hair that she wore in a heavy knot at the nape of her neck.

So far he and Kitty had not met Mr. Rossiter, who had been busy preparing for the pantomime when they arrived. As their small party moved off into the drawing room, however, their host made his appearance, still in costume, to a chorus of greetings and congratulations from the assembled guests. Kitty was calling out with the best of them, even though she hadn't been introduced.

"How Kitty does love a party," Mrs. Bond remarked in her falsely mild kind of way.

"Well done, well done, Mr. Rossiter," Kitty was crying, just as if she had known him for years; she was clapping her hands and smiling as he approached the spot where they were standing. "Oh, how we enjoyed it all!"

Impulsively, charmingly, she held out her hand to him and, equally charmingly, he bestowed a whiskery kiss upon it.

"You must be Rachel's delightful mother," he said. "How lovely to meet you, Mrs. Bond. And Mr. Bond. Such a pleasure to welcome you here—and the senior Bonds, of course. The Bearer Bonds, as you might say!"

Kitty squealed with laughter. "Oh, *Bearer* Bonds! Did you hear that, Ivor?"

Ivor smiled politely. Rachel, had she been present, would have recognised that smile. She had seen it often on other occasions. It meant that he was glad that his wife was enjoying herself, but was worried, too. Sometimes, it had to be admitted,

Kitty went too far. It was greatly to be hoped that she would refrain from any excesses on this occasion.

For her part, Kitty bloomed and blossomed at each introduction, sensing the admiration, almost purring with delight, not caring a bit that her mother-in-law's disapproval seemed to grow with every smile she bestowed. Already the gramophone in the corner was playing a tango—"Goodnight Vienna," one of her favourites—but she knew it would never occur to Ivor to ask her. He didn't like dancing, never had. She tapped her foot and twitched her shoulders in time to the beat, catching Hugh Rossiter's eye. Smilingly he came to her side.

"Have you ever danced with Santa Claus before?"

"Never! But there's always a first time."

Rachel and Alannah, coming downstairs together, saw them dancing together in the hall. For a moment they stood and watched as with exaggerated swoops and turns, making a mockery of the graceful dance and laughing gaily as they did so, the couple covered the floor.

"You're not like her, are you?" Alannah commented, and Rachel shook her head.

"I'm supposed to be like Daddy," she said.

Alannah continued her scrutiny.

"She's very—" she began, and paused while Rachel waited, suddenly a little anxious, for her to finish the sentence.

"Very what?"

"Well—" for a second Alannah hesitated, seemingly at a loss to describe Kitty. She shrugged after a moment, apparently unable to find words tactful enough. "Well, flashy, I suppose," she said at last. "I wouldn't think she was my mother's sort." Clearly this was in no way a compliment, for she added after a short silence: "If you'll forgive me saying so. She uses an awful lot of makeup, doesn't she?"

Rachel was speechless with anger. How *dared* Alannah be so critical? Honestly, she could be awful sometimes! Anyone would think that only Rossiters were any good—that anyone who was the slightest bit different was beyond consideration.

For a moment she continued standing next to Alannah, lips pressed close together in rage, her breathing ragged.

"I don't care what you think," she said at last in a furious whisper. "My mother's a lot prettier than yours, so there!"

Not looking where she was going, she turned and ran upstairs, away from Alannah. Blind with rage, she ran round the corner on the upstairs landing and went smack into Gavin who was just emerging from his room, having changed out of costume and into evening dress. The sight of him in his dinner jacket was sufficient to drive all else momentarily from her mind. Never had he looked so grown-up, so handsome, so altogether wonderful. Laughing, he held her by the shoulders.

"Hi, steady on! Where are you rushing to in such a hurry? What's wrong?"

"Nothing. I left something in the bedroom—"

Gavin looked at her searchingly, but appeared to take her word for it.

"Well, I'm glad you did because I wanted to say 'thank you' again. I loved my book and I feel terrible that I didn't get you anything."

"That's all right. I didn't expect it—I mean, I just wanted to say thank you to all of you because I'm always here—"

"Thank you for having me!" He was teasing her. They always teased her about insisting on saying "Thank-you-for-having-me" every time she said goodbye to Mrs. Rossiter, but on this occasion she didn't mind it at all. Her heart was banging in her rib-cage with nervousness, and with what remained of her anger with Alannah, but she managed to smile back at him.

"That's right! I hope you like Stephen Spender."

"I certainly do. He's got the right ideas."

"Like Auden?" Alannah had decided on the cigarette lighter, Rachel knew, but it seemed a good opportunity to air the name.

"Mm." He looked surprised. "You're well informed, aren't you?"

"I like poetry. There's one poem in the book I gave you—"

"Hey, Gavin! Gav-in!" From along the passage came Diana's voice, demanding and insistent. Rachel felt his hands tighten a little on her shoulders as he gave her a little shake of farewell.

"I must away. Thanks again." He raised his voice, looking down the passage in the direction of Diana's room. "All right, all right, keep your hair on, Di! I'm coming."

Biting her lip in disappointment, Rachel watched him go.

She'd wanted so much to tell him about "whispers of wind in the listening sky"—to let him know how much she loved it. It would, she thought, have been like giving him another present.

"What are you doing, mooching about here?"

Barney's voice took her by surprise and she turned round quickly, embarrassed that he should have found her staring at nothing.

"I'm not mooching!"

"Well, it looked jolly like it to me. What's up?"

"Nothing." She turned to go.

"Hey, wait a sec. I've got something for you." Barney dived back into his bedroom. "Here! I'm sorry it's not wrapped, or anything, but I didn't finish it until last night, and today has just been one big rush. I hope you like it." He held out a picture in a plain wooden frame.

"You did this for me?" Surprised, Rachel smiled at him.

"I said so, didn't I? Well, take it, silly."

It was a picture of the back garden in summer, just as it had been when she had first seen it. There were flowers, and leaves on the trees, and the high stone wall, and a figure in the hammock, with yellow hair. Diana, of course. And there was Mr. Rossiter with his panama hat tipped over his eyes sitting in a deckchair, and Mrs. Rossiter sewing her tapestry, and Gavin dressed for tennis, holding a racquet, and two distant figures huddled over a book.

"See?" Barney said. "That's you and Lannie doing *Hurrah for Dymphna.*"

"Oh Barney, it's lovely." The fact that she had quarrelled with Alannah—that probably she wouldn't be welcome in this house ever again—seemed to give the gift an added poignancy. "Thank you. I'll keep it for ever and ever. But where are you?"

"I'm drawing it, you dope!"

"You should have put yourself in it, just to make it complete. But I really love it," she added hastily. "It's awfully good."

"It's not really. I had to do Ma hundreds of times, and she still hasn't come out right."

"But I can see who it's supposed to be. Thanks *tons,* Barney."

"Is there somewhere you can have it at school?"

"Yes. Miss Rayner lets us have pictures over our beds. She's terrific—"

"You haven't got a crush on her!" Barney's nose wrinkled in disgust.

"No, of course not." Rachel refuted this indignantly. "It's just that she's nice, that's all. Miss Simkins wouldn't let us do anything."

"So school's not so bad now? I'm glad of that. I didn't like to think of you being unhappy."

"I'm not," Rachel assured him, her anger with Alannah almost gone at this revelation. It had not occurred to her that her happiness, or lack of it, was something that had ever crossed any of the Rossiters' minds, once she had left Warnfield.

"Shall I keep the picture until tomorrow?" Barney asked her. "You won't want to be bothered with it at the party."

He held out his hand, but grinned with embarrassed pleasure when she refused to be parted from it.

"I'll put it with my coat," she said.

Downstairs, all except the elderly guests seemed to be dancing, laughing heartily as the gramophone wound down and the music grew slower and slower.

"To the rescue!" cried Gavin, swooping across the floor to wind it up. The tempo picked up and dancers quickened their steps. Barney and Rachel stood on the stairs, looking down at them.

"I say," breathed Barney. "Your Ma's jolly good, isn't she?"

Rachel could have hugged him.

"She loves dancing. Daddy doesn't, much. She says he can't tell a waltz from an eightsome reel."

Diana was two-stepping with Guy, but neither looked happy. They weren't talking to each other and Diana was wearing what Rachel had come to think of as her snooty look.

"Is Di being beastly to Guy again?" she asked.

Barney sighed and shook his head as if defeated by his sister's moods.

"All their crowd went to a party over at Jean's place last night. I think he managed to upset her there, somehow. Don't know how."

"Who's Jean?"

"Haven't you met her? She's Gavin's new girl. Her family had loads of visitors so they couldn't come tonight, but you're bound to see her before long. He's absolutely soppy about her."

"Oh!"

She didn't mind; of course she didn't mind. It was enough to worship Gavin from afar. After all, he was nearly eighteen—a man, really—and she was only twelve. Well, thirteen next month, but even so, far too young for Gavin to notice.

Soppy he might be about the unknown Jean, but he appeared to be making do quite happily with a bouncy little dark-haired girl whom Rachel didn't recognise. How strange it was to think of life going on here in Warnfield—people meeting and getting to know each other, falling in love and falling out again, when all the time she was in that other world of St. Ursula's.

"Whatever happened to Marjorie Newton?" she asked Barney. "Gavin was all over her last holidays."

Barney shrugged his shoulders.

"It sort of fizzled out," he said vaguely. "Things do, don't they?"

"I suppose they do."

Maybe, Rachel thought, things would go on fizzling out until she was old enough for Gavin to notice her. Surreptitiously she counted on her fingers, pressing them against the pink silk of her party frock. In another few years—say by Christmas 1937, she would be almost seventeen herself. Was that old enough? Or would Gavin, at twenty-two, still think of her as a child?

"I say," Barney breathed, "Just look at your Ma!"

The music had changed to the Charleston. The dance had been out of fashion for years, but this record had long been lurking in Mr. Rossiter's record collection and had been deemed suitable for inclusion on this occasion.

It was, Rachel knew, her mother's *pièce de résistance*. She had seen her perform it at parties before this, but never with quite so much verve. This was a parody of the original dance, with the kicks, the shrugs, the vo-de-o-do hand movements, the facial expressions, all exaggerated for the maximum comic effect.

Kitty had been dancing with Mr. Rossiter's brother Kenneth; but now the floor cleared around her and while certain elements of the guests were clapping in time to the music and cheering her on, Rachel was horribly aware of strained smiles on the faces of others, notably other ladies.

Hearing the clapping, the more elderly among the guests who had been engaged in quiet conversation in the drawing room were enticed from their chairs and came out to the hall to see what all the commotion was about.

Rachel, standing on the stairs beside Barney, clutched the newel post and prayed that Grandma would not be among their number. She could see her father standing a little to the left of the door leading to the drawing room. He had been conversing with Mr. Seagrove, who was now among those who applauded.

"What's going on?" asked Mr. Rossiter's amused voice behind her. "Is someone putting on a floor show?"

She turned to see that he had been upstairs to abandon his Santa Claus costume in favour of a dinner jacket, a sprig of mistletoe pinned to its lapel.

"My mother's dancing," she said, inadequately.

"Why, so she is! How absolutely tophole! Quite a girl, your mother." Mr. Rossiter was smiling broadly, clearly delighted at the turn the party had taken. "Why isn't anyone partnering her?"

He didn't wait for a reply, but leapt down the remaining stairs and pushed his way through the crowd. Kitty blew him a provocative kiss and kept on dancing, spurred to even greater efforts now that her host was beside her. Her kicks became even higher, her movements more extreme, Hugh Rossiter matching her every move. Gavin, laughing like a maniac, wound the gramophone and began the record all over again.

Rachel stared at them, mesmerised. They looked—well, wonderful, really. Somehow Mummy and Mr. Rossiter *went* together. They both looked more alive, more colourful than most other people, but at the same time it was horribly embarrassing to have her mother so much in the limelight, attracting all this attention, and she felt quite certain that nothing but trouble would come of it.

Anxiously she flicked a glance towards the door where her father stood. He was smiling that strained, sick-looking smile she had seen before. And oh Lord—both Mrs. Rossiter and her grandmother were standing there together. Mrs. Rossiter was smiling faintly in a way that was reminiscent of Diana at her most superior; but her grandmother's expression was one of utter disgust, as if all her darkest suspicions regarding her daughter-in-law had been confirmed. Rachel was so worried by the look on her face that she didn't notice that Mrs. Rossiter, not generally given to swift movement, had made a sudden dive for the gramophone.

All at once the music stopped. The clapping continued for a moment but died away raggedly when it was perceived there was now no beat to accompany. Similarly, Kitty and Mr. Rossiter stood still and looked towards the gramophone, bewildered at the silence.

Mrs. Rossiter, it became obvious, had lifted the arm of the gramophone in mid-record, and now stood with it still held almost distastefully between finger and thumb.

"Supper is served in the dining room," she announced in her calm, mellifluous voice. "Please come and help yourselves, everybody. Mrs. Bond, you must be simply exhausted! Heaven knows, it was exhausting enough just watching you."

She smiled sweetly in Kitty's direction but moved away at once, almost as if fearful that Kitty would choose to join her; and, once she had turned away, she smiled no longer.

In a gesture of loyalty, Rachel ran down the stairs and slipped through the knots of people who stood between her and her mother.

"Come and have some supper with me, Mummy," she said, attempting to take her arm.

"Hallo, darling."

Rachel saw that her mother and Mr. Rossiter were still glowing, still smiling at each other, and the glance she received in answer to her plea was unfocused and very brief. She tugged at Kitty's arm, earning a quick frown.

"Oh darling, don't be a little pest! Run along with Daddy and Grandma."

"I want you to come."

"That," Kitty said to Mr. Rossiter, taking no notice of Rachel, "was the most fun I've had for ages."

"We make a good team. We must—"

Kitty was never to know what future plans Hugh Rossiter might be forming, for Ivor appeared at her elbow in that moment and grasping her arm firmly, bore her off to the dining room.

From then on, Rachel thought, it was downhill all the way. Grandma kept saying they never should have come and that as soon as supper was over, she intended to leave. Daddy was silent and worried-looking, trying to pacify his mother at the same time as keeping an eye on Mummy's glass, which kept, somehow, being filled up when he wasn't looking.

And Alannah cut her dead. There was no mistaking it. She walked right past the Bonds on her way to join the group around Diana and Gavin; and Rachel, seeking escape from the tensions surrounding her family group, had made as if to join her. Alannah had seen her, had tossed her head and, looking away, had kept on walking.

It's all over, Rachel thought, sick with loss. She still felt angry with Alannah, but the feeling of bereavement was even stronger. She heard Diana give a burst of laughter. At her mother's expense? Very likely! If Alannah thought her showy before, she would undoubtedly have more to say about her now. Well, let her. She was jealous, that was all. She couldn't bear anyone else to enjoy any of the limelight. What was so wrong about dancing?

But it wasn't just the dancing, Rachel had understood that perfectly well. It was the way they'd looked together, her mother and Mr. Rossiter. That was why Daddy was looking so frozen-faced; why he had spoken quite sharply at supper when Mr. Rossiter had come round with the wine.

"Kitty, *no*!" he had said, as if she were a naughty child. Mummy had been furious!

"For the love of heaven, aren't I allowed one night to enjoy myself?" she'd demanded, quite loud enough to make others nearby turn round to look at her. "I've had ten days of total boredom under your mother's roof. Ten days of criticism and pointed remarks. My God, it feels more like ten years! I'm not sure I can stand much more of it."

There was no doubt that it was not only people nearby who were looking at them now; or else studiously not looking, which was almost as bad. Rachel got up, hoping that Grandma was too busy being shocked by her daughter-in-law to notice that her granddaughter had left a large proportion of food on her plate. To take food and not eat it was, in Grandma's book, one of the most heinous crimes imaginable.

She collected up a few plates and glasses and made a rapid escape with them to the kitchen where, much to her relief, she found Barney looking neither more nor less aloof than usual, sitting on the kitchen table, swinging his legs, and drinking ginger beer.

"Enjoying yourself?" he asked her.

"Yes, thanks." Rachel avoided his eye as she found a place to dump the plates. "The food was lovely."

"There's trifle to come, and fruit salad and stuff. And then Dad says we can play Murder in the Dark."

"Oh." Rachel's response was markedly lacking in enthusiasm.

"What's the matter? It's jolly good fun."

"Come along Barney—do your bit in the dining room. I haven't got Pommy to help me today!" Mrs. Rossiter bustled into the kitchen carrying glasses, effectively preventing the need for Rachel to reply. "There are dirty plates to be cleared away, you know."

"I'll help." Rachel badly wanted to redeem herself, without knowing, quite, what her crime had been.

"Thank you, dear," said Mrs. Rossiter. The words were kind enough, but Rachel, looking up to smile at her in a placatory sort of way, saw that her eyes were cold, her full lips pursed. Was she, then, no longer "nearly a Rossiter"? "I believe, however, that your parents are preparing to leave—"

"Oh, they can't be! Not yet!" Barney, tray in hand, paused on his way to the kitchen door. "We haven't played Murder or done Sir Roger or anything! They haven't even had any pud! Rachel can stay, can't she?"

"Better not," Mrs. Rossiter said, still in that pleasant, impersonal way. "Rachel must do as her parents say."

"Well, it's jolly hard cheese, I must say."

Barney banged out of the kitchen, leaving Rachel with Mrs. Rossiter. For a moment, she hovered, silent and uncertain, while Mrs. Rossiter stacked plates and upended cutlery into a jug.

"Such a pity you have to leave, Rachel dear," she said at last. "But I suppose needs must."

"Yes." Still Rachel hovered, not knowing how to get out of the room. She couldn't just go, not without saying something. But what could she say? She couldn't say "Mummy isn't bad, she just loves parties and dancing.'' Or ''Mummy and Daddy don't usually quarrel.'' Or ''living with Grandma just makes everything worse.''

''I think you ought to run along,'' Mrs. Rossiter said, with another of those meaningless little smiles. ''Your parents will be wondering where you are.''

''Yes,'' Rachel said again. She looked at Mrs. Rossiter and sighed. There really was nothing more to say, was there? Well, only one thing.

She stopped on her way out, her hand on the door knob.

''Thank you for having me,'' she said.

''This house is like a morgue,'' Kitty said more than once in the days that followed Christmas. ''Thank heaven I have one friend.''

''Who?'' asked Rachel.

''Why, *you*, silly! You're my only friend in this place. Everyone else looks at me as if I were a scarlet woman—and why, in heaven's name? Because I enjoyed a dance! Is it possible, I ask myself?''

It was a miserable time. Rachel could still hardly believe that she had, in school parlance, broken friends with Alannah—and with Mrs. Rossiter too, unless she had imagined all that coldness in the kitchen. Which she was sure she hadn't.

She tried to keep on feeling angry with Alannah, but, as the days went by, all she felt was a sense of unhappiness. Miserably she remembered all the hours they had spent together, giggling over *Hurrah for Dymphna*. Were those days really gone?

Perhaps if she apologised—but what for, she asked herself? For standing up for her mother? She certainly wasn't going to do that. She did, however, pluck up enough courage to call at the house once, several days after the party, to find that Alannah was out with the other children.

''I'll tell her you called,'' Mrs. Rossiter promised; but there had been no answering call from Alannah and Rachel couldn't bring herself to try again.

''I'm sorry if I spoiled things for you, darling,'' her mother said one day, when they walked past Kimberley Lodge on their way to town where they planned to go to the cinema. ''But honestly, what did I do, I ask you? I merely enjoyed myself,

that's all. I thought that was the whole idea! The last thing I
expected, after all you'd told me about them, was that Mrs.
Rossiter would look at me as if I were something the cat had
brought in.''

"Mr. Rossiter liked you," Rachel said comfortingly, and
Kitty smiled.

"You know, I rather believe you're right," she said. "And I
rather believe that *that* was the reason for Mrs. Rossiter looking
daggers at me for the entire evening—or at least, such of the
evening I was allowed to spend there. The poor soul must have
a somewhat cataclysmic life if she has hysterics every time that
husband of hers looks at another woman. Any fool can see he
has a roving eye—''

"Mr. Rossiter?" Rachel was so shocked that she stood stock-
still on the pavement for a moment. "Oh no, Mummy, I'm sure
you're wrong. He and Mrs. Rossiter are absolutely devoted to
each other. He's always bringing her flowers and chocolates and
things.''

"Hmm. Maybe." Kitty smiled to herself, clearly unconvinced. "He's a handsome devil, though, isn't he, and she's really
frightfully overweight. And not at all what one could call stylish,
with all that hair and those strange clothes. One couldn't blame
him for looking elsewhere.''

"But—" Rachel was silent, not knowing how to express the
admiration she had always felt for Mrs. Rossiter—and still did
despite her coldness at the end of the party. She had never noticed that she was particularly overweight and had always
thought her clothes colourful and utterly right for her. "She
reminds me of a rose," she said at last. "Sort of creamy and
velvety.''

"Full blown," said Kitty, laughing. "And past her best.''

It seemed almost like blasphemy. Rachel made no reply, not
knowing which way her loyalties should lie. She felt rather glad
that another week would see her back at school, where life was
at least uncomplicated.

Meantime, it was fun to be taken to the pictures so often, for
Kitty was a great film fan and seemed anxious to make the most
of her time in Warnfield by visiting as many cinemas as possible. Together they watched Greta Garbo and Charles Laughton
and Jessie Matthews, laughing and crying by turns. They thrilled

to the obligatory galloping hoofs of the "B" feature and giggled when the organist rose from the depths, seated at what was billed as the Mighty Wurlitzer. The Mighty Wurtilizer, Doreen called it, to rhyme with fertiliser, which caused them much amusement.

Needless to say, Grandma was not amused, in fact she dismissed it all as "American rubbish."

"Filling the girl's head with nonsense," she grumbled to her son. "It shouldn't be allowed. I know *I* wouldn't allow it! You should put your foot down, Ivor."

It dawned on Ivor, very slowly because that was the way things always dawned upon him, that perhaps Kitty had some justification after all in wanting to live in a separate establishment, away from his mother. Perhaps a flat would, after all, not be a bad idea; and if it happened to be in London, then in the Easter holidays he would be able to take Rachel to museums and art galleries, classical concerts and so on. He would enjoy that, he thought. And Rachel would, too. Even Kitty. They could go about as a family, for once, as they hadn't seemed to do much in Uganda, and certainly didn't do here. Not since Christmas, anyway.

Perhaps it was time to forget Christmas, he thought. He was growing tired of the continuing strife, of trying to please two women with such entirely different outlooks on life. It would be nice, he thought wistfully, to have a contented wife again; for though life with Kitty was never without its ups and downs and a certain amount of jealousy on his part had always been an integral part of it, he couldn't deny that when she was happy, then she was a very different woman indeed from the waspish creature she became under her mother-in-law's roof. She was a good wife, really; had always stood behind him, doing her duty by entertaining the right people, putting up with petty annoyances—the vagaries of native servants, the clouds of lake flies.

London, then, it would be.

"London!" Alannah said, as if it was the last place on earth that anyone would want to live. "Gosh, how terrible."

It was over a week now since the party, and at last Rachel had steeled herself to make one more foray into Rossiter territory. Alannah had looked up from a jigsaw puzzle without surprise as Rachel had gone into the old nursery.

"Hallo," she had said, as if nothing had happened between them. "What on earth have you been doing with yourself? Haven't seen you for ages. I say, do come and help me with all this sky, it's an absolute beast."

Rachel helped her, and throughout the morning there was no mention of Christmas. Now that all the decorations were down, the festivities did, indeed, seem to have happened a long time ago. At Rachel's announcement that she would be spending the Easter holidays in London, Alannah seemed dismayed.

"What are we going to do about *Dymphna*?" she asked.

"Let's have a look at it now," said Rachel.

The notebooks were produced and Alannah read a page or two. Neither of them laughed. After a while Alannah stopped reading and looked at Rachel.

"It doesn't seem so funny now, does it? Gosh, when I think how we hooted when we wrote it! If you ask me," she went on, slapping the notebook down on the table, "I think it's time we gave dear Dymphna a decent burial."

"No," Rachel said, reaching out for the book and for the other which lay on the table unread. "I'd like to keep it, if you don't mind."

In spite of her undoubted relief that relations between herself and Alannah had apparently been restored, with no ill-feeling, she couldn't help feeling a curious sentimental sadness about the Dymphna project as she looked down at the shiny red covers of the two books. The story had seemed so good at the time.

'Sic transit gloria,' she said solemnly, wondering if it would always be like this—if it would ever be remotely possible for her to achieve something that was not, in the end, disappointing.

"Begging yours?" said Alannah, employing a phrase deplored by both Mrs. Rossiter and Rachel's grandmother, for once in harmony.

" 'The glory has departed,' " Rachel translated. But Alannah had lost interest in the matter.

"Come on, let's play a game," she said. "Let's find Barney and make him play Consequences—"

"Or Limericks," suggested Rachel.

"Or Battleships, or Racing Demon. *Something*, anyway.

Gosh, poor you, *London*," she added, remembering. "What on earth will you do with yourself?"

"Cornwall!" Nancy said, to the adult Rachel. "What will you do with yourself?"

"I shall write, of course. That's the whole idea."

"But here you have Beattie to look after Tess."

"I know, I know. I suppose it all seems crazy to you, but I have the feeling I must go. Don't you ever feel that things are 'meant?' That's the way I feel about this."

A city girl from birth, Nancy looked dubious.

"Are you sure you won't die of boredom?"

"Rubbish, of course I won't! It's a beautiful place that'll inspire me. You and George will have to come and stay."

"George and I," Nancy said, "aren't going to be able to afford to stop working until about the year 2000, at a modest estimate."

They could, indeed, hardly spare time for a wedding. Now that the decision was made, it seemed no time at all before George procured a special licence and they were married at Caxton Hall with just a few friends in attendance, all of whom came back to Inverness Street afterwards. It was a wild, noisy party which no one, least of all the bridal pair, dreamed of leaving before the small hours. Rachel, left contemplating the debris—the cigarettes squashed into half-eaten sandwiches, the half-empty glasses and bottles, the dirty coffee cups—collapsed into a chair and stared at it dumbly. At least, she thought, they'd had a good send-off.

"Please God, let it work," she prayed earnestly. "And let it work out for me, too.

She felt quite sure it would. Only sometimes, in the still watches of the night, did she think that Nancy might be right, that she might be bored so far from London. Most of the time she felt excited, as if something new and glorious awaited her—as if this idea of living in the country was something that had been buried in her subconscious for a long, long time, awaiting its moment.

⋧ SIX ⋦

To Rachel's delight, the advent of Miss Rayner had indeed brought the joy back into English lessons. Her enlightened attitude had its effect out of school hours, too. Her room became a place where the girls felt able to air grievances or discuss affairs of the day, and she cast a new and more compassionate light on such social phenomena as the hunger marches and the miners' strikes which were proving to be such a feature of the thirties. Ghandi's campaign of civil disobedience, President Roosevelt's New Deal, the rise of the Nazi party in Germany— all were subjects to be examined and discussed.

Janet Fanning said she was no better than a Communist and that she had a good mind to tell her father, but she was squashed by the others who were thoroughly enjoying the new regime. However, when Miss Rayner lent Julia Dodd an old copy of *Travels with a Donkey* which she had owned at school, they noted gleefully that her Christian name was Rosemary—and from then on she was known as Red Rosie.

Rachel drank in all Red Rosie's views as if they were Holy Writ, so well did they chime with those that Gavin expressed so forcefully in arguments with his father; and it was to Red Rosie's room that she went for comfort after the Christmas holidays, downcast by the thought that she would be going to London and not to Warnfield when term ended.

"Make the most of it," Miss Rayner urged her. "There's so much to see and do there."

Rather to her surprise she found that Red Rosie was right. The holiday in London proved to be a success, despite the absence of the Rossiters. Her parents were different away from

Warnfield and Grandma's disruptive barbs, though Kitty involved Rachel in little private jokes at her husband's expense, largely concerning his meticulous planning of expeditions.

"We muster at 9:10 precisely to catch train at 9:25. Mackintoshes will be worn," Kitty would say, with a wink at Rachel. There seemed no rancour in it, however, and Ivor suffered it with good humour. Rachel prayed that such harmony would last. There had been times when those insistent, low voices through the bedroom wall had made her fearful. People did get divorced, after all. There was a girl at school whose mother had gone off with another man and everyone knew about it and pitied her.

Back at school, knowing it would be at least three years until she saw them again, she felt bereft and miserable. Only Alice understood, for she had been through the same thing herself; and Red Rosie, of course, for she understood everything.

"I hate it here," Rachel wept, her longing for all the warmth and colour her parents would find in Africa having impelled her towards Red Rosie's study where she felt free to unburden herself. "Next time I'll go with them and I'll never come back."

"And what will you do in Uganda?" Red Rosie asked gently. "Wait for a handsome Colonial Officer to sweep you off your feet? Is that what you want?"

Rachel sniffed and scrubbed at her eyes. The Uganda dream really didn't tie in with the Gavin dream at all. It was very confusing.

"In my opinion, you ought to set your sights on University Entrance," Red Rosie went on, causing Rachel to forget her tears altogether.

"Gosh! I don't think I'm brainy enough."

"Nonsense!" Miss Rayner roundly dismissed such humility. "It's well within your grasp if you work hard. We'll take one step at a time."

It induced a secret glow, knowing that Miss Rayner considered her University material. It meant she was as good as Diana, Rachel thought; then laughed at herself, because she knew that she wasn't, and never could be. But she was pretty good all the same. Miss Rayner had said so. In her dreams she envisaged herself mixing with the Rossiters on equal terms, her assurance greater than it had been before.

Only occasionally did she think of Mrs. Rossiter's coolness

to her after the Christmas party. Friendly relations had been restored all round before she left Warnfield to return to school; but she still burned a little with indignation when she considered the matter, for after all, *she* had done nothing to incur displeasure. She couldn't help feeling let down. Mrs. Rossiter had been on something of a pedestal—the perfect mother, an ideal of womanhood. Now she knew she was capable of less than perfect behaviour.

But such thoughts were swept away and the pedestal restored when a rare letter arrived from Alannah. Would Rachel, she asked, like to come on holiday with them to Clearwater-on-Sea for two weeks in August? Her mother had been on to Rachel's grandmother and had persuaded her to agree to the idea.

"We'll have fun," Alannah wrote. "Do say you'll come!"

Diana wouldn't be with them. She was going to France, as guest of a French family.

"It'll improve her French, I suppose," Alannah said, "but why she wants to bother, I can't imagine. She's terribly good already."

The boys weren't going to be there, either—or at least, only intermittently. They were camping somewhere in the New Forest, but had promised to drop in from time to time, since Clearwater was relatively easy to reach on bicycles. And Mr. Rossiter couldn't get away from the office. He, it was explained, would come down for the two weekends.

"So it's only you and me," Alannah explained to Rachel. "That's why we asked you, really. None of my friends here were able to come, you see. I mean, we're jolly glad to have you and all that, but the idea is that you should keep me company so that Ma can go off and do her painting. It's not that she doesn't want to be bothered with me, exactly, but just that I do get rather tiring because I want to be doing things all the time."

"Oh," said Rachel.

It was a little deflating, somehow, to realise that she was merely a substitute for Diana and the boys and other, closer friends; and even more deflating to realise that Gavin wouldn't be there—at least, not all the time. She had indulged in many a daydream about him; little fantasies in which, with the rest of the family miraculously disposed of, the two of them strolled along the shore discussing poems and politics and life in general. Ever since she'd known about the holiday she had paid even more attention to Miss Rayner's views on current events, and followed her directions towards the latest trend in both novels and poetry—swotting up, as it were, in case the opportunity to air her knowledge to Gavin should arise.

The house rented by the Rossiters stood on its own at the end of a narrow concrete strip bordered by tussocky grass which led along the cliff in the direction of the main beach and the town of Clearwater. "Sea View," as, with conspicuous lack of imagination, the house had been called, was quite new, with white walls and a green roof and wrap-around windows of the kind that was very fashionable. Mr. Rossiter maintained that, architecturally, it was quite grotesque, but Alannah and Rachel were enraptured by its modernity, particularly by the tubular steel furniture in the sitting room and the curtains with their black and orange zigzags.

"Well, at least we have the sea to look at," Mr. Rossiter said resignedly, averting his eyes from the interior and gazing appreciatively out of the window. "Let us thank the good Lord for that."

And indeed, Rachel did thank the good Lord, for from the moment she opened her eyes in the morning, she was overwhelmingly conscious of the sea; first the sound of it as it threw itself on the rocks of the cove just below Sea View, then—with a never diminishing thrill of pleasure—the sight of it as she sat up in bed and saw it blinking placidly in the early sun.

She loved the freedom they enjoyed, too, though she vowed never to mention it to Grandma who had been gloomy and full of dire warnings on this very question. Though exaggerated, Rachel admitted to herself that her fears were by no means unfounded. She and Alannah were able to amuse themselves pretty much as they liked.

Mr. Rossiter caught the train back to town on Monday morning, and from then on, Mrs. Rossiter was engrossed in her painting, leaving the two girls to enjoy the pleasures of town and beach, of which there were many. You could rent things called Whoopee Boats, or watch Punch and Judy or sing jolly hymns with a red-faced, fat little parson with gleaming spectacles who smiled and smiled beneath his panama hat.

There were donkey rides, and a strange, swarthy man who made pictures in the sand. Passers-by were supposed to show their appreciation by throwing pennies down. Alannah and Rachel gazed at his creations in wonder but retained their pennies, preferring to spend them on entry to the pier which to them was the source of all delight.

Here there were machines that told your fortune, analysed your handwriting, guessed your weight. Machines that simulated football matches, showed them What the Butler Saw, sent silver balls spinning round with the chance of turning a ha'penny into a shower of coppers should they fall into the right hole. There were little cranes in glass cases that for a mere penny could be directed over glittering prizes nestling in a sea of noxious-looking green sweets. Breathlessly the girls watched their descent, desperately turning the wheels that were supposed to manœuvre them in the right direction; and always a cascade of green sweets was their only reward. Constantly disappointed, they were constantly hopeful. There was always next time.

For Alannah, the best thing of all was undoubtedly the Pier Pavilion and Uncle Frank's Follies. Uncle Frank was a strangely hairless man who, like the parson on the beach, smiled without ceasing. There were, however, no other similarities. Uncle Frank wore a bright sky-blue suit with silver lapels and a silver stripe down the outside of his trousers, and a silver top hat with a curly brim that he flourished a good deal. He told jokes, few of which made any sense to the girls, though the adults present laughed uneasily.

His small team of artistes consisted of two blonde girls billed as the Singing Shubettes; Tony Tonetti, who was pale and willowy and appeared to model himself on Jack Buchanan; a seedy, foxy-faced older man, known as Wally who acted as Uncle Frank's straight man; and a woman of uncertain age, ample proportions and improbable auburn hair who was invariably introduced as "Your Own, Your Very Own, Gloria Dawn."

Gloria Dawn, dressed in a flowing gown and carrying a long chiffon handkerchief, was clearly intended to add a little culture to the programme. While the Singing Shubettes dressed as Teddy Bears to sing and dance to "The Teddy Bears' Picnic," or Cowgirls ("Home on the Range") or Guardsmen ("Something about a Soldier"), and while Tony Tonetti crooned into the microphone popular songs of the day, Gloria Dawn's repertoire consisted of tear-jerking ballads of the kind sung in Victorian drawing rooms to the accompaniment of soulful glances. In fact, it might be said that soulful glances were her forte.

Rachel and Alannah thought her exquisitely funny. Away from the show they rolled around in helpless mirth as they invented more and more outrageous songs for her to sing, more and more exaggerated gestures. And at the show itself, they could hardly control themselves as Uncle Frank came on to the stage, his face rearranged into the serious expression he considered suitable for the introduction. If Rachel glanced sideways to see Alannah biting her lips, she was undone. If Alannah heard so much as a stifled sob from Rachel, an explosion was inevitable.

"We ought not to go any more," Rachel said. "I think Uncle Frank's getting mad." Indeed, this was true. Uncle Frank had turned a particularly murderous look upon them that afternoon when their giggles had proved impossible to control.

Alannah would not countenance staying away from the show, however, for there was one part of it she wouldn't miss for anything. This was the moment when children were invited up to the stage to give their own performance, the act attracting the most applause being rewarded with the princely sum of half a crown.

Uncle Frank disliked children who recited. He liked those who sang or danced—preferably both. In particular, he liked a diminutive, bubble-haired, cute little girl who sang "Keep Your Sunny Side Up," off-key and with a slight lisp.

In spite of his outrageously partisan approach to the whole matter, however, Alannah still succeeded in winning the prize on several days. Kipling was her speciality. With one or two well-chosen "Barrack Room Ballads," delivered in a cockney accent and with a great deal of pathos, she had the audience, many of whom remembered the Great War and had developed a somewhat cynical approach to it, in the hollow of her hand.

"Well, that's it!" Uncle Frank said, handing over the half-crown to her for the third time. "Three times only, that's the rule. And no more recitations for the rest of the week. Give the singers a chance, I say. And the dancers. Fair dos for all.''

''No one ever said anything about that before,'' Alannah said furiously as they walked home along the cliff. ''He made it up on the spot. He hates me!''

''Why?''

''Because he knows we laugh at Our Own, Our Very Own Gloria Dawn, I suppose. And also he's a snob. Yes he is,'' she went on as Rachel laughed. ''Inverted snobbery, it's called. Diana told me about it. He doesn't like me because I'm not working-class. I expect I make him feel inferior—for one very good reason! He *is* inferior! And he hates kids who recite. Did you see his face when that boy said he was going to do 'The Charge of the Light Brigade'? Oh, *spit*! I was counting on earning a bit more money this week. It's Ma's birthday on Saturday and I wanted to buy her something nice. Oh well, it'll have to be flowers as usual.''

'' 'Only a Rose,' '' carolled Rachel, throwing back her head and striking a pose in the manner of Gloria Dawn. Alannah stood still.

''You know,'' she said, ''*you* haven't got a bad voice. You could do it.''

''Do what? Oh—'' as realisation dawned ''—you mean, I could sing? Oh, I couldn't, really I couldn't, Lannie.''

''Yes, you could. What do you know the words of, all the way through?''

''Nothing. Honestly. Oh, I couldn't—''

Afterwards, Rachel couldn't explain why she gave in. Perhaps it was the idea of having money with which to buy a present for Mrs. Rossiter. Perhaps, secretly, she had longed to be up there on the stage, proving herself just as good as Alannah, not merely ''almost a Rossiter'' but one of their number. For whatever reason, she allowed herself to be coached in the words of ''Bye-bye Blackbird,'' even though she protested constantly, assuring Alannah she'd never have the nerve to respond to Uncle Frank's call.

''Nonsense,'' Alannah said briskly. ''You're miles better than that disgusting little curly-haired creature. All you need is to put a bit more expression in it. At least you're in tune!''

But she wasn't cute. Rachel, staring at herself in the mirror, could see that quite clearly. Her face was too thin, her hair too straight. Even so, Friday afternoon found her getting up, rather like a sleep-walker, and going towards the stage when Uncle Frank announced the contest. She didn't even need Alannah to push her, which assistance had been promised should she delay in answering the call. She went quite of her own free will—a matter which was, afterwards, no consolation at all.

Her heart was thumping madly, reverberating throughout her whole body, and her knees were trembling so much that she stumbled as she went up the steps to the stage. She tried to smile at Uncle Frank as he asked her the usual questions—her name and age and where she came from, but managed no more than a nervous twitch of the lips.

"So you're going to sing 'Bye-bye Blackbird,' eh? Well, don't look so scared. No blackbird's going to peck off your nose, not while you're in my capable hands!" Uncle Frank leered towards the audience as he spoke, and there were a few sycophantic sniggers in response.

Wally, who played the piano as well as acting as straight man, began the introduction, and for the first time Rachel looked directly out over the audience.

It was a full house, for it had rained earlier and the weather was still too unsettled to attract many to the beach. The sea of faces seemed to shimmer before her—old ones, young ones, hatted, bareheaded, their eyes all directed towards her. Her mouth was dry and she couldn't swallow, couldn't seem to breathe; and then, suddenly, her vision cleared, her attention caught by the sight of two familiar figures in the back row. Her jaw dropped in disbelief. It just couldn't be true, she thought, amazed and horrified. It just couldn't be. But alas, it was. There, to her utter astonishment, sat Barney and Gavin, grinning hugely.

They had been expected that weekend, but not here, not now. Why had they come? It was like a bad dream, a nightmare. She was paralysed, the words of the song completely gone from her mind, conscious of nothing but total panic.

"Well, between you and me, I reckon she'd rather be waving bye-bye to you lot than a wagon-load of blackbirds. You've scared her to death," Uncle Frank said to the audience, inviting them to laugh at her. "Come along, dear, no one's going to eat you. Once more from the top, Wally, if you please."

Wally played the introduction again, and still there was silence from Rachel, a silence that seemed to go on for several centuries. She wanted to die—or at the very least, to run away and hide. But she was incapable of movement, her feet apparently glued to the stage. Uncle Frank was doing his best to attract her attention, mouthing the words at her, beating time, but though she darted a look in his direction her eyes were drawn back to the sight of the audience and to Gavin and Barney.

With a sudden sob, she turned and bolted, down the steps from the stage, along the gangway at the side of the theatre. Someone—Barney?—tried to grab her arm in passing, but she shook him off.

Outside the shameful tears felt cool on her cheeks. She hurried back down the pier, towards the entrance, sensing that people were turning to look at her, certain that all of them knew of her humiliation. How could she have been such a fool? What on earth would the Rossiters think of her now? It was worse than Adverbs. Worse than anything. Oh, *why* had she ever agreed to attempt such a thing? They'd despise her more than ever, that was certain.

The tide was out and it was shadowy under the pier, with seaweed festooned on the rusty supports and girders. There was a rank, unpleasant smell and the damp sand was dark and discoloured.

Rachel didn't care. She knew she deserved no better. She sat down with her back against a broad wooden post, laid her head down on her bent knees, and sobbed, sure that her world had, finally, come to an end.

It was some time before she became aware of Barney. When she did, she would not look at him.

"Leave me alone," she said, ungraciously.

"You're being daft. Honestly, what the hell does it matter?" He squatted down beside her and began prodding the sand with a small piece of driftwood. "Coo, this place stinks. I bet all the sewers of Clearwater empty out here."

"I don't care." Rachel gulped and sniffed. "I don't seem to have a hankie."

"I have. Here, take it. It's not very clean," he added. He was right, but she was in no position to be fussy. "I bet it's really unhygienic here," Barney went on. "What a stink! Maybe we'll get sick."

"Go away, then. I don't care if I die."

"You're being daft," he said again. "Look, what does a potty show like that matter? You got stage fright, that's all it amounts to. Lots of people get it."

"I made a fool of myself!"

"Well, all right, maybe you did, but it doesn't matter. You'll remember it longer than anyone else."

"You and Gavin were laughing. I could see you."

"No, we weren't. Oh, we may have done when you first went up, but not afterwards. I knew how you were feeling."

"You couldn't have! Anyway, what were you doing there?"

"We arrived earlier than we thought, and Ma said you and Lanny were here so we thought we'd come too, just for fun. But it had started by the time we got there, so we just slipped in the back. Gosh, that man's a slimy toad, isn't he? And that awful Gloria woman!"

"Oh, Barney!"

Rachel put her head down and wept again, her tears coming to an abrupt halt when, to her total astonishment, she felt his arm around her. It was unexpected and embarrassing, especially when he landed a kiss somewhere close to her left ear.

The embrace, if such it could be called for Rachel's role was one of shocked immobility, lasted no more than a few moments. Sniffing and dabbing at her eyes, she drew away from him. There was silence between them and they did not look at each other.

"It'll be all right, Rachel, honestly," he said.

"You'll all despise me even more than you do already," she muttered, not admitting that it was Gavin's opinion that mattered above everything. To think that she'd made such a fool of herself in front of *him*! How could she bear it?

"Nobody despises you, idiot." He got to his feet and prodded with his toe at a half-buried bottle. "We like you."

This was so unexpected that Rachel stared at him directly, forgetting the embarrassment of the kiss.

"*Do* you? Honestly?"

"Of course. Why wouldn't we?"

She sniffed mournfully. "You're just being nice because you're sorry for me."

"Don't be so wet, Rachel. You're talking a load of rot." This was so much more the Barney she was familiar with that she began to feel that there was, perhaps, life after Uncle Frank. "Come on," he went on, stretching out a hand to pull her to her feet. "Let's have a go at that football machine on the pier. Bet I beat you."

Rachel gave her eyes one last wipe on his unsavoury handkerchief.

"I bet you do, too," she said, resignedly. But, as she followed him over rocks and pools and bits of driftwood, she felt almost cheerful.

They liked her! Barney himself even liked her enough to kiss her—and seemed to prove it further not only by paying for her to re-enter the pier but by buying a threepenny stick of Clearwater rock which he presented to her with a flourish.

And after all, she comforted herself as together they made their way home to Sea View, it could have been worse. Diana could have been there.

It was, however, too much to hope for that she wouldn't be teased about the incident. Gavin said that Uncle Frank was trying to book her for the entire season and that she was from now on to be known as "Our Own, Our Very Own Rachel Bond." Though she still burned inside, she knew how important it was to appear a good sport, so she laughed at the jokes and pretended not to care; but she was even quieter than usual during the evening and disappeared early to her bedroom, longing for solitude.

It was Mrs. Rossiter who eventually came looking for her. Rachel, who had been lying in bed gazing at the ceiling, reliving every ignominious moment, sat up hastily.

"My dear child," said Mrs. Rossiter, her voice honeyed with sympathy. "Are you still upset about that silly incident at the theatre? Alannah told me about it—oh, not to laugh at you, I promise, but just to explain. Really, you mustn't mind a little teasing! We all have to put up with it in this family."

"I made such an ass of myself," Rachel said, not looking at her and picking at the cotton bedspread, with her head bent and her hair hanging like two curtains on each side of her face.

"But from the best of intentions! I gather it was to make some money to buy me a birthday present. I think that's very sweet, and so do the others."

"Any of them could have done it without thinking twice. Oh, it was awful, Mrs. Rossiter! I just *stood* there!"

Mrs. Rossiter sat on the bed beside her, and taking Rachel's two hands in hers pulled her round to face her. Her expression, Rachel saw, was one of great sweetness.

"Now listen," she said gently. "You are our dear, timid little Rachel! We can't be all the same! Alannah and the others are life's fortunate ones. Not everyone has their showy kind of gifts—the ability to amuse, to be noticed. Just as important are the Marthas of this world, the steadfast workers. Your gifts are just as valuable, even if less obvious, so cheer up and don't make yourself miserable by longing to be different."

Tears threatened to overwhelm Rachel once more.

"You're awfully kind," she said humbly. But she couldn't help sighing to herself when Mrs. Rossiter had gone. Being a Martha didn't sound nearly as much fun as being a Rossiter— or even *almost* a Rossiter.

Back in Warnfield, she found that Alannah was spending more and more time at the Tennis Club, following in Diana's footsteps and winning much commendation. Rachel became a loyal and enthusiastic spectator but, feeling she had learned her lesson at Clearwater, declined to join in. There was one definite advantage to this interest in tennis: it was often possible to watch Gavin playing, either singles or with Diana. He usually won, and win or lose, he was always something to behold in his tennis gear. As indeed was Diana. Both had their admirers but, to Rachel's secret relief, there seemed no girl that Gavin favoured more than another. Jean, as so many others, had in her turn fizzled out.

Life at The Laurels was as dull and colourless as it had ever been, but at least her grandfather no longer allowed her to win every chess game, which was a relief. Rather to Rachel's amazement, since her grandmother did nothing but complain about her, Doreen still worked in the kitchen—less happily now, since Molly from Magnolia House had only this week left domestic service for more congenial work as an usherette at the Gaumont.

"S'all right for you," Doreen said, slumped over the sink

scraping potatoes. "You can go off next door whenever you feel like it. Go off to your precious Rossiters." Her shoulders heaved in what Rachel recognised as excessive mirth. "Makes me laugh, she does, that Lady Paint Pot of yours, what thinks so much of 'erself. All those colours and flowers on her hat and what-not, floating along like she was Queen of the May. If she knew what I knew—"

"What do you know?" Rachel couldn't resist rising to the bait. Doreen gave a malicious leer in her direction.

"That husband of hers. Mr. Hugh Rossiter. No better than he should be, Molly told me. And *she* knows because her brother's wife works up the Town Hall and hears what goes on."

What on earth could she mean? Rachel stared at her in bewilderment.

"Rot! You don't know what you're talking about!"

"Oho, don't I? All right, I won't say no more, then."

"You better hadn't." Rachel was very much on her dignity. "The Rossiters are friends of mine."

"Huh! Fine friends, I must say." For a moment or two Doreen scraped and said nothing, but she couldn't maintain her silence for long. "A roving eye, that's what your friend Mr. Rossiter has got," she said. "Molly'll tell you. Can't keep his hands off the typists, Molly says."

"Then she's lying."

"He's got a special lady friend."

"Shut up," Rachel snapped rudely.

None of it was true—if she was ever sure of anything, then she was quite sure of that. She forgot the shared film magazines, the times when, in desperation, she had sought Doreen's company. Now, seeing her lumpy figure in its shapeless overall, the cap with the elastic at the back and the upturned brim at the front pulled low over her brow, Rachel felt nothing but hatred for the girl. What did she know?

"You can finish these yourself," she said rudely, and banging a half-empty pea-pod down on the table, slammed out of the kitchen.

Doreen's allegations were so outrageous, so patently untrue, that she forgot them almost immediately. When, back at school, Julia asked her about the holidays, there was a multitude of other matters that were far more worth remembering, like the celebration when Gavin heard of his place at Christ Church, and when they all went to the zoo.

She felt sorry for anyone who didn't have the Rossiters living next door, though the last week of the holiday hadn't been entirely free from strife. There had been one of those mysterious conflicts of will between Gavin and Diana that had upset the whole household before it was just as mysteriously resolved; and a whole series of arguments between Gavin and his father. One, witnessed by Rachel, had concerned the rise of Fascism.

Mr. Rossiter was inclined to dismiss it as a minor, foreign kind of peccadillo that would soon pass—and as for Mosley, well, he wasn't preaching much beyond patriotism and devotion to the Royal Family, surely?

Gavin had exploded.

"God, you're complacent!" he'd raged. "You and all your lot! Don't you know what's happening in Germany—the persecution and the book-burning? And the rearming?"

Mr. Rossiter had remained calm, his faith in the League of Nations unshaken despite Germany's decision to withdraw. It wasn't any of Britain's business, he said—and he seemed amused at Gavin's apparent change of heart. Last year, he pointed out, Gavin had been a pacifist. This year he was sounding positively warlike. What, he wondered, would next year bring forth?

His smiling tolerance seemed to infuriate Gavin more than any argument; but later, from the bathroom window, Rachel had heard them all laughing heartily together in the garden so she knew that no lasting harm had been done.

"Tell me about the holiday in Clearwater," Julia begged. "Was it absolutely super?"

"Super-duper," Rachel assured her. She went on to recount some of their more amusing doings. She even described Your Own, Your Very Own Gloria Dawn. But she said nothing about her own excursion into show business.

Though the memory of that experience recurred at intervals when she least expected it, flooding her once again with a feeling of unbearable, disintegrating shame, there were other abiding memories of Clearwater that lasted equally long.

The sight of the sea from the bedroom window, for one, and the little curling waves that threw themselves against the sand.

Maybe she'd live by the sea, when she grew up. Yes, that's what she'd do—she'd live by the sea and write books.

With Gavin? In Africa? After she'd been to Oxford? (If Gavin was there, then clearly no other University was worth striving for.)

She wasn't quite sure where this dream fitted in with all her others, but it didn't really matter. That was what was so good about dreams. You could have everything.

"Look," Rachel said, standing at the living-room window and holding Tess up at shoulder level. "I always wanted to live by the sea and now here we are. There it is, in all its glory."

Tess, unimpressed, crowed and gurgled and made an attempt to grab a handful of hair which Rachel skillfully foiled. She allowed Tess to slip down to one hip and continued to gaze, entranced.

It was a cool, cloudy day and the sea was slate grey with touches of silver in the ripples that shirred the surface. It looked magnificent, Rachel thought, but formidable, unfriendly—not at all the same sort of sea in which she had frolicked at Clearwater all those years ago. But even as she watched, the sun came from behind a cloud like a spotlight bringing a stage set to life.

She found it fascinating, this early and brief lesson in the sea's changing moods. It seemed to promise so much and demand so little. It was all there, for her enjoyment.

The journey from Paddington had seemed endless and the autumn afternoon was darkening when the taxi finally deposited her in the street where six stone steps led up to Gull Cottage. Rachel had emerged gingerly from the ancient vehicle, feeling shell-shocked and decidedly the worse for wear, for the drive had taken place at breakneck speed through narrow lanes where at any moment she had expected to come face to face with another car—or a cow at the very least.

The driver—no impetuous youth as one might have imagined by his mode of driving, but a hefty, red-faced man with a bull neck and a check cap worn on the back of his head—had enlivened the journey by shouting disjointed and totally incomprehensible comments in an impenetrable accent over his left shoulder. In return she had made what she trusted were suitable noises, representing interest, disbelief or amusement by turns;

and apparently she hadn't erred too badly for he was geniality itself at their journey's end, carrying her cases up to the front door without being asked, and then returning just as cheerfully for the folding pram.

To Rachel's intense relief the cottage felt reasonably warm. She supposed Mrs. Hoskings must be responsible for that, and was thankful. Tess, who had behaved impeccably for the entire journey, was now tired and hungry, and feeding her had been Rachel's first priority. Afterwards, she prowled around, Tess in her arms, exploring her new territory.

She liked what she saw. The front door opened directly into a room with a fireplace at one side and a door to the kitchen in the far wall. Beside the fireplace were two wing chairs, covered in faded chintz. They were deep and comfortable, she found. Trust Sylvia! Though, as she looked around, she thought that probably it was Rex's unknown forebears who had been responsible for the furnishings, since they were decidedly Victorian. There had been a gilt mirror just like that over the fireplace at The Laurels, and a gate-legged table too, just like the one in the window. A telephone stood on a small drop-leaf bureau. Though she couldn't imagine who would want to call her, she was glad to see it; it made her feel that at least she was in touch with the known world.

There were two smaller armchairs, covered in some dark green material; heavy oil paintings of ships in stormy waters; shelves stacked, not with books but with china ornaments.

The ornaments would have to be packed away, she decided, if she were to find places for the books she had brought with her. It was all she could do not to get down to the task right away. Her spirits rose. With her books around her, this would be a lovely room.

By this time, darkness had fallen and she drew the curtains across the window—chintz, to match the chairs; but not before she had looked out to see the lights of Polvear spilling down the hillside across the river. It was not until the following morning, however, that the full glory of the view was revealed.

Gull Cottage was built on a kind of small plateau roughly halfway up the hill which led from St. Bethan quay. From the front window she was high enough to look over the rooftops of houses lower down. To the right she could look up-river, where hills, covered with trees in all their autumnal glory, folded down to creeks and inlets, where boats both large and small went about their business.

Below her the river was at its widest, with the small port of Polvear almost directly opposite, just as Rex had described it. Larger than St. Bethan, its grey stone church tower protruded from the cottages that surrounded it, while other houses clustered higgledy-piggledy down the hill, and lined the river's edge. There were warehouses and boatyards beside the water, too, and there in the centre was the quay and a small square of larger buildings.

To the left was the mouth of the river, guarded by two magnificent headlands, and beyond it the open sea.

"Just look, Tess," she whispered delightedly. "It's ours—all ours!" The thought that it was there to be looked at whenever she chose seemed, for the moment, totally unbelievable.

A knock at the door brought her back to more practical matters. A woman stood at the front door, smiling and friendly. She introduced herself as Mrs. Hoskings.

"I'm your neighbour," she said, in an accent which immediately entranced Rachel. "Your auntie will have told you about me. She left me a key, so's I could keep an eye on the place. I've brought ee a pasty and a few home-made buns, just to say welcome, like."

"How very kind of you! Thank you so much. Won't you come in?"

"Oh, just look at that liddle maid," Mrs. Hoskings said as she came into the room, tickling Tess under the chin. "She's some lovely, dear of her. Your auntie never said."

"Didn't she?" Rachel smiled sunnily. "This is Tess. I'm so grateful to you for making the house so nice and warm for us last night. Tess appreciated it, and so did I."

"Well, it struck cold, like, when I come in for a quick dust round. You'll be wanting to light the boiler today, I 'spose."

"Will I?"

"You won't get no hot water, else."

"Is it hard to light?" It looked it, Rachel thought. The stove had a malevolent, bad-tempered look about it.

"Bless you, no," Mrs. Hoskings said. "I'll do it for ee."

Rachel breathed a sigh of relief as Mrs. Hoskings removed

her coat revealing a serviceable wrap-around apron beneath, and
tackled the stove's mysteries, soon coaxing it into life. When
that was done she helped Rachel upstairs with Tess's cot which,
together with the packing cases, had been delivered a day or
two before and left in the outhouse. She then carried an odd
table into the main bedroom upstairs so that Rachel could set
up her typewriter there, established a friendly relationship with
Tess, and gave invaluable information regarding milk deliveries,
the whereabouts of the Food Office, and the best sources of meat
and groceries.

A busybody? Well, maybe. Over a cup of tea and one of Mrs.
Hoskings' own yeast buns, Rachel took stock of her. She was
sixtyish, she supposed, and rotund. Rather like a cottage loaf,
Rachel thought. Her hair was grey and skewered with hairpins
into a knot at the back of her head; but she had fine dark eyebrows and eyes that were a clear, peaty brown. She must have
been quite a looker in her day.

"Now don't ee forget, my dear," she said as she put her coat
on before she left. "I'm down the steps and to your left, no
distance away if you want me. 'Tidn't that I want to interfere,
like, but I'm ready to help if needed. I could give ee one morning a week seeing you're busy with your writing. I go up the
school other days."

"I'd love that," Rachel said warmly. "To have the place
cleaned through just once a week would be wonderful. Of
course, what I really need is a girl to look after Tess a few
mornings a week."

Mrs. Hoskings pursed her lips and nodded thoughtfully.

"Well, I'll look out for ee. 'Tis hard, being on your own with
a baby. Will your husband be coming soon?"

For a moment, Rachel hesitated. Nancy had suggested that,
in a small place like St. Bethan, she might consider buying herself a wedding ring and passing herself off as a war widow—
of which, as she rightly said, there were plenty about.

At the time Rachel had rejected the suggestion out of hand.
There were too many difficulties, she said; ration books, for one,
and the fact that one lie would undoubtedly lead to another, and
as one who was bad at lying, she would be bound to entrap
herself sooner or later. Besides—why should she lie? If the vil-

lagers of St. Bethan rejected her, then they would have to get on with it.

Now, however, faced with Mrs. Hoskings, she was conscious of a great need to be liked and accepted, and she wavered a little. Then, slowly, she let out her breath.

"There isn't a husband," she said. "I'm not married."

"Not married?" Mrs. Hoskings stared at her. "You and that dear little maid, you'm on your own?"

Rachel nodded.

"That's right."

"I see." There was an instant cooling of the atmosphere, like a cold wind suddenly blowing over them. Mrs. Hoskings looked embarrassed, as if she hardly knew how to react to this revelation. "Oh, well," she said awkwardly at last. "It takes all sorts. You're not the first and you won't be the last, I daresay."

The coolness remained, however.

"Will you still want to come and work here one morning a week?" Rachel asked.

For a moment Mrs. Hoskings considered the matter, her eyes narrowed. Then she nodded.

"I'll come," she said. "I don't know what they'll say up chapel, but I'll come."

"Perhaps," Rachel said, forcing a smile, "they'll say, 'let them that are without sin cast the first stone.' "

Mrs. Hoskings looked sceptical.

"What they'll say," she said, with some asperity, "is that the war's got a lot to answer for. A lady like you! Mrs. Courtney's niece! 'Tis awful, that's what 'tis." She sighed heavily. "Well, I'll see you Thursday, Mrs.—pardon—Miss Bond."

"Thursday, Mrs. Hosking," Rachel said. "Thank you for the buns and the pasty." She closed the back door, and for a moment rested against it, lost in thought.

Was this going to work? Clearly, it wasn't going to be easy— but then, what had she expected? Commendation? Hardly! After all, it wasn't so very many years since women in her situation had been consigned to mental institutions, accused of moral instability.

She would have to be tough, self-reliant. She wouldn't be accepted at once, that much was clear. She'd have to work her passage, prove herself, show that she was, after all, a reasonably worthy member of the human race. She closed her eyes, suddenly weary and a little afraid; then she pushed herself away from the door with sudden determination. She'd make it work, she thought. She would have to make it work. Somehow.

Later, with most of her unpacking done and a need to buy some provisions, she took advantage of a comparatively settled spell of sunshine to push Tess down the hill towards the quay and the few small shops.

Those she met in the street wished her good morning pleasantly enough, but she was conscious of curious glances. They would soon know, she thought. The word would spread. Well, let it! She was thankful she had told Mrs. Hoskings the truth, glad beyond words that she would not be called upon to remember a pack of lies.

The sun went behind a cloud and the light drained from the day. There was an autumnal chill in the air, and the grey stone cottages seemed to huddle for comfort around the tiny quay where, as she watched, the open boat that was the Polvear ferry unloaded its few passengers.

She could hear the slapping of the water against the dock, and leaning over, saw a frond of seaweed waving this way and that, just below the surface.

That's like me, drifting hither and thither, she thought, fighting depression. She lifted her head, and for a moment she watched the people leaving the boat, walking away from the quay, up the hill, back to their homes. The village seemed to absorb them, enfold them, welcome them, as if knowing they belonged. Could she ever hope to feel like that?

Give it time, she thought. And as she continued to look, the sheer beauty of the place brought its own peace.

It'll be all right, she thought, suddenly calm. Then she, too, turned for home.

⊰ SEVEN ⊱

Fifth-formers were awarded the coveted privilege of a room to themselves. Rachel joyfully celebrated her liberation from the hated dormitories by hanging Barney's picture on one wall and a reproduction of Constable's *Hay Wain* on another. With her books and family photographs on the shelves, she was delighted with her own small domain.

She had seen little of Gavin during the recent summer holiday for he had spent much of the time travelling on the continent with a group of student friends. A constant stream of picture postcards had arrived from various places in Austria, France, Belgium, Holland and Germany. They told his family little, except that he was still alive and still on the move, but Mrs. Rossiter kept every one of them on the mantelpiece and examined them constantly as if searching for clues concerning his activities.

"Montmartre," she said fondly, gazing at the one he had sent from Paris. "Oh, what memories! I was a student there, you know. I'm so delighted that Gavin's seen it. Such an experience for him! Such an education—"

"Such wine, such girls!" Diana added scornfully. She, alone among them, affected total indifference regarding Gavin's whereabouts, openly despising his friends whom she dismissed as long-haired poseurs. Even so, she had spent a week with him in Paris and had apparently enjoyed it.

"It's not fair," Alannah grumbled to Rachel. "I wasn't allowed to go. Gosh, I can't *wait* to be as old as they are."

It was a sentiment with which Rachel could only agree. By next summer, she thought with satisfaction, she would be nearly sixteen. Well, fifteen and a half, anyway. Maybe her skin would have cleared up by then, people said it often did. Alannah said so, anyway, though what she knew about it Rachel couldn't imagine. No one in the Rossiter family seemed to suffer from pimples or any other such unattractive adolescent manifestation, not even Barney who was one on his own when it came to looks.

Diana, now eighteen, had left school bearing a vast number of prizes and scrolls of honour. Various universities, it was said, were competing for her favour, but to her scornful astonishment Oxford was not among them. Lady Margaret Hall had failed to offer her a place.

"They must be mad," Alannah said loyally.

It did not seem, to Rachel, quite so extraordinary. Despite the fact that, according to Alannah, half the junior school swooned at the sound of Diana's name, it seemed quite feasible that others might find her as unattractively cold and supercilious as she, personally, had always done.

January, February; inexorably the year passed. Rachel's Oxford dream was now in the ascendancy, and two more years at school in the sixth form a virtual certainty. An unworthy thought spurred her on. What heaven it would be if she could achieve a place where Diana had failed!

Such prospective glory was still years ahead, however. If only all subjects were as enjoyable as Eng. Lit! Rachel didn't care how many hours she spent reading set books or how often she picked over the bones with Red Rosie when homework was done. Her happiest moments were spent in the housemistress's room with Julia and Alice. Together with a few of the sixth-form girls they spent hours drinking cocoa and arguing about such things as whether Portia would have been a suffragette and should *The Merchant of Venice* be produced at all, now that people were more aware of the evils of anti-Semitism, as practised in Nazi Germany.

Miss Rayner's views on that and other matters were widely aired. Italy's brutal invasion of poor, defenceless Abyssinia was bitterly deplored; and nearer home, she still agonised over the squalor that existed in northern cities and the inhumanity of the Means Test. The Industrial Revolution had abolished responsibility, she said. Human beings were a secondary consideration;

dividends were all important. Didn't they agree, she asked them, that men had a right to work or maintenance?

At least rearmament would give employment, suggested Vera Meadows, one of the sixth-form girls. There was a touch of defiance in her manner, for Red Rosie's views on this matter were well known. She, it went without saying, was a passionate believer in disarmament and the League of Nations.

"If you ask me," Janet Fanning said after one such discussion when the girls were on their own again, "Red Rosie's asking for trouble, sounding off the way she does. Scrimgeour doesn't like it. She told my father so."

"What on earth would we do if Rosie got the sack?" Rachel asked Julia, uneasy that Miss Rayner was the subject of conversation between Miss Scrimgeour and Mr. Fanning—and who knew how many other parents?

"There's no chance of that," Julia replied reassuringly. "Rosie's a wonderful teacher, and Scrimgeour knows it."

Rachel hoped she was right, but couldn't help worrying about it—until, that is, the beginning of March when, with the Easter holidays just over the horizon, she was presented with a more immediate cause for concern. A letter arrived from her grandmother saying that a troublesome gall-bladder meant an operation and long convalescence and that she would be unable, therefore, to have Rachel for the holidays as planned. Other arrangements would have to be made.

"She means Aunty Sylvia," Rachel groaned. "I can't bear it! What am I to do?"

"Come to us." Julia knew all about Aunty Sylvia. "Oh, *do*, Rachel! It would be fun. Mum won't mind a bit."

Rachel hugged her friend, genuinely grateful. Going to Julia's house was bound to be a million times better than going to Aunty Sylvia. But how could she bear not to see Gavin?

In fact, she bore it quite well, thanks to the kindness of the Dodds. The rain fell almost daily and the rectory echoed to the sound of the ping-ping of raindrops as they fell into receptacles placed strategically all over the house. Wet though it was, however, the atmosphere was one of warmth and acceptance, of gentle humour and dry, scholarly wit. Mr. and Mrs. Dodd seemed old to Rachel, a generation removed from her own parents, but from the beginning she had felt at home with them, parting from them at the end of the holiday with real affection.

"My dear, you must be sure to come again," Mrs. Dodd said. "Not, alas, next holidays since we are to undergo a prolonged visit from my niece and her husband and young family, home on furlough from China. But soon. We've enjoyed having you."

"I've had a lovely time," Rachel assured her with perfect honesty.

Back at school, the exams were now looming large; but beyond them; so sweet that Rachel could hardly bear to think of it, lay the summer holidays. Her friendship with Julia had grown and deepened during the weeks they had spent together, but nothing and nobody could quite compete with the Rossiters. With Gavin, anyway. Her grandmother reported a good recovery—adding gloomily, however, that at her age one never could tell. More cheeringly, Alannah wrote to wish her luck just before the exams began.

"Let's hope your grandmother is fit by next hols," she went on. "From what you tell me about your Aunty Sylvia, it would be a fate worse than death to have to go there. Can you beat it? Barney's going to some camp in Switzerland this summer, but I'm *still* considered too young to go anywhere! Never mind. I think Gavin and Di are going to be here most of the time, so it should be fairly lively at home. Bet you'll be glad to be here, with all the exams a thing of the past!"

Would she *not*! Rachel felt a tremor of excitement at the very thought, and inspected her chin closely for incipient pimples. She truly believed they were fading away. Another month might make all the difference.

The exams were spread over two weeks, and it was a relief when the long-awaited ordeal at last began. Geography, History, French, English—all went well. Rachel congratulated herself on having swotted the right things; fate, she thought, was being kind. But she was brought back to earth when, halfway through the second week, the post brought another letter from Grandma. It was her grandfather who was ill this time, struck down with shingles and suffering frightful pain and distress. Absolute quiet was essential, and devoted nursing—all the more exhausting, Grandma wrote, since she herself was not after all fully recovered. This time Rachel would have to go to Aunty Sylvia. Arrangements were already made.

"If only I could go to the Dodds' again!" Rachel said miserably to Red Rosie. "Julia wants me to, but they're full up with Mrs. Dodd's niece and thousands of children, home from China."

"What about your other friends—the Rossiters?"

For a moment Rachel hesitated, biting her lips. She could feel the tears, hot and swelling, behind her eyes.

Why hadn't they asked her? They must know the situation. Maybe they would offer a last-minute reprieve, she thought, hopeful to the end. No word came from them, however.

It was an unsmiling Sylvia who met her at the station.

"Do drop the 'Aunty,' " she said as the taxi took them back to the flat. "It makes me feel old. Whatever made you bring that enormous trunk? There's simply no room for it at the flat."

"But we have to bring everything—"

"I've no idea where we're going to put it. Schools really are the bitter end. I wonder who on earth designs those hideous uniforms? You must change into something more civilised the instant you get to the flat. I've a friend coming to tea."

In her narrow slit of a room, Rachel changed into a cotton dress, badly in need of pressing, and looked dolefully at herself in the mirror. Gosh, it was going to be awful staying here! Eight whole weeks. How could she possibly stand it?

"Tea's ready, Rachel," Sylvia called. Her voice was different now, trilling and sweet. "Come and meet Clarissa."

As Rachel emerged into the sitting room, she was aware of the slight frown on Sylvia's face as she took in the creased dress and the school shoes that she had forgotten to change. She saw the two women exchange glances, raise eyes to heaven.

Clarissa, platinum blonde and fashion-plate thin with orange lips and nails, extended a limp hand.

"So you're the niece," she said, unanswerably.

"How do you do?" Rachel said politely.

"I do frightfully well, thank you." Clarissa screwed up her eyes in a smile that failed to alter the shape of her painted mouth in any way. She turned to Sylvia. "Too old for the zoo and too young for civilised society. What on earth does one do with a child of this age?"

"There's no need to do anything," Rachel said coldly. "I'm not a child and I can look after myself."

"I'm rather banking on it, my dear." Sylvia smiled at her winningly. "Beginning with tonight. Rex and I have had tickets for *No, No Nanette* for simply ages—I'm dying to see it, couldn't bear to miss it. It seems too bad to leave you on your first night—"

"It's all right," Rachel said stiffly.

"I'll leave supper for you, of course, and you can always listen to the wireless. Let's see what's on. Oh look, there's a discussion on modern poetry. You like poetry, don't you?" Sylvia turned to Clarissa. "*Quite* the little bluestocking, our Rachel! Never with her nose out of a book."

"Well, she doesn't inherit that from you, darling!"

"What do you mean? I read *The Murder of Roger Ackroyd!*"

"Only because it was all the rage."

"Is there a library near?" Rachel asked abruptly. Both women turned and looked at her, then looked at each other.

"There's Boots, in Ken High Street," Sylvia said.

"Or Harrods," Clarissa offered. "That's quite near."

"I mean free ones."

"Oh, there's bound to be." Sylvia sounded vague.

Tea was brought in and handed round. Rachel, hungry by this time despite her misery, munched stolidly through several slices of sponge cake. She neither spoke nor was spoken to, and to the accompaniment of what she considered quite the most boring conversation she had ever heard, almost exclusively concerned with other people's infidelities, she made a survival plan.

From the time she had stayed in London with her parents, the capital had exercised a strong fascination for her. Miss Rayner, on that occasion, had assured her that there was a multitude of things to see and do there, and Rachel had proved the truth of this for herself.

All right, she thought now. It was clear that Aunty Sylvia (*Sylvia*, she must remember) would like it if she made herself as scarce as possible. She would, therefore, buy a map, find out about buses, and go *everywhere*! Museums, galleries—everything. Hampstead Heath, Soho, Kew—that wasn't far from London, was it? It said so in Noyes's poem.

And she'd buy a new, stiff-covered exercise book and write a daily report—a diary of everything she had seen and done. And she'd find a library—lots of libraries. She loved libraries and could spend hours in them, just browsing and looking up things.

She became aware, suddenly, that Sylvia and Clarissa were looking at her as if expecting her to say something. She licked a piece of icing sugar from her lip.

"Sorry?" she said.

"We were talking about the Rossiters," Sylvia said. "You'd think they might have invited you to stay with them."

"I expect they were busy."

"Thoughtless, more like. Mrs. Rossiter sounds frightfully odd."

"She's not odd, she's lovely!" Rachel spoke vehemently, the colour flooding her face.

"Hm!" Sylvia raised her eyebrows sceptically. "Your mother had a different tale to tell. Wasn't there some stupid rift that Christmas they were home? She's a real earth-mother type," she went on, turning to Clarissa. "Weaves her own skirts and knits her own stockings, by the sound of it. I thought she sounded a total yawn! Though of course," she added, "it seems she does have her cross to bear. Kitty told me that Mr. Rossiter is well-known the length and breadth of Warnfield as something of a ladies' man."

"That's rubbish! He's just nice to everybody," Rachel said, stung to anger. "It isn't fair, the way everyone says horrible things about him, when he's just being friendly and jolly." She got up from her chair. "I think I'll go and unpack properly, if that's all right, Aunty Sylvia." She laid particular emphasis on the "Aunty," just to pay Sylvia out.

"Quite all right," Sylvia said silkily, and Rachel heard both women laugh as she left the room.

"Well!" Clarissa sounded amused. "This provincial Romeo has one fan, at least. Of course—" Outside the door, Rachel paused to hear the rest. "She's just the age for a *grande passion*, isn't she? Oh my dear, *what* a trial for you!"

And for me, Rachel thought mutinously, depressed at the thought of the long, lonely evening ahead of her. But as the holiday progressed, she found the lonely evenings, of which there were many, almost more preferable to the ones when friends came for drinks or dinner when invariably she felt awkward and out of place. But at least these parties had one positive and highly satisfactory outcome.

From the moment of her arrival, Sylvia had openly and vocally regretted everything about her appearance—her clothes, her hair, her deportment. A certain amount of money had been deposited with her for Rachel's pocket money and essential replacements, and finally, unable to stand the shame any longer, Sylvia marched her niece round to Barkers in order to rectify all that could be rectified.

For the first time, Rachel warmed towards her and was grateful. Clothes were Sylvia's passion and she chose wisely. Looking at herself once they were home, Rachel could only marvel at the unrecognisable image she could see in the mirror. Dressed in the full blue and white skirt that emphasised her waist and the pretty white blouse with the butterfly sleeves, her hair thinned and shaped and held back with a blue band, she looked almost pretty and certainly more grown up than she had ever looked before.

Hanging in the wardrobe was a printed silk dress for better wear, another new blouse, and a little dark-blue jacket that Sylvia had donated from her own wardrobe. There were sandals, too—not the flat regulation things that Rachel had worn ever since she could remember, but pretty ones with a bow on the front.

"We mustn't buy anything else," Rachel said to Sylvia guiltily, remembering the new skirt she would need next year in the Sixth Form. "There can't be much money left."

"I'll wire to your father and tell him to send some more," said Sylvia gaily; but Rachel, mindful of Grandma's comments regarding poor Ivor's pocket, looked worried.

"I don't think you ought—"

"Oh, nonsense! I refuse to have you mooching about the house looking like a scarecrow."

Something of Rachel's pleasure in her fine feathers evaporated; but she rallied again when, next evening, she appeared at one of Sylvia's little drinks parties, dressed in the printed silk. Gordon Boothby, Clarissa's husband, was a bulky, thick-lipped, red-faced man with a loud laugh; she had disliked him on sight, but even so it was impossible not to feel just a little gratified, if embarrassed, by the compliments he paid her.

Sylvia had no idea what she did with herself during the day, for Rachel—knowing instinctively that her aunt would object to long and solitary excursions on the tube to areas of London she considered undesirable—usually said she had been to the library or to the Science Museum or the V & A. There had, it was true, been some disturbing encounters: a seedy and persistent man who had followed her from St. Pauls, and another, coming to sit close to her in a railway carriage suddenly vacated by other passengers.

Neither had bothered her unduly. She felt perfectly capable of dealing with such pests, and said nothing when she got home, for her rambles about London were the only things that kept her sane. She delighted in her discoveries; the sweep of Regency crescents, the grandeur of St. Pauls and, by contrast, Wren's small, city churches. She loved the squares and the parks and the markets.

It was after a river trip to Greenwich that she returned to find that Sylvia had been speaking to Grandma on the phone.

"She says you can go there for the last two weeks," Sylvia said, and smiled a bitter little smile at Rachel's exclamation of delight. "Has it been so awful?" she asked.

"No, of course not." Rachel knew she sounded stilted and insincere, and tried to remedy matters. "You've been very kind," she said.

"Well, it hasn't been altogether easy for us," Sylvia said. "We're just not used to having young people about the place. It might have been different if I'd had children of my own."

"I know." Rachel smiled at her a little awkwardly. "I'm grateful, really."

There was a moment's silence. Rachel hovered indecisively as Sylvia, on the point of going out, picked up her handbag and searched through it. She was conscious that something more ought to be said; that perhaps, after all, there was the chance of some sort of communication with her aunt, some possibility of *rapprochement*. Then Sylvia snapped her bag shut.

"Well, now we'll be able to go to Biarritz with Clarissa and Gordon," she said. "I was afraid we'd have to cancel."

The moment had gone, and Rachel went to her room.

One more week in London—then Warnfield!

Rachel had heard nothing from Alannah in response to the

letter telling her of her holiday plans; still, she felt certain that nothing would have changed, once they were together again. Communication between them had always been like that. There had been long silences between them, even quarrels, but it never mattered, they always seemed to pick up the friendship again.

They were all like that, all the Rossiters. Barney would look up and grin at her as if she'd only been away for a day or two. Gavin would make a joke and maybe tweak her hair. Mrs. Rossiter would enfold her in an embrace. Mr. Rossiter would give her a quick hug and kiss the top of her head. Diana would—well, Diana would greet her with total indifference, but then that was normal, too. She'd probably lift her eyebrows and say "Look what the cat's dragged in," but Rachel wouldn't mind that. Gone were the days when she'd agonise over such remarks. Now she would just pull a face, or throw a cushion, or something.

Would they notice her new clothes, see that she'd changed? Her shape had, anyway. Her chest had got bigger, it seemed to her, even since she'd been in London. You could almost call it a bust. Would Gavin be aware that she was very nearly a woman?

Sitting on top of the bus that was taking her from Trafalgar Square where she had been visiting the National Gallery up the Haymarket towards Piccadilly, she pondered such things, making plans. This was the last day she would wear the new skirt before washing it, she thought. Then she would iron it and keep it for making an entrance at Kimberley Lodge. Maybe she ought to buy another blouse.

There was a small gathering of taxis outside Swan & Edgar in Piccadilly, forcing the bus to a halt. Rachel looked idly out of the window in the direction of Eros where today, in the sunshine, there were people sitting around the base of the statue. Tourists from all over the place, she thought, feeling proud because now she felt that this was *her* city. And as she looked, she saw a backview that seemed suddenly familiar; a backview that made her gasp with astonishment and delight.

Gavin! Surely it was? She'd know the shape of his head anywhere, from any angle. Oh, why didn't he turn round? He was sitting on the steps talking to another young man. The bus would go on in a second. He *had* to turn round!

And he did—and it was Gavin! Her heart was leaping like a wild thing as she pushed past the woman in the seat next to hers and stumbled along the now moving bus.

" 'Ere, 'ere, steady as you go, ducks," called out the conductor, punching tickets at the rear of the bus; but she took no notice, clinging to the rail beside the stairs as they swung into Regent Street, remembering too late that she hadn't paid and dismissing the thought without a qualm, not caring if the entire Metropolitan Police Force pursued her and thrust her into Holloway for the crime. Gavin was *there*, in Piccadilly, and she had to get to him before he went off somewhere else.

She lurched down the stairs and stood on the platform, leaping off the moment the bus came to a halt a little way up Regent Street. Regardless of other pedestrians, she ran back the way they had come. People looked at her over their shoulders, but she was unaware of them, for Gavin was her only thought. Suppose he had gone when she got back to the Circus? She wouldn't have a hope of finding him in these crowded streets.

But he hadn't gone. He was still sitting on the base of the statue, one knee drawn up, an elbow resting on it, smiling a little as he watched the passing show.

A taxi hooted as she darted across the road and a motor bike swerved dangerously, its driver shouting a startled insult. She was unaware of both of them.

"Gavin!" she shouted, and as he turned to look in her direction she saw his smile widen in delighted recognition. She flew towards him, and though he had never embraced her before, he held out his arms to her and she rushed into them.

"If it isn't our Rachel," he said, swaying from side to side, still holding her tight. "And all grown up, too. Who'd have thought it! Just look at you, girl!" He held her at arm's length, grinning widely. "You've cleaned up a proper treat!"

Thank heaven she was wearing the new skirt and the hairband and everything! Rachel couldn't believe her luck. Yesterday she'd gone out in the awful, outgrown printed cotton that she couldn't bear the sight of. Just imagine if she'd seen him then!

"What—what are you doing here?" she managed to stutter at last.

"Just seeing life," Gavin said. "Here—meet Peter." He turned to the brown-haired young man who was still sitting on the steps, regarding them with a smile. He stood up when his name was mentioned and proffered a hand.

"Peter Merrick," he said, politely.

"Rachel Bond," Rachel said, shaking his hand and instantly forgetting him.

She felt quite sure she must be dreaming. Nothing seemed quite real and when, a little while later, she found herself sitting opposite Gavin at a table for two in Lyons' Corner House, she could hardly remember how they had got there.

Gavin ordered egg and chips and a pot of tea, and she said she'd have the same, even though she'd had tea and a doughnut only half an hour before. She demanded news of Warnfield and the family, but this Gavin was unable to give her. He'd been staying with Peter, he told her. In Gloucestershire, he added.

She looked at him curiously. There was something about the way he spoke that made her think he was hiding something. Maybe there was a girl, she thought resignedly. Maybe he hadn't been staying with Peter at all. She pushed the unwelcome thought away.

"How long are you here for?" she asked.

"Just for two nights. We're going to see *The Seagull* tonight—Edith Evans and Peggy Ashcroft."

"Oh, lucky you! It's wonderful!"

"You've seen it?"

"No, only heard about it." Everyone had been talking about it at Sylvia's last drinks party, but afterwards Sylvia had said it didn't really sound her sort of thing. Rachel thought she was probably right.

Gavin frowned as he shovelled a forkful of chips into his mouth.

"It seems a pretty rotten thing, doing something so enjoyable when all hell is let loose in Spain."

Yes, Spain, Rachel thought. People had been talking about Spain too, but current affairs weren't discussed very much in Sylvia's household and she had no idea what was going on. There'd been something on a newsreel, though, when she last went to the pictures. Something about Franco bombing British ships at Gibraltar. Honesty, she felt, was the best policy.

"I don't really understand it," she said humbly.

Gavin explained. There was the legally elected government

on one side, he told her, and General Franco on the other, fighting to bring it down. How, he asked her, could anyone defend that? It was contrary to all democratic beliefs, made a nonsense of all human rights. General Franco pretended the fight was about Catholicism against Communism—but clearly he had no more regard for religion than the man in the moon. Less, in Gavin's humble opinion. The fight was about Left against Right—a legally elected Communist government against filthy Fascists. And what did the British Government do? They drew up their skirts like the collection of puritanical old women that they were and refused to intervene, said it wasn't their quarrel; and what was worse, they were persuading other countries to follow their example. They should, Gavin assured her, be tarred and feathered. And then shot.

"But—" Rachel began.

"It's good against evil, Rachel old girl—as simple as that."

"War is evil. Rearmament is evil." Miss Rayner said so, didn't she?

"Well, maybe we have to make a choice between two evils. Look what old Musso has done in Abyssinia! Horrible things are happening, Rachel."

"I know."

"I was in Germany last year. It's frightening. Hitler's a madman. Believe me, he's not wasting time while the British draw back from rearming! He'll help the Fascists in Spain. He *wants* a world war, and he'll provoke one if he can."

"Gosh," breathed Rachel. He knew such a lot! She loved his fire and enthusiasm, the way his eyes flashed. Even eating egg and chips, he looked magnificent. She poured the tea, scarcely taking her eyes off him.

Finishing his food, he sat back in his chair and smiled at her.

"I know what you're thinking," he said. "That I'm nothing but a windbag, spouting a lot of hot air. That's what Di thinks, anyway."

"Oh, I don't!" Rachel assured him. "I just wish—well, it seems awful not being able to *do* anything, doesn't it?"

Gavin glinted a smile at her as he stirred his tea.

"Shall I tell you a secret?" he asked her. "Can you keep mum?" Could she! Eyes shining, Rachel nodded vigorously. "Well," he went on, leaning towards her confidentially, "don't tell a soul, but I've joined the University Air Squadron. I'm learning to fly. It means when the balloon goes up, as I'm quite convinced it will, I'll be ready for it. Ma would go mad if she knew—in fact she and Dad positively forbade it, but I forged Dad's signature.''

''Gosh,'' Rachel said again.

''Ma was dead against it. She had a brother, you see, who was a flyer, and he was killed in the last war. She simply can't bear any talk of another one. Well, nobody welcomes the prospect, of course, but she's practically psychopathic about it. She almost had hysterics when the subject was raised about my learning to fly, and Dad said I wasn't to mention it again. Di had hysterics, too. She went into one of her spitting rages.''

''You haven't told Diana?''

''I haven't told anyone except you.''

Oh, the pleasure this gave her! She felt as if her heart would burst.

''You know last year, when I was supposed to be abroad?'' Rachel nodded. ''Well, part of the time I was, but for three weeks I was at camp near Oxford. Same this year.''

''But all those cards—!''

''Oh, I wrote them in advance. I had friends who posted them for me wherever they happened to be. This year I'm supposed to be staying with Peter.''

''They'll surely have to know eventually.''

''Sufficient unto the day.''

''Is it fun?''

''Flying? I love it!''

''You're not frightened?'' He laughed at that.

''We learn on Avros—they're the safest things in the world. It's safer than riding a bicycle. This year I've been learning to fly on instruments.''

He'd be the best one in the whole Squadron, Rachel was quite sure of that. Her eyes shone as she looked at him. Just imagine—she was the only one he had chosen to tell—the only one in the whole world!

''London's great, isn't it?'' he said, grinning over his teacup. ''Have you enjoyed yourself?''

''Well, sort of. I've been exploring—''

''Sounds fun.'' He looked at his watch. ''I mustn't be too

long. I've got to meet Pete and some others around six thirty, to make plans for tomorrow.''

''What's happening tomorrow?''

''Didn't I tell you? We're joining an anti-Means Test March. There's a whole crowd of us from the camp. The thing's a disgrace, an obscenity.''

''Oh, I agree.'' Rachel, on more familiar ground, spoke earnestly. She knew all about the Means Test. ''It's entirely wrong for people who are prevented from earning their living to be subjected to that kind of—''

''Must go, love.'' Gavin cut her short, reaching out to squeeze her arm. ''It's been absolutely great to see you.''

''I'm coming to Warnfield next week.''

''Wonderful! You'll be in time for Di's birthday party. I've sworn to be back for that, on pain of death. There's going to be a dance.''

''Gavin—''

About to rise from his seat, both hands grasping the table, he looked at her.

''What is it?''

''Oh, never mind.'' She had wanted to ask if she could come on the March, too, but knew he wouldn't be keen on the idea. It didn't matter. She would be seeing him in no time.

On the way home, she hugged herself in her delight. What luck, what incredible, marvellous, stupendous luck it had been, to pass through Piccadilly at just that moment—and in her new clothes, too. What on earth would she wear at Diana's dance? She couldn't, just *couldn't* wear her old party dress, which was much too short and too tight and too juvenile for words.

Poor Ivor's pocket, she thought with a sigh. Sad as it might be, she was going to have to make still more inroads upon it.

Through the trees she could see the bulky shape of The Laurels. She could even see the bathroom window where, more than once, she had stood and listened to the Rossiters enjoying themselves in their garden on a summer's evening. Now she was on the right side of the fence.

A wooden platform, just a few inches high, had been put over the grass for dancing. Alannah said that her father had borrowed it from the Council; it was the one, she said, that they'd used in the park at the Silver Jubilee celebrations.

There were lights strung in the trees, and a three-piece band that played quicksteps and foxtrots and waltzes—all of which Rachel could do quite well, thanks to dancing classes at school and Julia's willingness to take the man's part.

In floating pale blue georgette over blue satin, with a wide satin sash (approved by Sylvia and bought in C & A's summer sale, drastically reduced) she felt transformed; but only Mr. Rossiter and Barney had asked her to dance.

Barney had seemed shy and abrupt at first, rather as if she were a stranger. Was he remembering that kiss at Clearwater? Surely he didn't imagine that she had attached any importance to it?

She did her best to put him at his ease—which seemed odd, when she remembered that first day when he had sat on the wall and looked down on her, like some lord of creation.

"You seem a bit peculiar," she said, when he settled down next to her at the supper interval. They were sitting on the low wall that edged the rose bed, with a fine disregard for Rachel's new dress, and were eating ice-cream. "Have I changed, or something?" She wasn't exactly fishing for compliments, she told herself; not really. Still, it would be nice to hear that she did, indeed, look different.

He turned and looked at her, his mouth twisted as if in thought.

"Well, I thought so at first," he said with a grin. "You looked so much more grown-up. But as soon as I saw you with a dollop of ice-cream on your nose, I knew you hadn't changed at all."

"Oh, no!" Hastily Rachel felt her nose. "You beast! I've got no such thing!"

"Caught you, though, didn't I? Tell me what you've been doing with yourself."

"I've been exploring," Rachel told him, just as she had told Gavin. But Barney was interested, and asked questions; he even seemed to envy her.

"To be honest," she said, for somehow it was easy to be honest with Barney, "it was a bit lonely. Some days I didn't talk to a soul all day—not more than 'please pass the salt,' anyway. You wouldn't have liked it really.''

"It does sound a bit of a far cry from the Rossiter household. You never know, I might welcome a bit of peace.''

"It's good to be back.''

Why hadn't they invited her to stay? She hadn't asked Alannah, and Alannah hadn't told, but instead had prattled of the play she had been in at the end of term, and the tennis match she'd won, and a new friend she'd made—*American*, of all things—whose father had been over on some temporary assignment at Burnetts, the big electrical manufacturing plant on the edge of town, and of the marvellous party they'd given before they went back. She'd been glad to see Rachel, though. They had laughed as they had always laughed together, and it seemed, Rachel told herself, as if she had never been away.

But she knew she had, when she looked at Diana. This was Diana's nineteenth birthday party, and she was undoubtedly grown up now. Her skin was smooth and tanned and she wore her blonde hair cut close to her head—rather like a young Greek god, Rachel thought. Her eyebrows were plucked, thin and arched, which did much to add to her air of sophistication. Her dress was very plain, sage-green satin with narrow gold shoulder straps. She looked, Rachel thought, quite devastating.

There were a number of her college friends at the party; but she still queened it over the old ones, too. Guy Seagrave was obviously as adoring as ever, and Gavin's friend, Peter Merrick, clearly had eyes for no one else.

Gavin was having a good time, but didn't seem to be dancing with any one girl in particular. Would he remember that they were special friends, now that she knew his secret? Would he ask her to dance before the evening was out?

Whenever the band began a new number, she couldn't resist a quick glance in his direction, just in case; then, finally, when she had almost given up hope, it actually happened. He came across to where she was sitting with Alannah, made a little, mocking, courtly bow, and led her to the floor.

She would never again, she knew quite well, hear "These Foolish Things" without remembering this night. There was the scent of stocks in the air, and the stars were at last appearing, adding their own magic to the summer night. It was a dream

come true, a fantasy. If her hands weren't otherwise engaged—
one resting on his shoulder, the other clasped in his—she would
pinch herself to make sure she was awake.

They didn't talk very much. It was all passing far too quickly,
she thought with sudden panic—and her hand must have tightened on his shoulder, for he looked at her quizzically.

"What is it?" he asked her.

"Nothing."

"You will remember that what I told you in London is a
secret, won't you?"

"Of course!"

"You won't tell Alannah? I know you and your girlish secrets! You're all the same—"

"We're not, and I won't say a word. If you don't trust me,
you shouldn't have told me."

"I do trust you." He smiled into her eyes and she felt light-
headed, as if she were going to faint.

The music stopped, but he didn't move away.

"How did the March go?" Rachel asked him. "I read about
it in the paper."

He had no opportunity to answer, for Diana had approached
from behind and had pulled him round to face her.

"Pray excuse me, little Miss Cinderella!" She smiled at Rachel over Gavin's shoulder, but it was there, that edge of derision that Rachel had always been aware of. "Time you went
back to the nursery slopes."

"What a bossy-boots she's become in her old age," Gavin
turned to smile at Rachel too, but he made no demur and together he and his sister drifted away to the strains of "Smoke
Gets in Your Eyes."

Rachel stood for a moment watching them, feeling a strange
twist of pain at her heart that was almost pleasurable.

They're so beautiful, she thought. Both of them—almost as
if they were made of something more than the flesh and blood
of ordinary mortals.

"They do me credit, don't you think?" said a voice beside
her.

She turned to see that Mrs. Rossiter had joined her. She nodded, smiling; and together, Mrs. Rossiter's hand through the
crook of her elbow, the two of them stood watching Gavin and

Diana. When the older woman spoke again, her voice was no more than a whisper.

"What mother could help but be proud?" she demanded softly. "I ask you. What mother could help it?"

⟩ EIGHT ⟨

The journal that Rachel had begun while in London had become something of a habit. Back at school, enjoying the minor privileges of the sixth form, she continued, intermittently, to record her doings and her thoughts. For posterity? Hardly! Who, she thought, would be interested in her wild delight that she was now excused obligatory games—reprieved from the boredom, for so she saw it, of chasing a ball up and down a hockey pitch or leaping ineffectually around a netball court? And could anyone appreciate her overwhelming gratitude for the fact that sixth-formers were allocated studies, to be shared with two others?

She and Julia and Alice ("We three, we happy three, we band of duffers," as Julia put it, for all had failed to distinguish themselves in any sporting activity of any kind) had turned to each other quite naturally, and so far had cohabited in perfect harmony.

Alice was fair-haired, fresh-faced, and rather earnest. She worried constantly about being overweight, which in no way inhibited her intake of doughnuts, freshly made and sold every day at the tuck-shop. So determinedly tearful when she had first come to St. Ursula's, she still tended to be over-sensitive and a little slow to see the point of any joke until it was explained to her very carefully. Julia and Rachel teased her, but only with the greatest affection.

"And she is improving," Julia said. "She actually made a joke herself yesterday. I had to think about it very hard, but there it was. Almost a wisecrack."

"She'll have us rolling in the aisles before too long," said Rachel.

They all knew they would never achieve sixth-form stardom. The positions of House Captain or Head Girl would, inevitably, go to those whose talents were more to Miss Scrimgeour's taste—*rounded* girls, as she was fond of saying, with team spirit as well as intelligence.

"I'm as rounded as they come," Alice grumbled, looking at herself in the mirror. She wasn't happy at the reflection she could see there, but was plainly delighted with herself for making a joke out of it.

"Ah, but rounded in which direction?" Rachel asked darkly. "And where, may I ask, is your team spirit? Do you lose one wink of sleep if St. Ursula's fails to beat Norwood House? Are you on the sidelines, cheering your nicely rounded throat hoarse?"

"No, she's not," Julia said, answering on Alice's behalf. "She's sitting on her nicely rounded backside, sunk in decadence, reading *Gone with the Wind*."

The shiny-covered notebook that Rachel had bought to record her explorations in London was full, and she had bought another. It was on the first page of this that, long after lights had been dimmed in the dormitories—and indeed, long after even a sixth-former should have been asleep—sitting up in bed with the book resting on her knees, she inscribed the date.

18th November, 1936—Today a European War moved a step nearer, according to Red Rosie, for Germany and Italy have recognised the government of General Franco and are providing him with assistance despite agreeing to non-intervention. This year has been a dreadful one, what with the activities of the Italians in Ethiopia, and now this terrible war in Spain. I have never seen R. R. so down. She has a friend (lover?) who has gone to Spain with the International Brigade and though she had a letter from him a few days ago, posted in Madrid, since he wrote Madrid has been under siege and there has been hand-to-hand fighting in the streets. Unimaginable! Think of it happening in London!

Had a long discussion tonight in R. R.'s room (me, Julia,

Alice, Vera, Morag, Jill) about whether war can ever be justified. R. R. thinks not, but says in spite of herself she can't help being filled with admiration for the idealistic young men who have joined the I.B., because there is something splendid about those who are prepared to fight for what they see as a war of good against evil. We all knew she was thinking of her friend. How terribly torn she must be, between respecting his ideals and her own hatred of war.

Not all the talk was of Spain. We also talked about prayer, and holidays. Can't remember how we got from one to the other, but R. R. believes that though prayer is useless for altering physical things (i.e. like praying for fine weather if a depression is already forming over the Atlantic, or a safe journey if the car's brakes need attention), it's the manifestation of love for another and is a force which can be transmitted through the ether, creating a positive field of influence surrounding the person who is being prayed for. I'm almost sure she loves the man in Spain and was thinking of him. I shall go on praying for Gavin anyway, just in case. I think one should give God a chance.

Re holidays, R. R. loves France, especially Provence. She cheered up a lot while she was talking about it. She made us aware of the warmth and the colour of it—or was it just that it made me think of Uganda? No, I don't think so. The feel was quite different. She talked about sitting on the side of a mountain, drinking wine and eating nectarines and smelling the thyme, and somehow I could just see it all. She's clever like that, she can make you see the things she describes, and she looked so happy while she was speaking of it. I think she was there with The Lover, but she carefully avoided saying so. I wonder how old she is? About 35, I think, but is still very attractive in spite of her age. Not pretty, exactly, but good-looking. She reminds me of that line in Rupert Brooke's poem about the girl who "tossed her brown, delightful head, amusedly among the ancient dead." Being in the sixth form is so different! She always seemed more like a friend than a teacher, but now there is an even greater feeling of barriers being down. She *almost* admitted tonight that she didn't like Scrimgeour!

Not quite, of course, because that would never do, but she did say they didn't always see eye to eye, which I imagine is putting it mildly!!

Letter from Mummy this morning. She and Daddy have been on safari in Kenya—not real safari, with guns and things, but travelling around quite a lot staying at up-country hotels. It sounded wonderful! Sometimes I *thirst* for Africa. We went once to Kenya before I came to England and reading Mummy's letter brought it all back to me. I remember how funny it was to feel cold in the evening and to sit in front of a roaring fire, when the days were so warm and the air so very clear and still. Quite different from Entebbe. I stood on a hillside once and could hear the sound of a tractor below me in the valley. It looked like a toy, but I could hear it so plainly. Oh, when will I see it all again? Mummy still thinks I'm coming home after a year in the sixth form. They were pleased about my good exam results, of course, but it doesn't seem to occur to anyone that I might like to take a degree, and I haven't said a word, I don't know why. I suppose because I still can't really believe I'm good enough. I'll wait until I've done a year in the Sixth and then see how things go.

She chewed the end of her pencil, thinking about it, wondering why she found the subject so difficult to talk about. It was all right at school, of course, with Red Rosie, and with Alice and Julia. They all knew what she wanted to do, and didn't see anything particularly remarkable about it. Julia cherished similar ambitions, and her parents took it for granted that these would be fulfilled. Grandma, however, had a strange and almost scornful attitude towards higher education for women, and Mummy and Daddy seemed to think it irrelevant—a waste of time unless one was going to be a teacher. Even the Rossiters—who, Rachel felt, might have taken a different view since their own daughter was at London University—assumed that she had reached saturation point with School Certificate. Mrs. Rossiter had urged her to take a shorthand and typing course—"*such* an advantage for any girl," she had said, adding that Mr. Rossiter always maintained that a good secretary was worth her weight in gold.

"And you would be an *excellent* one, Rachel, I'm certain of it,'' she had said earnestly. ''You're such a dear, methodical, unobtrusive little creature.''

''You make her sound like Mrs. Tittlemouse,'' Barney said, sounding irritated on her behalf, and Rachel was grateful for his intervention. She hadn't followed up the conversation, though, or attempted to state her very different ambitions. Had she done so, she would have felt like Yeats:

> I have spread my dreams under your
> feet;
> Tread softly, for you tread on my
> dreams.

Yawning, suddenly overwhelmed with sleepiness, she put the book down on the table beside the bed, hopped out to turn off the light, and, with the room in darkness, went to the window to pull the curtain aside and look out at the night.

She was in a room high up in the east wing; a servant's room, no doubt, in the old days when the house had been occupied by landed gentry. It had been raining earlier in the evening, but now the sky was clear and the moon was shining. It shone on the handsome bulk of the school with its sweeping drive, glinting on the puddles, palely lighting the front porch. It would be shining on Gavin, too, wherever he was. She knew that to be no more than a cliché, well used by poets and lovers through the ages, but all the same she liked to think of it.

The school faced south—a feature made much of in its glossy brochure, which also spoke at length of its extensive, park-like grounds. Rachel had long ago worked out that Oxford lay vaguely to her left, and it was in this direction she looked now. Tightly she closed her eyes, summoning every bit of positive thought that she could muster, putting her last ounce of effort into a prayer for Gavin.

Afterwards, she continued to look out over the bleached gardens, the moon so bright that she could almost see the individual leaves on the trees. Had he felt it, she wondered? Had he felt surrounded by her love, just for that moment? Would he ever feel it?

Suddenly aware that her feet were cold on the bare lino, she scampered back to bed. She could, she thought, think of Gavin just as easily under the bedclothes.

There was no Rossiter pantomime at Christmas any more; but there was still a party at which they played charades and all the old-time favourites, or most of them. The game of Adverbs seemed to be forgotten, much to Rachel's relief, for she had never been able to come to terms with it.

It was during a game of Sardines that, as they huddled together in the airing cupboard, Barney kissed her again. She couldn't in all honesty say that it was an enjoyable experience, mainly because—as on the last occasion—she was utterly unprepared for it. Which shouldn't, she recognised, really make any difference. If it had been Gavin, she would have rallied from the shock in short order and would have given as good as she got. With Barney, however, it was like being kissed by a brother; not unpleasant, exactly, but rather pointless.

She made no comment, and nor did he, mainly because they were almost immediately joined by Alannah and her friend Daphne Baker who, amid many giggles, squeezed into the cupboard beside them.

Daphne had a crush on Barney, so Alannah had told her. What a pity it was, Rachel couldn't help reflecting, that it hadn't been Daphne who found Barney first. Maybe he would have kissed her instead, which would have given a lot more pleasure. Sometimes life could be so unsatisfactory.

Rachel, with a shelf jutting painfully into her back, began to think that perhaps Adverbs hadn't been so bad after all, and was heartily thankful when they were all discovered and were able to troop back to the drawing room where dancing was being organised by Gavin. He had a new girlfriend called Jacqueline who was not only extremely attractive but seemed nice as well. Try as she might, Rachel could see nothing to her detriment.

I ought to be used to it, she thought drearily. Heaven knows there have been enough girls over the years, and none of them last very long; but even so, she couldn't avoid feeling an aching desolation at the sight of them laughing together.

The dancing took place to the same gramophone and the same records, she realised, as on that Christmas Day three years before when Mummy and Mr. Rossiter had danced together and caused such a lot of unnecessary fuss. Christmas 1936 passed without any such upset, but Rachel did wish Barney hadn't kissed her. It unsettled her. She didn't know what to make of it. And she did wish Jacqueline didn't have such pretty dark curls and such a flawless skin. That night, in yet another new journal, she wrote:

I have a horrible feeling that this might be *it*, for Gavin and Jacqueline looked so right together. I hope not. And what on earth does Barney mean by kissing me like that? Does he want me for his girl friend? Or is he just trying to get a bit of practice? If the former, I fail to see how it's possible he could be attracted to me when all I feel for him is mild affection.

She studied this for a moment, chewing her lip, then crossed out "mild." The affection she felt for Barney was more than that, she decided on reflection. But it was still only affection. She went on,

Actually, I feel that the second alternative is more likely. He's not a bit like Gavin—I bet he was twice as experienced as Barney when he was sixteen! I got the feeling that Barney is as green as I am, so if he's experimenting then it's just too bad for him! What I know about kissing (as he must recognise by now) you could write on the back of a postage stamp in block capitals and still have room left over for the Gettysburg Address. He didn't say one word when we were dancing—not about that, anyway, just went on and on about whether or not he should go to Art College. Mrs. Rossiter is passionately keen that he should go, but he doesn't think he's good enough. I didn't know what to say, except that I supposed if his mother thought he was good enough, then he probably was. He's not happy about it, though.
   You'd think, if he really liked me, that he'd have said *something* nice, just for once. It was Gavin who said I was looking pretty. I don't honestly think he meant it, but it was nice of him to say it. And you never know, he might have meant it, in spite of Jacqueline.

Jacqueline or no Jacqueline, it was good to be among them all again, part of the family. Even Diana seemed more friendly than in the past. One afternoon soon after Christmas, Rachel found herself involved in a brisk argument with her, regarding *Emma*—was she too bossy and too much of a prig to be a likeable heroine? Diana held that she was—that she was totally impossible and that Mr. Knightley wouldn't have looked at her twice in real life, but Rachel argued that it was her faults that made her human.

"And after all, she's very honest about herself," she went on earnestly. "She does learn."

"But of all the interfering busybodies in fact or fiction, she takes the cake," Diana maintained.

Rachel was diverted afterwards to see that they had been talking, actually conversing, for over five minutes—and as equals, too. It must, she thought, be some kind of a record. Had the time come at last when Diana accepted her as one of them?

It seemed quite a possibility; and she certainly felt a true member of the family when, alone in the kitchen with Mrs. Rossiter one morning, she was the recipient of certain confidences regarding the distant courtship of the Rossiter parents.

"My father never cared for Hugh," Mrs. Rossiter said. "He was a rather austere man, you see, and he thought Hugh a lightweight, which was terribly unfair. Of course, he might give that impression, I can see how people might think it of him, but it's quite untrue. I knew right from the beginning that it was he I wanted as the father of my children."

"Really?"

Rachel was a little startled at this aspect of the relationship. In her book, people fell in love and they got married. Children, surely, hardly came into the picture at that stage.

"Oh yes!" Mrs. Rossiter's eyes glowed with a reminiscent light as she paused in drying a milk jug. "He had such vigour and vitality, such a *glow* about him! 'I want sons like that,' I thought. Well, Barney is more like my father to look at than his own, except for the eyes, but Gavin, you'll agree, is the image of Hugh."

"Yes, I suppose he is. Taller, though."

"He gets that from my family. But he has all of his father's charm, don't you agree?"

"Oh, yes!" How could Rachel disagree with that?

"And such intelligence! It shows in his face, of course. There's a fineness there, a liveliness. And of course," she went on more matter-of-factly, resuming the drying briskly, "he's full of affection for his home and family. I know I'm lucky to have such a son. I suppose one day I shall have to share him with another woman, but not yet, not yet!"

"You don't think Jacqueline—" began Rachel, diffidently.

"Jacqueline? That little dark girl who came to the party? My dear Rachel, give Gavin credit for some taste! She's pretty enough, I grant you, but hardly his intellectual equal. Oh no, when Gavin chooses a girl it will be someone very special, I promise you. Well, well! I mustn't go on. You'll think me a doting mother, and no mistake. It's not that I don't think anyone good enough for him, you understand, or that I don't care for the other children. I'm proud of all of them, and with good reason. There's something about the first-born, though . . . Oh, I can't explain! You'll find out, in time."

Rachel smiled guardedly and said nothing. She—who better?—knew how easy it was to dote on Gavin, yet there was something in Mrs. Rossiter's enthusiasm that caused a flicker of unease, as if she had revealed herself naked in the High Street. People just didn't go on like that, Rachel thought. They spoke of their children with detached affection, however proud they were of them underneath. She tried to imagine her own mother conversing in the same vein, and failed miserably.

But when later she was in the old nursery with all of them— Barney making toast in front of the fire, Alannah lying on her back on the floor with her legs upright, pressed against the wall (which she had read somewhere was recommended practice for anyone who required shapely ankles), Diana elegantly draped in a chair reading *This Gun for Hire*, Gavin sitting in the window seat with his profile turned towards them all, drumming his fingers as if lost in thought—she couldn't help thinking that Mrs. Rossiter's fervour was understandable. They were a pretty impressive and unusual lot. Especially Gavin.

As she looked across at him, he turned from the window and looked straight into her eyes. She smiled a little nervously, feeling somehow caught out, but the smile he gave her in return was perfunctory, as if he was not really seeing her. With an exaggerated movement, lifting his hands before pressing them down on the window seat to lever himself upright, he stood for a moment, looking now not at her but at Diana who, blissfully unconscious, went on reading.

"I wish to make an announcement," he said abruptly.

"Is it worth getting my legs down for it?" Alannah asked, not moving.

He didn't reply. Diana looked up, but slowly, unwillingly, one finger keeping her place. Then, seeing his expression, she shut the book and put it to one side.

"It looks as if it might be," she said.

"Toast's ready!" Barney, his fair-skinned face reddened by the glow of the fire, was sitting back on his heels. "Who wants first bit?"

"Leave it!" Gavin's voice was curt, making Barney look up in astonishment.

"What on earth is it?" Alannah asked, now sitting the right way up.

"I'm going to Spain," Gavin said harshly, without any preamble. For a moment there was silence. Then Diana spoke.

"You surely couldn't be such a damned fool," she said coldly.

"I'm not going to fight. At least I don't think so. I've volunteered to drive a supply lorry out there, full of stretchers and blankets and clothes and primus stoves and so on. They're all badly needed. You can't object to that!"

"Why can't I? Have you seen today's paper? They're bombing Madrid, it says."

"Ma won't let you go," Alannah said fiercely. Gavin laughed briefly.

"She can't stop me! I shall be twenty-one in three months' time."

"Maybe you'll never be twenty-one." Diana's face was bone-white, drained of colour. "Have you thought what that would do to her?"

"Of course." Hands thrust in his pockets, he flung himself on the arm of the chair where Rachel sat. Because it was the nearest; she told herself, sitting very quietly. Not for any other reason. Still, it felt good having him so near. Maybe, instinctively, he had turned to her for the support he knew he wouldn't get from his own family. "I've thought about what it would do to me, as well. I've thought about it endlessly, but in the end it boils down to one thing. Have I the guts to do what I know to be right?"

"You idiot, it's not our fight," Diana said through clenched teeth, leaning towards him. "Even your precious Labour Party says that."

"I'm disgusted with the Labour Party! It's a collection of lily-livered time-servers. The Labour Party can only live when it leads. It'll die for certain if it continues to flounder around dodging the issue like it's doing at the moment."

"Better the Labour Party should die than you."

"Oh, shut up, Di! I've told you, I'm driving a lorry, not fighting."

"That's what you say now." Abruptly Diana jumped to her feet, her book falling to the floor. "I know you. You'll get into it if you can. You're just a stupid kid, that's all—a stupid kid who's spoiling for a fight. Well, go then!" Her voice rose. "Go then. Go and find your bloody corner of a bloody foreign field and see what comfort it is to you when you're dying, with your guts hanging out. And what about your degree? You're in your final year, for God's sake—"

"Di, listen—" He rose from beside Rachel and made a move to hold her, but she shrugged away from him.

"Don't touch me! You're a selfish, self-centered, self-deluding, utterly, utterly stupid *moron*, and I want nothing more to do with you." Her lips were drawn back, her face contorted as she pushed past her brother. "I said, don't touch me—and don't ever speak to me again, either! I tell you this, Gavin—" She paused on her way to the door and with hands clenched by her sides, turned to glare at him. "If you go, I never want to see you again, never, never—"

Turning, she slammed out of the room, leaving silence behind her.

"Toast, anyone?" Barney asked at last, in one of his funny voices. No one took any notice.

"Do you have to go, Gavin?" Alannah asked, more subdued than Rachel could ever have believed.

"Yes, I think so." Gavin sat down on the arm of Rachel's chair again.

"Do us a favour," Barney said. "Stick to driving the lorry, won't you? That I can understand. But fighting? We neither of us believe in that, do we?"

Rachel looked at him with interest. Barney was not one to parade his beliefs and it caused her some surprise to find that he had any.

"I'm not making any promises," Gavin said.

"Then you jolly well should!" Alannah was glaring at him from her position on the floor. "Don't you care anything for us? And surely it's mad to leave Oxford now."

"It'll be all right, Lannie. A number of us are involved. We'll get special dispensation, we hope."

"You *hope*?" Barney's voice soared with dismay, all thoughts of toast forgotten. "You must get that sorted out, surely? You can't waste the better part of three years. Are you sure you're doing the right thing, Gavin?"

"I'm sure," he said quietly.

"Well, I'm not!" Alannah's voice was tight with misery. "Di's right! You're just being selfish, not thinking of us at all."

"He's not selfish!" His nearness made Rachel brave and the words seemed to burst out of her. "I think it's perfectly splendid. Don't you know what's going on out in Spain? Aren't you proud that Gavin's standing up for what he believes in? I would be, if he were my brother. He's helping the cause of democracy—"

"Oh, do dry up, Rachel!" Alannah snapped the words, angry now. "What do you know about it? He's not your brother."

"I know it's a war between good and evil. I think it's marvellous that Gavin wants to stand up and be counted."

"Bless you!" Gavin turned, and putting an arm around her shoulders, leant to kiss her cheek. "Listen to Rachel, you lot! She's got the right of it. This is a fight I want to be part of."

"Fight? You said you were only going to drive a lorry," wailed Alannah.

"So I am. But if I should get a chance to fly a plane, then I will—"

"*Fly?*" Alannah and Barney chorused the word together.

"Yes, fly! I've been learning—haven't I, Rachel?" Still holding herself stiffly within the circle of his arm, Rachel nodded. "I'm part of the University Air Squadron—a pilot, and a damned good one, though I say it myself. Soon we'll be part of the RAF Reserve.''

"Ma will die," Alannah said dramatically. "You know how she's always been about flying."

Gavin was more down to earth. "No she won't," he said. "She'll be upset but she'll get over it. A lot depends on your attitude. Why can't you see my point of view? Surely you can, Barney?"

"Maybe. Have you talked to Dad?"

"Not yet. I intend to tonight. I just wanted to tell all of you first—get you on my side, as it were. I seem to have failed dismally, with the exception of Rachel here." He hugged her again and she smiled at him tremulously, the smile fading as she caught sight of Alannah's expression.

"Rachel," Alannah said bitterly, "is not family. She never has been, she never will be."

"Rot!" Gavin was almost breezy again now that he had got his confession off his chest, at least to his siblings. "I always think of her as an honorary sister. Well—" he stood up and consulted his watch. "Dad should be arriving home any moment. I want to beard him and talk to him first."

"He'll kill you for what you're going to do to Ma," Alannah shouted after him as he left the room. "And as for you, Rachel Bond," she went on when he had gone, leaping to her feet and thrusting a twisted, enraged face close to Rachel, "you can just go home!"

"Hey, steady on, Lannie," protested Barney.

"She's nothing but a snake in the grass—taking Gavin's part against us! What does she know about it? They're bombing people out there and killing them with machine guns." A thought occurred to her and she turned back to Rachel again. "And what was that about flying? Why did you know about it when we didn't?"

"I told you I met Gavin in London, just by chance. He told me then."

"That was ages ago! Why didn't you tell us?"

"He told me not to. It was a secret."

"How *dare* you!" Alannah glared at Rachel, her face as white as Diana's had been. "Keeping a secret like that about *our* brother! Well, if he dies, it'll be your fault."

"Lannie, don't be so bloody silly," Barney said wearily. "Rachel, don't take any notice of her. She doesn't know what she's saying."

"Oh, yes I do! I never want to see you again, Rachel Bond. I never want to see your smug little face. When I *think* what we've done for you over the years—"

"Shut up, Lannie," Barney said again, more sharply. "If Gavin said it was a secret, than Rachel was right not to tell."

"Alannah—" began Rachel.

"Oh, go to hell," snapped Alannah. "You make me sick, both of you. I'm going to find Diana."

"I'd better go," Rachel said, when the door had slammed behind her.

"No, wait." Barney got up from his position on the hearthrug and came close to her. "Don't let Lannie upset you, Rachel. You know what she's like—she makes a drama out of everything."

"Should I have told? I couldn't, could I, Barney? It was Gavin's secret."

"Of course you shouldn't. Anyway, what difference would it have made? Gavin does what he wants."

"I hope he's right about going to Spain." Suddenly Rachel was a prey to doubts. Even if the cause was a just one, maybe— just maybe—it was futile to risk dying for it.

"You sounded sure enough just now."

"Did I? Yes, I suppose I did. I don't honestly know what I think, really. It was just that everyone seemed so against Gavin . . ." her voice trailed away. Oh, why did everything have to be so mixed up?

"I almost felt like enlisting myself!"

"Oh no, don't, please!"

"Would you care?"

"Of course."

There was a look in his eyes that made her think he might attempt another kiss, and to forestall him she turned away towards the door.

"I must go," she said. "Tell Lannie—" she hesitated.

"What?"

"Tell her I didn't mean to upset anyone. Tell her I hope we're still friends."

"Oh, you know Lannie! She'll get over it."

"I wonder." Rachel went to the door and opened it, then looked back to where Barney still stood. "Do you think Gavin's right?" she asked. "Honestly?"

Barney gave a short, derisive laugh.

"I think he's a dope," he said.

It was during the course of the following morning that a note arrived from Mrs. Rossiter asking Rachel to call and see her after lunch. It was a very formal letter with no hint of the close relationship that had marked their conversation in the kitchen only a day or two before, and Rachel's heart sank a little as she read it; however, it seemed so manifestly unfair that she should be blamed for Gavin's decision that she approached the interview with no more than mild uneasiness. She was totally unprepared for the sight that confronted her when a tight-lipped Diana ushered her through a strangely silent house into her mother's presence.

The interview took place in her bedroom—a large colourful room with a gilt, roccoco bedhead. At some distance from the bed there was an ornate bureau with its top down in the writing position, and here Mrs. Rossiter sat, pen in hand. Rachel could see several pages of blue writing paper covered in her flowing hand.

Though it was afternoon, she was still wearing a loose wrapper and feathered mules, and her hair, usually caught up in a knot, was streaming down her back. Her eyes were swollen and red as if she had been crying without ceasing for hours on end, grief making her almost unrecognisable.

Rachel's nervousness had grown as she followed Diana up to the room, for it was clear that Diana was as angry as ever—and not only with Gavin. Now her anger appeared to encompass Rachel as well. However, in the face of Mrs. Rossiter's misery, Rachel forgot her nervousness and hurried towards her.

"Oh, Mrs. Rossiter, please, please don't be so upset!" she implored her. Mrs. Rossiter turned tragic eyes upon her.

"You ask that of me?" Her voice was rough, as if it hurt her to speak. "*You!* If you'd spoken out earlier, we might have been able to knock this ridiculous scheme on the head. You've a lot to answer for, Rachel."

Taken aback, Rachel faltered for a moment, then rallied.

"Honestly, I don't see why," she said.

"You don't see why?" Diana, who had been hanging back, now entered the fray. "You encouraged Gavin in his stupid ideas. Oh yes, Alannah told us everything you said yesterday about it being grand and glorious for him to stand up for what he believes in. You little fool! What do you know? You're encouraging him to go to his death, you realise that?"

"No, no, that's not fair!" In desperation Rachel turned from one to the other. "His mind was made up. He doesn't take any notice of me."

"He told you about learning to fly," Diana said bitterly. At this Mrs. Rossiter gave a low moan, and burying her face in her hands began to cry again.

"But he's only driving a lorry to Spain—"

"He'll fly, given half a chance. Permit me to know my brother a little better than you do. You should have told us."

"It was a secret!"

"Don't be so infantile. We had a right to know."

"That's enough, Diana." Mrs. Rossiter made an effort to compose herself, wiping her eyes and straightening her back so that she looked directly at Rachel. Her lips were pressed together in a straight, uncompromising line. "I want to speak to Rachel myself."

"Oh, please Mrs. Rossiter—" began Rachel, attempting to forestall her.

"Be silent and listen to me! I am distressed and hurt—very, very hurt by your attitude, Rachel." Her voice quavered and she bowed her head, gathering her resources. "Our family," she went on tremulously after a moment, "has shown you nothing but friendship and kindness over the years. I have done my best to treat you as one of my own." Emotion overcame her once more and she looked away from Rachel until she succeeded in composing herself again. "We have taken you on holiday, included you in family celebrations, and asked for nothing in return but your friendship and loyalty and love—"

"But you've had all of that, Mrs. Rossiter. Always!"

Mrs. Rossiter gestured feebly to silence her, a handkerchief clutched in her hand.

"I feel betrayed, Rachel," she went on brokenly. "Betrayed that you, *you* of all people, to whom we have never stinted our hospitality, should have been so grossly ungrateful as to behave in this way.''

"But Mrs. Rossiter, I haven't done anything!" Rachel fought back tears of unhappiness and frustration.

"You encouraged him. We know from Alannah that you yourself have political views quite different from our own—"

"No!" Desperately, Rachel denied it. "Well—" she amended. "It's true I agree with Gavin up to a point, and I can't help admiring anyone as brave as he is—"

"Exactly! You have encouraged my son to risk his life for some wild political ideal that neither of you understand."

"I don't know why you're blaming me—"

"You knew about his flying," Diana put in. "You can't deny that."

"It was a secret!" Rachel's voice emerged as a desperate wail. She felt as if she was on some mad roundabout, coming back each time to this same point. Surely they understood that she couldn't betray a confidence? It was like a nightmare, none of it making any sense. Gavin had always defended his beliefs strongly, they knew that. It was ludicrous to think that her opinions would have swayed him, one way or the other.

"There is no need to raise your voice," Mrs. Rossiter said icily. "I want you to leave now. It will, I think, be a long time before I can bear to see you in my house again—"

"If ever," put in Diana.

"If ever," echoed Mrs. Rossiter. "I feel our hospitality has been abused, our generosity set at nought. There is nothing more I wish to say."

"This isn't fair," whispered Rachel, tears now streaming down her face. "This isn't fair."

Emotion drove sensible argument from her mind. Later she would be able to think of all she ought to have said. Now, helplessly, she stumbled from the room.

The house was silent, with no sight or sound of Barney or Alannah. Then she heard the front door bang, and thinking it might be one or the other of them, she ran down the stairs; but, to her surprise, it was Mr. Rossiter who stood in the hall, taking off his overcoat.

"Well, hallo," he said a little awkwardly, seeing her.

"Oh Mr. Rossiter," she began, scrubbing at her eyes with

her handkerchief. "Mrs. Rossiter's so angry with me, and honestly I don't know what I've done—''

"Yes, well, there there!" He patted her shoulder in an embarrassed way, uncharacteristically subdued, as if there had been a death in the house. "You meant no harm, I'm sure. Carina tends to get upset sometimes. You must understand what a great shock Gavin's announcement was to her. She's not herself. That's why I've come home so early. I felt she might need me.''

"I didn't mean any harm.'' In spite of her best efforts, Rachel began to cry again. "Oh, can't you talk to Mrs. Rossiter?''

"Well—'' Mr. Rossiter, already edging up the stairs, shrugged his shoulders. "You have to realise, Rachel, that my wife—and the girls, too, are very fond of Gavin.''

"Do they imagine I want him to be killed?''

"No, no, of course you don't! Look, Rachel my dear, please calm yourself. This will all blow over.'' He looked around the hall as if desperately seeking a way of escape. "Really, these upsets—'' he paused, sighed, ran fingers through his hair and shook his head in desperation. "They're so damaging, so unpleasant for everyone. I simply can't bear having the house in such a turmoil. Carina is not, generally, an unreasonable woman, but where Gavin's concerned . . .'' his voice trailed away and he stood looking at Rachel helplessly and with some exasperation as she wiped her eyes and nose. "It will blow over,'' he went on, almost as if he were trying to convince himself. "It always blows over. Eventually. Now run along home and—'' he hesitated for a moment, not knowing what panacea to suggest. "And have a nice cup of tea,'' he finished lamely.

He gave her a bright and encouraging smile, and left her, marching rather self-consciously up the stairs towards his wife's room, as if he knew quite well that he had failed to help Rachel but was determined not to admit it. Halfway up, he turned to look back at her, saw her still standing there, and came down a step or two, looking more exasperated than ever.

"Do go home, Rachel,'' he said. "Look, I know that none of this was your fault, but you must try to forgive Carina. She has to find someone to blame, you see—''

"Why me?'' Rachel asked tearfully. But he had said all he had to say, dispensed all the sympathy of which he was capable, and was proceeding up the stairs.

"Women!'' she heard him say under his breath.

* * *

Grandma saw Rachel's grief and demanded explanations which, when received, filled her with a righteous and self-congratulatory fury. Hadn't she always said that the family next door were unstable, unreliable, unfeeling and generally undesirable? Hadn't she always deplored the fact of Rachel's friendship with them? Perhaps, she said, Rachel would in future take a little more notice of her knowledge of the world and of human nature.

Not that Rachel had told her everything, by any means. It was only slowly that the whole story emerged, but when it did the resentment of years coalesced to form a white-hot anger. She had to be persuaded not to march round to Kimberley Lodge there and then to give Mrs. Rossiter a piece of her mind.

"It wouldn't do any good, Grandma," Rachel assured her hastily, knowing that this could only make a bad situation worse. "I don't feel I want any more to do with them."

"I should hope not! The woman sounds completely unbalanced. Mind you, I've always thought there was something very strange about her—haven't I said so a hundred times? It was a mistake for you to get so involved with them. I've a good mind, in spite of what you say, to go round there and tell her that she's behaved despicably."

"Grandma, no! Honestly, I just don't care any more."

She did care, though. She seemed to care more rather than less as the hours passed, for more and more of Mrs. Rossiter's accusations, unregistered at the time, came back to haunt her.

Oh, why didn't Alannah call round to tell her it was all a mistake? Now that they'd had time to think about it, they'd surely see that nothing she had said would affect Gavin's actions. Should she write? Should she attempt to explain all over again? Maybe she should call at Kimberley Lodge herself; come to think of it, Alannah still had the copy of the *Diary of a Provincial Lady* that she'd lent her, and she had no intention of losing that! It surely would be in order for her to go and ask for it before she went back to school. It took her some time to pluck up her courage, but on her last afternoon she went next door and rang the bell.

It happened to be Alannah who answered the door. Rachel knew at once from her expression that nothing had changed, she was still unforgiven. She was invited to stand in the hall while Alannah went to find the book and, unsmilingly, handed it over.

"Alannah—" began Rachel appealingly. "We've been friends for a long—"

"Goodbye, Rachel," Alannah said, cutting her short, holding open the door.

"Oh, *Lannie*—" Rachel tried again, but stopped at the sight of the stony face that looked back at her. For a moment she hesitated. "Tell your mother," she went on resolutely, "that I have never been ungrateful. Not ever."

Alannah raised a supercilious eyebrow, a trick she had been practising for some time and had now, apparently, perfected. Her lips curved in a small derisory smile, but she said nothing. Rachel turned and left, hearing the door shut behind her.

Rain was falling and sodden laurels dripped on to the path. The whole world seemed utterly without hope, as if no one, ever, would smile again; but as she reached the gate she met Barney coming in, and he greeted her with welcome warmth.

"Rachel! I've been wanting to talk to you. I was coming to see you later on. Can I come back with you?"

"Grandma will be there." And would give them no privacy, Rachel knew—in fact she would undoubtedly relieve herself of the piece of her mind she had been threatening to give Mrs. Rossiter for the past three days.

"I want to talk to you." Barney caught hold of her arm and looked around wildly. "Tell you what—let's go in the shed."

It smelt of wood and creosote; a summer smell, Rachel thought, associated with deckchairs, and games of cricket, and tea in the garden. They perched uncomfortably on a crate and looked at each other.

"I'm sorry I haven't seen you before this," Barney said. "I've been away. I drove Gavin to Oxford and stayed the night."

"He's really going, then?"

" 'Fraid so. And guess what—he's engaged!"

"*Engaged?*" Rachel stared at him blankly.

"To Jacqueline. Well, I'm not surprised myself, but Ma and the girls are almost as upset over it as they are about his going to Spain!"

Rachel gave a brief and mirthless laugh.

"Well, at least they can't blame me for that!"

"Rachel—" He edged nearer to her and put his arm around her shoulders. "I'm sorry—I'm so terribly sorry for the way they've treated you. It's so unfair."

Rachel, who had managed all day so far without crying, suddenly felt the tears prick her eyes again and merely nodded in reply, biting her lip.

"You've got to understand that where Gav's concerned, they're not rational."

"I think I do understand," Rachel said. "I understand that I'm the scapegoat. Gavin can't be blamed for anything, so they've fixed on me—your father said as much. I wonder if *you* can understand how frightening it is when all you Rossiters close ranks! I feel as if I'm in some sort of outer darkness."

His arm tightened around her.

"Not all the Rossiters," he said. "I've stood up for you, honestly. They're behaving like idiots, and I've told them so."

"What does your father say?"

"Dad?" Barney shrugged. "He's angry with Gav, not you, but it's anything for a quiet life with Dad. He hates it when Ma gets into one of these states and he'll agree to anything, just so long as she calms down."

"Does she get in these states often? I've never seen it before."

"Not often, thank God, but sometimes. So does Di."

"I know about Di! I've never understood it."

"Who could?"

Barney sounded gloomy, and for a few moments they sat in silence. Rachel was conscious of his arm still around her and, for once, was grateful for it, for the comfort it gave her. She leaned her head against his shoulder and closed her eyes.

"Rachel—" Barney's voice was rough. "I'm not like the others. I still think an awful lot of you."

"Do you?"

"You know I do! I wouldn't hurt you for anything."

She twisted her head round to look at him. The lock of hair was over his forehead, just as it had been that first time. She was really awfully fond of him. Perhaps if she really tried, she thought, she might be able to fall in love with him. If that was what he wanted.

His arm tightened round her. He was going to kiss her again, she realised. She closed her eyes and tried very hard to persuade herself that she was enjoying it as he held his lips unyieldingly against hers. Maybe that's all kissing *was*! If so, it was a dreadful con.

"I—I think you're sweet," he said awkwardly. "Will you be here next holidays?"

"I don't know. I haven't thought that far." But now that he'd mentioned it, she had a sudden vision of the Rectory in Little Milbury, and she felt the first peace that she had felt for some time. The atmosphere there—the quiet, the gentle good-humour, seemed to her, at this point, the most desirable thing in the world. "I may go to my friend Julia's, if they'll have me," she said.

"Can I write, then?"

"Oh, please! I want to know what happens—whether Gavin is safe. And what you decide to do with yourself," she added hastily, realising that she had been somewhat deficient in tact.

"I shall miss you," he said.

For a moment they looked at each other without speaking. Then Rachel smiled.

"I was so scared of you that first time when you accused me of spying on you," she said. "You glared down at me from the top of the wall like some High Court judge."

Barney laughed. "That seems a long time ago."

"It can't all be over, can it?" The thought was so shocking that she felt sick.

He shook his head, then bending his head he kissed her again.

"It isn't over," he said softly. "It can't be."

Rachel sighed.

"Well, it feels as if it is," she said.

She had never been more glad to get back to school. The weight of misery around her heart seemed to ease a little as she went up the steps and through the front porch—a phenomenon that she would have found it hard to believe a year or two ago. Now she could hardly wait to see Julia and Alice and Red Rosie. Even the indescribable and unmistakable smell of polish and girls and the memory of thousands upon thousands of school meals, once so depressing, now seemed welcoming.

Girls called out to her as she made her way to her room.

"Hallo, Rachel. Good hols?"

In reply she smiled and nodded and asked the same of them.

"Seen Julia?" she added, as she went on her way. "Any sign of Alice?"

She was arranging books on the shelves in her room when Alice arrived looking distraught. She closed the door behind her and stood leaning against it, panting as if she had raced along the corridor to impart her news.

"Guess what," she said, without any preamble. "Red Rosie's left."

"*What?*" Aghast, Rachel seemed not to notice that one of the books she was holding had slipped to the floor. "She can't have! Who told you?"

"I've just seen Scrimgeour in the entrance hall. Honestly, there's no mistake. She introduced me to the new Housemistress—and oh Rachel, she's awful! All sort of mincy and scrunged up—I hated her on sight."

"She can't have left," Rachel repeated, refusing to believe it. "Maybe she's just ill, and this woman is temporary." Alice always looked on the dark side. It simply couldn't be true!

"No! Julia's ill with flu and won't be coming back for a few days—Scrimgeour told me that, too—but Rosie's resigned. Taken up an appointment in Wales, Scrimgeour said. I bet they had a fight, don't you?"

"I bet they did," Rachel said. "And I bet it was about Rosie's politics. Someone's made trouble for her." The desolation was complete. No Rossiters, no Miss Rayner. "How are we going to stand it?"

"I can't imagine. It's just awful, isn't it? Julia's going to be devastated."

"Aren't we all?" Slumped on the bed, all the spirit gone out of her, Rachel contemplated the future and could see no joy in it anywhere, nor any possibility of joy.

Alice sighed.

"I suppose I must go and unpack," she said. "Actually I feel like going straight home. Oh, by the way," she added, half out of the door. "Scrimgeour wants to see you after supper in her study. She asked me to tell you."

"What on earth for?" Rachel asked the question listlessly, not caring.

"She didn't say. Maybe she's going to make you a Prefect."

"Ha ha!" Rachel was grimly amused at such a far-fetched idea, but no alternative reason for the summons suggested itself and for the moment she dismissed it from her mind. The sight of Miss Spalding, Miss Rayner's replacement, was enough on its own to occupy her thoughts. Never had she seen anyone less attractive. Her long thin nose was reddened, her shoulders rounded, her teeth protruding, clearly she was devoid of all dress sense; and none of the girls, Rachel least of all, appreciated that her ingratiating manner was due entirely to a paralysing shyness. As a replacement for Red Rosie, Rachel considered, she was a total disaster. How Miss Scrimgeour could ever have thought otherwise it was impossible to imagine.

Alice had to remind Rachel that she was required to present herself to the headmistress. Hastily straightening her hair and her blouse, she knocked at the door. She found Miss Scrimgeour sitting at her desk, regarding her unsmilingly.

"Alice said you wanted to see me, Miss Scrimgeour," Rachel said politely.

"Indeed, I did." Miss Scrimgeour laced her fingers together in the steeple position and looked at Rachel over the top of them, a cold gleam in her pale eyes. For a moment she said nothing.

Rachel's own eyes alighted on an exercise book on the desk that separated them. How odd, she thought idly, that Miss Scrimgeour should have a book so like her own journal. Her gaze intensified and sharpened. Surely it *was* her own journal? There was the smear where she'd spilled cocoa, and the crease on the corner. There could be no doubt about it—it was one of the old ones she had left at school, for she'd taken only the current one to Warnfield.

"You recognise this?" Miss Scrimgeour asked her, holding the notebook up between finger and thumb as if it was something unsavoury she barely liked to touch.

"That's mine! It's private! Where did you get it?"

Miss Scrimgeour replaced the book on the desk and laced her fingers together again.

"You left it in the study, did you not?"

"It was locked in the cupboard. I'd never have left it if I'd thought anyone was going to go snooping about."

"No one," Miss Scrimgeour said icily, "was snooping about, as you so inelegantly put it. It is common practice to clean out the cupboards during the holidays—the same key fits all of them, as you must surely know, and we've found this necessary since even sixth-form girls tend to horde food and other perishables."

"There was no food in my cupboard. You had no right to read that."

"The first page was seen quite by chance, and quite rightly brought to me." Picking the book up again, she handed it over the desk to Rachel. "Read it," she ordered.

Rachel looked down at it. It was the entry for the 18th November where she had written of the discussion in Rosie's room about the Spanish Civil War, where she had said what she had parroted almost word for word at Kimberley Lodge—that there was something splendid about those who were prepared to fight for what they saw as a war of good against evil.

"I shan't read it to you," she said defiantly. "No one but me was meant to see it."

For a moment Miss Scrimgeour looked at her through eyes narrowed with anger.

"It is quite clear to me," she said at last, "that Miss Rayner has a very great deal to answer for. I had my suspicions all along that she was indoctrinating you senior girls with all manner of undesirable political ideas. This gives me proof of it—and not only of her suspect politics, but of immoral behaviour as well. All this talk of going to Provence with her lover. It's quite, quite disgusting! And in addition," she went on, holding up her hand as if to stem Rachel's protest, "I have received a letter from Mrs. Rossiter, whom I know full well has been a good friend to you over the years. She told me what took place during the holidays—how disappointed she was in you."

Speechless now, Rachel stared at her.

"I have spoken to you now, like this, before the term begins in earnest, to give you due warning," Miss Scrimgeour continued. "I wish to hear no Communist nonsense from you—no left-wing political claptrap that could contaminate any of the younger girls—"

"It wasn't like that—"

"Enough!" Miss Scrimgeour banged the desk with the flat of her hand. "If it weren't for the fact that your parents are abroad, I'd very probably expel you. As it is, I shall give you one more chance to behave sensibly."

A burning desire to clear Miss Rayner's name gave Rachel more courage than she might otherwise have possessed.

"Please, Miss Scrimgeour, please try to understand," she begged, coming a step closer to the desk. "It truly wasn't like that. Miss Rayner didn't try to make us think one way or the other. We discussed different points of view, that's all. She made it seem interesting, all the things that were going on in the world. Don't you see—"

"That will do."

"Where is she?"

"That is no concern of yours."

"I'm not a child, Miss Scrimgeour. I want to write to her."

"I should not be doing my duty by your parents were I to allow any such thing. Kindly go, and see that you behave with more circumspection in future."

For a moment, still clutching the notebook in her hands, Rachel stared at the woman behind the desk, wanting to speak, longing to find the words that would make her see how mistaken she was. She looked at the narrow face, at the rigid, thin-lipped mouth, then hopelessly she shook her head. There was no talking to her, no way of explaining, no hope of understanding. Anyway, she thought with a flash of insight, it wasn't really anything to do with politics. That was just the excuse. Miss Scrimgeour had, for some reason, disliked and feared Red Rosie from the beginning. Jealousy? Perhaps. Rosie had seemed to command the love and respect of the girls almost effortlessly, which Miss Scrimgeour had never done. And now that she came to think of it, wasn't there something in that journal entry about the two of them not seeing eye to eye? Something about Rosie implying her dislike of Scrimgeour? Yes, it all added up. Without another word she left the room.

That night sleep eluded her for a long time. She stared dry-eyed into the darkness, conscious of an overwhelming weight of misery that seemed to be crushing her; and not only misery, but fear, too, as if, inexplicably, the worst was yet to come.

Which was, as she told herself, moving her head restlessly

on her pillow, quite ridiculous. What more could happen? She'd lost Gavin, the entire Rossiter family, and Red Rosie, all in one fell swoop. That was enough, wasn't it? Nothing more could possibly go wrong—unless, of course, the unthinkable happened and Gavin was killed, just as his family feared. She felt cold and sick at the very thought.

Oh God, keep him safe, she prayed fervently. Please keep him safe. Jacqueline didn't matter. She'd manage, somehow, to cope with the idea of Jacqueline, just so long as he was safe.

Funny, she thought; she hadn't really cried for him yet, and for the end of all her dreams. It was as if all her tears had been shed before Barney had told her the news about his engagement. Or as if, even now, she couldn't really believe it. Yet she knew it to be true, knew that the Gavin dream was over. And what about the Oxford dream. Was that over too? Without Rosie, it just wasn't the same, somehow.

But that was ridiculous! She owed it to Rosie to keep on; owed it to herself to go as far as she could. Once Julia was back, she thought, she would feel better. Julia was such a dear— such a staunch, funny, rock of a friend who would never, not in a million years, treat her as Alannah had done. Exposed to a few doses of Julia's down-to-earth common sense, everything would look different. Calmed by the thought of her, and of her gentle parents who would, she felt certain, welcome her again to their home, she slept at last.

When both she and Alice were called once more to Miss Scrimgeour's study the next morning, she felt both angry and rebellious.

"What now?" she demanded of Alice as they made their way there. "What more can she possibly say? She said it all to me last night." She had an uneasy feeling, though, born of those irrational night-time fears, that there was something worse in store, and her heart was beating fast when together she and Alice went into the study.

Miss Scrimgeour's face was grave.

"Sit down, girls," she said, in a very different tone from the one she had used to Rachel the evening before. "I'm afraid I have some very bad news for you. I felt it only fair to tell you first before I make an announcement to the school."

She paused and looked at them and Rachel's heart seemed to

shrivel with dread. With sudden, heart-stopping certainty, she guessed the truth.

"Julia?" she whispered.

"I received a telephone call this morning. I'm afraid she died yesterday of meningitis."

There was a sudden, strange sensation as if the room was tilting sideways. Tearless, Rachel stared at the carpet, concentrated on it, noting its red and blue lozenges and the squiggly pattern each contained. Squashed beetles, she thought. They had always reminded her of squashed beetles. There were girls' voices, happy voices, coming faintly from the corridor outside. Inside, Alice was giving small gasping sobs—Alice who had cried so much and for so long when she had first come to school, but never quite like this.

Looking up, Rachel saw Miss Scrimgeour's eyes upon her, saw the criticism in her face. She thinks I don't care, she thought. She thinks I'm unfeeling. And she's right, because somehow I can't seem to feel anything.

But the pain would come, she knew, and she feared its coming. Because she also knew that once she began to weep for Julia, she might never be able to stop.

❧ NINE ❧

Izzy Pollard, who ran the St. Bethan Stores halfway down the hill that led to the small quay, was as free with her endearments as all the Cornish. "My dear," "my bird," "my 'andsome," "my lover" all fell trippingly from her lips, but Rachel, seeing her hard, snapping eyes and pinched mouth, knew they were not to be taken at face value.

"Oh, the dear liddle soul," she said now, bending down to look at Tess. She had come out from behind the counter to serve Rachel with vegetables. "Don't favour ee though, do un? She'm like her daddy, I s'pose."

Rachel said nothing but smiled noncommitally, glad to see that Tess showed enough perspicacity to favour the shopkeeper with an impassive stare even if she herself lacked the courage to do so. It didn't do to antagonise Izzy Pollard, for she it was who wielded power—if not over life and death, then certainly over such little luxuries as made life worth living. The odd extra egg, for example, or good quality marmalade. It paid to keep on the right side of Izzy Pollard, but even so, Rachel saw no need to pander to idle curiosity.

Izzy retreated behind her counter and, reaching beneath it, brought forth a tin of salmon with the air of a conjurer producing a rabbit from a hat.

"There," she said, lowering her voice to a conspiratorial hiss. "I'll let ee 'ave it for half a crown, never mind the points."

"Half a crown?" It seemed an exorbitant sum but even so Rachel wavered. It would be a change, she thought; and if she refused it, Mrs. Pollard would undoubtedly be offended and offer her nothing more in future.

"No points!" Izzy glinted her sly little smile towards Rachel. " 'Tis worth summat, that."

"Yes. Yes, all right." Rachel made up her mind. "Put it with the rations and the vegetables. They will be delivered this afternoon, won't they?"

"Soon's my Billy's home from school, Mrs. Bond, you can rely on it."

Rachel opened her mouth to correct this form of address, then closed it again, convinced that Izzy Pollard knew the truth but merely wanted the satisfaction of hearing the malefactor confirm with her own lips that, despite the baby in the pram, she had no husband.

She had been in the village for three weeks now; ample time for the word to get around. She was not entirely sure if the curious glances and the muted response to her "Good mornings" and "Good afternoons" were the norm. Perhaps they were, and she was seeing slights where none were intended. Perhaps this arms-length treatment was no more than any stranger would have received.

She accepted it philosophically, thankful that at least Mrs. Hoskings, having registered her disapproval, seemed now to have decided to overlook the matter. Or perhaps she was just naturally fond of children. For whatever reason, she seemed to have taken to Tess and had already knitted her a woolly bonnet ready for the cold winds of winter and had stated her intention of knitting matching mittens, if Rachel would provide the wool.

In spite of this strange and rather detached existence, Rachel found, somewhat to her surprise, that she was content. She was busy with proofs of *With This Ring* as well as the first draft of the new book, and she had no time to worry overmuch about the village's reaction to her presence.

She and Tess had settled into a way of life that seemed to suit them both. As if the River Tamar had proved to be some hitherto unremarked dateline, Tess had changed her habits from the moment she arrived in Cornwall and now slept for two hours in the afternoon, waking about three thirty and being once more ready for bed by seven. If only, Rachel thought, she could find a replacement for Beattie so that she had a few mornings free, she could ask little more of life.

From the room she had designated her study, she had a narrow, interrupted view of the river. More a glimpse than a view, as she wrote to Nancy, now living in a flat in Norwich and apparently thriving on marriage to George, despite a constant panic about the health of the aged Lancaster and a life spent hustling for freight.

"But from the living room, the view is—if you'll forgive the hackneyed phrase—breathtaking," she wrote. "Literally. Every morning, it's just as if I'm seeing it for the first time. You and George must come! Why not spend Easter here? You must surely be able to take a break at some time, though it certainly sounds as if you are frantically busy. I hadn't appreciated the problem of getting freight for the return journey as well as the outward one. It sounds enormously difficult. *What* a time George had in Nyasaland! Oh Nancy, dear Nancy, how I hope it works out! I'm keeping everything crossed—eyes, toes, the lot.

"You're going to need St. Bethan by Easter. The ability to feast one's eyes so liberally has a therapeutic effect. I have found it makes for a feeling of serenity and contentment. Or is it just that I'm not worrying about the Rossiter factor any more? A bit of each, perhaps. Somehow, I can't imagine being angry or worried or frustrated, ever again."

She would be, she knew. Perfect contentment was surely an unattainable state—which perhaps, for a writer, was no bad thing. A time would come when she needed the stone in the shoe, the unscratchable itch—stimulation, fresh people, a dash of culture. A man?

Her thoughts swerved away. One day, she thought. Maybe. But not yet.

Mrs. Hosking's efforts to find a girl to look after Tess had proved so far unsuccessful, but one morning she came up with what appeared to be a sensible suggestion.

"Your best bet," she said to Rachel one day, "is to have a word with Teacher—Mrs. Laity, that is." She paused, duster in hand, to add the customary potted biography. "She'm a lovely woman, Mrs. Laity. A widow, she is, married a Polvear lad who died very young on a motor bike, poor soul. 'Tis likely she'll know a good girl leaving school soon. Maybe one whose mother wouldn't be too fussy, like.''

Rachel ignored this throwaway line and welcomed the suggestion with enthusiasm.

''That sounds a good idea. Where do I find her?''

''She'm up at the schoolhouse. Master's house, it used to be, only we don't have no Master now, only Teacher for the big ones and a wisht little thing as comes over from Polvear every day for the Infants. Poor soul, pale as a whitewashed wall, she is, true as I'm 'ere.''

Rachel, diverted by this graphic description, nevertheless resolved to follow up Mrs. Hosking's suggestion as soon as possible. She thought of phoning, but decided instead that a personal approach would be better, and pushed Tess up to the schoolhouse that very afternoon at an hour when she guessed lessons would be finished for the day.

Mrs. Laity welcomed her warmly, inviting her into the house at once, even though it was clear she had not long been home. She brushed aside all apologies for disturbing her peace after what, surely, must have been a tiring day.

''I'm pleased to see you, believe me,'' she said. ''A cup of tea and a little adult conversation is most welcome after the undiluted company of the eights-to-fourteens. Come in, do. I know exactly who you are! You're Mrs. Courtney's niece, and a famous author—''

Rachel laughed at that.

''Hardly! I've written one book that isn't published yet and I'm about one third of the way into another.''

''Oh, do allow the village a little bit of excitement. It's an achievement any way you look at it. Congratulations!''

''Did you know my aunt?'' Rachel asked.

''Only by sight.'' Mrs. Laity looked faintly amused. ''We moved in different circles. She's not the reason for this call, is she? I don't think she was aware of my existence.''

''Oh, no! It was actually about the fourteen-year-olds I wanted to see you.'' Rachel, now settled with Tess on her lap in the comfortable, book-filled little sitting room, hoped very much that these different circles would not prejudice the schoolmistress against her, for she had taken to her on sight. Mrs. Laity had a lively, interesting sort of face; rather like a bird,

Rachel thought, with her bright eyes and the way she had of cocking her head on one side to listen attentively. "I wondered," she continued, "if there happened to be a potential mother's help among their number."

"Well—" Mrs. Laity looked thoughtful and Rachel had the distinct and uncomfortable feeling that she was being assessed, weighed up, to see if she were a fit person to employ one of her girls. "There might be. Look, why don't you put Tess down on the carpet? We can corral her with the cushions—she can't do any harm. May she have a biscuit?"

"I don't want her to mess up your things."

"She won't. Not irretrievably, I'm sure. There—what a lovely baby! You must be very proud of her."

"I am. But—" Rachel paused and Mrs. Laity tilted her head in enquiry.

"But what?"

"About the help I need," Rachel went on after a moment's hesitation, "I realise that it might be embarrassing for you—that—you might feel my home isn't a suitable place for any of your girls."

Mrs. Laity, now pouring tea, shot her a mischievous look.

"Yes, I know all about that, too," she said. "Well, I suppose there are those who might hold those views, but your situation isn't exactly unique in St. Bethan, you know. Many a bride is married with a distinct bulge under the white satin."

"But at least they've donned the white satin! They're regularising the situation."

"Hm. Some do, some don't. I daresay we have a few Yankee toddlers among us with fathers who delightedly embraced all the dangers of the Normandy landings as an alternative to facing their responsibilities here. Plus, of course, many little mistakes of the home-grown variety. Oh, there'll be those who hold up their hands in horror because it gives them the appearance of virtue—and they're the worst, in my experience. I could tell you a few things about some of those Holy Joes—but I won't! Believe me, I've had my share of malicious gossip. Teachers are supposed to live lives of blameless rectitude, attend chapel regularly, never darken the doors of the Ship Inn—"

"And do you?"

Mrs. Laity laughed.

"I think 'mostly' is the answer to your question—but it's not always easy to conform and I've rather given up trying. As long as what I do feels right to me, then I'm afraid I can't worry too much about what St. Bethan thinks. The important thing is that I'm devoted to the children. I think they know that.''

"Have you been here a long time?"

"I was born in Polvear. My father was the Methodist minister and we lived there until I was about five. After that we moved about—Southampton, London, York—that's the way it is, in the Methodist church—but I always spent holidays here and vowed I'd return one day. Then I met and married Jim. His parents ran the big hotel you can see over the river, the one towards the end of the point. They were quite old, nearing retirement, and we were in the process of taking over when Jim had his accident—''

"I heard about it. I'm so sorry."

"All that was twenty years ago. I went back to teaching, my first love. I had no stomach for the hotel without Jim. I taught in Truro and then Penzance and then, during the war when women were given a somewhat better crack of the whip than ever before, I took over this place. Temporarily, it was said, but I can't think they'll demote me now, though one never knows. The ways of the County Council defy understanding sometimes.''

"So I believe." Deftly Rachel fielded a piece of soggy biscuit and wiped clean Tess's hands and mouth. "About the girl—" she reminded Mrs. Laity.

"Yes, the girl. There is one who'll be leaving after Christmas. She loves helping with the little ones. Marlene Pengelly, her name is—''

"Heavens!"

"Don't hold it against her. She's a good girl and I think she might be interested. I'll talk to her, if you like. Sound her out.''

"Would you? I'd be awfully grateful. The only thing is that I couldn't afford to employ her full time.''

"That might just possibly be an advantage. Mrs. Pengelly does bed and breakfast in the season and needs Marlene's help. I'll send her down for a chat and you can talk to her yourself. You'd like her, I think.''

"But would she like me?"

"Why not? She's had plenty of experience with babies. She's the middle one of seven—not all of which, I am reliably informed, are the guaranteed progeny of Mr. Pengelly, so there aren't any stones to throw."

Tess, who had been happily engaged with her biscuit and the few toys that Rachel had brought with her, now embarked on more adventurous exploration, crawling over the cushions to pull herself up on the settee.

"I'd better take her home," Rachel said, raising her voice above the crows of delight that were beginning to make conversation difficult.

"She's an awfully good baby," Mrs. Laity said. "But how on earth you manage to work, I can't imagine. Do you ever get out in the evening?"

Rachel shook her head as she got to her feet to gather up Tess and the toys. "That's when I work—when Tess is asleep. Anyway, I haven't anywhere to go out *to*."

"Then come here—please do!" Mrs. Laity, seeing that Rachel was intent on leaving stood up too and began helping with the clearing-up process. "Leave the work, just for once. I'm having a few friends round for a meal next Saturday. You'd like them, I think. It won't be wildly exciting—just pleasant chat. Marlene would sit in for you, I'm sure. Do say you'll come!"

"I—I think I'd like that very much." Rachel spoke hesitantly, but with dawning pleasure. She had felt instantly drawn to the schoolmistress despite the age difference between them and was glad to think that she, too, was not averse to pursuing the friendship. "Yes, I'd love to come, if Marlene really will look after Tess for me. Thank you very much for asking me, Mrs. Laity."

"The name's Emma," Mrs. Laity said.

"And mine's Rachel."

Emma Laity laughed aloud.

"I know," she said.

She would, of course, Rachel thought as she went back down the hill towards Gull Cottage. St. Bethan was like that, and there was nothing to be done but accept the fact.

She couldn't settle to her writing that evening; couldn't, somehow, think of the right words. Which was, she told herself, just plain daft when she knew, more or less, what she wanted to say. Surely it wasn't the prospect of a night out that had put her in such a turmoil? She swore and tore yet another page out of the typewriter. Why couldn't she write? Where now was all that tranquillity she had boasted about to Nancy?

She sighed and put her head between her two hands.

She knew perfectly well why all inspiration had deserted her. It was because of the letter she had received from her mother a couple of days before, redirected from London. She'd put it behind the clock on the mantelpiece, promising herself that she would reply to it as soon as she had a free moment. So far that moment hadn't arrived and meanwhile the sight of the letter seemed to accuse her more with every passing hour.

It had carried, understandably, a plaintive note.

"I know things go astray. Your father had a letter from his bank in London yesterday posted four months ago. Still, I can't help worrying. It really is such a long time since we heard—not since the marvellous news about your book. Daddy and I are so proud of you—I tell everyone about my daughter who is an author! I'm sure you're busy, but we long for more up-to-date news. Please write soon.

"It seems now that we are unlikely to get home before March at the earliest. *Such* a long wait, but of course you know your father—everyone else has to go before he can get away! 'Twas ever thus. I can't tell you how I'm looking forward to seeing you again. Little did we know, when we said goodbye at Mombasa in 1939, that it would be 1947 before we were all together again! Such a long, long time. What a lot has happened to us and to the world."

Indeed, indeed, thought Rachel, abandoning the book as a lost cause. She made up the fire with some driftwood she had found on the beach and sat beside it, staring into the flames with her chin in her hand.

She knew she would have to reply. It was sheer cowardice to dodge the issue like this—but oh, there was so much at stake! Should she string them along for a bit longer? Tell them that she had rented out her house in London and come to live in Sylvia's cottage to write her next book? Maybe that's what she'd do. Once they were here and could see Tess in the flesh, it would all be a great deal easier.

On the other hand, was it fair? Nancy had always urged her to tell—said it was wrong to hide the truth from them. If only she could be sure of their reaction!

They were proud of her, her mother had said. They boasted about her. Would they still be proud of her when they knew the truth?

Hardly! They'd be ashamed and disgusted. Her mother might say it was no more than she expected, given the perverse way Rachel had behaved in Uganda, the unsuitable friends she had insisted on associating with. Not for them the apportioning of blame elsewhere.

Not like the Rossiters.

"*Damn* the Rossiters! If it were not for them—" Abruptly she got up, went to the kitchen, made tea, then brought the cup back to the armchair beside the fire.

If only she knew for certain that her parents loved her, that they wouldn't turn their backs on her. What a complicated business it was, she thought miserably, this parent-child relationship! Surely, if there was one thing that was proved beyond doubt it was her strength and independence; she could never have got anywhere without it. Yet their love and their forgiveness mattered so much. She supposed it always would.

There were times in the past when she'd fought with her mother, times when they'd said unforgivable things to each other. On the surface they were forgotten, smoothed over; but had they left rancour behind them? Alannah had always said—

Damn Alannah! Why had Rachel let those sly little remarks get under her skin? They were only made to show the superiority of all things pertaining to the Rossiters. Why, knowing that, had they affected her so much, and still affected her? They don't love you, she'd said. How could they, when they send you away like this?

It wasn't true. She was certain it wasn't true. And yet—and yet—

Oh God, what was she to do?

The tea, forgotten, cooled on the table beside her.

Into her mind, suddenly, came the memory of that awful time; that long-ago September of 1937. She'd felt sure of her mother's love then. When she'd needed her more than she had ever done before in the whole of her life, her mother hadn't hesitated. She'd come flying halfway round the world to her rescue. She'd taken on Miss Scrimgeour and the whole of St. Ursula's in a way that, even now, provoked amusement and admiration. She'd been on Rachel's side then, all right. Blood had proved thicker than water.

Dare she hope that it was still the same?

She couldn't think what her mother was doing there. This was school—the san, she realised dazedly, looking around at the white-walled room with the four beds, one in each corner. She'd been here twice before, once when she'd had flu, once when she'd broken her ankle. But this time? She couldn't remember being ill or hurting herself.

Gradually a picture emerged and she remembered. She remembered the uncontrollable weeping, and Miss Spalding's consternation. She remembered Miss Scrimgeour's flushed face and her unconvincing concern. She remembered faces, hundreds of faces, staring at her.

"You had a little breakdown," her mother said gently.

Rachel stared at her.

"You mean I went potty?"

"Not at all. The doctor explained it to me, and he'll explain it to you if you're well enough to take it in. There was just too much for you to bear all at once."

The Rossiters, Red Rosie, Julia. She remembered it all and was conscious of the dull weight of sadness, and of bewilderment, too.

"You came home because of me?" The thought was astonishing. Her mother had always seemed so far away, so unreachable.

"I flew! Just imagine! I came Imperial Airways—oh, such an adventure, I can't tell you, and so quick. Only five days, door to door—can you imagine it? Miss Scrimgeour phoned Grandma, and seemed in such a state about you that Grandma cabled us to tell us you were ill, and I couldn't bear not to come just as quickly as I could. Daddy's coming later by sea. We were due for leave anyway in four months."

"How long have I been ill?"

It had been almost three weeks, she learned with astonishment. More than sufficient for her mother to take an intense dislike to Miss Scrimgeour, Miss Spalding, Matron and everything pertaining to St. Ursula's. Her intention, Rachel gleaned over the next few days, was to take her away from school at the earliest possible time sanctioned by the doctor.

"I'm not leaving you here with that woman," she said forcefully. "I've told her you're not coming back, and she can whistle for her next term's fees in lieu of notice. If she makes a song and dance about it, I'll report her to the Headmistress's Conference, or whatever it is, and write to *The Times*. I blame her entirely for what happened to you."

"Where are we going, then? Not Warnfield? Please not Warnfield!"

"Certainly not. We're going to rent a little place in the country somewhere. I'm arranging it with an agency—it's all in hand. Then we'll all go back the long way, round the Cape."

No Oxford, then. No university at all. Rachel felt too tired to argue, far too lethargic to do anything but accept the plans that others had made for her. And if the truth were to be told, she had no enthusiasm now for study. The thought of seeing Africa again seemed the first good thing that had happened for a long time; she craved it, hungered for it, could see it in her mind's eye as bright and as colourful as on the day she had left it and it called to her now like a comfortable, undemanding womb that she longed to re-enter. If anything could heal the hurt inside her, then it was the sight of Lake Victoria, gleaming blue in the sunlight. She felt quite sure of it.

"Oh, I'm so glad," she said, more enthusiastic than she had been about anything for some time past.

The place in the country where they spent the next eight months proved to be twenty miles distant from Warnfield, which Kitty Bond considered far enough from her mother-in-law to be well outside daily contact, yet not so far as to prevent Ivor getting over to see her fairly frequently, once he arrived in England. April Cottage, the house they rented in a village not far from Aylesbury, was damp and rather cold, but though Kitty complained, Rachel barely noticed it.

It was a strange time; a limbo sort of time. Her grief did not lessen, exactly, but it grew manageable, helped in part by a wonderful letter she received from Julia's mother, full of comfort, asking her to stay at the Rectory just as soon as she felt fit enough.

It was a letter that filled her with admiration and astonishment—how *could* people go on believing in a merciful God when such awful things happened?—and she replied with gratitude. She knew, however, that the invitation was one she would never accept. Julia belonged to the past, to the St. Ursula's-Red Rosie-Rossiter time, and though she would never forget her, Rachel knew instinctively that she had to move on, somehow.

She felt herself to be distanced from humanity as if nothing had the power to affect her very much. Sometimes she shopped with her mother in Aylesbury, and together they went to the cinema. There was no dissension then. She was meek and docile, like a small child. Afterwards, she could never remember much about the films they saw. She took walks in the country, borrowed books from the library, helped in the house. She smiled and was agreeable, arguing with no one, even when her father made reactionary political statements that would once have had her quoting Red Rosie at her reddest. Now nothing seemed to matter enough to risk rocking the boat.

She knew no young people locally, and did not want to know them. Sometimes she would see a group of them at the bus stop or cycling along the road and would hear them talking to each other. It was as if they spoke a foreign language, meaning nothing to her. She felt sad, bereft, no longer young, as if part of life she had once enjoyed was dead to her. Summer turned into autumn, and though she acknowledged the beauty of the golden woodlands which surrounded the village, she did not thrill to it as once she would have done.

Then suddenly, one day in early November, towards the end of their tenancy of April Cottage, right in the middle of watching Ronald Colman in *Lost Horizon* at the Regal Cinema, she felt an inexplicable irradiation, as if a light had been switched on. She lost the thread of the story, impatient with it and with herself. It was as if a commanding voice had said to her: "OK, that's it, the mourning's over. There's a life out there waiting to be lived." The rest of the film passed over her head for she was too occupied in thinking about her future to take it in. Suddenly she was restless, even excited. There were plans to be made.

A few days later she enrolled for typing lessons. She'd need to learn to type, she told her parents, if she was ever to write.

"Good idea," her father agreed heartily. "And who knows, you might find it useful in Uganda. I daresay there'll be some little voluntary job crying out for a typist."

If Rachel thought of Red Rosie who had been so scornful of using her time in this way—or, indeed, of Mrs. Rossiter who had promoted typing skills with a fervour equal to her father's— she gave no sign of it. In the event, she rather liked her typing class. She found it strangely calming to sit banging out meaningless phrases in time to a wind-up gramophone, and was pleased that she seemed to show an aptitude for it, progressing through the exercises with gratifying speed.

Though she made no close friends among the other girls, she was on good terms with them and found it fun to exchange notes and measure progress, to commiserate and to giggle; and when a boy she had noticed about the village drew her into conversation at the bus stop and asked her to go to the pictures with him, she found herself agreeing to do so. He was quite nice, she told Kitty afterwards, but no, she didn't think she would bother to see him again.

The truth was, she still couldn't get Gavin out of her mind. He had been there all along, she realised, even though for a long time she had refused to acknowledge it. She longed for news of him. Was he safe? Was he well? Was he married? It was agony, not knowing.

There had been a letter from Barney waiting for her when she recovered from her breakdown, but it had been written three weeks earlier and contained no fresh news. She had not, somehow, been able to muster the energy to reply to it at the time, and had not done so since. Somehow the longer she left it, the more difficult it seemed to write at all, as is the way of such things.

Now, in her new no-nonsense mood, she sat down and wrote to him, saying that she had been ill but was now better and was looking forward to going to Uganda just after Christmas. How was everyone? she asked. And what was the news of Gavin?

Her mother, hearing the sharp bark of laughter with which

Rachel greeted Barney's reply, looked up enquiringly from reading her own letter, spectacles on the end of her shapely nose.

"What's the joke?" she asked. For a moment Rachel made no reply; then she shook her head.

"It's nothing," she said. "Nothing at all. I must fly—I'm late for my class."

On the bus to Aylesbury and her typing lesson, she read the letter again.

Gavin, Barney had written, never got to Spain. He went down with mumps a few days before the lorry was due to leave and had been far too ill to drive. By the time he'd recovered, disillusioned members of the International Brigade were already trickling back with stories of maladministration and muddle, and he had thought better of the whole enterprise. He'd managed to get a good degree, and the engagement still seemed to be on, though Mrs. Rossiter was much against it . . .

So it was all futile, all that upset. Seeing nothing of the countryside, Rachel stared out of the bus window. If she'd just kept her mouth shut, she thought bitterly, how differently things would have worked out. She would still have the Rossiters—but did she want them, now that she had seen them in their true colours? The sight of Mrs. Rossiter, distraught and accusatory, deaf to reason, not kind any more, was almost as great a shock as any other she had sustained. Mr. Rossiter, too, who had always seemed so warm and friendly, had proved a broken reed. He'd known she was innocent and had seen the distress she was suffering, but could only see things from his own point of view. It would have cost him so little, she thought now, to stand up for her.

And Alannah—how quick she had been to turn on her! Past friendship had appeared to mean nothing. She was better off without them.

She wouldn't write any more, she decided, now that she knew Gavin was safe and still engaged to Jacqueline. She would forget them, cut them out of her life, look forward instead of back. She tore the letter into small pieces and deposited it in a convenient litter bin in Aylesbury High Street.

There was the voyage to look forward to now. They were going round the Cape, so she'd see Table Mountain, and the beaches of Durban, and Lourenço Marques, and Dar es Salaam. Magical names, all leading home.

The Rossiter days were over, she said to herself. Africa was waiting.

⊰ TEN ⊱

The supper party at Emma Laity's house was a great success. Rachel, who agonised for some considerable time over what to wear, finally settling on a multi-coloured wool skirt and black sweater enlivened by Grandma's amber beads, realised from the moment of arrival that she needn't have worried unduly. Emma's friends were clearly a fairly motley assortment, characterised not by their style but by their entertainment value.

Conversation was lively. It encompassed the deeds of the Labour Government, which member of it one would least like to entertain for a long weekend, Jean-Paul Sartre, the magnificence of the St. Bethan Male Voice Choir, the possibility of civil war in India and the awfulness of Izzy Pollard, among other things. There were strong opinions, much argument, and a great deal of laughter, and at the end of it Rachel felt as if a door had opened on a world she had all but forgotten.

It was in the middle of a conversation with a mild, bespectacled teacher from Truro called Derek on the subject of post-Butler education that she found her attention wandering. It wasn't that the topic was dull; far from it. It was simply that suddenly she wasn't enjoying herself any more.

Tess never woke at night unless she was ill or teething. But suppose, just this once, she did? Suppose she had a nightmare? After all, it was surely possible for a baby to have a nightmare. The world must be full of frightening things—buses and cars and aeroplanes. Well, not buses in St. Bethan, perhaps, but other noisy things. Dogs. Seagulls. Seagulls could make the most terrifying noise when they put their minds to it.

She found herself unable to concentrate on Derek any more,

though she presented a listening mask towards him.

Suppose Tess woke up and found only a stranger to comfort her? Marlene seemed a nice enough girl, bright and competent, but hardly more than a child herself. Would she know what to do in an emergency? Suppose the house burnt down?

"I think," she said to Derek—but gently, because he looked the kind of man who could be easily hurt—'I ought to go home now. I'm a bit worried about my baby."

"Oh?" He looked confused. "I hadn't realised—I mean, I didn't think you were—"

Married, he meant. Rachel smiled at him, but made no explanations. She would leave all that to Emma.

"I'm sure you're worrying unduly," Emma said as she escorted her to the door.

"I expect I am. I hope I am. Emma, it's been a lovely party. I had a wonderful evening."

"In spite of the untimely departure?"

"In spite of. Forgive me. I know I'm being a neurotic idiot."

"That's right," Emma said; but she laughed sympathetically as she spoke and Rachel knew she understood and that the dawning friendship had not suffered.

"Emma, come and see me, won't you?" she said.

"You can count on it."

In spite of her sudden panic, Rachel had indeed enjoyed the evening and could only agree with Emma, when she found Tess sound asleep in her cot, that her sudden flight had been unnecessary. She would have to be on her guard against being foolishly over-protective, she told herself, and a complete bore into the bargain.

It was therefore rather ironical that only the following day she should lay herself open to criticism regarding her care of Tess.

It happened in the afternoon. She had desperately needed a fresh supply of typing paper—a commodity unobtainable in St. Bethan, but available, so she was told, from the newsagents in Polvear. Accordingly she put Tess in her pram immediately after lunch and went over the river on the ferry.

She had been in Polvear only twice before, and though it was a cold November afternoon, she enjoyed walking through the narrow streets, looking at the unfamiliar shops and the attractive architecture of the small port. Compared to St. Bethan, it seemed a veritable metropolis.

Tess quickly fell asleep which meant that Rachel could browse in peace. She spent a happy half hour in the bookshop, bought some vegetables from the greengrocer which looked a great deal fresher than those offered by Izzy Pollard, and stood for a moment on the quay. A man was rowing, his oars gleaming silver as they rose and fell; and slowly, almost majestically, a cargo boat with an unfamiliar flag slid past the quay, on towards the loading dock a little further up-river. Throughout all, Tess slumbered peaceably, not even disturbed by the noise of the ferry when finally Rachel decided it was time they were getting back to St. Bethan.

The village, seen from this perspective, seemed almost deserted, with only a few black match-stick figures standing about the quay waiting for the ferry to return to Polvear. There was no colour now. The river was slatey-grey, and grey, too, the cottages that looked as if they had hunkered down to wait for spring. A few lights had already appeared, piercing the gathering gloom of the afternoon.

Rachel thought of the busy London streets, the press of people on the tube, and regretted nothing. This was beginning to feel like home.

The man who ran the ferry helped her lift the pram out on to the quay; and still Tess slept. Rachel took a deep breath. The hill leading up to Gull Cottage was steep, particularly down here on its lower slopes, and it needed an effort to get under way. As she passed Izzy Pollard's shop she paused. The rations weren't due until the following day, but they might be in stock already. If so, and she could pick them up now, then it would save a trip tomorrow.

There were two steps up to the shop—always difficult with the pram. She wouldn't be more than a minute, she thought, and Tess would be perfectly safe outside.

She was less than that, for the rations were not in stock. Impossible not to think that Izzy Pollard took delight in saying so, she thought, turning back towards the door.

To her horror, she saw that the pram was moving downhill. With a cry she leapt for the door, only to run full tilt into a woman who was already on the step.

"The pram! My baby!" Almost incoherent, she pushed the woman aside and rushed out into the street where already the pram was gathering momentum on its short, steep journey towards the quay.

She had never run so fast, never felt such panic. There seemed no one about to halt its progress; only the ferry, now leaving the quay, the faces of its passengers, like circles of white paper, turned towards the land and the flying pram.

Then suddenly, out of nowhere, a tall thin figure materialised, grabbed the pram and brought it to a halt. Still Rachel ran.

"Oh, thank God!" she sobbed. "Thank God."

The man who held the pram watched her approach. He was breathing hard, and his face, she saw as she came close to him, seemed contorted by extreme emotion, his teeth clenched as if in anger. She'd seen him about the village before, she realised, but had no idea who he was. She had thought him odd, different, with his pale, thin, unsmiling face. He was always alone, always dressed in an old Navy-surplus donkey jacket.

"Thank you," she said, reaching out to take the handle of the pram. "Thank God you were there!"

"What is it you think of?" His words, uttered in broken English, seemed to be flung at her like a handful of pebbles. He was shaking, she saw; as she was herself. "Are you mad woman? Why do you not take care of your child?"

"The brake was on. I don't know what happened."

"Is not on now! You have no right to have baby. Perhaps your child drown, if I am not here!"

Tess had begun to cry. Rachel lifted her out of the pram and held her close.

"You think I don't know that?" Angry herself now, and still shocked at the near-accident, Rachel was close to tears. "If you don't mind letting go of the pram," she said, her voice trembling, "I'll take my baby home now. Thank you again."

Without a word the man swung round and strode off across the quay, in the direction of a small shipyard that had recently re-opened after being closed throughout the war.

Others had collected now, and all were sympathetic, ready with words of comfort.

"Don't take no notice of ee, the bloody foreigner! 'Tis they brakes," said a man whom Rachel recognised as a fisherman, always about the quay. "They'm not like the pre-war ones. Proper ramshackle, they are."

" 'Twasn't your fault, my 'andsome," said a woman who had come out of one of the nearby cottages. "The very same thing happened to me when my Jackie was a tacker. Is the little maid all right?"

"Right as rain," Rachel said. "Better than I am, I think. She was startled by the shouting, that's all."

She refused the kindly woman's offer of a cup of tea on the grounds that she wanted to get Tess home as soon as possible; and more shaken by the strange man's anger than she cared to admit, she once more pushed the pram up the hill towards home, the mood of well-being that she had experienced on the ferry now thoroughly dissipated.

She made up the fire and sat before it, rocking Tess against her shoulder, a prey to agonies of guilt. Not fit to be a mother, she thought. The wretched man was right! But she had put the brake on, she *had*, she was sure of it!

Tess, quite recovered, gurgled contentedly, and slowly Rachel's fears subsided. She couldn't get the stranger's words out of her mind, however, and at intervals—throughout Tess's bath time, giving her a bottle, tucking her into her cot—they continued to accuse her.

Not fit to be a mother. And, with that letter still unwritten, not fit to be a daughter, either. All in all, it had been some time since she had felt so low in her own estimation.

Emma called the next afternoon.

"Are you all right? I heard about what happened. Betty Pearce told me."

"Who? Oh!" Of course, Rachel thought. Betty Pearce was the wisht little soul, pale as a whitewashed wall according to Mrs. Hoskings, who had been one of the passengers waiting for the ferry as she left it, and therefore one of those on the boat who had looked so helplessly towards the near-disaster. "Yes, we're fine," she assured Emma. "Tess was all right in no time, but I seem to have taken a bit longer. Do come in! I couldn't be more pleased to see anyone."

She made tea, recounting the event as she did so for Emma's benefit.

"Who is that man?" she asked as they both settled down by the fire. "He looked as if he would take great pleasure in tearing me limb from limb. I quailed before him!"

"Tall, and rather cadaverous?"

"That's the one! I've seen him once or twice, always alone and always wearing that awful jacket. He went off towards Carthew's Yard."

"That's the Pole," Emma said. "Stefan Something. No one can pronounce his last name."

"What's he doing here?"

"Working at the shipyard. I don't know much more about him than you do." Emma laughed. "You'd better ask the fount of all knowledge—Mrs. Hoskings!"

"I will," said Rachel.

The conversation turned to the recent party, and to Marlene.

"She's agreed to come after Christmas," Rachel said. "I'll manage till then. She's going to work in the Neptune Cafe in Polvear in the afternoons, so it couldn't be better. She's a dear little thing, isn't she? And so sensible! When I think of myself at the age of fourteen—"

"She'll be fifteen next month."

"She seems much older. I think we'll get on very well."

"She seems to have fallen for Tess already," Emma said. "Which, I have to confess, is a fairly easy thing to do."

"You're going to warn me now about being over-protective and over-anxious," Rachel said, laughing at her. "Maybe I should get you and Stefan Whatsisname together. You'd cancel each other out."

"I'd be terrified, if what you tell me about him is true! I wonder why he's come to St. Bethan? There's a story behind it, mark my words."

"Which you will ferret out?"

"Hm. I take exception to 'ferret.' Investigate is better."

"Investigate, then," Rachel agreed, laughing.

Conversation between them seemed to flow, easy and unstrained.

"Look," Rachel said at last. "I must give Tess her bath and bottle now—"

Emma jumped to her feet immediately.

"Heavens, how the time has gone! I had no idea it was so late. I must be off."

"Oh, do you have to go? Stay for pot luck! I'll rustle something up once Tess is in bed."

Emma, looking at her, saw her need and sat down again. Rachel, she recognised, needed company, needed to talk—and there was, really, nothing to make her rush home to the schoolhouse at the top of the hill.

"Well, if you're sure," she said.

With Tess duly bathed and fed, a more ordered, peaceful atmosphere descended on Gull Cottage. The "something" that Rachel rustled up proved to be toasted cheese and baked beans—a repast that she surveyed, as she placed it before Emma, with an expression of disgust tinged with resignation.

"What a nerve, to give you something like this," she said, taking her place at the table. "Could you pretend it's lobster, do you think?"

"I'd really rather pretend it's smoked salmon, if it's all the same to you. I'm allergic to shellfish."

"Whichever. I suppose the day will dawn when we'll be able to indulge ourselves—though you don't appear to do too badly, judging from the spread you prepared the other night. I made an absolute pig of myself."

"That was the object of the exercise. I have a tame farmer in my power, you see. By the grace of God, I managed to get his far-from-bright son through his grammar school entrance, and he seems to feel in my debt for evermore. I'll bring you some bacon and eggs for your breakfast next time I come."

"How wonderful! My stomach's rumbling at the very thought." Rachel took a forkful of toasted cheese. "D'you know what I crave more than anything?" she said. "A slice of paw-paw! In Uganda we had it every day for breakfast, all pink and dewy, with a slice of lime and a touch of sugar. I would have killed for it when I was pregnant."

"I've never tasted it; never travelled at all. I've always longed to, though. Africa, in particular, has always held a great fascination for me. I envy you, being brought up there. You must know it in a way mere visitors can never do."

"Know it?" Rachel shook her head regretfully. "Oh no, Emma. I didn't know it at all. I loved it—or thought I did—but we lived a strange, detached kind of life in our little European enclave. It wasn't Africa. That was somewhere at a distance, red in tooth and claw, violent and pulsating and totally incomprehensible to us.''

"You couldn't have been aware of that as a child, surely?''

"No,'' Rachel said thoughtfully. "No, I wasn't. But later I was—and I could never live there again.''

"How old were you when you went back?''

Rachel smiled.

"I was seventeen,'' she said. "Younger and greener and more innocent than any girl has a right to be.'' She laughed a little. "It was a million years ago, Emma. Thinking of it, it all seems to have happened to someone else.''

"Youth viewed in retrospect always seems like that.''

"I suppose so. By the time I came back—'' She paused, memories crowding in.

"You were older and wiser?'' Emma suggested.

Rachel laughed again.

"Well, older, anyway. Look, do finish the beans. They'll only go to waste.''

"Is there any more of that delicious smoked salmon?'' Emma asked. Cataclysmic events were taking place in the outside world, but in the Entebbe of 1938 reports of them were little more than a disquieting whisper, easily disregarded. News was brought by a daily paper published in Kampala, and there was also a wireless set beside Ivor's chair that could be tuned to receive the authoritative, if faint, tones of the BBC. Rachel, however, found it a simple matter to ignore both.

For her, the return to the scenes of her youth was every bit as pleasant as she had imagined, the scents and sounds just as she had remembered them. The hibiscus was as red, the plumbago as blue, the frangi-pani as sweet-smelling, the sun as warm. The lawns, tree-shaded, that sloped down to the lake still fringed the small township, and the golfers were, surely, the selfsame golfers that had played there in earlier years.

"Oh, it's heaven—*heaven*!'' she had cried on the evening of her return, spreading her arms wide, as she looked from the verandah towards the lake. It lay limpid and calm in the fading evening light beneath a sky tinged with pink and gold and pale,

pale yellow. "Nothing's changed! It's just wonderful to be back!"

She was not entirely correct. Some things had changed, of course. Mateo, the friend of her childhood, had graduated from his position as Kitchen Toto and had gone as houseboy to the home of a railway official in Kampala; but Melika, though she had left the Bond household for another where there were two small children, was still in Entebbe.

Juma, his face split in a broad grin, came to tell Rachel, that first evening, that there was someone to see her at the kitchen door. Finding Melika standing there, flanked by her two small, sun-hatted charges, she cried out with delight and hugged her warmly.

"Oh, Melika, it's wonderful to see you!" she said in English—then, a little haltingly, repeated it in Luganda, angry with herself because she had forgotten so much that had come naturally before.

"So big, so big!" Melika, laughing, reached up to put her hand on Rachel's head. "A real memsahib now. Soon you find a bwana."

How people went on about it, Rachel thought. It didn't seem to matter how much she denied it, it was apparently assumed by everyone that she had come to join what she had heard referred to on board ship as "the fishing fleet"—i.e. girls who went to the Colonies in order to find a husband.

She'd first heard the term from Mr. Nicholls, the handsome young Assistant Purser. She had blushed and disclaimed the notion; but he had been so much fun that she hadn't minded his teasing too much.

It was her mother who had minded, she remembered uncomfortably. But not about the "fishing fleet" accusation. She minded because Mr. Nicholls bore Rachel off to look at the phosphorous glinting in the water that creamed beneath the bows. Anyone would have thought that they had been caught in some compromising position, instead of merely leaning companionably side by side on the ship's rail.

It had sparked a row that had marred the last few days of the voyage which, until then, Rachel had found wholly enjoyable. For the first time she had been treated like a grown-up—well, almost; and as for her seventeenth birthday, it had been the most heavenly birthday she could ever remember, with the ship's orchestra playing "Happy Birthday to You," and a phalanx of waiters marching to her table with a wonderful cake.

"Your mother's jealous," said Judy Gambell, a young married woman going out to Kenya to join her husband. She was several years older than Rachel, but still young enough to become a friend and confidante. "It's the old green-eyed monster. Haven't you noticed how palsy-walsy she is with Mr. Nicholls?"

"Well, yes," Rachel said uncertainly. "I suppose I have. But I didn't think—" She paused, worried and defensive. "I mean they're just friends, that's all."

Could there be any truth in Judy's assertion? It seemed unlikely; but the row took a few days to smooth over. Her father, throughout, had remained aloof. He had, in fact, been aloof from most of the social life of the ship, spending a great deal of time studying and writing reports in the saloon. He had heard while on leave in England that he was to be put in charge of a special commission which was to look into salaries and conditions, involving a great deal of travelling around the Protectorate on his return, and with his customary thoroughness he was determined to be fully prepared for this new task.

Shipboard life in general, its friendships and jealousies, so absorbing and important while she was living it, faded quickly from her mind now they were back in Entebbe. This new life was so different from anything she had experienced before, even though superficially the place looked the same.

In the innocent and heedless sub-world of childhood that she had inhabited in former days she had been unaffected by the somewhat oppressive rules that governed life in this small outpost of the Empire. The dressing for dinner, the protocol, the dropping of calling cards—Rachel was astounded at the importance her mother placed on such rituals considering her nonconformist attitude when on leave in Warnfield.

"Do we have to?" she asked when her mother mentioned the necessity of signing the book at Government House, and was quite taken aback at the vehemence of her reply.

"Well, of course we have to," Kitty said explosively. "Honestly, you are a little goose, Rachel! You want to be asked to things, don't you? You don't want to be a social pariah? What on earth would one do in this place if one weren't asked to things?''

It was all too, too Jane Austen-ish, Rachel thought with lofty amusement; and if this had been all there was to Entebbe, then she would have been bored to tears in a week, as bored as her mother had been in Warnfield. But there was a great deal of fun to be had, too—and she needed fun. She seemed to have been starved of it for a long time and she rushed with open arms to embrace it, happily dancing at the Club until dawn lightened the sky over the lake, and agreeing, rather diffidently, to take the part of Edwina, the *ingénue* young sister of the heroine, in a somewhat insipid comedy called *Skylarks in Suburbia*.

This involved a considerable number of entrances through french windows, tennis racquet swinging, but mercifully few lines to speak. Somewhat to her amazement, despite doubts induced by the memory of her stage debut at Clearwater which still had the power to make her blush, she found herself able to manage the undemanding part quite adequately. The rest of the cast, being kindly disposed towards the young newcomer, had no hesitation in telling her so.

Her self-esteem burgeoned. She found it easier now to converse with her elders at dinner parties; she even flirted a little, taking discreet lessons from her mother who was adept in the art. Most amazing of all, she allowed herself to submit to golf lessons from a handsome young Administrative Officer called Clifford Bailey, whose hands lingered over hers as he demonstrated the correct grip.

Clifford Bailey was a young man considered by the matrons of Entebbe to be the answer to any maiden's prayer. Such a *nice* young man, they all agreed. The Bond gel would be doing well for herself if she could get him to the altar.

The Bond gel, after a steamy session in Clifford's car one moonlit night, thought differently. Kissing was acceptable. Rachel was getting a considerable amount of practice at it these days and felt, modestly, that she was now quite good at it and could possibly show Barney Rossiter a thing or two. However, the kind of insistent, intrusive, even painful fumbling that Clifford had considered appropriate was something different, even frightening. He had ignored her demands to be taken straight home, ridiculed her prudery, accused her of leading him on and

giving him the wrong signals. She hadn't know how to deal
with it, how to emerge from the situation with any self-respect;
and the whole incident had shown her how ridiculously inex-
perienced she still was, how totally at sea in her dealings with
the opposite sex.

The awful thing was that, though she had struggled and
fought against him, there was no denying that, in retrospect,
she'd found the whole incident exciting in a weird kind of way.
Which was pretty despicable, because the truth of the matter
was that not only was she *not* in love with Clifford, but she
didn't even like him very much, winning smile and golf lessons
notwithstanding. Quite apart from his venom at her rejection
which had been unattractive in the extreme, she had discovered
a mean and arrogant streak, well hidden by the surface charm,
that was positively repellent.

Perhaps the whole thing was her fault, after all. Had she, in
the phrase that was so often bandied about among the matrons
of Entebbe, "led him on"? Oh, why did everything have to be
so confusing? How did people like Diana manage, flirting as
they did with a dozen different young men at once?

"Don't give him another thought," Paula Garfield said comfortingly, when Rachel confided in her. "He's not worth it. I've
always thought him a slimy piece of work. Have you seen him
sucking up to the bosses' wives? It's enough to turn anyone's
stomach."

Paula, who had quickly become a friend, was one of the
younger wives whose husband held a junior position in the Public Works Department. Kitty Bond regarded her with a great
deal of dubiousness for that very reason. There was a definite
pecking order among the various Government Departments,
with the Secretariat—naturally—at the top and the PWD at the
bottom.

"You know, you can't be too careful in this life," she said
to Rachel. "I do wish you'd be warned by someone who knows
a great deal more about society than you do."

"You're beginning to sound just like Grandma," Rachel said
angrily.

It was not a remark calculated to please her mother, already
put out by the ending of Rachel's friendship with Clifford and
inclined to say so, over and over. Rachel, however, continued

to see much of Paula, whom she liked better than anyone else she had so far met. She liked her commonsensical attitude to life, and her irrepressible, irreverent sense of humour. If it were not for Paula, she now realised, life in Entebbe, for all the fun, would be frightfully tedious, with acres of time lying vacant and unused. A kindred spirit made all the difference and now, more often than not, they spent their afternoons together at the swimming pool.

"Mummy is absolutely maddening," Rachel confided to Paula when she had been in Entebbe for a full six months. "She always wants to know everything. Honestly, I had more freedom at school."

"You'd feel upset if she didn't care what you did."

Rachel sighed, but admitted the truth of this.

"Yes, I suppose so." She was silent for a few moments. "We seemed such friends in England," she went on. "Well, we're still friends a lot of the time. She can be so much fun when she wants to. But now all she seems to think of is finding me a suitable husband. *Why*, for heaven's sake?"

"She hasn't got enough to do," Paula said. "Planning a wedding would be marvellous entertainment. Or maybe she's jealous. Perhaps she wants to see you settled, out of harm's way."

"That's nonsense," Rachel said; but it was an echo of Judy's remark on board ship, and it made her uneasy. Surely it couldn't be true? Mothers weren't like that. Or shouldn't be. She was silent for a moment, then sighed heavily. "It's such a shame," she said. "For years I've longed and longed to come back to Entebbe, but now I'm here, my mother and I seem to do nothing but argue."

"Maybe you should try to find some kind of job—"

"I have. There isn't one."

"Well—" Paula hesitated. "Should you really be here, then? Look, this may sound like unwarranted interference, but I think you're wasting your time. You ought to be out in the real world—learning something, living life, not sitting here letting it all roll by. But until then, cheer up and think of the good things. After all, it's a beautiful place, the climate is wonderful, we have servants so that entertaining is easy—which reminds me! You're going to accuse me of match-making now, but I promise you I'm not! There's a chap from up-country coming down for a short spell. His name's Tom Whitcroft and he's going to be working for Bob for the next few months. Priscilla and Brian Martin are coming to dinner on Saturday night to meet him. Will you come too, to make up the numbers? He's a bit of a rough diamond, Bob says, but an interesting chap. Intelligent. I haven't met him yet, but he sounds the sort you might enjoy talking to. Do say you'll come. I swear I'm not match-making!''

"You'd better not be." Rachel's fierceness was merely assumed, for the implied compliment hadn't been lost on her. She smiled at Paula, happy again. "Thank you," she said. "I'd love to come."

She found refuge in her journal that night.

"I can't help wondering what Red Rosie would say about this life I'm leading," she wrote. "It seems so purposeless, somehow. I've offered myself for Good Works, but nobody needs me, and I've read nothing worthwhile for ages. I hereby resolve to take myself in hand."

In England, Mr. Chamberlain flew back from Berchtesgaden, with his death's-head smile and his winged collar and his umbrella, to announce to the populace that he brought "peace for our time."

It was quite like old times, Rachel thought, as she listened to Tom Whitcroft holding forth at the Garfield's dinner table the following Saturday. He was a wireless buff, a great listener to the BBC, and utterly contemptuous of Neville Chamberlain and his policy of appeasement.

"He caved in," he said, his thin dark face showing his disgust. "Gave Hitler everything he wanted—and the Czech representative wasn't allowed to say a word. Nor was Russia. The poor bloody Czechs were just sold down the river—"

"Rubbish," snapped Priscilla Martin. She was a blonde vivacious girl with a wicked gift for mimicry, star of the Dramatic Society. She was also a notorious flirt, but had clearly not found it worthwhile going into action for Tom. "Nobody wants war."

"Have you looked at a map recently?" Tom asked her derisively. "The Rhineland's remilitarized to the west. Now Germany's snatched the Sudetenland to the east. If you imagine the threat's over, all I can say is there's none so blind as those who won't see."

And because of his accent—the accent, in Priscilla's view, of comedians and men with daft grins who played ukeleles—they were words that she garnered and relished and improved upon; so that "Noon so blaind as them as worn't see" became a catch-phrase, bandied about among the younger set long after Tom Whitcroft had returned to his home station at Masaka.

It was, of course, the accent that did for him as far as Kitty was concerned—that and the fact that he had, as she told Rachel after the first and only time that he came to the house, a working-class face. In vain did Rachel say that he was intelligent and had opinions she found interesting; her mother continued to assure her that she was committing social suicide by continuing to associate with such an impossible young man.

Rachel set her lips stubbornly and continued to enjoy Tom's company, not admitting even to herself that her mother's opposition in any way increased his appeal. He was interesting, she said—a whole lot more interesting than most of the people she was forced into conversation with at all the dinner parties she had to attend. Her mother should be glad, she insisted, that she'd met someone who at least encouraged her to find out what was going on in the world, and to read the more serious magazines that arrived spasmodically in large, out-of-date bundles.

Few others in Entebbe seemed to share Tom's disquiet. Did Gavin, Rachel wondered? Was he even now burning with righteous zeal on behalf of the Czechs, just as he had done for the Spanish Nationalists? And had he joined the RAF yet? He would, she felt sure, at the first opportunity—unless, of course, his fiancée talked him out of it. Or was she his wife by this time? She'd had no news of him since leaving England. Grandma wrote from time to time, but she made no mention of the family next door and Rachel was too proud to ask.

Oh, you fool, she said to herself. Stop thinking about him! It wasn't as if she loved him any more, was it?

Who would have thought that the Spring Ball would have been the catalyst that brought everything to a head? It started so innocently—a celebration of spring, Kitty told Rachel, with the Club decorated with garlands of spring flowers (paper flowers, of course) and a collage of skipping lambs and fluffy chicks all over the walls, and a competition for the best Easter bonnet.

"What's that got to do with Uganda?" Rachel asked.

"That's hardly the point. We're English."

"Mrs. McTavish isn't. Nor Mrs. Muir."

"British, then. Don't be absurd, Rachel! Anyway, we're going to start making the flowers next week. That'll be fun, won't it? It'll give you something to do."

"Mummy, I can't! I'm useless at that sort of thing."

"Well, you can cut out, or something."

"Over my dead body," Rachel said. "Honestly, I've never heard of anything more futile."

"What on earth has got into you?" Kitty's eyes were blazing. "There's no pleasing you these days. You seem to enjoy being as contrary as you know how."

It wasn't true, Rachel thought, as her mother swept angrily off the verandah. She didn't really enjoy much about Entebbe these days. It all seemed so petty and time-wasting and pointless. Take this so-called Spring Ball, for example. What did springtime mean to anyone in Entebbe? What on earth would the Africans make of it?

The stewards at the Club, in their long white khanzus and their red fezzes, watched everything that went on with flat, opaque, unreadable eyes. The plays, the reviews, the skits, the dances; the drinking, the flirting; the mighty Europeans with their hair down. What did they think—*really* think?

Nobody cared. Oh, people cared about building roads and schools and hospitals, about tending the sick and administering justice and planting trees and husbanding the land. They cared on a grand, cosmic scale.

Perhaps, Rachel thought, it was different for those who lived close to the people; the District Officers who administered justice and were witness to the daily struggle for existence. Perhaps they became more intimately involved. But here, in Entebbe, it sometimes seemed as if Africans did not exist as individuals but only as a crowd of film extras.

That night at dinner, with her father recently back from one of his up-country safaris, she ventured to voice some of these thoughts.

"I was thinking about the boys," she said. (Boys? Juma was old enough to be her father—even grandfather! Did he mind that he and his kind were called boys? Why hadn't it struck her before that to do so was ludicrous? Maybe she would ask Melika about it. She saw her quite often and sometimes sat with her under the huge tree on the greensward where the children played.)

"What about the boys?" Kitty asked. She sounded wary, clearly prepared for more criticism of her way of life.

"I was thinking that we are just like the Victorians, aren't we? They treated their servants as if they were somehow of lesser importance, without the same feelings and emotions as the upper classes. We're the same with the Africans."

Kitty gave a gasp of outraged laughter.

"Rubbish!" she said. "They wrap us all around their little fingers. The whole household revolves around Juma. I bend over backwards to please him. With what result? This very day he's told me he has to go back to Mbale to bury his father—*again*! That's the third time to my certain knowledge."

"Are you going to let him go?"

"Well, of course I am. I don't want to lose him, do I? I'm just illustrating the point that they've got us where they want us. Juma had better be back by the Spring Ball, because I intend to take a party."

Rachel found her heart sinking. Who would have thought it? Once she would have been thrilled at the prospect; now everything had gone flat, as unexciting as Tizer without the bubbles. She knew exactly who would be invited, what they would talk about. Suddenly it seemed unendurable.

A few days later, when she was walking with her father in the cool of the evening, she nerved herself to speak of her feelings.

"I don't think I can stay much longer, Daddy," she said.

For a few moments he continued walking in silence. She glanced at him sideways. He looked sad, she thought. Disappointed. But not altogether surprised.

"I thought, perhaps, that this would give us all a chance to get to know each other," he said.

"But it has!" She took his arm, pressed close to him. "It's been lovely. It's what I needed *then*. But now—"

"Now it's claustrophobic?"

"Yes. That's it, exactly. I keep thinking, is this *it*? Mummy wants me to find a suitable man and settle down here—"

"I suppose we both want that, really."

"But it's not what I want. There must be something else in life! I'm bored stiff, Daddy, that's the truth of it. Anyway, what suitable man? There isn't one. I could die, waiting!"

"I doubt that. You're growing into a lovely young woman, Rachel."

"Hark to my proud and prejudiced father!"

"Do you have some sort of plan in mind?"

"I want to go back to England. To London. Alice is working there now, living with her Aunt Susan. I met her once, at school. She's awfully nice, and she says that I could live there too. She'd be glad of the money, Alice said."

"And if war comes?"

Rachel said nothing for a moment.

"It may not," she said. "But if it does, I'd rather be there. Oh Daddy, I *must* be there!"

"Yes." His voice was reflective. He understood, Rachel saw, rather to her surprise. She heard him sigh again.

"You know, Rachel," he said, "I've always loved my job, loved living here. It's always seemed to me something worth doing. Don't dismiss all that we've done as unimportant, or self-seeking, or trivial. For me, it hasn't been like that."

"I know," she said softly.

"I can see that for the women, for the families, then it's different, though. I wonder, sometimes, if it's all been worth it— worth the separation and all the pressures of living this rather artificial life. I suppose one can never be sure. One can only hope that something is gained and not too much lost. I can't imagine any other life that could have been so rewarding for me."

"But you see how I feel?" she asked him.

"I do." He glanced at her sideways and gave a short and rueful laugh. "But don't expect your mother to," he said.

❧ ELEVEN ❧

Alice's Aunt Susan lived in Shawcross Street, Chelsea, not too far from Sloane Square. Number 29 was tall and thin with a flight of steps to the front door and area steps to the basement. It looked, Rachel thought, a little forbidding—an impression enhanced rather than lessened by the fact that it was identical to all the other houses in the street, give or take the odd brass knocker or window-box. Even so, her heart swelled with excitement. This, after all, was the beginning of a new life.

"Gosh, I've missed London," she said to Alice as, having paid off the taxi that had brought her from Victoria, she stood on the pavement surrounded by her luggage, inhaling the mingled aromas of smoke and petrol, cat-soured earth and summer heat. A man, sorting through parcels at the back of a delivery van across the road, was whistling "The Lambeth Walk." The whole cocktail brought back the summer she had spent with Sylvia—not the loneliness, but the rewarding voyages of discovery she had embarked on with such determination and eventual enjoyment.

"The last time I saw you, you were missing Africa," Alice pointed out, not unreasonably. Rachel laughed, but attempted no explanations.

Inside the house she found a comfortable, untidy clutter; an elderly dark-red carpet covered the hall and stairs, and there were far too many coats on a stand. A tall Chinese vase contained umbrellas and two peacocks' feathers, a pile of books on the bottom stair waited to be taken up to a more permanent home, and just outside the kitchen door was a green felt board pinned with notes and telephone numbers and reminders. On this, a plain white foolscap sheet of paper stood out. Its bold black message read: "Alice. Eric rang."

"Oh!" Alice grinned and tore it down. She stuffed it into the pocket of her skirt, looking both pleased and embarrassed.

"Who's Eric?" Rachel asked. "You haven't told me about him."

"All in good time!" Alice tried to look mysterious, but giggled instead. She had lost much of her puppy fat, Rachel noticed, and seemed a great deal happier than when she was at school; her face, however, did not lend itself to mystery. It was round, almost childish still, her little rosebud mouth as vulnerable as ever.

"Come on," she said now. "I'll take you up to your room. Aunt Sue is out for the moment. You're up two flights, so we'd better leave the trunk in the hall and just take up the small cases. Someone will be around to help us later."

It was, Rachel found in the days that were to come, that sort of a household. Someone was usually around. The key was on a string and could be pulled through the front door letter-box, enabling out-of-work musicians, wives on the run from violent husbands, refugees from Nazi Germany, Members of Parliament in search of a kind word, any and all manner of people to gain entry and help themselves to friendship and a cup of tea. Aunt Susan worked in an Agency that liaised between refugees and the Home Office, and her circle of friends and acquaintances seemed enormous.

Eric was one such, Alice told Rachel on that first day, as she sat on the bed and watched her unpack.

"Aunt Sue met him at some political function. He wants to go into Parliament," she said.

"What party?"

"Oh, Labour, of course."

"There are others," Rachel pointed out.

"Not for Eric. He's very earnest—"

"Oh, dear!"

"Yes, well . . . I feel a bit guilty, really, because I confess I stop listening sometimes and just look at his mouth. And his chin. It's sort of pointed, with a cleft—"

"His mouth?"

"His chin, idiot! And the tip of his nose has a super way of moving downwards when he smiles. Not that he does very often. Honestly, politics are all very well and I know we have to have them, but you can get tired of them. There's an awful lot of them in this house, I can tell you. Oh Rachel, it's so wonderful to have you here! I've got to know a few girls at the College, but there's no one who speaks the same language, no one I want to *do* things with, like go to theatres or the pictures, or anything.''

Rachel turned and grinned over her shoulder.

''It will be fun, won't it?''

''If only Julia—''

''Yes,'' Rachel said flatly. The loss of Julia could still hurt so piercingly that, from time to time, it took her breath away. ''Tell me about the College,'' she added, changing the subject. ''Will I like it?''

Her father had decreed that typing on its own was woefully inadequate to meet the needs of business life, and she was to join Alice for three months to learn the intricacies of shorthand and bookkeeping.

''No, of course not. You're bound to hate it, the same as I do, but what's the alternative? Teaching? Nursing?''

''Sword-swallowing? Bareback riding? You'd think there'd be something, wouldn't you?''

''What happened to the writing?'' Alice asked.

''It—simmers,'' Rachel said. ''I've decided that what I need is Experience of Life.''

''Didn't you get that in Entebbe?''

''A bit, I suppose. I learned I didn't belong there, anyway. But where do I belong? I don't know!''

''You have to Find Yourself,'' agreed Alice earnestly. Rachel could almost see the capital letters. ''It's terribly important. Eric Found Himself when he discovered politics.''

Rachel perceived that, for Alice, finding Eric had been important, too. She knew what it was like to have the urge to bring the beloved's name into the conversation at every opportunity and experienced a surge of affectionate sympathy.

''Well, good for Eric if he's managed it,'' she said. ''What do you want to do with your life, Alice?''

Alice sighed wistfully.

"Get married eventually, of course. It's the only fulfilling thing for a woman, isn't it?"

"Is that what Eric says?" Rachel asked guardedly.

"It's what *I* say! But of course, Eric agrees."

He would, thought Rachel. She didn't think, somehow, that she was going to like Eric very much.

There was general amazement, not least from Rachel's grandmother, that she should be sent back to an England which, on all sides, was making preparations for war.

"I think your mother must have taken leave of her senses," Grandma said, setting the telephone wires buzzing with her outrage.

"You can't blame Mummy. She didn't want me to come, but I couldn't go on wasting my time there, Grandma. I had to get on with doing something. Daddy agreed with me. After all, they'll be home themselves early next year."

"Next year? Next *year*? We'll be at war long before then!"

"Nobody knows that for sure. It might be over by then. Or it might not happen."

"Your grandfather says it will. And then where will you be? It's a well-known fact that London will be bombed to bits in the first week."

This, indeed, was the current speculation. Trenches were being dug in Hyde Park, and air raid shelters delivered and installed in back gardens. People in Entebbe, Rachel was forced to admit, didn't know the half of it. She presented herself at the local Police Station to be given a gas mask, to bring her into line with the rest of the population who had been issued with them at the time of Munich, and in August, when she had been in London only a month, there was a trial blackout.

And in spite of it all, she wouldn't have missed a moment of it. She was frightened, but there was a thrill, too; the thrill of being part of it, right here in London, where the news was immediate and the discussion constant.

Aunt Sue, to the rest of the world, was Susan Greaves. Rachel had tried calling her Miss Greaves, until her look of astonishment prompted her to ask if she would prefer to be called Aunt Sue.

"Why not Susan?" she had replied. "That goes for you, too,

Alice. It's what everyone else calls me. God knows you're big enough and old enough."

She was a small, olive-skinned woman with warm brown eyes and a big smile, her grey-streaked dark hair pulled back in a knot at the back of her head. She dressed carelessly in men's shirts and hand-woven skirts, but in spite of the fact that she spent the minimum possible time on herself, she had style. Rachel admired her from the first. She liked her casual warmth, the friendly, no-nonsense way she treated her many visitors, her lack of pretence. She was brisk and efficient and could mix a salad or make a toasted cheese sandwich faster than Rachel had ever seen before, but beneath the efficiency and the forthright manner there was real kindness.

The house had been left to her by an uncle she had cared for until he died, but there was no money for its upkeep beyond her inadequate salary, and she made no secret of the fact that she was glad of Rachel's contribution. There were two more empty bedrooms, but though she allowed some of the droppers-in to stay a night or two under exceptional circumstances, she refused to let any more rooms on a permanent basis.

"Not to any of this lot, anyway," she said privately to Rachel and Alice. "If I'm to share hearth and home, it has to be to someone who'll pay the rent. These, on the whole, are not good payers."

They were, however, excellent talkers. Rachel, listening avidly for echoes of Red Rosie, was astonished to find a remarkable unanimity among almost all of them. None of the old attitudes seemed relevant any more. The days of the Peace Pledge Union were over. The Nazis, it was generally agreed by everyone no matter what shade of politics they preferred, were evil; and a war, sooner or later, was inevitable.

Grandma, on the telephone, begged her to visit Warnfield "before the balloon goes up."

"There'll be no travel afterwards," she said dolefully. "Railway lines are bound to be the first target, mark my words."

Though not everyone shared Mrs. Bond's apocalyptic view of wartime Britain, it was true that no one knew what to expect. Sylvia, whom Rachel attempted to contact by telephone for courtesy's sake, had elected to stay on in Cornwall after her summer holiday.

Rachel dreaded going to Warnfield, dreaded the possibility of seeing any of the Rossiters. She knew nothing of their current doings. Grandma never mentioned them in her letters which, invariably, were concerned with items which she considered of more burning interest: namely, such matters as Doreen's insolence and her departure to work behind the sweets counter in Woolworths, and the vicar's distressing tendency to repeat everything three times, despite having been told, over and over, that his sermons were far too long.

Only once had the family figured, rather obliquely, in her litany of complaints. The grass verge outside The Laurels had, so Grandma wrote much earlier in the year, been "ploughed up and totally ruined" by a car driven without due care and attention "shooting like a rocket" out of the drive of the house next door. The driver, Grandma informed them, was apparently a friend of the Rossiters, an officer in the Royal Air Force, from whom, surely, more responsible behaviour was to be expected.

"Heaven help us all if he flies his plane in the same way as he drives his car," she wrote, adding with bitter sarcasm: "Who needs Hitler and his bombs when the RAF will devastate your property?"

"Three cheers for the boys in blue," Kitty had said as she handed over the letter for Rachel to read.

Rachel, equally unsympathetic, had spared little thought for Grandma's grass verge, but seized immediately on her mention of the RAF. It seemed to imply that Gavin had already joined, if the Rossiters were entertaining friends from the Service. Surely, surely, if he had married, even Grandma would have found it worthy of mention? Not that she personally cared if he were married six times over. It wasn't as if she was in love with him any more. Gavin Rossiter, she told herself, could do exactly as he liked, and good luck to him. She just would like to *know*, that was all.

It was the others—Alannah, Diana, Mrs. Rossiter—she really dreaded seeing. Those last days in Warnfield had taken on the aspect of a nightmare, the participants grotesque and larger than life. The desolation she had felt then still made her feel hollow with grief.

"I'm a fool," she confided to Alice. "The chances of seeing them are remote. I'll go up next weekend."

"You can't! We're going out with Eric and Kenneth on Saturday."

"So we are." Rachel felt depressed. Nearly two months in London, and Kenneth was the only man who had asked her out—and that merely because he was Eric's friend and had been pressed into service to make up a foursome. He was an angular, awkward, bespectacled youth who tended towards Communism but was undergoing agonies of self-examination now that Stalin and Hitler had formed an unholy alliance. It did not make for lively social chitchat. "Do I have to?" she asked. "I don't think Kenneth likes me much."

"He does, I promise you. He told Eric. Anyway, you said you would and I can't cope with them both."

Rachel sighed. She didn't think Eric liked her much, either, and certainly she was not enamoured of him, finding him dull and pedantic and seeing little attraction in the cleft chin and strangely mobile nose that Alice found so fascinating. How inexplicable it was, this business of love. Alice was clearly enraptured, hanging on his every word, apparently oblivious to the self-importance and sheer egotism of his endless monologues. It was enough, she thought, to make any girl long for the spurious charm of a Clifford Bailey.

"All right, I'll come," she said, capitulating reluctantly. "But next weekend, I must go."

And she wrote on the notice board in the hall: "Sept. 2nd and 3rd. Rachel in Warnfield."

"Well," Grandma said, passing the cabbage. "Better late than never!"

She'd been saying it on and off ever since Rachel arrived on the train, which had been greatly delayed owing to the evacuation of children from London to the country. She was not, however, referring to the hour of the train's arrival, but to the fact that Rachel had been in the country two months before making the journey to Warnfield. This observation, in various forms, together with her remark concerning Rachel's inexplicable arrival in England at such a period in the country's history, had meant that there had hardly been time to talk of anything else. Now, as they sat at lunch, she produced the phrase once more just in case Rachel had not taken it in the first time.

"Now, now," Grandpa said jovially, wagging a finger at her. "Don't spoil things, Maisie. Rachel's here now, and very glad we are to see her. May this be the first of many visits."

"I hope so, Grandpa." Looking at him, Rachel felt, after all, a few pangs of guilt. He looked unexpectedly frail, his nose sharper, his flesh fallen away a little. Her grandmother, on the other hand, was unchanged, at least to the naked eye. Even the dress she wore was one that Rachel remembered well: small white leaves on a grey ground, with a white guipure modesty vest showing at the neck.

"It seems like only yesterday," Grandpa went on, "that you were here in your white blouse and gym slip! Such battles we had over the chessboard, didn't we?"

"You used to let me win."

"No, no. Well—" twinkling at her "—maybe sometimes, but only when you were very young. I soon learned to fight with the best." The light seemed to die out of his eyes. "And now we've a real fight on our hands, haven't we? That dreadful man—"

"Not Hitler, please. Not at the lunch table." Poland may have been invaded, diplomatic exchanges had reached crisis point, children were fleeing the cities, but the mention of the man who had caused all this chaos, Grandma implied, must not be allowed to sully a civilised meal. "Rachel dear, do tell me more about your father. He's so conscientious and works so hard, I can't help worrying about his health, especially in such a climate. It's not as if—" she broke off sharply, cleared her throat. "More potatoes, dear?" she asked.

Not as if he has a wife who looks after him, she was about to say. Rachel could hear the words as clearly as if she had actually spoken them.

"Daddy's fine," she said. "And so is Mummy."

"Well, at least he's safe," Grandpa said. "He won't have to fight in this war."

"He'll *want* to." Grandma's eyes flashed belligerently. "He's not the kind to sit back and let others do the job. Last time he volunteered, Rachel, did you know that? He didn't wait to be called up. I was so angry—but proud too, of course, underneath it all. He looked a picture in his uniform." She sighed and shook her head reminiscently. "Saying goodbye to him at Warnfield station that last time was the hardest thing I've ever been called on to do.''

"But he only went to Edinburgh,'' Grandpa pointed out, with a touch of amusement. "He was one of the lucky ones.''

"We weren't to *know* that, were we?'' Grandma reacted as if her son's patriotism had been impugned. "We weren't to know he'd be stuck in Scotland for the rest of the war. He obeyed orders, that's all, like everyone else. When I waved him off in that train, it could have been next stop Flanders.''

"He would have been taking a somewhat eccentric route,'' Rachel remarked, in a neutral kind of voice.

Grandma looked at her pityingly. "Smile, Rachel, as much as you want to,'' she said. "You young people don't know what life's all about. You've no experience of the worry and the heartbreak—war's just excitement to you. Mark my words, you'll learn, you'll learn.'' She spoke almost as if this would be a process she, personally, would greatly relish—as if it were about time this generation suffered as hers had done. Rachel was conscious of a sudden chill, a goose walking over her grave.

"I expect we will, Grandma,'' she said.

Although it was warm, that afternoon and evening were spent indoors, making black-out curtains. Grandma had prudently bought a huge roll of black material when last in town—enough for Buckingham Palace, Rachel thought with a sinking of the heart when she first saw it—and together they measured and cut and sewed.

If Rachel had been called upon to nominate her least favourite way of spending an afternoon, sewing would probably have been top of the list. However, at least for the first hour or so, she was bolstered by a feeling of virtue, the consciousness that she was doing her bit, being of genuine help to her grandmother who, after all, had given her a home when nobody else would do so.

So she sewed with a good grace, and listened to Grandma's complaints about the vicar, and Miss Bickerstaffe of the haberdashery counter at Drake's Stores, who had promised to get in some navy ric-rac braid but had taken three weeks about it, and the boy from Hobbs Groceries who whistled in a particularly piercing and unmusical way, point-blank ignoring any requests to desist.

"What about the Rossiters?" she brought herself to ask at last. "Do you see anything of them these days?"

Grandma, busy with Rufflette tape, made a noise indicating disdain.

"As little of them as possible, thank you very much," she said. "If I'd known what sort of neighbours they'd be, I'd never have come to live here. Not content with ruining our grass verge with cars running out of control, it's been nothing but mess and noise around here for months. They've had some sort of elaborate air raid shelter built in their garden. There's been a lot of talk about it, actually. Of course, I'm not accusing them of using Council labour and Council materials, but you can imagine what's being said."

Rachel imagined; but not for long, for Grandma had further grievances.

"Mrs. Rossiter is on some committee or other to do with billeting. She had the effrontery to call the other day to ask if I could accommodate three teachers from London, in case of wholesale evacuation. She said she didn't think I'd welcome children! I was put out, I don't mind telling you. What a thing to say! Anyone would think I was some sort of monster. I felt it was a slur, bearing in mind the years I'd had you! I said to her 'Mrs. Rossiter, you make me sound like Herod—' "

"But would you welcome children?"

Grandma shrugged and pursed her thin lips.

"Well," she said defensively after a moment. "It's hardly a question of what I want. Your grandfather isn't as strong as he used to be."

"There you are, then," Rachel said. "Mrs. Rossiter was only being considerate."

"Nonsense!" Grandma was having none of that. "She was making a point. Underlining the fact that when you were here, you spent more time at their house than you did at home."

"But Grandma—" Rachel began, then sighed. It was an old bone of contention, best ignored. "So you opted for the teachers, then?" she said.

"Certainly not! I have very little help in the house. No live-in staff any more since Doreen left me to go to Woolworths. Just Mrs. Harkness three times a week, and heaven knows she's all but useless. And as I pointed out, I have a duty to my family.

You could well need to come back here to live when the bombs start falling. And then there's Sylvia. I have to think of her—''

"She's staying in Cornwall."

"I know that now, but I didn't then. It's so *like* Sylvia to find herself a safe little haven—''

Not for the first time, Rachel felt that the nature of Grandma's conversation made responding to it highly complicated.

"What about Alannah? Is she still at home?" she asked quickly, hoping to get back to the Rossiters.

"You're not going to look her up, surely, after the way she treated you?"

"I just wondered what she was doing."

"Oh, she's here, all right. I happened to see her from the window only a few days ago."

"And Barney? Is he away?"

"The younger boy? I heard he went to Art College. In London, I suppose. He comes back from time to time in a dreadfully noisy little car—''

"And Gavin?" Rachel's head was bent over the never-ending hem of a bay-window curtain.

"In the RAF. It was his friend who ruined our verge. I sent your grandfather round to complain, and of course he let them get away with some kind of apology. What about compensation? I said. No mention of that, of course. I should have known."

"Did he get married?"

"Married?" For a moment, Grandma looked perplexed, having lost her thread. "Oh," she said at last. "The Rossiter boy! Not that I've heard. Now Rachel, do look what you're doing! You've tacked the top of that curtain to the bottom of the other."

"Oh dear! What an idiot!"

How she hated sewing. Even so, she felt, all at once, ridiculously happy. Which proved without doubt that she was indeed an idiot.

The following morning Mr. Chamberlain's voice, tired and regretful, emerged from the wireless set to tell them that the nation was at war. So it was now a fact.

Even Grandma was silenced. Or almost.

"Well—" she said, hands gripping the arms of her chair. "Well!"

"At least we know where we are and what's to be done," Grandpa said.

The aroma of the weekend joint roasting in the oven brought Grandma back to more immediate concerns.

"Business as usual," she said briskly, rising to her feet. "That's what they used to say the last time. I must go and baste the lamb."

Rachel caught her grandfather's eye and he smiled.

"Brace up, my darling. We'll muddle through somehow. Right's on our side." His voice sounded frail and rather touching. Rachel nodded, wanting to believe him but at the same time remembering all that Tom had said about Germany rearming and taking over the Czech factories that supplied military equipment. Being on the side of virtue wasn't always enough. "I think," Grandpa went on, getting up from his chair, "that on this occasion I'm going to forget your grandmother's views about drinking in the middle of the day. I need a good strong Scotch. Can I get something for you?"

Before Rachel could reply, the air raid siren sounded, swooping up and down in a way that chilled the blood. Halfway between his chair and the drinks' cabinet, Grandpa stood transfixed.

"Did you hear that?" Kitchen spoon in hand, Grandma appeared framed in the doorway. "I knew it. I *knew* it! They'll bomb us out of existence—"

The noise of the siren died, and from the street, through the open window, could be heard stentorian tones:

"Take cover, take cover."

Forgetting her rules regarding the vulgarity of peering out of windows, Grandma went over and pulled the lace curtains aside.

"It's only that Sid Parker from the butcher's," she said. "A dreadfully common little man. You'd think they could find someone with a bit more authority. He looks quite ridiculous in that tin hat."

"Come away from the windows, Maisie." Grandpa, for once, was taking charge. "We'll sit under the stairs, as we'd planned. The canvas chairs are there, and a torch. Don't forget your gas mask—" He broke off as the doorbell rang.

"Oh, who can that be at such a time?" Grandma was fretful. "How very thoughtless."

"I'll go," Rachel said.

She opened the door to find, to her total astonishment, that Barney was standing in the porch. Stunned into silence, they gaped at each other. It was Barney who recovered first.

"Rachel! Good Lord! I didn't expect to find you here."

"Who is it? Come away from the door, Rachel." Grandma came up behind her. "This is no time for a social call! What on earth do you imagine you are about?" she said severely, seeing Barney. "We're supposed to be taking cover."

"That's why I'm here," Barney said. "My parents sent me round to ask if you'd like to come and share our air raid shelter. There's plenty of room in it, and its very comfortable. We thought that perhaps you hadn't had time to make your own arrangements." His eyes went back to Rachel. He seemed to be unaffected by the prospect of danger and was grinning widely, delighted to see her. "You'll come, won't you?"

"Are you sure—?"

"We'll stay here, in our own home," Grandma said firmly; but Grandpa, as if the outbreak of war had brought out a streak of decisiveness hitherto undiscovered, overruled her.

"This is most kind of you, my boy," he said. "Come along, Maisie. Get your gas mask. We can't stay dithering here, and if the Rossiters are kind enough to offer us a place of safety, then we owe it to Rachel to take it. It's not as if we have only ourselves to think of."

"I'm all right. Don't worry about me," Rachel assured him. The thought of confronting Mrs. Rossiter seemed, at that moment, worse than anything Hitler might throw at her.

Sid Parker's shouts could be heard once more as he approached the house, riding slowly back down the street on his bicycle, tin hat worn very straight on his head, ARP armlet much in evidence. He stopped when he drew level with The Laurels, seeing the small knot of people standing at the open door.

"What the 'ell do you think you're doing? Take cover!" he yelled.

"That's *quite* enough, Mr. Parker!" Grandma was icily outraged; but at least she was galvanised into action, and without further argument, went to get her gas mask, turn down the oven, and join the others as they went next door.

"I don't believe any of this," Rachel said to Barney. "It's surreal!"

"I certainly can't believe you're here. I thought you were in Uganda."

"I came back a couple of months ago."

"*Here?*"

"No, no. London. Barney, what will your mother say when she sees me?"

"She'll be all right," he assured her.

And she was. Not frighteningly angry as she had been at their last meeting; not even coldly polite, but serene and smiling, apparently delighted to see her. She sat in an old wicker arm-chair imperturbably sewing her tapestry as if there had been no past rows or tears, no present air raid. Her calm was monumental, her air that of a Lady Bountiful welcoming guests to her castle.

"You were surely going to call on us before you went back to London, weren't you?" she asked when they were comfortably sitting in the concrete shelter, sipping the coffee Alannah made on an ingenious little camping stove. Rachel's experience of air raid shelters was limited, but she felt sure that this represented a highly superior model. The walls were bright with painted murals—undoubtedly Mrs. Rossiter's work, judging by the impressionistic nature of them—and rugs covered the cement floor.

"Well—" she felt some embarrassment at Mrs. Rossiter's question. She could, she felt, hardly say, "You were so hateful the last time I saw you that wild horses wouldn't have dragged me." "There wasn't, actually, very much time," she said. "I only arrived yesterday, and must go back this afternoon."

"There won't be any trains," Alannah said.

She, of all the Rossiters present, was alone in seeming awkward. She had greeted Rachel with polite surprise but with no intimacy. Their eyes had not met when Alannah had handed Rachel her coffee cup.

"Oh, I'm sure some will run," Mrs. Rossiter said vaguely.

"Always supposing," Grandma said, "that London still stands."

"Now, now, Mrs. Bond. That doesn't sound like your normal optimistic self." Mr. Rossiter gave a private, conspiratorial wink in Rachel's direction. "We mustn't give way to gloom, must we?"

His manner was as lively as ever, and Rachel expected, any moment, the suggestion of a quick game of Adverbs, or even I Spy.

Barney, who had gone aloft once more to retrieve the gas mask he had forgotten on his first journey, came down the steps again.

"There's an old man with a white beard wandering around outside," he said.

"What a dreadful omen! Does he happen to have a scythe about his person?" Alannah asked—at which Rachel giggled and Alannah, for the first time catching her eye, joined in.

"That'll be old Jimmy Bancroft, poor old chap," Mr. Rossiter said. "He's one of the doormen at the Town Hall. Tell him to come down, Barney. He's a funny old fellow," he explained in an undertone to the others. "Talks a lot—cleft palate—all alone in the world. He lives just round the corner. He seemed worried when I spoke to him yesterday so I told him to come if the balloon went up."

Mrs. Bond pressed her thin lips together in disapproval, but naturally said nothing. If Mr. Rossiter wanted to share his shelter with every Tom, Dick or Harry, that was, of course, up to him. For her part, she was not accustomed to mixing with Town Hall doormen on a social basis, still less funny old fellows with cleft palates, and had no intention of allowing this war to lower her standards.

Jimmy Bancroft proved to be a mine of information. Enemy bombers had been sighted over the southern counties of England, he told them—except that he said "schighted over," which made Barney bite his lip and stir his coffee with great concentration. Gunsch, he told them, were already firing in Hyde Park. The entire Government was moving, lock, schtock and barrel, to Wooshter, or was it Leamington? (Maybe it was Schirenschester, Barney whispered to Rachel in Jimmy's voice, making her giggle again). And patientsch in all the London hoschpitalsch, not exschepting the dying, had been schent home to make room for air raid caschualtiesch. He had it all, he said, on good authority.

"Really!" Grandma, coldly scornful, was the only one present prepared to break the trembling silence which could, so easily, have erupted into hilarity. "I suppose Mr. Chamberlain was in touch with you personally, this very morning?"

Barney, to create a diversion, went up to ground level once more to see what was happening. He returned a moment later to announce that the All Clear had gone and with jokes concerning the rapidity with which the good old RAF had been able to scare Hitler away, the party prepared to disperse. Jimmy Bancroft, with effusive thanks, tottered off down the garden, leaving Rachel, Alannah and Barney free to indulge their mirth.

"Come along, Rachel," said Grandma, clearly wishing to put a stop to this kind of childish unseemliness. "We're most grateful for your hospitality, Mrs. Rossiter."

"You don't have to go for a minute, do you?" Barney asked Rachel, who glanced interrogatively towards her grandmother. Lunch, she was told, would be a little later than usual; half past one, and mind she was there on the dot.

"I think I ought to leave immediately afterwards," Rachel said. "Getting back to London might be difficult. It was bad enough yesterday. It was a ridiculous day to travel, really."

"You could have come at any time over the past two months," said Grandma, with perfect truth, but Rachel made no reply. She had run out of pacifying remarks.

"I'll drive you back to London," Barney offered. "No trouble."

"Oh, I couldn't possibly—"

"Yes you could! I insist."

In the event, Alannah came too. The constraint between the girls was shortlived, past differences ignored, and Rachel found she was glad, in spite of everything. It had always been thus—childish quarrels, so important at the time, had invariably been forgotten when they next met.

But this hadn't been a childish quarrel, and she surely couldn't have forgotten, Rachel thought, herself remembering all too clearly the tears, the accusations, the coldness—even the letter to Miss Scrimgeour, for heaven's sake! How could they have forgotten?

Perhaps it was the war, she told herself. The smaller crisis had been swallowed up in the larger; and the same spirit that had urged the Rossiters to ask Grandma to share their shelter after so many years of sniping, had enabled them to erase the uncomfortable memories of almost two years ago.

Gavin, she was told, had joined the RAF at the earliest possible moment and was now flying Blenheim bombers up in Lincolnshire. He'd been home last weekend, but had been recalled by telegram and gone back immediately. So perhaps, Rachel thought, they realised they had been wrong. Gavin had been determined to fly, and nothing she had said could have influenced him, either then or now. But if so, she knew better than to expect them to admit it openly.

Perhaps this present friendliness meant they were sorry. She would give them the benefit of the doubt, anyway, for she knew that this was the best she could hope for by way of an apology. And it was good to be friends again! To giggle with Alannah who, for all her little ways, could be so funny when she tried. No one's perfect, Rachel thought. Life's too short and too uncertain to bear grudges.

"But what happened to Jacqueline?" she asked. "The last I heard she and Gavin were engaged and going to get married."

"They weren't at all suited," Alannah said. "We all saw it—"

"I didn't," Barney said. "I liked her."

"Ma couldn't abide her, and nor could Di. She was frightfully bossy, Rachel, always telling Gavin what to do. He saw it would be a disaster—"

"But Jackie chucked Gav," Barney pointed out.

"*Anyway*," Alannah said, dismissing the point as irrelevant. "They broke off the engagement, that's all that matters. She didn't fit in, that was the top and bottom of it. She kept wanting to drag Gav off to her family."

"How very unreasonable," Rachel said dryly, causing Alannah to give her a sharp look. "And Diana?" she pursued. "Where is she now?"

"Oh, Di did absolutely brilliantly at University," Alannah told her. "Well, we all knew she would, of course. And now she's doing some post-graduate research at Cambridge. Something to do with Minoan Culture. She was home last week, too, but she was anxious to get on with some particular bit of work so she went back with Gavin and he dropped her off. They're not so very far from each other."

"Is she going to teach or lecture or something?" Rachel asked, and Alannah laughed.

"I can't see it, can you?" she asked. "She'd be the world's worst teacher. I don't think she knows what she wants to do, exactly."

"Maybe she'll join the Army," Barney said, at which they all laughed. The thought of Diana subject to Army discipline beggared belief.

As for Alannah, she had left school at the end of last term, she told Rachel, leaning forward with her arms resting on the two front seats of Barney's Austin Seven. And she'd managed to get a place in the Rose Kelly Academy of Dramatic Art in London. Only she supposed it wasn't in London any more, because they'd said in the event of war they would be transferring to Cheltenham.

"The parents aren't at all keen, even on that," she said. "They feel we ought to stick together. It's funny how different parents can be, isn't it? I mean, yours have never minded you being miles away from them, have they?"

She hadn't changed, Rachel realised with some amusement. If she was going to be friends with Alannah, she would have to accept her as she was, tactlessness, egotism and all.

"The circumstances are different, you idiot," Barney said, ever defensive of Rachel.

"Aren't you terrified of being in London?" Alannah asked her.

"Not terrified, exactly." Rachel struggled for honesty. "I don't know what I'll be like if there really are air raids, but so far being in London is rather exciting, especially living where I am. Alice's aunt knows so many interesting people. We had two Members of Parliament for dinner the other night—"

"Now that's what I call gluttony," Alannah said; but she looked impressed, just the same. "I must say," she went on, "I'm dying to go to Drama School. Honestly, Rachel, I don't know how you can possibly settle for secretarial work—it's always sounded the dullest thing in the world to me. I've positively refused to have anything to do with it. But then, I've always known what I wanted to do, so I suppose it's different for me, in a way. For someone like you it's probably the best thing.''

''Don't be so damned patronising,'' Rachel said. She spoke without heat and with the utmost good humour, but the remark caused Alannah to regard her with the same sharp interest she had shown before.

''You've changed,'' she said.

''She certainly has,'' Barney agreed, giving Rachel an appreciative sideways grin. ''She's a knock-out.''

''You're too kind,'' Rachel said, returning the grin.

''I didn't mean just looks,'' Alannah said.

The kitchen of 29 Shawcross Street gave the impression of being full to bursting point, and the atmosphere was one of nervous excitement, even elation. Several people were talking at once: Eric, who appeared to know exactly what strategy should now be adopted by the Government; Rudi, who being Polish and having lost his home, had a different and more bloodthirsty approach; and Carla, a wild-eyed woman who had left her husband in Guildford and now did social work among the more deprived families of the East End. Her line was to trace, in detail, the mistakes made by the Conservative governments of the past which had led the world in general and Britain in particular into the folly of war.

Others—Alice, Susan, a French violinist (old) called Jules and another (young) called Paul—sat around the pine table drinking tea and eating bread and jam and arguing or agreeing as they saw fit.

Into this maelstrom came Rachel, Barney and Alannah.

''Thank God!'' Susan called by way of a greeting. ''Come and be a diversion. I'm going quite mad, being told on all sides how we should conduct this war. Come on, draw up a chair, if you can find one.''

Introductions were made, tea was poured, plates provided.

''Oh, you're the *Rossiters*,'' Alice said. ''I've heard so much—'' She pulled herself up short, remembering just what she had heard. ''Anyway, I'm glad to meet you. Did you have the air raid warning? Wasn't it terrifying? I was still getting dressed and didn't know whether to finish or come down here as I was.''

The babble broke out again. Everyone had a story to tell, even Jules, whose English was all but incomprehensible. Susan, looking resigned, cut more bread and butter.

''Well, I'm grateful for it,'' Barney said. ''Because it was only when I went to ask the Bonds to come to our shelter that I discovered Rachel.''

''Their shelter is quite incredible,'' Rachel told the assembled company. ''You've never seen such comfort! Pictures and rugs and all mod. cons.—''

''Plus another shelterer who gave us real up-to-the-minute information,'' continued Barney, which led to an hysterically funny, if exaggerated, representation by Alannah of Jimmy Bancroft, which reduced all of them, even Jules, to helpless laughter.

Afterwards, Paul kissed his fingers in Alannah's direction.

''I 'ave 'eard, always, of ze Engleesh sang-froid,'' he said. ''Now I see it! To cause laughter on such a day—'' Words failed him and he gave an eloquent shrug. His dark, expressive eyes were full of admiration and Alannah rewarded him with a dazzling smile.

''The show must go on,'' she said.

''It's getting the show on the road that's the problem,'' said Eric, who felt he had been out of the limelight long enough. ''What the Government should do is—'' He was off again and Susan, catching Rachel's eye, shrugged with helpless amusement.

It was Barney who finally brought the peroration to a close by getting to his feet and announcing his and Alannah's departure.

''I promised my parents we'd be back early,'' he said. ''Thank you for the tea, Miss Greaves.''

''Thank you for your company. Come again.''

''I'd like to, very much.'' His eyes sought Rachel's. ''I live in London myself, during the term.''

''You'll be most welcome. Any friend of Rachel's—''

''She's nice,'' Alannah said to Rachel who had come out into the hall to see them off. ''Gosh, you're lucky, finding such a super place to live. Who was that *gorgeous* Frenchman? I didn't catch his name.''

"That's Paul. He's a violinist. He doesn't live here. He and Jules live in a terrible place in Earls Court and just come to have baths every now and again."

"A thought strikes me," Alannah said. "If by any chance the Rose Kelly doesn't move to Cheltenham and I need to find digs in London, do you think I might come here?"

A feeling of panic, a kind of claustrophobia, seemed to sweep over Rachel.

"That would be up to Susan," she said faintly.

"Maybe I'll get Ma to contact her, if the need arises. 'Bye for now."

She flapped a hand and made for the car. Barney let her go, turning halfway down the steps for a last word.

"Rachel—" he sounded tentative. "Will I really be welcome if I come again?"

"Of course," Rachel said. "You heard what Susan said."

"I mean, would you welcome me?"

For a moment Rachel hesitated, not knowing why. Surely she would welcome Barney? He'd always been a friend, hadn't he? Whatever reservations she might have about Alannah, she had never had cause to doubt Barney's friendship and there was no possible reason for this instinctive feeling that no good would come of encouraging him. "Yes of course I'd welcome you," she said, dismissing her doubts. "Come any time."

"I'll give you a ring," Barney said, and smiling, went to the car where Alannah waited.

It was, so everyone agreed, a funny kind of war. Nothing much happened, though all around was dramatic evidence that these were dangerous times. Hotels and shops were protected with high walls of sandbags, and above London floated the barrage balloons, shining silver in the sunlight of late September.

There were no more air raids; indeed, there never had been any, the warning on that first day of the war being a somewhat hasty response to an unidentified aircraft over the coast. However, gas masks were now an essential accessory and the traders in Oxford Street cashed in by selling fancy cases designed to cover the square, cardboard boxes. Rachel bought a plain and functional one in olive green with white piping—but couldn't help wishing, afterwards, that she had been a little more adventurous. Alice's scarlet case matched her new shoes and looked well against her navy blue coat.

Late September brought Barney back to London, and though petrol was short, he phoned Rachel at the first opportunity to suggest a run out to the country the following Saturday. They went, on a day of sunshine and scudding clouds, to Box Hill.

"This is wonderful," Rachel said, sitting on the grass with her arms encircling her knees, looking out over the surrounding countryside towards the South Downs. "Such space! I love it."

"I knew you would."

"It reminds me of *Emma* and the Box Hill picnic."

"I had a bet with myself about how long it would take you to mention her."

"How well you know me. I love seeing the English countryside spread out like this. Nothing must change it—not Hitler, not anybody!"

"I'll say not." Appreciatively, Barney looked about him. He had seemed strangely remote all afternoon, not talking very much, but now, for the first time, Rachel thought he looked more relaxed.

"Is something bothering you, Barney?" she asked now.

"Bothering me?" He sounded surprised. "No, of course not." He paused for a moment, apparently engaged in contemplation of the distant view of Dorking. "Well," he went on after a moment. "I suppose that's not strictly true. Yes, something is bothering me. Something like—what the hell am I doing at Art College when there's a war on? Of all the irrelevant occupations, it does seem to take the biscuit. Don't you agree?"

Rachel opened her mouth to disagree violently, then closed it again. Maybe he was right. He wasn't saying that art wasn't important, just that other things, at this moment, took precedence. She could imagine feeling the same herself, if she were a young man. On the other hand, there seemed a distressing familiarity about the whole question.

"Don't you inveigle me into your plans," she said. "I don't want to be accused of sending yet another Rossiter into the Valley of Death."

"I wouldn't dream of involving you!"

"You'll be called up eventually. Can't you wait until then?"

"I suppose so. God knows, I'm not in any hurry in one way.

I hate the thought of the Army. I know I'll be a rotten soldier—''

"Why should you be?"

"Well, I've always been bad at doing things en masse. I've always been a loner.''

"An unlikely claim for a Rossiter,'' Rachel said dryly. But she had to acknowledge that he was right. He was always the nonconformist among them.

"We have a lot to answer for, haven't we?'' She sensed that he was looking at her. "As a family, I mean. We treated you so badly, and you've been very forgiving.''

"That's not entirely true,'' she said. "*You* didn't treat me badly. And I don't think I'm as forgiving as all that. Nothing will ever be quite the same again as it was before.''

He was silent for a moment, wholly occupied, it seemed, with breaking a small twig into even smaller pieces.

"I've thought about you often,'' he said. "I was afraid I'd never see you again.''

"Were you?'' Rachel frowned in disbelief. She had not really thought it possible that her absence could have affected any of the Rossiters in any way.

"I used to imagine you having a whale of a time in Uganda, with hosts of dashing hunters dancing attendance, laying their trophies at your feet.''

"Hunters!'' Rachel laughed at him. "It wasn't like that.''

"There must have been men, though.''

"Well—'' Rachel considered the question. "Some.''

"Are you in love with anyone?''

"Good Lord, no! Would I have come back to England if I had been?'' Barney said nothing in reply to this, but sat up straighter and grinned at her, his gloom apparently lightened.

"What about you?'' Rachel continued after a moment. "Are you in love with anyone?''

"No,'' he said at once. Then amended it. "Yes.''

Rachel, laughing, looked at him.

"Make up your mind,'' she said. He reached out and took her hand.

"I think I did that a long time ago,'' he said.

She sobered, and for a long moment looked down at their two

hands joined on the grass. His fingers were quite short and blunt; not an artist's hands, one would have thought, but capable. Slowly she lifted her eyes and looked into his, those bright, blue eyes that she had once found so intimidating.

Was it possible? she asked herself. Was it Barney, all the time? He had teased her, laughed at her—ignored her quite frequently; but at the same time she had always known she could depend on him. And when she had opened Grandma's front door and seen him standing there, she had experienced a moment of pure joy.

He was a Rossiter, sure enough, and a staunch one; yet alone among them, he had taken her part when it came to a showdown.

"Barney?" Her voice was soft and full of wonder, full of questions.

One hand still clasping hers, he put his other at the back of her head and slowly, inevitably it seemed, they drew together. And this time, unlike its childish forerunners, the kiss was not perfunctory but long, searching, exploratory.

But still, in the end, unexciting. At least to Rachel. Unmoved, and disappointed to find herself so, she drew away from him, only to see from his face that he had experienced a quite different reaction. His expression was luminous with love, his eyes full of happiness.

"There's never been anyone else but you, Rachel," he whispered, a catch in his voice. "Never! You must believe me. It seems too good to be true, that I've found you again."

"I'm glad too," she said. And she was. He was a good friend and she had missed him.

With a sudden change of mood, he gave a whoop of joy and leapt to his feet, and pulling her up beside him he put both his arms around her and hugged her tight.

"It's going to be all right," he said, his voice exultant. "I'll stay here in London until my call-up, just so long as you're here too. Oh Rachel, this changes everything! You're wonderful, do you know that? And you're my girl, aren't you? Say you are!" He was laughing now, his problems forgotten.

Was it possible, she asked herself again? Could Barney be the one? He was highly presentable and fun to be with. They laughed at the same things, shared so many memories. Maybe she was being silly and childish to expect more.

And it would be awfully nice, she thought, to be someone's girl.

4 TWELVE 4

Barney was rather dazzled by the menage at Shawcross Street. Rachel, introducing him to a political columnist in a popular newspaper, saw it and was secretly amused, feeling it put her, for once, one up on the Rossiters.

It meant that he exerted himself to be acceptable to Susan. Or perhaps, she thought, relenting a little, she was being unfair. Maybe he would have exerted himself anyway. Maybe the fact that he proclaimed himself in love with her was enough to subdue the normal Rossiter arrogance.

His efforts were rewarded, for everyone liked him. He endeared himself to Susan by uncomplainingly helping with the washing up—an activity totally ignored by many of the droppers-in—and making her laugh as he did so. He also fixed the bolt on the back door which had somehow dropped out of true and been impossible to shoot home for many months.

"I had no idea you were so domesticated," Rachel said admiringly. "You never were before."

"There wasn't the call. Actually, I quite enjoy it."

"Well, you've made a big hit with Susan."

"Good! That was the idea."

Rachel tried not to let Susan's approval affect her view of him, but subconsciously she was influenced nevertheless. She had always liked him; now, it seemed to her, that love was a distinct possibility.

Alice, also, was impressed by him.

"He's awfully attractive, Rachel," she said.

"Do you think so?"

"I certainly do! Those eyes!"

"Rossiter eyes," said Rachel. "Diana and Gavin are the same. They get them from their father."

"What a good thing you went to Warnfield that weekend and met up with them again."

"I suppose," Rachel said doubtfully, "I ought to go again."

In fact Barney had several times suggested going home for the weekend. Always she had resisted the idea, partly because the prospect of spending time with her grandmother held few charms; but, more urgently, she felt far too tentative about her new relationship with him to allow it to become public property.

"Why on earth?" Alice asked, when Rachel mentioned the matter to her. "I know your grandmother doesn't like the Rossiters, but she'll have to get over it if you're going to *be* one!"

"For heaven's sake, don't jump the gun! Nothing like that has even been mentioned. We just, well, go around together, that's all."

"I've seen the way he looks at you," Alice said. "The other night when we were all packed into the sitting room and Paul was playing that violin sonata, he was absolutely *devouring* you with his eyes!"

Rachel laughed dismissively.

"Heavens, Alice, you really will have to stop reading lurid magazines," she said. "You're beginning to think like them."

But she was pleased, nevertheless. It was good for her prestige to have such a devoted boyfriend, and there was added kudos in the fact that he was so presentable. Though Barney would never have Gavin's film-star looks, he was tall and straight, with good teeth and a friendly smile—not to mention the much-remarked eyes. And the lock of hair which still insisted on falling over his forehead was undoubtedly endearing. Compared to Alice's Eric, he was desirability personified.

"It's not just Grandma," she said.

It was, in fact, far from just Grandma. Going back to Warnfield with Barney would be making a statement to his family that she was not yet prepared for, and perhaps never would be; but any suggestion to Barney of dissembling when in the bosom of their respective families met with astonishment.

"But you're my girl, for heaven's sake!" he said. "Why should you want to keep it dark?"

"Because I'm not really sure that I'm in love with you," she might have said; but she kept her silence. How could she not be sure, when everyone in the whole world told her how lucky she was? Maybe she was searching for something that didn't really exist, except in the imagination. Maybe this was *it*, the thing that people wrote poems and sang songs about.

Certainly, she felt nothing but affection for him, liked being with him, was delighted to have him as an escort; even, up to a point, enjoyed his lovemaking. Not that he ever—well, he was pretty circumspect, really, though he'd been venturing a little further recently. Alice, regaled with details, as indeed she regaled in her turn, was envious. Eric, she confided, had very high standards and didn't seem to be interested in that sort of thing. He was, she said, more cerebral—which didn't prevent her speculating on what *might* happen, should his iron control falter.

"Not that I'd ever Go All the Way," she assured Rachel earnestly. "Not before marriage. Would you?"

Rachel was less dogmatic.

"I honestly don't know. I suppose it's possible to imagine being carried away."

"But wouldn't you be afraid that you'd lose Barney's respect? You wouldn't want to be known as That Sort of Girl, would you?"

"I wasn't thinking of Barney, exactly."

"Who, then?"

Rachel shrugged her shoulders impatiently.

"I don't know. Someone I haven't met yet, maybe. Oh, don't look at me as if I fling myself at the feet of every man I come across! It's just that I can't help thinking that I could meet someone, one day, who would make me throw caution to the wind."

Among Barney's friends, a raggle-taggle band made up in almost equal number of dedicated talent and preposterous poseurs, she was well aware that it was assumed that they went to bed together—not that there was a great deal of opportunity, since Barney shared a small bed-sitter in Bloomsbury with another student, Clive Chambers.

Clive played the role of artist far more realistically than Barney, Rachel considered, being thin and dark and tortured-looking, as well as hopelessly untidy. He talked openly about sex, discussing his needs and his conquests in a way that embarrassed Rachel.

Barney, ever the gentleman, told him to shut up in her presence, but once Clive had left them, he appeared to regard his friend's excesses more indulgently. "Take no notice of him. It's all hot air," he said. "He's just trying to shock you. Don't let him see he's succeeded."

"How Barney puts up with him, I'll never know," she grumbled to Alice. "He says the rudest things about Barney's work, but flies off in a huff if there's the smallest criticism of his."

"Doesn't Barney mind?" Alice asked.

"Not really. He doesn't have any great opinion of his own capabilities. Never did have! He still says he only came to Art College to please his mother." Rachel gave a sudden giggle of amusement. "He took offence the other day, though. He produced one of his mother's pictures. Clive laughed fit to bust when he saw it. He said it was the most god-awful daub he'd ever clapped eyes on."

"Gosh, how frightful! What did Barney say?"

"Not much. He just put it away without a word, all huffy and on his dignity."

"And was it a—" Alice, not used to such language, gulped a little. "A god-awful daub?"

Rachel laughed a little and shook her head.

"How do I know? I don't know the first thing about art. There was lots of splashy colour about, the same as always, but apparently the technique and the composition were all wrong, according to Clive. I'm inclined to take his word for it. Everyone seems to defer to him, as if he knows what he's talking about. Funny thing," she went on after a moment. "I've heard Barney criticise pictures for the same sort of thing heaps of times. It's as if all the Rossiters kind of suspend their critical faculties when it comes to their own family. I knew Mrs. Rossiter was like that, but I never suspected it of Barney."

"Still, it's too bad of Clive to say awful things about his mother, even if she deserves it," Alice said. "Why does Barney put up with him?"

Rachel shrugged. "Convenience, I suppose. Lack of money. He'd love his own place, but he can't possibly afford it. And he likes Clive really, in a funny kind of way. He respects his talent."

"Well, it's not hard to see that you don't like him much," Alice said.

Rachel considered the question. She supposed Alice was right. Certainly she found Clive unattractive, even offensive, and would be thankful never to clap eyes on him again—but at the same time she welcomed his presence because it meant that a certain restraint was forced upon Barney.

"Life," she said somewhat obscurely to Alice, "is incredibly complicated."

"Mine isn't," Alice said wistfully.

Not for the first time, Rachel reflected that Eric was a pain of the first magnitude, but naturally kept her silence. Once or twice she and Barney had gone out with Alice and Eric, but Barney had implored her to enter into no more such arrangements. He and Eric, he claimed, had said all they ever wanted to say to each other within the first five minutes of meeting.

"You know what your trouble is?" Rachel said. "You're just not cerebral."

"No wonder I can't sing in tune," Barney remarked.

Alice, who finished her secretarial course a few weeks earlier than Rachel, had managed to find lowly work at the Ministry of Information, which had taken over the London University main buildings in Bloomsbury. She did little, she said, but carry files about from one office to another. No one seemed to know who was dealing with what, and no matter where she took the files, she was invariably told to take them somewhere else.

Rachel would cheerfully have settled for this, but was less successful when her turn came to look for a job. She finally managed, with a great deal of difficulty and many disappointments, to find an equally humble position in the typing pool of National & Domestic Insurance. It was not, she had to admit, quite what she had hoped for. Something more intimately connected with the war effort had been her goal, but such appointments seemed hard to come by—at least to someone of her limited experience.

"Insurance is very important. Day-to-day life has to go on," Susan assured her—but with sympathy and understanding, since a feverish desire to do what was generally known as one's bit had the entire population in its grip. She herself had moved to a job in the War Office, which gave her an oracle-like status in the eyes of all her friends and acquaintances. On all sides she was appealed to for up-to-the-minute news, predictions of future tactics and explanations of strategy—as if she now had a direct insight into the minds of the greatest powers in the land; and she became adept at noncommittal pronouncements that gave nothing away.

Rachel sighed.

"It's so incredibly dull," she said mournfully. "And the woman in charge of the typing pool is such a dragon."

"Look on it as practice, Rachel dear," Susan urged her. "Sharpen up your skills. Something will turn up, I'm sure. I'll keep my eyes and ears open for you, I promise. It's only too clear that the war is going on for some time yet, so your turn will come, you can depend on it."

Some said the war had barely started. Apart from raids against German ships involved in mine-laying around the coast, the action seemed mostly to be confined to words. Hitler, in a Reichstag speech, had declared that he had no war aims against Britain and France and that warmongers like Churchill were wholly responsible for the present deplorable state of affairs. British bombers infiltrated enemy territory, but dropped propaganda leaflets, not bombs. The British Expeditionary Force, sent to France at the very onset of war, waited behind the supposedly impregnable Maginot Line for the Germans to make the first move.

Despite the official news bulletins from the BBC, rumours abounded. Germany was said to be on the brink of revolution, or about to invade Holland, or soon to make more peace proposals. It was, said Miss Pargeter, the typing pool supervisor whom Rachel had disliked on sight, what she would call a very peculiar war. Very peculiar indeed.

"Not like the good old Crimean," Pam Compton whispered to Rachel out of the side of her mouth. At which Rachel suppressed a giggle. Pam Compton was the only thing that made National & Domestic Insurance even partly tolerable.

"They don't make wars like that any more," she whispered back; and was the recipient of a disapproving glare from Miss Pargeter.

Disapproving glares were her stock in trade, and Rachel was the target for the worst of them when, towards the end of November, Barney phoned her at the office. Even at the best of times, Miss Pargeter's face was severe; matters such as girls who spent too long in the lavatory, girls who dawdled in the corridors, girls who failed to clean their typewriters, and girls who received private telephone calls, were inclined to sharpen her expression still further to the point where her thin lips all but disappeared and, Punch-like, her chin and nose seemed almost to meet.

"Kindly tell your friend," she snapped as she called Rachel over to her desk, "this is not the place for private chitchat."

"Don't bother," Barney said, as Rachel took the receiver and put it to her ear. "I heard that."

"Well, we're not supposed—"

"It's an emergency! Is it OK if I pick you up about six thirty tonight? I've arranged to meet some people in a pub."

Rachel's heart sank a little. There were, among Barney's friends, individuals whom she liked very much. Clive was not entirely typical. On the other hand, en masse she found them overpowering. They used a language she did not understand, talked of people and techniques about which she knew nothing, made in-house jokes that to her were incomprehensible. Among them, she was the outsider once more, with no identity other than Barney's girlfriend.

"You wouldn't rather go on your own?" she said.

"No, definitely not! I want you to come."

"OK," she said resignedly—for after all, being wanted was not something to be lightly ignored. "I'll be ready."

Inexplicably, the chosen pub was in Hampstead, not one usually patronised by Barney and his friends.

"We thought a change would be nice," he said easily.

"On a night like this?" Rain was dashing against the darkened windows of the bus. Outside, headlights reduced to pencil-thin beams and shaded torches did little to pierce the gloom of the black-out.

"Cheer up!" She could barely see his face, but knew he was grinning down at her. "It'll be fun."

"Who's coming?"

"Oh, people."

"Will Clive be there?"

"Mm? Shouldn't think so."

His voice was offhand; and as, at that moment, he was delving in his pocket for the fare, she did not pursue the subject. She didn't care very much anyway. It was always, with a few additions or subtractions, the same crowd.

Once deposited in Hampstead they dashed to the Hollybush, huddled together under one umbrella; but though there were many people inside who looked as if they might be artists, Rachel could recognise no one as they stood just inside the curtained threshold, shaking the rain off themselves, peering through the pall of smoke.

There was a fair sprinkling of uniforms; a mass of khaki just inside the door, and more at the far right-hand side of the long bar.

"There they are," Barney said, and reaching for her hand began to plunge through the crowd. He appeared to be making for an elegant blonde whom she did not recognise, noticing only the shining pageboy hairstyle and the black saucer-shaped hat with an emerald-green feather. She looked, somehow, expensive and out of place in this far from pretentious pub.

Beyond her was an Air Force Officer with his back towards them. He turned as they approached; and all at once Rachel felt as if she had been hit by a ten-ton truck.

Gavin. Gavin and Diana.

"Surprise!" Barney was crying. "See who I brought? It's our own little girl next door."

"Rachel!" Diana was coolly welcoming. "Hallo. How nice to see you again."

"Wow! Look at you!" Gavin opened his arms wide and hugged her. "You look wonderful. Isn't she lovely, Barney?"

"I think so," Barney said, grinning at her.

She couldn't speak, could barely breathe. For a brief moment it seemed as if she had turned to stone—as if all physical activity normally taken for granted had simply stopped in its tracks; then suddenly everything seemed to lurch into action at several times the normal rate. Her heart was thumping madly and she was breathing as if she had run a race.

Somehow she contrived to say the right things. She was, she said, with just the right amount of amused, if affectionate, detachment, frightfully impressed by the uniform. And Diana looked as if she had stepped out of the pages of *Vogue* (dismiss the memory of the wild-eyed fury who had all but forbidden her the house)—and just fancy Barney not telling her who to expect! Honestly, he didn't improve, did he?

Thank heaven, she thought, that she had taken Alice's advice and worn her new Stewart tartan wool dress with the white collar. She almost hadn't.

Drinks were ordered and taken to a table which suddenly became free.

"Why Hampstead?" she asked again, her voice very bright and social. "What are you two doing here?"

"Di's staying with a friend up the road, and I managed to get a forty-eight, so I'm staying there too," Gavin said. "Well, well, will you look at the girl? How you've changed!" He lifted his glass to her. "Here's to old times, and times still to come."

He had always turned heads, but now, in his uniform with the wings over the breast pocket, he looked, Rachel thought, like every woman's dream. He knew it, too. There were two girls at the next table staring at him, nudging each other. Briefly he looked at them before, smiling a little, he turned back to his own circle, like a film star mildly pleased by the idolatry of his fans but not making anything of it, accepting it as his due.

And quite right too, Rachel thought, breathless with wonder at being in the same party as such a god-like being.

"Well, Barney-me-lad," he said to his brother. "When's your call-up?"

"Any time."

"You'd do better to volunteer. They might send you to the Pay Corps or something equally ghastly if you don't."

"Leave him alone," Diana said. "Why should he join up before he has to? Just because you couldn't wait to show your manliness—"

Dangerous ground, Rachel thought uncomfortably. She should change the subject. But her mind was a blank and she could think of nothing to say. The thump, thump, thump of her heart was the only reality.

"And what is your contribution to the war effort, sister dear?" Barney asked sweetly.

"Standing By, duckie." Equally sweetly, Diana smiled at him. "It's the fashionable thing to do, didn't you know? It's something I'm awfully good at. Actually, now I have my doctorate I'm being pressed to lecture, at least for a couple of terms.

After that, I'll think again.'' She took a small sip of her gin and orange. "Oh!" she went on, putting the glass down with a thump. "Have you heard the latest? Dad's thinking of enlisting!''

"*What?*" This was news to Barney.

"They want architects, apparently, because of requisitioning big old houses and turning them into Army HQ's and offices and things. I've told him he's quite mad. He'll send Ma into a decline.''

"Rubbish!" Gavin gave his slow, devastating grin. "Ma is a tough old boot. Look how she created about me learning to fly. But she got over it.''

Involuntarily Rachel looked at Diana, to find her eyes upon her. They exchanged a brief, blank glance before Diana turned to fumble in her bag for a cigarette.

"Give me a light, Gav," she said. He flicked a lighter and held it to her cigarette. The green feather dipped as she bent her head.

"Don't hand them around, will you?" he said, satirically.

"It was my last one.''

"A likely story! Generous to a fault, is our Di.'' He grinned at her and in return she wrinkled her nose at him. They seemed so close, so friendly. Rachel wondered if they had outgrown the rows they used to indulge in. In his turn Gavin lit a cigarette, offering one first to her and then to Barney. Both shook their heads in refusal.

"Rachel," Gavin said, turning to her, "when was it we last saw you? Darned if I can remember. It seems ages ago.''

"It was just before you didn't go to Spain," Rachel said after a moment, and he gave a short, amused laugh.

"Good Lord, yes! What a fiasco! Imagine getting mumps at such a juncture. I was absolutely mortified.''

"No long-term effects, we're all thankful to say," Barney told her.

"Not nearly as thankful as I am, old boy.''

He knew nothing, Rachel realised; nothing of all the trouble that had followed his announcement that he was going to Spain, and nothing about the cataclysmic effect on her life and her relationship with the rest of his family. No one had told him. Or if they had, he'd forgotten.

Diana remembered well enough. How could she not? She drew on her cigarette, looking at Rachel through the smoke with narrowed eyes. Her lips were curved in a small malicious smile.

"Actually," Barney said, "Rachel fought your corner and suffered for it, Gavin. I told you at the time."

"Oh, please! Don't let's drag all that up," Rachel said quickly. "It doesn't matter now."

Gavin blew her a kiss.

"My belated thanks," he said, dismissing the subject. "I say, what a pity young Lannie isn't here to make the party complete. How's she getting on? Anybody heard?"

She liked Cheltenham, Barney said, but had reservations about everything else.

"She says that she hasn't learned much yet."

"Cocky little beast," Diana said affectionately.

"She says she's going to shorten her name to Alannah Ross, so that it will be easier when it's up in lights."

"She'll make it, too," said Gavin. "Now!" He leaned forward with the kind of eager vitality that reminded Rachel of his father. "What are we going to do this evening? Let's find somewhere to eat and dance, shall we?"

"I'm skint, Gav," Barney said.

"I've just been paid. Let's eat, drink and be merry, for God's sake."

The implication of possible death was not lost on Rachel, but Gavin gave no impression of being weighed down by the thought. He stood up, reached for her hand, pulled her to her feet and stood smiling down at her.

"Gosh, it's good to see you again," he said. And as, speechless, she smiled back into those blue, blue eyes, she saw them cloud for a moment as if with sudden surprise. He tilted his head and frowned. He looked, she thought, as if he were trying to get her into focus.

Her heart, which had been behaving erratically from the moment she saw him, now felt as if it were turning somersaults. Her throat was dry and her head was whirling.

This, she knew without any doubt, was love. It wasn't imagination, wasn't anything to do with the affection she felt for Barney. That was all of the mind. This was of heart and nerve and stomach. This was a giant hand squeezing the gut and closing the throat and stopping the breath. How could she possibly have fooled herself, pretended that she was over him, even for a moment? Nothing had changed—not one thing!

No, she was wrong. Something had changed after all, for he was looking at her in a different way. There was a softness about his mouth, a look of uncertainty, as if for the first time he was truly seeing her. And, unbelievably, as if he were attracted to her. She had seen that look before, seen other girls melt before it.

"Come on, you two," he said to the others. "Before I whip this lovely creature away and keep her all to myself."

He put his arm loosely around her waist as if to guide her to the door and, to Rachel, his touch burned like fire.

Sometimes there were days enlivened by reports on fraudulent insurance claims, or claims of such a bizarre nature that it was possible to extract some amusement from them. The day following the meeting with Gavin and Diana was not one of them. Dull, routine letter followed dull, routine letter. Miss Pargeter found numerous careless mistakes in Rachel's work, and was sharply angry, slapping them down on her desk for her to re-type them.

"Perhaps, Miss Bond," she suggested acidly, "if you had a little less social life and went to bed at a reasonable hour you might be able to keep your mind on your work."

"Yes, Miss Pargeter," Rachel said dully.

Her mind, she had to agree, was very far from her work, split as it was between remembering all the glories of the previous night—every word Gavin had spoken, every look cast in her direction, every touch of his hand—and wondering what she was to do about Barney.

He had taken her home (in a taxi he couldn't afford, which made matters worse) and had kissed her goodnight. He had made no mention of the fact that she and Gavin had apparently got on so well, had danced together far too often and found so much to talk about.

He had seemed as affectionate as ever and said that he'd come round to Shawcross Street the day after next. He'd promised, he said, to go and see a mate in hospital the following night. One of his fellow students had fallen down a flight of steps in the black-out and broken his leg. The rest of them were taking it in turns to visit, as he had no family nearer than Sheffield.

She hadn't prolonged the farewells, guiltily thankful that owing to the unfortunate friend she had a day's grace. She tiptoed up the stairs, careful not to waken the sleeping household, and went to bed, there not to sleep but to indulge herself by thinking of Gavin. And Barney, of course. What on earth was she to do? She'd have to do something, that was certain. Even if she never saw Gavin again, she now knew without doubt how she felt about him.

Dawn had brought no solution; nor had the hours spent at the office. Surreptitiously she looked at her watch. Fifteen more minutes left of this ghastly day. She just about had time to type the letter to the Birmingham branch.

"Miss Bond?"

She was fitting her paper into the typewriter (top copy and three carbons) when she heard Miss Pargeter call her name as she came hurriedly through the swing doors from the outer reception area. What now? Rachel thought wearily, looking up. More mistakes? Take a hundred lines and stay after school, maybe.

"Yes, Miss Pargeter?"

Astonishingly, Miss Pargeter was smiling, her normally pale face quite pink and bright with animation.

"Miss Bond, you have a visitor. As a special favour, I'm willing to let you go now, even if it is a little early." She wagged a finger that was positively roguish. "Just this once, mind. We mustn't take advantage, must we? But nothing's too good for Our Brave Boys."

Had she gone mad? Rachel wondered.

"What about this?" she asked, indicating the paper in her typewriter.

"What's that? The Birmingham letter? Oh, tomorrow morning will do. Perhaps you could come in a little early. But run along now, dear, because the gentleman has to get back to camp quite soon."

Gavin, Rachel thought. In all his glory. It could be none other; and indeed, there he was, in Reception, making the whole dreary place crackle with excitement. The girl behind the counter was sorting through files in an important kind of way, taking great care not to look at him but at the same time self-consciously fluffing out her hair and tossing her head. And even Mrs. Spooner who had a face like a dried lemon was smiling and wished Rachel a cheery "good night, dear" in a way she had never done before; adding, saucily, "Don't do anything I wouldn't do!"

"And what, I wonder, might that be?" Gavin asked as he took her arm and led her into the dark night outside. Rachel giggled.

"Heaven knows! You've got a nerve, Gavin, coming here like that."

"My dear girl, what are so many dragons to one who dices with death? I thought maybe you'd have an early dinner with me. I've got to leave London about nine o'clock at the latest—hence the sob-story to Miss Thingummy."

"She said that nothing was too good for Our Brave Boys."

"Quite right too. I trust you're of the same opinion."

"In a modified form," Rachel said.

She felt quite pleased with her ability to converse lightly when inside she was in such a turmoil. She'd had a chance to powder her nose, apply lipstick and comb her hair when she went to the cloakroom to get her coat, and while she could have wished to be wearing something other than her black skirt and pale blue jumper for such an occasion, and regretted the fact that her hair wasn't newly washed, it might have been worse.

He took her to a restaurant in the City, not far from the offices of National & Domestic Insurance but a million miles away in atmosphere. It had red plush banquettes with high backs, pink tablecloths, and framed posters advertising Naughty-Nineties entertainments: lists of musical-hall turns superimposed on high-kicking, black-stockinged legs, huge hats and feather boas.

The food was unremarkable, but the waiter apologised only to Gavin as he served the tired vegetables, proffering wartime and shortages as an excuse. Other customers, Rachel noted, had to take it or leave it.

For herself, she could have been eating cotton wool garnished with wood shavings, so little impact did the food make on her. Afterwards she could only remember Gavin, his apparent pleasure in being with her and her pride in being with him, sitting by his side on a velvet banquette. People would think he was her boyfriend—even, perhaps, her fiancé.

He went on, she thought, about how much she had changed, but he had changed too, in a way that was hard to define. Now that they were alone together he seemed altogether quieter— almost as if the handsome, extrovert, archetypal RAF officer was merely a role he adopted for the outside world to see and admire. He had told her the previous evening that he flew regularly on the leaflet-dropping raids over Germany, but when pressed to say what it felt like to fly over enemy territory, he seemed unwilling to make any kind of a drama out of it.

"It's bloody cold," he said. "So cold you ache with it. Could cry with it, sometimes. And all for what? Leaflets! Why not bombs, for God's sake? Still, I suppose it's all experience. It's flying."

"You love it as much as ever, don't you?" Rachel, studying him, tried to understand. "Do you remember telling me all about it when we met in Piccadilly?"

"Of course. I must have bored the socks off you about it. And Spain. Funny," he went on, "I was so sure about everything then. I'm still sure about some things but not, I truly believe, quite so didactic."

"I thought of you often when I was in Uganda. I met someone who was always sounding off about politics and policies and the awfulness of Chamberlain. I thought you were probably thinking the same."

"I think he's a good man, Chamberlain. Honest and honourable—too honest and honourable, probably. At least he bought us time. We need someone else now, though. God, how we need someone else!"

"Churchill?"

"Probably. We need his drive and sense of urgency. This inactivity isn't doing anyone any good. Are you glad you came back? What was it like, that time you spent in Uganda?"

This was new, Rachel thought, as he listened with apparent interest to her replies. As he himself had said, in the old days he had sounded off about numerous issues, but he had never seemed greatly interested in what anyone else had to say, least of all little-Rachel-Bond-from-next-door.

Now he listened, laughed at her jokes, asked supplementary

questions. Perhaps he had always been like that with his successive girlfriends. How could she tell? Did it mean—? She couldn't bring herself to speculate what it might mean. She only knew that she was happier here, with him, than she had ever been in her life before.

"What are you grinning at?" he asked her, catching her unawares.

"Was I grinning?"

"Like the cat who caught the canary."

"I was just thinking," she said artlessly, "how seldom it is that one's happy and realises it at the time. I mean, you look forward to being happy sometimes, only to find that you're not; and sometimes you look back and realise that you have been, only you didn't know it."

He smiled at her, his eyes warm.

"Complicated sentence construction," he said. "But I get the drift. Am I to take it that you're happy now?"

She was giving away too much, Rachel thought, but she couldn't help it.

"Yes," she said softly, smiling back at him. For a while he said nothing, but the look was there again; that puzzled, seeing-her-for-the-first-time look. He reached out and touched her cheek with a gentle finger.

"Dear Rachel," he said. "Dear little girl next door. How sweet you are! Thank you very much for growing up."

Could one faint from sheer happiness? Instead, Rachel smiled warmly back at him.

Barney called at Shawcross Street as promised the following night with the intention of taking her to a Deanna Durbin film she had wanted to see. Instead she suggested a walk and a talk.

The rain had started before they reached the Kings Road and they dived into a Milk Bar for shelter. It was not a particularly sanitary place, Rachel noted as she sat at a smeared table by the thickly curtained window. The ashtray was overflowing, and dirty glasses and a half-eaten bun on a plate still remained as a souvenir of the last customers.

Barney, returning to the table with two pallid coffees, pulled a face.

"This place has solved the problem of where the flies go in the wintertime," he said. "Why don't we go to the flicks? I don't fancy spending the evening here, and the rain looks as if it's set in.''

"Barney, we must talk," Rachel told him.

Barney, taking the bentwood chair opposite her, looked wary.

"Could that be, do you think, the most ominous sentence in the English language?" he asked. Then, as she sat with bent head, finding it difficult to begin: "It's Gavin, isn't it?"

Rachel, lip caught between her teeth, looked up at him and nodded.

"I'm sorry, Barney. I'm afraid it always has been."

"I see," he said. For a while he stared down into his cup. "And Gavin?" he asked, not looking up. "Does he feel the same way about you?"

"I don't know, Barney. I only know how I feel."

He looked at her then, and her heart smote her. He looked so miserable, almost as if he were about to cry. And it was all her fault! She'd been guilty of leading him on, just like she had Clifford Bailey, only worse because Barney really cared.

"Oh Barney, I'm sorry," she said again.

Still he said nothing. He looked down again at his unappetising coffee.

"You don't know him," he said. "You don't know the first thing about him. He's a complicated sort of a bloke."

"Don't be ridiculous! I've known him for years and years. I fell in love with him the very first time I saw him."

Barney gave a small, hopeless kind of laugh.

"I know when I'm beaten," he said.

"So there you are," Rachel said to Alice, much, much later. "No more Barney."

Three short words; so easy to say to Alice, but so painful to convey to Barney. She'd felt like a criminal.

Alice, who had managed to buy some toffees now in very short supply, looked at her, one cheek as round as her eyes.

"You're an idiot," she said, indistinctly.

"Maybe."

"You are—there's no maybe about it!" She sucked furiously for a few moments in order to deliver some well-chosen words with greater clarity. "Barney is here, on the spot," she said at last. "Dancing attendance, you might say. It doesn't matter how marvellous and glamorous Gavin is, you can't get over the fact that he isn't *here*! And you don't even know how he feels about you.''

Rachel said nothing. It was true that there had been no declaration, no promise of a further meeting. How could there be? Gavin was in the RAF, subject to all kinds of restrictions on his movements. But things had moved on in an indefinable way. There was in his manner an implicit understanding that the relationship between them had changed, the age difference reduced now to vanishing point. His goodbye kiss had not been entirely brotherly either, even if it fell short of a passionate embrace.

But none of this was of importance anyway. What mattered was the way she felt about him. How could she go on being ''Barney's girl'' when she felt like this?

''If you ask me,'' Alice went on, ''you're throwing away the substance for the shadow. I don't think it's fair on Barney, when he might be called up at any time.''

''Being fair to Barney is what it's all about,'' Rachel explained with commendable patience. ''I've always been mad about Gavin. It wouldn't be honest to pretend I felt remotely like that about Barney.''

''Well, I don't think Gavin's behaved very well,'' Alice said priggishly. ''I mean, taking over one's brother's girl isn't really *on*, is it?''

''Gavin didn't know anything about Barney and me. You can't blame him. Anyway, all he did was take me out to dinner. I expect Diana would have come too if she hadn't been doing something else.'' (And thank heaven for that, she thought.)

''It must have been awful for Barney when you told him.''

''Actually,'' Rachel said thoughtfully, ''he'd kind of guessed. He said he noticed that night we all met up in the pub that I came alight for Gavin in a way he'd never seen before.''

Alice sighed despondently.

''I come alight for Eric,'' she said after a moment. ''But I don't think he notices.''

By Christmas, both Eric and Barney had gone to serve King and Country—Eric in the RAF somewhere in Leicestershire and Barney as a Private in the Royal Hampshires in Aldershot.

Rachel went to Warnfield to celebrate Christmas with her grandparents and spent the evening of Christmas Day next door with the Rossiters. Neither Gavin nor Barney were given Christmas leave, and though the Rossiters did their best to make the occasion as much like other years as possible, there seemed, to Rachel, a hollow feeling about it all.

Alannah was in complete agreement.

"I hate it without the boys," she said when Rachel came over to Kimberley Lodge to say goodbye before going back to London. "There just doesn't seem any point in it."

"Business as usual, the show must go on, are we downhearted?" Rachel chanted, running all the words together.

"Frankly, yes." Alannah yawned as if exhausted and took up a studied pose on the window seat in her bedroom. Her fine blonde hair was swept up, Edwardian style, wisps escaping to fall around her face. Her mouth was painted pillar-box red and, at this moment, looked discontented. "I'm glad you came, anyway," she said. "I'm desperate to talk. Tell me, do you know anything whatsoever about how I can get into ENSA? It's a branch of the Ministry of Information, you know. Didn't you say your friend Alice works there?"

"Yes, she does. And what's more," Rachel added proudly, "so do I now. Alice told me they wanted someone for the Overseas Division, so I applied and I got it. Isn't it great?"

"Gosh, you never said!"

"No." Nobody, Rachel reflected with a touch of inward amusement, had given her much of a chance. Par for the course, she thought.

"Well, what about it? Can you do anything?"

"About what?"

"About *me*, of course! I would give," Alannah said dramatically, "ten years of my life if I could get into ENSA."

"I can't do anything, Lannie. I just type things for people."

"But you must know someone. Who's in charge of it?"

"ENSA? Heaven knows!"

"Can't you find out?"

Despairingly Rachel thought of the Ministry, with its far-flung offices in different buildings, its staircases, the rabbit-warren corridors, the utter impossibility of locating almost anyone.

"I don't know that I can," she said.

In an angry, sinuous movement, Alannah rose from the window seat and began striding up and down the bedroom. Rachel watched her with enjoyment.

"I thought they hadn't taught you anything at that school of yours," she said. "How come you've learned to do that?"

"What?"

"Getting up from your seat in one easy movement and swooping around like an enraged prima donna. It's most impressive."

"Well, yes, there's quite an art in it." Alannah's voice was now normal, undramatic. "There's an art in sitting, too. When you cross your legs, they're supposed to go in the same direction, not splayed out in different ones like yours are now. See, like that."

"Oh, very elegant!"

"Never mind all that. You will try to find out something, won't you?"

"About ENSA? I can't promise anything, Lannie. Wouldn't it be better to stay and learn your trade—"

"There's nothing, absolutely nothing, so good for teaching you the trade as actually working," Alannah said passionately. "Travelling around, taking plays to the forces, learning on the hoof—that's what will teach me the trade."

"Maybe you're right."

"I know I am. Oh, I wish I were in London! It's the only place to be. I wish I could come and live at your place."

"Susan's place," Rachel corrected her. "She says she doesn't want any more lodgers, I'm afraid."

She felt guilty about feeling so thankful. Gavin had been down once more since the time he had taken her to dinner, and she never knew when he might be able to come again. The last thing she wanted was to have Alannah on the spot—advising, analysing, wanting to *know*. The relationship with Gavin was a delicate one, far from resolved.

He seemed to like to talk to her. His last trip had taken place in cold, bright weather. Snow had fallen recently and still covered the vast acres of Richmond Park, where they walked all the way from Robin Hood Gate to Richmond Gate via Pen Ponds. The collar of his greatcoat had been up around his ears, and he had taken her right hand and held it inside his pocket.

Her left hand in its too-thin leather glove had felt frozen, but she didn't care. Her feet were cold and wet, too, but she didn't care about them either. She could have gone on walking for ever, just so long as Gavin was there at her side.

He had talked and talked and talked; not in the didactic way he vowed he had forsworn, but musingly, reflectively, about war and bombing and the rights and wrongs of it. About how much he wanted to get on with it, but how he couldn't help wondering . . .

"Do you still read poetry?" Rachel asked him. "You used to like Auden and Spender—"

"Still do."

So at last she could quote to him the poem she had longed to present as a gift so many years before: " 'Through corridors of light where the hours are suns—' "

" 'Endless and singing.' " He took up the lines, delighted that she knew and loved them. " 'Whose lovely ambition/Was that their lips, still touched with fire,/Should tell of the Spirit clothed from head to foot in song.'

"That's flying for you," he said. "That's how I feel— 'clothed from head to foot in song.' "

She glowed with the glory of her discoveries about him.

"That's wonderful. I'm so glad."

The look of strain that she had noticed when he first arrived had quite definitely gone, she thought, when she faced him over the table at the little teashop on Richmond Hill where they finally found their way.

Just imagine if Alannah had been there too! He would have wisecracked—they all would have wisecracked—and she would be no nearer knowing him than she had been before. Now she felt closer to the real Gavin, the man behind all the glamour, the adult, authoritative pilot who took seriously his responsibility to his crew and his country.

He was, she thought, so unlike the man he appeared to be. Oh, he exerted charm to get his own way, and he wasn't averse to a swagger here and there, and if he saw admiration on the faces that were turned to him, then he enjoyed that too.

But that wasn't all of him. She knew him now to be thoughtful, vulnerable; even afraid. How could she not love him?

It froze that evening. They went—where else?—to the pictures, sitting in far better seats than Rachel was accustomed to, with a box of chocolates to pass between them.

His arm was round her shoulders. All around them there were service men and girls in the same position. It didn't mean anything, Rachel told herself; but even so she was far more conscious of him than of the film. She didn't want it to end. If there were to be no more than this, she thought, then at least she would have had this little piece of him, this one weekend.

No—a thousand times no! she didn't want Alannah in London. Even so, she did, eventually, ask about ENSA, and managed to find an address for her to write to. Probably nothing would come of it, she thought; and forgot the whole matter when Gavin phoned a few days later to say that he would be coming to London once more on the following Saturday.

"About lunch time, I think," he told her. "If that's convenient."

Convenient? Rachel gave a breathless laugh. Her heart was hammering with excitement at the very thought and she could hardly speak. It couldn't, as it happened, have been more convenient, for Susan had already announced that she was off to Brighton to some conference or other, and Alice had been invited to a family gathering in Wimbledon with Eric, currently home on seven days' leave. She and Gavin, therefore, would have the house to themselves, which could lead to almost anything. Not that she expected—not that she would—well, she didn't think she would, anyway. Oh, it was ages until Saturday! Was it possible to *die* from sheer excitement?

The week passed somehow, a confusion of hopes and dreams and soaring emotions. By twelve thirty on Saturday she was dressed and pacing. She had opened a can of tomato soup which she knew to be one of Gavin's favourite things, and it waited in the saucepan, ready to be heated at a moment's notice. She'd made an egg salad, too. She'd tried to buy ham but the corner grocer was out of it—or said he was—and she had rejected Susan's kindly meant offer of a tin of corned beef because Gavin had always turned up his nose at it. That was in the old days, of course. Maybe he was less finicky now.

It didn't look a very exciting meal, she thought, gazing at it without enthusiasm as she paused momentarily in the kitchen. Maybe she should have prepared something hot. It was just that a salad seemed easiest, since she didn't know exactly what time he would get there. Anyway, he liked egg mayonnaise, she remembered that very well, and it was too late to do anything else. He'd surely be arriving any time now.

She went and stood by the fire in the front sitting room, absently warming her hands—waiting, waiting. She'd lit it in case they decided to stay in that afternoon. She didn't know—couldn't guess—what would appeal to him, but if he wanted to sit on the sofa with her listening to records and—well, doing other things—then that was all right with her.

By half past one there was still no sign of him. The house seemed to wait for him, empty and expectant, with no sound but the ticking of the grandfather clock in the hall. Rachel waited, too, each minute that passed making her a little more anxious, a little more certain that something had happened to prevent him coming at all.

By three o'clock, she was seriously worried. Unable to read or settle to anything, she sat with her hands clasped tightly on the kitchen table in front of her, her eyes fixed on the salad which she could not bring herself to eat.

The phone shrilled through the empty house, causing her to jump with alarm and race to answer it, certain that it would be Gavin saying his leave had been cancelled, not knowing how she would bear it if it were. But it was only someone wanting Susan; nothing of any importance.

He'd been shot down, she was convinced of it. If he'd just been delayed, then he would have phoned. He'd never submit her to this waiting, not without a word of explanation, not in wartime when anything could happen. It was always the finest and the best—think of the poets in the last war, Rupert Brooke and Wilfred Owen, and—and—oh, lots of others.

There was a strangely hollow, fluttering feeling in her stomach. This couldn't really be happening, could it? It wasn't real. She couldn't face a world without Gavin. She sat very still at the kitchen table and tried to imagine it; tried to remember what it had been like, all those months when she'd worked so hard to convince herself that she didn't love him after all—times when she'd laughed and danced and flirted and tried to fall in love with someone else, telling herself that she would never see him again, that he was gone from her life for ever and ever; but at the same time knowing deep within herself that he hadn't gone and never would, not while she had breath in her body. She hadn't thought then of death, of *his* death; had made no allowances for it—for its cruelty, the irrevocable quality of it.

The doorbell, when it rang, made her jump and catch her breath. She ran to answer it. Gavin, standing on the step, saluted with a flourish as she flung the door open.

"The late Flying Officer Gavin Rossiter, at your service, ma'am."

"Oh!" She was incapable of doing more than gape at him as if she could hardly believe the evidence of her eyes, so irrevocably had she consigned him to the grave. For one moment she thought she was going to faint, like a Victorian heroine, and put out a hand to steady herself against the wall. "Oh, Gavin!" she said, helplessly. "I'd given you up."

"Always a mistake," he said, bending to kiss her lightly as he came into the hall. "You can't keep a Rossiter down, you know."

With the door to the outside world closed behind him, she took hold of his lapels and looked into his face. Though he smiled, though his words were flippant, there were strains evident. His eyes were bloodshot, his mouth tense.

"I was so worried about you," she said softly.

He gave a grunt of laughter and pulled her close to him, rubbing his face against her hair.

"Strictly between us, I was worried about myself," he said. "Our little trip over enemy territory last night was not, as they say, without incident. I say, have you got any grub? I'm absolutely ravenous."

"Yes, of course. Come into the kitchen." Rachel ran to turn the gas on under the soup. It all seemed hopelessly inadequate, this small repast, now that he was there. How could she have thought it would satisfy him? "I remembered this was your favourite," she said, making the best of it. "You said once that it didn't taste like any recognisable vegetable, least of all like tomatoes, but that you liked it just the same."

"What a memory you have!"

"I hope it's enough. There's egg mayonnaise, too. I'm sorry it's cold, but I didn't know exactly when you'd arrive—"

"It'll be fine," Gavin said. "You shouldn't have waited for me."

Again she noticed the weariness behind his eyes, the deadness of his expression. She took her place at the table opposite him, passed him the bread and the butter, all the while looking at him anxiously.

"What happened, Gavin?" she asked softly, after a few moments. "Can you tell me?"

He gave another short laugh and shrugged his shoulders.

"I probably shouldn't," he said. "But what the hell? We were out on a leaflet raid last night over the Ruhr. It was just routine. We should have been back by two, two thirty at the latest. But coming back—" his voice seemed, suddenly, unutterably weary, as if he could hardly bring himself to recount his misadventures.

"You were hit?"

"No, not hit. I told you how cold it was, didn't I? Well, the wings iced up to such an extent that we went into a steep dive. It took the strength of both Jock and me to pull her out of it." Jock, Rachel knew, was his co-pilot. "When she did come out of it," Gavin went on after a moment, "we found that the rudder and elevators were stuck and the port engine on fire. All the time we were losing height like mad."

Rachel stared at him in horror.

"So what happened?" she asked at last when he fell silent.

"There was a lot of cloud cover. Because of the rudder we'd drifted a long way off course and didn't know where the hell we were. Finally, flying very low, we saw an airfield of some kind—a strip and hangars and huts and so on. Didn't have a clue which side of the Maginot Line we were, of course, but I didn't have any choice, we'd lost so much height. I had to put her down."

"And where were you?"

"In France, thank God, just over the border. It was getting on for three by that time. We had to wait until around nine thirty this morning for things to be fixed sufficiently for us to fly home. Then, of course, there were reports to be made— endless reports . . ." Wearily his voice trailed away, then picked up again. "I kept looking at the clock, seeing the time tick away, knowing you'd be waiting. I'm so sorry, Rachel. I guessed you'd be worried.''

''It doesn't matter now,'' she said gently, dismissing those frightful empty hours that had echoed with her nightmares. ''Eat your lunch. You must be exhausted. You can't have had any sleep.''

''We managed to get a couple of hours' kip in France. I'll be all right.''

But later, when she persuaded him to go into the front room to sit by the fire while she made coffee, she discovered when she brought the tray in to him that he had fallen asleep where he sat, stretched out in the winged armchair, arms hanging loosely over the sides and legs stretched out in front of him. His tunic was unbuttoned, his tie loosened.

For a moment she stood and looked at him. She had never seen him so helpless, so utterly without pretension. His exuberance, his vitality, his charm, his egotism—all had drained away, leaving him without defences, not a leader of men but a child once more.

Weak with love for him, she sat down to drink her coffee, feasting her eyes on him, noting again the curve of his mouth, the way his hair grew, the shape of his fingernails, just as if she had not, long ago, learned him by heart. The thought that he could so easily have been killed—could even now be no more than a heap of broken bones and torn flesh—was beyond bearing. The relief of having him here, safe, still living and breathing made her feel strange; sick and breathless and hollow inside.

For a while she sat and watched him sleep. He stirred once and muttered to himself. She felt guilty then, as if she were invading his privacy, and stood up, irresolute, before going noiselessly out of the room, back to the kitchen. She'd write a letter, she thought. It was high time she wrote home.

Three times she pushed open the door a crack to peer in and see if he had woken up and three times she saw that he had not stirred. She made up the fire, looking round at him anxiously when coal grated against coal, but still he slept.

On her fourth visit, she found that he was awake and sitting up, leaning towards the fire. He did not hear her cautious opening of the door. Instinctively she opened her mouth to speak to him, but was shocked into silence, the words shrivelling and dying. She thought, in that moment, that she had never seen such grief before, such utter desolation. She could see what he would look like when he was old and his good looks ravaged by sickness.

Something was wrong. Her heart seemed to lurch with fear.

"Gavin? Gavin, what is it?" Swiftly she went to him and knelt beside his chair. "You look awful! Are you really all right? Has something happened to you, something you haven't told me?"

"Hey, what's all this about?" He turned and smiled at her and the look was gone. "I always look like death when I wake up. You've drawn the curtains! What time is it?" He looked at his watch. "My God, it's almost seven! You shouldn't have let me sleep so long."

"You needed it." Rachel sat back on her heels, looking at him with a puzzled frown. Had she imagined that ghastly expression, then? Or was it born of the nightmare hours he had endured in the crippled plane, the responsibility he bore for his crew, something he must feel himself unable to share with any civilian? But she wanted to share it—wanted to share everything with him.

"Poor Rachel," he said, stroking her hair. "This is hardly the kind of day you expected, is it? Let's go out somewhere really grand tonight, shall we?"

"Not unless you want to. It's a horrible night. I'm perfectly happy to stay in, if you'd rather."

"When will the others be home?"

"Alice is going to be late and Susan isn't coming home at all."

He grinned at her and twirled an imaginary moustache.

"Ho ho! I have you at my mercy, my pretty wench."

"Completely," she said.

His smile slowly died; then he reached out and pulled her towards him, shifting a little so that there was room for her, too, beside him in the chair. For a long moment he seemed to study her face.

"You know," he said at last. "You could be the saving of me."

"Oh?" She gave a puzzled smile. "How's that?"

"Every man needs something to live for."

"But you have—"

"Everything to live for?" He gave a breath of laughter. "I know. But there are times—" He broke off, and very gently, almost thoughtfully, brushed her cheek with his lips, not finishing his sentence. Rachel held her breath, feeling as if all her nerve endings were concentrated in that one spot.

"Finding you again was the best thing that's happened to me for a long time," he went on after a moment. "I was always fond of you. You were such a funny, anxious little thing—"

"Thanks!"

"Well, weren't you? Always minding your manners and saying thank-you-for-having-me, and trying so hard at those ghastly games."

"But you enjoyed them! You were so terribly competitive and so good at them—"

"We weren't that good. We just didn't care. You cared so much it was painful."

"You make me sound such a ninny."

"You were endearing."

"Diana thought I was a ninny."

He pulled a face.

"Yes, well, Di would. She judges everyone harshly." He sighed. "Me, most of all."

"Nonsense! She adores you."

"Well, I suppose I adore her too, sometimes. Unfortunately." His voice diminished to a mere thread and his expression was sad. "And there are other times," he said, "when I hate her guts. Family relationships are the damnedest things, aren't they?"

"I—I suppose so." Rachel sounded uncertain. "I haven't actually had many of my own."

"Well, never mind Di," he continued after a short silence. What had he been thinking? Rachel found herself unable to make any guesses. "She's an unwelcome third at this moment. I want to concentrate on you."

Could she ever have imagined, in all her wildest dreams, hearing such heavenly music as those words? She closed her eyes in sensuous pleasure as his mouth sought hers; and this, she soon realised, was the kind of kiss that must surely signal the abandonment of brotherly embraces for ever. The kisses of all the other young men who had been tried and found wanting were forgotten. She felt his hand on her breast, tasted the sweetness of his searching tongue, gasped with the joy of it.

"Oh Gavin, I love you so much!"

As, tremblingly, they drew apart the words seemed to surface of their own volition, terrifying her with their boldness. What would he think of her now? No girl should be the first to say such things. That was one of the rules, the received wisdom, handed down from mother to daughter and friend to friend.

"Honestly?" he asked, as if there might be some doubt about it.

"Honestly. I always have. I'm sorry," she added foolishly—meaning the embarrassment, the burden, the feeling that he might be expected to do something about it.

But he was smiling, apparently not burdened at all. He touched her forehead, her nose, her eyelids with small, light, butterfly kisses.

"Then marry me," he said.

⊰ THIRTEEN ⊱

It was a Sunday in late March, with the sun shining out of a cloudless sky and daffodils and forsythia and all the pink almond trees that were such a feature of the gardens of Ranelagh Avenue shouting aloud the glories of spring. It was a day made for celebration, but beneath the delight Rachel felt at walking from The Laurels to Kimberley Lodge with Gavin by her side, there was an undeniable feeling of apprehension.

She was reminded of the time when, sick with nerves and dreading the scorn of the Rossiters, she had gone next door for the first time. She had been doubtful then of her reception. The doubts were even greater now.

"I can't believe they took it so well when you told them," she said to Gavin. "I can't believe that your mother was really pleased." She hadn't, after all, been associated with the Rossiter family for all these years without knowing that there was no one in the entire world good enough for Gavin.

"Why wouldn't she be? Just because she was a bit miffed with you that time, all those years ago—"

"Three years," Rachel said. "Not long, really." And "miffed" was hardly the word, she thought, remembering the tears and the fury and the total rejection. How could anyone forget it? Gavin squeezed her hand.

"Cheer up, sweetheart! I honestly don't know what you're so worried about. It's all right, believe me. Look, Ma's waiting for us at the door—"

And holding her arms wide in their voluminous sleeves, Rachel saw, like some beneficent priestess.

"Come, come—let me give you a kiss, Rachel dear. Welcome to the family—a *real* Rossiter at last!''

"Thank you.'' Rachel succumbed to her embrace. "Thank you very much. Are you really pleased? I thought—''

"That I'd bear a grudge? Oh no, child. That's not my way. I believe in letting bygones be bygones. All that's forgotten and forgiven—''

How very magnanimous, said the small cynical voice in Rachel's head. But it was swamped, drowned, by the welcome from Mr. Rossiter.

"Look what I've got,'' he said triumphantly, holding aloft a bottle of champagne. "The last brace of bottles in Warnfield, I shouldn't wonder. I had to get something special to drink your health. Where are those girls? Give Di and Alannah a shout, Gavin.''

Di and Alannah. Best to get it over, Rachel thought, resignedly. She couldn't begin to imagine what they would say, let alone think, but at least she was spared Barney's reaction. She felt guiltily thankful that he couldn't get home that weekend.

Alannah was the first to come downstairs, and seemed genuinely friendly.

"*What* a dark horse,'' she said when she had kissed Rachel. "But you were always crazy about him, weren't you? We used to have a bit of a giggle about it, Diana and me. It seemed such a hopeless cause! It never crossed our minds that he would ever—'' she caught herself in mid-sentence and apparently realised that, even by her standards, she was about to be more tactless than was acceptable on such an occasion. She gave Rachel another hug. "But at least you're One of Us, aren't you? I couldn't be more pleased, honestly.''

"Thanks, Lannie.''

"Show me the ring. Oh, it's lovely! What a dear little diamond! Bags be a bridesmaid! When's the wedding?''

"Soon,'' Gavin said, his arm round Rachel's shoulders. He bent and kissed her lightly on the tip of her nose. "Very soon,'' he added.

"What's the hurry?'' Placidly, Mrs. Rossiter smiled at them from the large armchair in the window where, as always, she had taken her place, the queen on her throne. "You're both very young.''

Gavin's face seemed to grow very still.

"Not as young as all that," he said. "Times aren't what they were, Ma dear."

"Don't you think I recognise that?" His mother's smile had died and her remark was gravely reproachful. "I worry about you constantly, Gavin. Believe me, you're never out of my thoughts or my prayers."

"Wow—let joy be unconfined!" Diana said ironically, making her entrance at this point. "What's this? A wake or a celebration?" She looked stunning in a plain black dress relieved by a black and yellow scarf tied with the kind of jaunty expertise that succeeded in making Rachel feel dowdily schoolgirlish in the tartan dress that had, up to that moment, seemed fashionable and becoming. She smiled brilliantly at Rachel but made no attempt to kiss her. "Congratulations are in order, I understand."

"You congratulate the man and give the lady your good wishes," Alannah instructed fussily. "I read it in Mrs. Beeton."

"Then congratulations Gavin, and good wishes Rachel." Again Diana smiled as she raised the glass that her father had given her.

"I am about to make a speech," Mr. Rossiter said. "Oh yes I am—"

"Oh no, you're not," chorused the family automatically.

"Silence, *mes enfants*! We have all known and loved Rachel for a very long time," he continued despite the groans from his children. "She has always seemed like a member of the family, and I, personally, am delighted that now she will be one in fact. As for Gavin—well, he knows how proud we are of him. He deserves nothing but the best—"

"Which I've got," Gavin said, looking down at Rachel.

"Stop stealing my lines! I was about to say that."

"Can't we get on with the drinking part?" Diana asked plaintively.

"Here's to both you dear young people. To long life and happiness, and may the sun that's shining today shine on you both for ever and ever."

"Amen," said Alannah irreverently. "To Gavin and Rachel."

"Gavin and Rachel."

"I and my future wife," Gavin began, in tones of pompous mock-solemnity that had the party groaning again, "wish to express our heartfelt thanks to you all. We wish," he went on, his voice throbbing with drama, "to ask of you one crucial question. It is a question that strikes at the very heart of family life; a question that comes from the very depths of our being— and, of course, when I say 'our,' I refer to my future lady wife and myself—and one that demands an honest answer." His voice reverted to normality. "When the *hell* are you going to fill up these glasses?"

Amid laughter, Mr. Rossiter brought the bottle round once more. It was going to be all right, Rachel thought, the hard, icy knot of nerves in the pit of her stomach beginning to unfreeze itself. Alannah had been nicer than she had expected, admiring of the ring, thrilled at the prospect of a wedding in the family. Even now she was speculating about bridesmaids' dresses. Not pink, she was saying. Please not pink. I look awful in pink.

"What about you, Di?" she asked her sister, raising her voice to reach Diana who still stood on the fringe of the small group as if reluctant to commit herself absolutely to the day's celebration.

"Me? What's it to do with me?" Diana's voice seemed to ring out across the room. Rachel, looking across, was struck by the look of contemptuous amusement on her face. "You can count me out," she said. "I'm not the bridesmaid type."

"My dears, there's plenty of time for all that," Mrs. Rossiter said comfortably. "Plenty of time."

Gavin, catching Rachel's eye, gave her a small, reassuring, heart-warming wink.

It was going to be all right. She was almost sure.

Sending letters to Uganda was something of a lottery. Sometimes they arrived in reasonable time, sometimes they were delayed for months and sometimes they didn't arrive at all.

"I wonder," Rachel wrote to her parents in the letter which told them of her engagement, "when you will get this. Soon, I hope. How I wish you were here! I am so happy, and I want someone of my own family to be happy *with*! You are happy for me, aren't you? I wonder if you've got

Gavin's letter yet, and what he said to you. He wanted everything to be very proper and above board, and said he was going to ask you for my hand in the time-honoured way. I trust you won't withold your permission. You'd better not! I do love him so.

"Grandma isn't best pleased because she 'took agin' the Rossiters ages ago and nothing they do can make her change her mind. I pointed out how kind they were on the first day of the war when they invited us to their air raid shelter, but she said that one shelter doesn't make a summer, or words to that effect. They invited her and Grandpa to the celebration lunch, but she refused because of gastric trouble—which none of them believed for one minute! Still, her presence wouldn't have added much to the gaiety of nations. Barney was soldiering on Salisbury Plain and couldn't get home, but all the others were there and were very nice to me."

She paused a while, chewing her pen. That was hardly the whole truth, she thought. Diana wasn't nice. Diana had more or less said the right things, but her smile was strained and her eyes had been hostile. Later, after lunch when Rachel had carried glasses out from the dining room, she had come across Diana and Gavin facing each other just inside the kitchen with the atmosphere crackling with tension, taut with remarks just uttered or about to be uttered. Seeing her, Diana had turned and without a word had left them.

Rachel had wanted to ask what was wrong, but Gavin gave her no chance.

"It's such a gorgeous day, we ought to go out somewhere this afternoon," he said brightly, taking the glasses from her hand. "What about Chuffington Common, for old times' sake?"

"Is Diana—?"

"Oh, never mind her! She's in one of her moods."

He dismissed the incident lightly, but Rachel was under no illusion. Diana was dangerous. Diana had scuppered Gavin's engagement to Jacqueline. He hadn't gone into details about that particular episode in his life, but that much had been clear between the lines. And Mrs. Rossiter, with her smug, platitudinous

"No hurry" remarks. Was she truly as delighted as she had maintained?

With Gavin to put his arm around her, to give her smiles and kisses, it was easy to be lulled into a false sense of security. She knew, however, that she had to keep on her guard. The insidious power of the family was not to be underestimated.

It was the week following her visit to Warnfield that Germany invaded Denmark and Norway—for those countries' own protection, it was said—and a naval battle raged off the Norwegian coast. It marked a new phase of the war, for at last British bombers were permitted to attack a target on the mainland of Europe and were dispatched to bomb Stavanger airport.

Though Gavin was not among those who made the flight, everything was in a state of change and confusion, and all leave was cancelled with personal matters forced to take a back seat. Rachel's spirits were raised in early May when he phoned to say that he hoped to manage a quick trip to London the following Saturday. She made a chart: so many days, so many hours, so many minutes—but at the last moment he phoned again to say he couldn't make it. He was being sent to another station, Chilbury, still in Yorkshire, but further east, transferring to Whitleys. There was no hope of leave just yet.

"Sorry, darling," he said. "I'm so sorry."

"Just so long as you're all right—"

"I'm all right. Longing to see you."

"Mm. Me too. When do you think—?"

"Can't say. Things are hotting up."

"Take care."

"You bet. I love you, Rachel."

"Love you, too."

"Not coming?" Susan, passing through the hall, put a sympathetic hand on her shoulder. "Poor love! Bloody war."

"Isn't it just?" Rachel agreed.

T-Tango was the name of Gavin's new aircraft. She had a letter from him a few days later, referring to it as if it were a living, sentient being; and she learned about his crew, too. There was Griff, the first officer, an ebullient Welshman; Prof, the wireless operator, who had been a teacher—an old man of twenty-eight; Jimmy, the navigator, who had a girlfriend who was the spitting image of Dorothy Lamour; Mike, the rear gunner.

She became aware that Gavin had moved into quite a different phase of his life where T-Tango and the crew were all-important. She understood, she told herself. She absolutely understood. Personal relationships, love, marriage—all had to wait. At least he phoned and wrote to her when he could, and she wrote back. Every day.

Though she thought of him and worried about him constantly, her life had taken on a distinctly more interesting aspect lately and, day-to-day, she was not actively unhappy. For several weeks, when first appointed to the Ministry of Information, she had dutifully typed the reports dictated to her by Colin Milner—the ageing, sometime writer of thrillers, now employed not so much to thrill as to ensure that news favourable to the Allies was given the widest possible publicity overseas.

Rachel was, at first, much in awe of him. He was, after all, a real writer, someone she had actually heard of. Further acquaintance, however, demonstrated that though able, he was constitutionally lazy. He was, it transpired, only too happy to allow her to compile the reports and was delighted with the ability she showed.

"You can actually write the King's English!" he said, pleased and astonished.

"Of course."

"No 'of course' about it. Most people can't."

"I can't do anything else, really," Rachel admitted. "English was my only good subject."

"Nonsense! You have a good analytical mind. You can see what to put in and what to leave out."

"Can I go on doing it, then?"

"Certainly," Mr. Milner agreed, visions of long lunches and soporific afternoons floating before him. "I'll have a quick run through and make a note of suggestions, and you can take it from there. I suppose I'd better see the reports and approve them before you send them upstairs."

"Of course."

It didn't matter to her that they went out under his name while her pay stayed at the very bottom of the typists' scale. At least life had become more challenging. She took pride in describing events economically, honing her sentences, selecting the right word. And when, as sometimes happened, Colin Milner took her up on some matter of syntax or scored his blue pencil through passages he considered could be better expressed, she took his strictures seriously and learned from them.

Worry about Gavin became part of everyday life, no more and no less than that suffered by most other women in the country. She had little direct knowledge of his activities, but since the invasion of Holland and Belgium and the bombing of Rotterdam by the Germans, any British scruples regarding raids on Germany had disappeared altogether. The nights of the leaflets were over. Now more dangerous missiles were dropped east of the Rhine and news bulletins frequently reported that ''one of our aircraft failed to return.''

Whenever she heard the dread statement, she felt certain it must, this time, refer to T-Tango. To the warning by Churchill, now Prime Minister to the relief of almost everyone, that he had nothing to offer but blood, sweat and tears, she felt she could add another promise. There was nothing, now, but the twist of fear in the gut that underlay everything—every action and every thought.

Gavin was long overdue for leave, but with the German Army marching inexorably through France, all leave was cancelled. Now there was Barney to worry about, for he had been sent to France at the beginning of May. No one knew quite what was happening there. On 20th May, Amiens fell in the morning and Abbeville in the afternoon; and less than a week later tens of thousands of British and French troops converged on Dunkirk to wait on the beaches under bombs and shell fire for the Armada of boats of all kinds that were to bring them home.

It was at the very beginning of June that Rachel, answering a ring at the doorbell, found Alannah standing on the doorstep. The clutch of fear intensified and she couldn't speak. It had to mean bad news, surely?

But Alannah was laughing.

''What's up?'' she asked. ''It's me, not a ghost! Aren't you pleased to see me?''

''Yes, yes of course. Come in. I just thought—''

''I tried to phone but there was a queue at the station and the one in the kiosk in Drury Lane didn't seem to be working.''

"Drury Lane?"

"Yes—Drury Lane!" Inside now, bubbling with excitement, Alannah hugged her. "I got tired of waiting for an answer to my letter, so I bunked off college and came down. I've been there since crack of dawn, but at last I got to see Mr. Fairman—the chap you said was more or less in charge, remember?—and he took down my particulars!"

"And?"

"He seemed impressed. He did, honestly! I swore I would do anything, go anywhere, could learn lines in less time than it takes to read them. He got me to read a bit of *Hay Fever*. I gathered they're trying to cast it—gosh, how I'd *love* to be Sorrel! And then he said what else could I do, so I did my lightning impressions of Shirley Temple and Gracie Fields and hundreds of others—even George Formby! He actually laughed at George Formby. Though I says it myself what didn't ought, my George Formby is really rather good."

"So what did he *say*?"

"Well, the usual. You know—don't call us, ducky, we'll call you—but he did ask if I would be free at a moment's notice and I said 'You bet!' He liked me, Rachel, I know he did. Listen, can I stay here tonight? I could share your room, couldn't I? Then I'll go there again tomorrow first thing and start pestering all over again. It's the only way."

"But what about—?"

"I told the old Queen Bee that I simply had to go and see my fiancé who was wounded in France and just back from Dunkirk—which reminds me, Barney is OK."

"Oh, thank God!" It was entirely typical of Alannah, Rachel felt, that this news should have taken second place to the other.

"He's not home yet, but he phoned from Folkestone and he's fit and well. Expect him when they see him, he told Ma."

"What a relief for her, and your father. They must have been out of their minds with worry."

"I knew he'd be all right." Alannah spoke airily, looking into the hall mirror and tucking little tendrils of hair into place. "Barney could always look after himself. He'd suit you a lot better than Gavin, you know."

Rachel stared at her.

"I happen to love Gavin," she said distantly.

"Don't we all know it!" Alannah grinned and flapped a hand at her. "Love's Young Dream just isn't in it! Listen, it is all right if I stay, isn't it? I know you've got a double bed in your room because I saw it that time I came before, so yah-boo, sucks to you, you can't pretend there's no room."

"Of course you can stay." Rachel took her arm. "But we'd better sort of ask Susan, just for politeness's sake. Come on, everyone's in the garden tonight. It's such a wonderful evening."

"Is that gorgeous French violinist there?"

"Paul? Good Lord, no! He went into the Free French Army ages ago. We can do a nice line in sailors, though. One of Alice's cousins is here—"

"Less drippy than she, I trust."

"Shut up! Alice is all right. Mind you behave yourself."

"Don't I always?"

She did, of course. She had always, like all the Rossiters, been able to switch on the charm when it suited her. Susan seemed delighted to see her again, and old Mr. Spivey from across the road, who had taken a fancy to Susan and was now a constant visitor, sat up a little straighter and stroked his moustache. Rachel was, however, quite pleased to see that although Alice's sailor cousin was perfectly pleasant, his eyes still rested on Alice rather than the newcomer. In Rachel's opinion, Lieut. Keith Bessemer was a far more attractive propostion than the odious Eric. She only hoped that Alice recognised it too.

For a long time they sat in the narrow walled garden where the evening sun lingered, talking of matters large and small. Mr. Spivey was wrestling with his conscience over the matter of the newly formed Local Defence Volunteers. He was too old for them. Too old *on paper*, he said, over and over; but not a bit too old in fact. He could defend the gas-works just as well as Mr. Hubbard next door who'd joined up the day the force was formed and, even as he spoke, was drilling in the park with a broom-handle instead of a rifle because rifles were in short supply.

Age was relative, Mr. Spivey said. Mr. Hubbard, now, was an old man—bent, crippled with rheumatism, could hardly see a hand before his face, no matter what his birth certificate said. On the other hand, he, Wallace Spivey, was spry. Trim.

"Look at that," he said, banging his midriff with his clenched fist. "Not an ounce of spare flesh. Not an ounce."

What should he do? Perjure himself by lying about his age? Find some other war work? All he'd been offered was the job of collecting waste paper, he told them disgustedly. What kind of job was that for a man of his capabilities? Was that the sort of thing to make Hitler sit up and take notice?

"If you ask me," Keith Bessemer said, "I'd advise you to hold your fire. Air raids on London are bound to start soon, then you'll all be in it and there'll be jobs for everyone. I wish you and Alice would get out, Aunt Susan."

"My job is here," Susan said calmly.

"And so is mine."

Alice spoke bravely, with no evidence of the fear which Rachel knew was beneath the surface, for she had confided in her one night and had spoken of her nightmares.

"Everyone else seems so brave," she had said. "But I can't get it out of my mind. Just imagine houses falling down on top of you. Imagine being trapped!"

Now, however, she lifted her chin and smiled at her cousin, inviting his admiration. Rachel, mentally, rubbed her hands. It all, she thought, seemed to be going very well. She was thankful that Alannah hadn't succeeded in putting a spanner in the works of this budding romance; not, it had to be said, for any want of trying.

Susan was, of course, perfectly agreeable that she should stay there that night. It seemed to Rachel, as they prepared for bed, that the old relationship between them had been utterly restored and, despite all that had happened, she was glad that the friendship had endured. Even if she now regarded it with more caution, was less starry-eyed than in the past, she still valued it.

It felt quite like old times, listening to Alannah rattle on about her dreams and her hopes—how Mr. Fairman had looked at her; how he had asked the woman with the clipboard to make sure she had her address; how (once more) he had laughed at the George Formby impression; how she, Alannah, was sure, absolutely *positive* that he'd rather fancied her.

"You can't mistake that look in the eyes, can you?" she demanded; and Rachel agreed that you could not. "Of course he was old," she went on. "Oldish, anyway. Nearly as old as Dad, I suppose."

"Your father's not really old," Rachel said as she climbed into bed.

"He's forty-six. But he has the kind of looks that wear well, don't you think?" Alannah wiped some surplus cream off her face and got in beside her.

"Like Mr. Spivey?" Rachel suggested, and they both giggled.

"Imagine craving to drill with broom-handles and wear those pathetic armbands," Alannah said.

"He'd feel he was Doing His Bit. Everybody's the same. All right if I turn out the light?"

"OK. You know," Alannah went on out of the darkness, "I reckon Gavin will wear well, don't you? He's got Dad's sort of gloss and energy."

"I don't care if he does or not," Rachel said softly after a moment. "Just so long as he goes on *being*."

"Oh, he'll be all right. We're all survivors, we Rossiters. Look at Barney! An awful lot of his battalion got taken prisoner, apparently."

A sudden and totally unexpected rage gripped Rachel so that for a moment she was unable to speak. Who did they think they were? Did they honestly imagine themselves to be immortal? Was Barney inherently more worthy of being saved than his friends? Every night, to her certain knowledge, Gavin was in the most fearful danger—danger which Alannah seemed to dismiss without a thought. Yet it hadn't always been like that.

"You didn't seem to think that when he wanted to go to Spain," she said.

"Oh, gosh, that was ages ago! You're not still harping on that, are you? You really must learn to be less sensitive, Rachel. You'd think you'd know by now that it really doesn't *do* in our family. Tell me—" she leaned up on one elbow. "What have you and Gavin decided about the wedding? Have you fixed the date?"

"Not yet. There hasn't been much of a chance."

Alice sighed, and sank back on to her pillow.

"I suppose not. Poor Gavin! They're keeping him busy, aren't they? Di says he's looking awfully tired."

Rachel, in the middle of a yawn, became rigid with shock. "Diana's seen him?"

"Yes. I think he spent the weekend before last with her. Yes, it must have been then, because last weekend she went home. I phoned up on the Saturday and she answered—that's when she told me about Gavin. Why?"

Couldn't she honestly see why? No, of course not. It would seem quite natural to her, that one Rossiter would spend the weekend with another Rossiter rather than come to London to spend time with an outsider, even if that outsider were a fiancée.

"No reason," she said stiffly. "Good night. I'm going to sleep now."

" 'Night," responded Alannah, unaware of any hurt. "Roll on the morning and darling Mr. Fairman. Oh, please God, bless Mr. Fairman! He must take me, mustn't he? You do think he will, don't you?"

But Rachel, feigning sleep, said nothing.

When towards the end of June Gavin was finally rested and came to London on a weekend pass, Rachel taxed him with it. She had vowed to herself that she wouldn't mention it. Told herself that if she married a Rossiter, this is what it would be like; especially with Gavin and Diana, who had always been so close. It was just something she would have to learn to put up with.

Maybe, she thought, he had just driven over one afternoon; after all, Cambridge was nearer to Chilbury than London. But not *that* near! That theory wouldn't wash. He must have had at least a twenty-four-hour pass. And anyway, why hadn't he mentioned it? He had phoned her often enough and said how much he wished he could see her, hold her in his arms, kiss her; but never once had he said that he'd been able to spend time with Diana.

Somehow, despite her vow of silence, the words seemed to speak themselves.

They were lying on a grassy hillock that seemed a million miles from London, yet was no more than twenty miles away overlooking peaceful Hertfordshire woodland. Though the country held its breath, imminently expecting invasion, here it seemed unimaginable, totally ludicrous. A honeysuckle bush was close beside them with wild roses clambering over its higher branches, and the air was redolent with all the scents of summer, birdsong and the murmuring of bees.

Rachel had lain in his arms all afternoon, happy at last. Their lovemaking had been low-key, for from time to time others had walked along the footpath close by, and once a child's large rubber ball had come to rest in the small of Gavin's back.

Still it was a time of great sweetness and contentment. They had talked and kissed, made plans and kissed again. They must marry soon, Gavin said. Somehow he would find accommodation for her. He wanted her to be with him—and in addition, he wanted her to leave London. There would be raids, he was certain of it.

"That's what Alice's cousin said."

"Alice's cousin was right. Come on, fix the day—"

"It depends on you. When can you get leave?"

"I should think—say, six weeks from now? The first week in August? How about the 3rd? That's a Saturday."

"I don't think I've anything important planned," Rachel said with assumed offhandedness; and he laughed and held her close and told her to consult her diary, just to make sure there was nothing vital like a hairdresser's appointment which could interfere.

"The sun's given you freckles," he said, tickling them gently with a long stem of grass.

She reached out and touched the face, so much loved and now so close. Diana was right, she thought; he did look tired.

"Alannah mentioned that you saw Diana." There it was— the statement that had lain all afternoon in her subconscious.

"Did she?" He had been lying on his stomach, cap and tunic abandoned. Now he rolled over on his back and stared up at the sky, one arm shielding his eyes.

"You—you didn't mention it."

"Didn't think it important." Then, when she didn't speak, he removed his arm and turned his head to look at her. "Do you think it was important?"

"No. Well, not really." She half sat up and began, idly, to encourage a ladybird to move from a blade of grass on to her finger. "I did sort of wonder," she said at last, "how you managed to find the time."

"When I couldn't get to London? Now, come on, darling!" he reached for her arm and pulled her down to his level again. "You're surely not jealous of my own sister, are you?"

Yes, yes, Rachel wanted to scream. But she said nothing and could not meet his eye.

"Look," he said persuasively. "One night, I was scheduled to fly. Was intending to fly. But Griff let on to the CO that I'd been ill all day with a touch of God-knows-what. Delhi-belly, Montezuma's Revenge—call it what you like. The quack grounded me. Put me off-duty for twenty-four hours. I didn't fancy hanging around the Mess feeling lousy, so I went down to Di's and felt lousy. OK? Understood?"

"Yes, of course." Rachel felt overwhelmed with guilt. "I just wish you'd said—"

"It was such a last-minute, off-the-cuff thing. I was back on the station by twelve the following day. I could hardly have been down to London and back in the time."

"No, of course not. Honestly, I'm not complaining, darling. It's just that I never stop thinking of you and worrying about you."

He pulled her into his arms once more, and covered her face with small kisses.

"Silly one! Nothing's going to happen to me."

"Of course not," Rachel murmured dryly. "You're a Rossiter, aren't you?"

Back in London, much later, he took her out to a French restaurant in the King's Road, where the owner and his wife were still in mourning for Paris which had fallen the previous week.

"Just imagine if it was London," Rachel whispered, seeing their stricken faces. "It doesn't bear thinking about, does it?"

"*Vive de Gaulle*," Gavin said, raising his glass towards the restaurateur, unleashing, at last, smiles and straightened backs and expressions of patriotic fervour.

"*Vive le* RAF," responded Madame from behind her cash desk.

Gavin rose, raised his glass once more, and bowed. There were more mutual expressions of esteem. He was smiling when, finally, he turned back to Rachel, taking both her hands in his.

"So much for the *entente cordiale*," he said. "Now about

us. Let's take a run up to Warnfield tomorrow and get everything settled. We can ring Ma tonight to warn her."

"She's not going to like it."

"Then," Gavin said hardily, "she'll have to do the other thing. Don't worry about it."

"I'll have to ask Grandma about a reception."

"It'll be at our place, naturally."

"I don't know, Gavin. Grandma might be hurt if I don't ask her first."

Gavin groaned.

"Oh, Lor'! Maybe we ought to get a special licence and elope."

"I wouldn't mind."

He seemed to give the matter his serious consideration, then shook his head.

"No—no, we can't do that. The family would be upset. Especially Alannah! She seems to think we're arranging the whole thing so that she can be a bridesmaid. Besides, you'll want a splash, won't you? White tulle and a bouquet and all that?"

"I suppose so. That's not what's important, though." Even as she spoke, however, she felt a tremor of excitement. Yes, she thought. Oh, yes! Marrying Gavin was the important thing, not how it was done, that went without saying; but the thought of floating down the aisle of Warnfield Parish Church on Grandpa's arm was utterly beguiling, she had to admit. She could see it all—could see Gavin waiting for her at the altar, looking, as he always did, so wonderfully handsome in his uniform, and everyone else dressed to the nines. How her mother would love to be there, and what a thousand pities that her parents were so far away! The rows, the harsh words that had been uttered in Entebbe now belonged to the forgotten past. She owed it to them, she thought, to have the best of weddings and thousands of photographs. She could just imagine her mother showing them round to her friends in Entebbe; could imagine the pride with which she would display pictures of her daughter on the arm of such a devastatingly handsome hero.

"Don't worry about a thing," Gavin said. "I'll talk Ma round, see if I don't. And if the worst comes to the worst— well, I don't need parental permission, do I? Not like you, my little child bride."

"I am nineteen," Rachel said with great dignity. "And a half," she added, with slightly less. "You can't call me a child."

"I shall call you whatever I like," Gavin replied with mock ruthlessness. "Love, honour and obey, don't forget."

"Till death us do part," Rachel said softly.

She had made a bed up for him in one of the top rooms, on Susan's instructions. Did Susan really expect him to sleep there alone? Rachel thought about it as, sitting up in bed with her arms about her knees, she waited impatiently for the hush of night to descend on the house.

Alice expected it. Alice had popped in for a few moments before going to bed to say that Keith had phoned earlier. He was coming up to town the following week and wanted to take her out. Did Rachel think, she asked, that it would be fair to Eric if she went to the theatre with Keith? He was so nice, such good fun and he was, after all, a cousin. On the other hand, she had sort of promised to keep herself for Eric—

"Go," Rachel advised her without hesitation.

"Gosh, Rachel, you're always so decisive!" Alice had looked at her admiringly. "You know," she added a little shyly, "I've been meaning to say—I was wrong about you and Barney. I can see what you mean about Gavin. Barney's nice, but Gavin's something special."

"Well, I think so, anyway," Rachel agreed.

"I'm so awfully glad that you're happy, Rachel. And I must say—" Alice bit her lip and went pink. "I must say, I do admire you," she finished in a rush. "I mean, I know how crazy you and Gavin are about each other, but you still stick to your principles."

"Oh?" Rachel raised her eyebrows in surprise and some amusement. "What principles are these?"

"Well, saving yourself for after marriage, and all that." Alice's voice was earnest. "I do realise it can't be easy."

"How do you know I have saved myself? It's not a thing one would be likely to advertise, is it? I mean, you'd hardly put an announcement in *The Times* in the Virginity Lost column."

Alice giggled in spite of herself.

"You mean you—oh, you're having me on, Rachel! You

haven't, have you? Gone All the Way, I mean?''

Teasingly, Rachel grinned at her.

"Wouldn't you like to know?'' Then, seeing Alice's expression, she took pity on her. "No,'' she went on. "Not yet.''

"Well, good for you! It's always a mistake.''

"That's what you've found, is it? In your experience?''

"Oh, shut up! You know I haven't. And won't, what's more.''

But I will, Rachel thought. And soon. She hoped that she proved to be good at it. How could a girl know? How could you learn? Some people said it hurt a lot the first time; even Mrs. Marryat and Evelyn Home, those two oracles who had always been her mentors in such matters, often stressed to enquiring correspondents that the initiation into the mysteries of sex was sometimes disappointing.

She felt she would be good at it. She wanted it enough; wanted Gavin, anyway, and was fully prepared to exercise patience and fortitude and any other quality that might be necessary. Oh Susan, *please* hurry up and come to bed, she thought, as after Alice left her she did her best to will her lively landlady into tiredness, into switching off the radio, turning off the lights, and coming upstairs.

And at last she heard her; heard the tread on the staircase, and the click of the bathroom light; heard the bathroom door shut behind her, heard taps running and the flushing of the lavatory. Heard, finally, the sound of the bedroom door being closed.

She gave her half an hour after that. And then, with great caution, she opened her own door and looked out. There was no line of light under any door. No sound anywhere.

Slowly, cautiously, her bare feet silent on the carpeted stairs, she began to make her way to the next floor. "It's no good,'' Gavin said at last, lying rigid beside her. "It's no bloody good. God, what's the matter with me?''

"It's all right. Honestly.''

"No, it's not. How can you say that?''

Angrily, as if disgusted with himself, Gavin flung the bedclothes aside and went over to the chest of drawers, fumbling for a cigarette. The lighter flared, then dwindled, but not before

Rachel had seen his face. It looked drawn and old, contorted by self-disgust.

Drawing on his cigarette so that the end of it glowed in the darkness, he went to stand by the uncurtained window. The moon was almost full and his profile was sharply defined.

Rachel felt a great sadness—not so much for herself, though she couldn't deny that her disappointment was great, but for him. He had wanted her so much. They had planned this at the restaurant, holding hands and smiling at each other with excitement.

He had drawn her into his bed and his kisses and caresses had quickly brought her to the point where any lingering doubts and fears were swept away. But as her passion mounted, his seemed to languish and die.

"Don't worry," she urged him now. "It doesn't matter. You're tired."

On the back page of Alice's magazine, she remembered, it had been clearly stated only last week that it was necessary for wives to be aware of the problems often suffered by their husbands. ("Wives," not "women," for no unmarried woman would get herself in this position, if she took Mrs. Marryat's advice.) Husbands, said Mrs. Marryat, often suffered worry and stress which their wives, confined as they were to the daily round within the four walls of their home, were unable to comprehend. Sometimes the strains and tiredness consequent upon their work made it impossible for them to make love. Any wife worthy of the name would be patient and loving and understanding.

"What on earth are you going to think? You're better off without me."

"Gavin, it's all *right*. Why don't you come back and let me hold you? Let's be like we were this afternoon. I want to feel close to you."

"Do you still want to marry me? How could you?"

"Don't be idiotic! Of course I do. I love you, don't I?"

"I feel so damned useless."

"There'll be lots of other times. Maybe you're inhibited by being in someone else's house. All this creeping about."

She heard him sigh. He opened the bottom half of the sash window, ground out his cigarette on the sill and threw it out.

For a few moments he stood motionless, leaning out, as if communing with the stars. Then he turned and looked towards the bed where she sat waiting for him.

"You're a girl in a million, Rachel," he said. His voice sounded strange, almost as if he were crying. He came and sat on the side of the bed, holding her hands. "God knows why you love me. I'm a pretty worthless type, if the truth were to be known."

"What nonsense!"

He gave one great sob and pressed the heels of both hands to his eyes.

"The last thing I want is to disappoint you."

"I know. Oh, Gavin! Darling! Don't be upset. Another time it will all be different, you'll see."

"I don't mean just this. I mean—oh, in all sorts of ways. I know how I seem. All brash and cocksure and the-world-owes-me-a-living kind of thing. But inside I'm not a bit like that. I'm—I'm jelly, Rachel. Just jelly."

She had a sudden vision of a bomber trapped in the crisscross beams of searchlights, tracer bullets falling like rain.

"Who wouldn't be?" she whispered. "Come back to bed, darling. Come."

It was getting light when she crept back to her own room, leaving him asleep. He came down to breakfast looking and behaving just as usual and it was not until they were on their way to Warnfield that he referred to the incidents of the night.

"You were right, of course," he said. "It'll all be different another time. It'd better be!"

She kissed him.

"It will be. Don't give it another thought."

By the time they drove back to London, all the necessary arrangements had been made. Perhaps compensating for his previous night's shortcomings, Gavin was forceful and determined and would brook no talk of delay from his mother. He was brutal in his arguments.

"Ma, I'm risking my neck every night," he said. "I want to marry Rachel now, and I want her with me. Surely you can understand that?"

"But you're both so young!"

"Not that young. Twenty-four! I've got seventeen-year-old

boys in my squadron who think I'm practically in my dotage."

"Gavin does have a point, Carina," Mr. Rossiter said, rather surprising Rachel by his support. "If he's old enough to fight for his country, then I think we should respect him when he says he wants to get married, and not put difficulties in his way."

"Put them in our way if you like," Gavin said flatly. "All that would mean is a special licence and a London registry office. You pays your money and takes your choice."

So Mrs. Rossiter with her "No hurry" talk was silenced. Gavin even managed to charm, moderately, Rachel's grandmother, and get her agreement to holding the reception in the garden of Kimberley Lodge, a marquee to be provided by the Council.

"It's bound to be disruptive," Gavin argued. "The last thing we want is to put you to any trouble."

"Well, I don't know—"

"Our garden will be at its peak just then," Grandpa said wistfully. "Still, perhaps you're right. You Rossiters are so much more practised at catering for numbers."

Alice and Alannah were to be the bridesmaids, and Rachel undertook to get a suitable pattern and samples of material from John Lewis's the very next week. And for Rachel herself, said Mrs. Rossiter, beginning to get into the spirit of the thing in spite of herself, she knew the very women—her own pet seamstress who had made for her many, many times over the years and who would produce a wedding dress that would look as if it had come from a Paris couturier. At a fraction of the cost, of course.

"All we need is somewhere to live," Gavin said as they drove away from Warnfield. "I'll get on to that right away."

"I suppose I'll have to put my notice in."

Rachel felt a pang of regret at the thought of losing her congenial job, but it lasted no more than a second. How could she compare it with being Gavin's wife?

"Oh darling," she said softly. "I can't wait, can you?"

Meat and tea and fats might be rationed, but somehow a wedding breakfast was to be scraped together. Friends sacrificed stocks put down for Christmas, grocers turned blind eyes, farmers in the country were visited and proved to be generous with butter and eggs when it came to the wedding of an heroic RAF pilot.

Little by little, Mrs. Rossiter collected the ingredients for a cake. Rachel, visiting Warnfield to be fitted by the dressmaker, was thrilled with the dress and excited by all the discussion regarding the great day, coming closer by the minute.

A telephone call from Gavin in mid-July brought her the best news of all. He'd managed to get hold of a tiny cottage, he told her—a bit primitive, standing on its own at the edge of a field, but perfectly suitable. It had been occupied by a fellow officer, now posted to Kent. His wife, a Scottish girl, was imminently expecting a baby and had elected to go back to her home in Edinburgh for the birth.

Rachel caught a train at the crack of dawn on Saturday morning and was with him by eleven o'clock. He took her straight out to see the cottage. It was plain, square, unadorned, without any fancifully romantic appurtenances such as thatched roof or roses round the door, but it had all the necessary conveniences. The bathroom had to be approached through the kitchen, but who cared about that? There was a front door to close against the outside world, that was the important thing.

It had a tiny living room and a short steep flight of stairs leading to the bedroom which looked out over the fields that Gavin had mentioned.

"The other bedroom's hardly worthy of the name," said the present occupant, who, heavily pregnant, had left her task of packing the kitchen equipment into boxes and had followed them upstairs. "Still, it's useful to put things in. There's not much storage space."

"You must be sad to go."

"Yes." The girl sighed. "Still, that's the way it goes. We've been happy here. I love the view from this window."

Rachel looked towards it once more. There was a field of ripening wheat directly in front, with a broad, grassy path to the side of it leading uphill towards a five-barred gate in a grey stone wall. Beyond the gate, the path curved around the side of a wood, one hill folding gracefully upon another.

"It's lovely," she said. "I know we'll be happy here too."

"You can bet on it," Gavin said, smiling down at her.

Any hopes Rachel might have cherished that there might, this night, be an opportunity to wipe out the memory of the last she had spent with Gavin were to be dashed, for he was on duty and she lay alone in the high white bed under the eaves of a cottage close by the pub. The sound of the planes flying overhead just before midnight made her feel much nearer him, much more immediately involved in his day-to-day danger.

Many hours later, she heard them coming back, but it was not until some time after that she knew T-Tango was safe yet again. How would she cope, going through that vigil night after night? It would take, she thought, a special kind of strength.

Back in London, the countdown to the wedding began. Alice's dress was ready and pronounced beautiful. Alannah, as yet still at the Rose Kelly Academy, required one more fitting, so her mother reported. As for Rachel's own dress, Mrs. Rossiter said that it was almost finished.

"You'll be up this weekend, won't you?" she said.

"Yes, I'll be there Saturday afternoon."

Saturday morning was her last day at the Ministry, for she had given herself one week at leisure in Warnfield before the wedding. It had seemed, like so many other things in life, a good idea at the time; however, once the final details of her dress had been decided, and a list made of all the wedding presents that had so far arrived, she felt strangely out of place.

Somehow, here in Warnfield, it seemed that the wedding was nothing to do with her and with Gavin. It had been taken over by others, its main purpose forgotten amid the welter of arrangements that had to be made. She knew such things were inevitable, but she longed to see him just once more before the day— to feel his arms around her again and to hear his assurances that being together was the only importance.

And she *would* see him! She would go by train to York and would get a bus from there to Chilbury. She knew the way now, after her last trip. Nothing could be easier. After all, she had settled the problems connected with the dress. It wasn't as if her presence was really required—in fact the opposite was the case. Even the few tentative suggestions she had made regarding the reception had been swept aside by Mrs. Rossiter.

"I don't think you should go chasing after him," Grandma said dourly when she was told of Rachel's planned trip.

"Grandma, I'm marrying him! Any chase is over. And I'll be back on Wednesday."

There was no telephone at the cottage, so she was unable to tell him of her plans. She enlivened the journey by picturing his surprise. With any luck, she could be there by lunch time. If he'd been flying, he might probably still be in bed. Her heart raced at the thought. This time would be different, perfect, a forerunner of many, many other times.

The train was crowded with servicemen of all kinds; and if she hadn't known that happiness had made her pretty, then their reaction would have told her so. But though she smiled and replied to their overtures, she kept her distance, sat in her corner, and watched the countryside go by.

The train was so slow—much, much too slow! And there were far too many stops. But at last, inevitably, it arrived—and there, right outside the station was her bus. She sprinted and caught it, and stood, strap-hanging, laughing with triumph and all those around smiled in sympathy.

It dropped her at the end of the lane. The wheat, she saw, was yellower than it had been on her last trip. There were bright poppies on the edge of the field and the sky was cloudless.

She could see the cottage ahead of her, and quickened her footsteps. The little wooden gate squeaked as she opened it. There was a tiny front garden, choked with weeds. She would do something about that—and she would polish the knocker and the doorhandle. Oh, there was so much she would do! It was going to be their place, their palace.

The door opened at her touch. There was no need for locks and bolts out here. Who would want to come in? Only friends, she thought.

"Gavin?" she called.

There was no answer. Perhaps he was asleep. She smiled to herself. She'd waken him with a kiss, she thought; Sleeping Beauty in reverse—the handsome prince being woken by the princess.

Quietly she went upstairs and pushed open the door to the bedroom; but this, too, was empty. He had been here quite recently, though. The bedclothes were pushed back, his uniform jacket was slung on a chair.

And also on the chair was an ivory satin dressing gown, unmistakably feminine. Rachel stared at it, bewildered. Her gaze travelled round the room. There was a blue enamelled brush and comb on the small dressing table; an open jar of face cream, a drift of powder.

Gavin must have let someone else use it, she thought. That was it, of course. He had lent the cottage for the weekend to one of his crew, perhaps. Well, she hoped they'd made good use of it. It was quite clear two people had used the bed—hopefully with more success, she thought wryly, than she and Gavin had enjoyed.

A sudden breeze gusted the curtains inward from the open window, and with it came the sound of laughter. Time she got out of there. She turned for the door, glancing as she did so towards the view that she had so admired on the previous occasion.

Her heart seemed to stop beating. Gavin and Diana were sauntering down the path, arms round each other. Like lovers. They looked happy, without a care in the world. As Rachel watched, they came to a halt and Gavin, laughing, stuck poppies in Diana's hair.

She couldn't move, couldn't turn her eyes away from them. She felt desperately, physically sick—sick with disbelief, yet somehow, beneath the disbelief, she recognised the truth and saw that it had always been there, waiting to be discovered.

Gavin and Diana. How could he? How *could* he?

She had no memory of going downstairs, but found herself, somehow, standing at the open front door. And still they came towards her, happily dawdling, engrossed in each other, unaware of her presence.

Then Diana looked up, stopped in her tracks and pointed. Rachel saw Gavin look towards her. His face seemed blank, wiped of all expression; then, giving a hoarse cry, he began to run towards her.

And she, weeping, waited for him.

"Well, at least she knows now," Diana said to Gavin.

"Just leave us a minute, Di." Gavin's eyes were on Rachel; but though all three of them were standing awkwardly in the small living room, he made no attempt to touch her and Rachel was glad of it. Once Diana had gone upstairs, however, he came closer. He reached out a hand towards her, but let it drop as she shrank away from him.

She was trembling, and had wrapped her arms about herself as if for warmth and comfort.

"Rachel," Gavin began falteringly. "I—I'm sorry. I don't know what to say."

What was there to say? She tried to frame the words but could not speak. Blindly she shook her head.

"Rachel, darling, please—let me explain."

"No." At least she managed that. "You can't."

"I didn't mean this to happen. I didn't know she was coming." Rachel sank into a chair, her head bent, not looking at him, not speaking. "Honestly, that's the truth." Gavin crouched down beside her. She looked at him then.

"What difference does it make?" she whispered. "You and she—you're lovers. It's horrible!"

"I know." He got up and walked away from her, towards the window. It had old-fashioned wooden shutters; so useful, the previous occupant had said. You didn't need black-out curtains. Idly he pulled one side towards him, then pushed it away again. "I know how this must seem—" He stopped, turned towards her. His face was wearing that haggard, tortured look she had seen before. He ran his hand through his hair, a gesture of desperation. "Don't you see," he went on, his voice rising, "I need you so badly! She won't leave me alone—"

Sick at heart, Rachel closed her eyes, saying nothing, and he too fell silent as if he were suddenly aware of how pathetic he must sound.

"I loved you," Rachel said at last. "I loved you so much. But I suppose, really, for you, almost anyone would have done."

"No, it wasn't like that." He came swiftly to crouch beside her again. "It wasn't, Rachel. You seemed so—so sweet. Complete. Contained. Oh, I don't know! I felt good with you, able to cope with everything. Don't leave me now."

She stared at him, without comprehension.

"You think I can marry you in four days' time?"

"Rachel, nothing's changed."

The tears began again, streaming down her cheeks, soundless and unheeded.

"You're wrong, Gavin," she said. "Oh, how wrong you are!"

❧ FOURTEEN ❧

Rain had been falling in a dismal, long-term way since early morning, and now the lights of Polvear which normally added a magic touch of festivity to the wintry evenings were no more than an insubstantial blur.

It had been a miserable day altogether. Tess had woken before five thirty that morning after a restless night and had been less than her amenable self all day, demanding and difficult to please. She was teething. There were two bulges in her top gum that looked sore and angry and Rachel felt the pain as if it were her own; more, perhaps, for she had the additional mental anguish of knowing that there was little that could be done to help matters, plus a lurking feeling of guilt at feeling even a moment's exasperation with the constant crying of a suffering child. Teething powders, warmly recommended by Mrs. Hoskings, had little, if any, effect. Only time, she suspected, was going to heal, in this case as in so many others.

She was thankful when Tess went down for her customary afternoon nap, but the ensuing peace was wasted to a large extent for her writing had not gone well. Somewhere along the line, she realised, the book had taken a wrong turn—but where? Was it David, the rather raffish charmer with the heart of gold? She had a shrewd suspicion it was, and that she had caused him to act in a way that no raffish charmer would ever act. She hadn't *got* him, somehow. Didn't really know what made him tick. She wasn't, she thought gloomily, very good at men. Maybe she didn't know what made any of them tick.

Whatever her problem, it made for a highly unsatisfactory and frustrating afternoon, particularly as Tess had woken earlier than usual despite her premature start to the day. She was glad, at last, to draw the curtains, shutting out the dark and the rain, wishing as she did so that it was as simple to shut out her other nagging worries.

She had not, after all, told her parents about Tess. The letter she had finally written in reply to the one she had received from her mother had been apologetic, cheerful, superficial, but essentially unrevealing. Yes, she was working hard, she had said, and had taken Sylvia's cottage in Cornwall. She guessed they'd be surprised at that! It was just the most inspirational place to live, and a wonderful part of the country for them to stay when they came on leave. She was so looking forward to seeing them. Spring was beautiful in Cornwall, she had been led to believe, with loads of flowers all over the place. *With This Ring* was coming out in March, too. She'd hold the champagne until they arrived.

Not one word about Tess.

Later, she thought. She'd tell them later. When they were actually here, on the spot—away from Entebbe, where they had the opinions of friends and superiors to worry about. Then she'd tell them.

Tess seemed a little better after her sleep and was happily sitting in her high chair gnawing a rusk when there was a knock at the door.

Emma? Tess wondered, going to answer it. Or maybe Marlene. She'd given the girl a warm invitation to come any time, so that Tess would get used to her, and she had already dropped in once or twice.

But it was neither. Standing on the doorstep, his face shadowed by his peaked naval cap, was the man she had dubbed in her mind the Angry Pole. He looked not so much angry now as anxious and unsure of his welcome. In his hands he held a bunch of chrysanthemums wrapped around with soggy paper.

"Please," he said, holding them out stiffly towards her. "To apologise for other day."

"Oh!" Taken aback, Rachel was for a moment speechless, not yet quite prepared to unbend. "That's—that's very kind of you. Really, there was no need."

"Please." He thrust the flowers closer, and automatically she took them from him. "I was wrong," he went on. "Cruel. I am sorry. Forgive me." He gave a stiff little bow, turning to leave without another word.

"Wait," she said, relenting. "These are lovely. Thank you very much." She looked at him as, half turned from her, he waited on the step. "Look, I know I was careless. I've had nightmares ever since. I can't tell you how grateful I was that you were there."

"The little one—she suffered nothing, I hope?"

"She's fine." For a moment longer Rachel hesitated. He looked cold and wet and rather tired, and his duffle coat was soaked through on the shoulders. She was surprised to see how young and vulnerable he looked. Somehow, at their last encounter, the intensity of his emotion had given his gaunt face an appearance of age which she now realised was false.

"Come in and see her," she said impulsively. "I've just made some tea."

She regretted the words the moment they were out of her mouth. She was in no mood for making conversation with a stranger, particularly with a stranger like this who seemed so odd and abrupt; and since Tess's sleep pattern had been so disrupted that day, she had made up her mind to start the bedtime ritual earlier than usual. This unexpected visit was bound to delay things.

And the cottage was a mess! She and Tess had been confined to the house all day because of the weather, and the living room was strewn with toys, with nappies airing on the fire-guard, a half-chewed rusk on the floor, and a general air of seediness everywhere. The whole picture would do nothing, she felt, to improve the impression of neglectful and incompetent motherhood that she had clearly given on their first meeting.

Still, too late now. He had accepted the offer with polite, if surprised, thanks, and was even now wiping his shoes with great care on the doormat. There was nothing for it but to go through with it with a good grace. It had, after all, been kind of him to bring the flowers.

He took off his cap and removed his coat, dangling it helplessly from one finger.

"Is so wet!" he said.

"Never mind. I'll hang it in the kitchen by the boiler."

He bowed again.

"You are very kind. More kind than I deserve. These days, I am sometimes not myself. I am sorry."

"Please, don't give it another thought."

(Why not? He'd been rude and offensive and horrible—but somehow, now that he was here, it was hard to see him as the same person who had shouted at her the other day.)

"Look, here's Tess," she said. "None the worse, as you can see." Tess smiled at him engagingly, banging the tray of her high chair with a wooden spoon that Rachel had offered her when all else seemed to pall. "And I am Rachel Bond."

"Stefan Wisniowiecki." Yet again he bowed.

"I think," Rachel said, "I'd better call you Stefan."

For the first time his smile was something more than a nervous twitch of his lips.

"Please," he said. "Stefan is best, I think."

"I think so, too. Please excuse me. I must put these flowers in some water and hang up your coat in the warm. Do sit down, won't you?"

He had not done so, she found when she returned with the flowers and an extra cup, but was stooped over the high chair playing with Tess, making her crow with laughter. He straightened up as Rachel appeared.

"She is lovely child," he said.

"Well, I think so." She smiled at him, pleased as always by praise of Tess. She stood the flowers in their pottery jug on the mantelpiece, then busied herself with the tea things. "She's not always so angelic, though. She's been a little fiend all day. She's teething, poor child."

"Ah, teeth! A trouble coming, a trouble going."

"You have children yourself?" It was a casual question, made without looking at him as she poured the tea. "Do you take milk and sugar?"

When no reply to either question was forthcoming she glanced up at him. His face was thin, with high cheekbones and a strong, slightly curved nose. It seemed, at this moment, a harsh face, a face without warmth, the mouth drawn down in something like the angry snarl she had seen before. Then, as if with an effort, a polite neutrality returned and he smiled thinly.

"Milk, no sugar," he said, coming to sit at the table in the window. "Thank you."

There was a short and awkward pause. Rachel was angry with herself. From the days when she had lived in Shawcross Road and been in contact with Susan and her refugees, she knew that direct questions about families were to be avoided. Especially were they to be avoided with lone, bitter-looking men like this one. He'd lost a child—that much was clear as day.

Tess began to cry and Rachel, glad of the diversion, lifted her out of the high chair, putting her down on the floor amid the toys.

"The poor darling doesn't know what she wants today," she said.

"How old is she? Nearly one year? I thought as much." Stefan reached out a hand which Tess clutched with enthusiasm. "Is a frustrating age, no? They are learning that there is much to explore in the world, but as yet are not able to do so. They are like prisoners who look out of the window at sunlight and green fields but cannot reach them."

"Yes, I suppose you're right."

Rachel looked at him curiously. On reflection, he seemed an unlikely person to be a manual worker. There was intelligence and refinement in that hawk-like face. How old was he? Late thirties, early forties, perhaps. He looked, she thought, more like a musician or an artist.

"What in the world are you doing in St. Bethan?" she asked impulsively.

He glanced at her, sharing with her the smile that Tess had coaxed from him. He wasn't, Rachel thought, at all bad-looking when he smiled; not, that is, if you liked the lean and hungry type of man.

"Working in boatyard," he said. "Don't tell me you don't know! In St. Bethan, everyone knows everything."

"That's true. Yes, I knew that much—but why here?"

"Oh—" He turned back to Tess. "A long story, and not so interesting. This is nice house," he said, firmly changing the subject away from himself.

"It belongs to my aunt. I'm afraid you're not seeing it at its best."

"No? To me it seems like home. Warm and comfortable, with books."

"There were china ornaments on those shelves when we

came, but I wrapped them up and put them away for safekeeping. I was afraid Tess would make short work of them now she's crawling. Anyway, I needed the space. I seem to have so many books—''

''You are author, they tell me.''

''Who told you that?''

''The lady on the quay who was there when the pram ran away. She told me where to find you, too.''

Rachel laughed, shaking her head with resignation.

''I've never spoken to her in my life before that day.''

''But she is right? You are author?''

''After the day I've had, I'd hesitate to describe myself as such—I don't seem to have been able to construct two coherent sentences. But yes, on the strength of one book, not yet published, I suppose you could call me an author.''

He did not reply, apparently engrossed in making a pink fluffy teddy bear hide in the crook of his arm only to pop up into view to the accompaniment of shrieks of delight from Tess.

''I, too,'' he said after a moment.

''You—you're a writer, too? *Really*?'' Rachel looked at him with interest. ''What sort of thing do you write?''

He held up his hands in an attitude of repudiation, still holding the pink bear.

''No, no. I am not a true writer. I write one book, no more. A textbook.''

''On what subject?''

''On synthetic resins. Interesting, yes?'' He cocked a mischievous eyebrow in her direction.

''If you say so,'' Rachel said, laughing. ''Does that mean you are a scientist?''

''Of a kind.''

''Then why—'' on the brink of asking more questions that might seem intrusive, Rachel hesitated.

''Why do I make boats?'' He spread his hands out before him. ''For me there is much joy in working with wood. It is, for me, therapeutic.''

''He seemed so different from that first time,'' Rachel said a few days later when Emma came to call and they were sitting drinking coffee together. ''He was so kind and gentle and sweet with Tess—yet at the same time, you could feel a kind of—'' she hesitated, her face screwed up with thought as the appropriate word eluded her.

"Bitterness?" Emma suggested.

"Maybe. No, I don't think that's quite the word. Sadness, I think. Even despair. Something very weighty and powerful, anyway."

"I know a little more about him than I did," Emma said. "I happened to meet Mrs. Carthew the other day—Mrs. Joseph Carthew, that is, wife of the chap who owns the boatyard. It seems he—your Stefan—had a horrendous war. He was in a prison camp at the end of it, starving and debilitated, and when he finally managed to make his way back home he found his wife and little girl had both died on some sort of forced march to Siberia. She said he was quite a wealthy industrialist before the war."

"He told me he'd written a book on synthetic resins. I think that's what it was, anyway."

"Plastics, in other words. Interesting! Apparently he succeeded in getting to England, and went to the home of some business associate he'd had dealings with before the war. I don't know the full story. Anyway, he managed the journey, but then he collapsed—had a breakdown, mental and physical."

"Understandable," Rachel said.

"It seems he's a good craftsman as well as everything else, with a knowledge of boatbuilding. The friend happened to be someone who spent all his time sailing on the Pol before the war and he knew Joe Carthew very well, so through him your Stefan came down here. Mrs. Carthew says he's still recuperating, really. His doctor thought that working with his hands in the peace of the countryside would be excellent therapy for him."

"Yes, he said as much. Poor man." Rachel was silent for a moment, thinking about him. "The bloody war," she said bitterly at last. "So many lives thrown into chaos! I guessed about the family, of course."

Emma seemed absorbed by her own thoughts.

"Sometimes," she said, "it seems quite despicable that I should have spent the war here, going on with my work so peaceably."

Rachel laughed at her.

"Don't be ridiculous! Children need teaching even in war-time. Perhaps most of all in wartime."

There was a touch of self-mockery in Emma's smile.

"Yes, I know. But I longed sometimes for a little bit more involvement—something more exciting. I had fantasies about being parachuted into occupied France, or being one of those women who plotted aircraft in the Battle of Britain. Still, I've only to hear a story like your poor Stefan's to realise that I had—and still have—much to be thankful for."

"He's hardly *my* poor Stefan," Rachel objected.

"Tell me," Emma said, leaving the subject aside and pursuing a further path of her own. "What did you do in the war, Rachel?"

For a moment it seemed that Rachel had not heard her. She added some milk to her coffee, offered Emma the plate of biscuits.

"Go on," she urged. "Have another. I've got plenty, thanks to an unprecedented burst of generosity on the part of La Pollard. The war?" she went on, after a small silence. "Well, for a while I worked for the Ministry of Information." She paused as if she was speaking of times long past that she could barely remember. "Then, in 1940, just before the Battle of Britain, I joined the WAAF."

"That must have been fun."

For a moment Rachel continued to look thoughtful; then she gave a laugh that was almost a sigh. "Yes, I suppose it was." Then, more certainly, "Yes, of course it was. A lot of it, any-way."

"What job did you do?"

"I trained as an RTO—Radio Telephone Operator. We talked the aircraft down. I was in Kent until the end of 1941, so we had our share of air raids—"

She paused again, remembering. She hadn't cared, she thought. She really hadn't cared. People had thought she was brave or reckless or stupid or all three, but the truth was that she hadn't cared one jot or tittle whether she lived or died, not at first. She had felt as if she were dead already.

Life had returned, however. She found, rather to her astonishment, that the world, post-Gavin, still held things to enjoy: friends, laughter, books and music.

"And then?" Emma prompted her.

"Then Bothley," Rachel said. "A bomber station near Leamington."

Dances in the Sergeants' Mess; silk stockings, for once, instead of the hated lisle, bought with precious coupons that were supposed to be used for essential non-issue items; hair combed down in a Joan Bennett style instead of rolled up, off the collar; a band, more or less in tune, thump-thumping out the beat of songs that she knew, even as she heard them, would always mean wartime and Bothley and the living-for-the-moment excitement that motivated them all.

There were tragedies, of course.

"Isn't Ken coming to the dance tonight?"

"He bought it over the Ruhr."

And Ron. And Ginger. And Scotty. And Titch.

All friends; but no one close. No one that touched her more than superficially. No one that she shed tears for.

"You're so hard, Ray," Mary said to her, the day they heard about Titch. He was a rear gunner with an enormous grin and a wicked sense of humour. They'd all loved Titch in their various ways. Rachel, in particular, was looked upon as a special friend of his, though they'd never done more than go for a few drinks together. Titch's heart, he had confided, was with the girl he left behind in Rotherham. Rachel, on the other hand, had no heart at all. Or so the other members of the WAAFery thought.

She smiled in response to Mary's accusation, the rather enigmatic smile that sometimes made others uncomfortable, unable to see what, if anything, had amused her.

"Rubbish! I'm not in the least hard," she said.

"Then I don't understand—?" Mary—wholesome, innocent, unmade-up Mary, eyes still pink from the tears she had shed—blushed to the roots of her flaxen hair.

"Why I don't cry?" suggested Rachel. "How do you know I don't, in the dim watches of the night?"

She was looking in the mirror as she spoke, touching up her lips with Scarlet Flame lipstick.

"Well, do you?" Mary asked.

Turning from the mirror, Rachel smiled again.

" 'Tears, idle tears. I know not what they mean,' " she said. "Tennyson. Lord Alfred of that Ilk."

Mary, eighteen years old and fresh from school, felt a million years younger than Rachel who would be celebrating her twenty-first birthday in two months' time. She was greatly in awe of what she perceived as Rachel's sophistication and savoir faire even as she criticised her lack of feeling. She bit her lip and nodded thoughtfully.

"You're right, of course. I suppose it's the only way to be in wartime," she said. "The only professional way, I mean. It's just that it's so awful, when you get fond of people, and then you lose them—"

Rachel snapped her shoulder bag shut, straightened her tunic and swivelled her head round to check her stockings.

"Are my seams straight?" she asked. Satisfied, she looked back at Mary and smiled a rallying sort of smile. "Cheer up!" she said. "Live for the moment."

The smile remained as Rachel walked smartly away from Mary towards the Watch Office, but it changed in character, became thoughtful, self-mocking. Look who's talking, she thought. You weren't so bloody cheerful last year.

Strange, really, how the terrible events of the summer of 1940 seemed to have happened to someone else. In a way, they had. She was a different person now. She had been like Mary then— trusting and innocent and ingenuous. The whole thing was like a nightmare she could barely remember, frightening and fragmented, faces looming and fading, events out of sequence.

Had Gavin put her into a train at York? If so, how had they got from the cottage to the station? She couldn't remember; she only knew that she had sat on the train with tears streaming down her face. A woman with fat pink cheeks had spoken to her—offered help, tea, coffee, sympathy. She didn't know if she had accepted; and if she had spoken, what she had said.

It had seemed, at the time, natural that Alice should meet her in London and bear her off to Shawcross Street; only long afterwards had she realised that Gavin must have phoned to alert her.

Susan had dealt with the Rossiters and her grandparents and

the cancelled wedding. Suddenly her grandfather was there, in London, offering kind but ineffectual support; and as suddenly he was gone without her noticing his going.

A letter arrived from Mrs. Rossiter, heightened emotion causing her normally confident, loopy writing to straggle down the page in uneven lines.

"I simply cannot imagine what has possessed you to behave in this unforgivable way, after everything was arranged (against my better judgment, I may say), and for such a frivolous reason! Can you imagine how upset Gavin is, having the wedding cancelled at such a late hour? And why? Because of his fondness for his sister! I am appalled and disgusted that such petty jealousy could motivate one who has been part of our family for many years and has therefore been fully aware of the closeness between us all. Did you truly imagine that you would be able to take the place of the family in Gavin's affections?

"There is no doubt in my mind that my son, and indeed my entire family, has had a most fortunate escape, which in no way lessens my anger at the thought that you, who surely might have thought herself the luckiest girl in the world to have captured the love of a fine young man such as Gavin, should have wantonly brought such heartbreak upon him at a time when he is risking his life for all he holds dear, and at a time when any lapse of concentration could mean the difference between life and death."

"Petty jealousy?" Rachel repeated with astonishment to Barney when he came round to Shawcross Street some two weeks after the debacle. "Hasn't anyone explained to her—?"

Barney, now in the uniform of a Second Lieutenant, looked miserable.

"You know Ma," he said. "She simply doesn't take it in. She believes what she wants to believe."

"You knew, didn't you?"

For a moment he said nothing. He stood, head bent, running his finger round and round the bevelled edge of a small table that stood in the sitting room.

"I—I kind of had my suspicions," he admitted at last, looking up at her. "I didn't know for sure."

"How could you let me—?"

"I thought, maybe, it would all be all right. He told me he loved you."

"Did he?" It seemed unbelievable now.

"I'm sure he did, Rachel. I thought that once he was married he and Di would see that it wasn't on."

"Wasn't on?" Rachel repeated the words and gave a short, incredulous laugh. "What a masterpiece of understatement! It's disgusting, Barney. It's incest."

She saw him wince at the word, biting his lip. He looked at her then, and sighed.

"Oh, Rachel," he said helplessly. "I'm sorry. About everything. About you and me, and you and Gavin." He sighed heavily. "Especially about you and me. I have a kind of feeling there'll never be anyone else—" He broke off and shrugged his shoulders. "Oh well, too late now, I suppose."

"Much, much too late," Rachel agreed. "But if you felt like that, I can understand less than ever why you didn't say something. You put up no fight at all, did you?"

"I should have done. I can see that now, but you were so mad about him—"

"Yes," Rachel agreed sadly. "I always was. More fool me. I see now that there was always something weird about them, something I didn't understand."

"He wants to see you, Rachel."

"No!" Her response was immediate and implacable. "I couldn't, Barney. I couldn't bear it. Anyway, there's no point."

"He wants to explain."

"I don't want his explanations."

"I honestly think it was Di's fault."

" 'The woman tempted me'? That won't wash, Barney."

"What are you going to do now?"

She was silent for a long time; then she sighed.

"I don't know," she said. "I've lost that job at the MOI that I quite enjoyed. Susan's being marvellous about the rent and everything, but I'll have to look around for a job soon. Maybe I'll join up."

"You could do worse," Barney said.

*   *   *

The Blitz had started by the time she had an opportunity to prove him right. Every night now she and Alice and Susan huddled in the Anderson shelter in the back garden dressed in what were popularly known as siren suits. They slept—or attempted to sleep—in deckchairs, wrapped in layers of blankets against the cold, fortified at intervals by tea from the several thermos flasks they took with them.

They never knew, each morning, if they would emerge to find the house standing; but in fact 29 Shawcross Street survived unscathed, apart from broken windows. Mr. Spivey—so anxious to join the Home Guard—was killed outright when a landmine hit his house and its neighbour, and the street that ran parallel was almost totally destroyed.

At the end of September, she enlisted in the WAAF.

"Why the WAAF?" Alice had wailed when Rachel had come home with the news that the die was cast. "Of all things! You'll be surrounded by RAF uniforms—you might even be posted to the same station as Gavin!"

She was convinced that Rachel's choice of the Air Force over all other services had been born deep in her subconscious. Freudian influences were not ruled out.

"That's nonsense," Rachel said. "I didn't care where I went or what I did—with the possible exception of the Land Army! I stepped off the bus, and there was the WAAF recruiting office, so I went in. There's nothing more to it than that. It's a million to one against that I'll get posted anywhere near Gavin. And even if I do it won't matter. It's finished, Alice. Over. I'm not wasting another ounce of emotion on him or any other Rossiter."

Easily said; but the posting to Bothley towards the end of the following year had undoubtedly caused something of a setback in her erratic recovery. The sound of the bombers taking off on her first night caused tears to pour down her cheeks, just as they had so long ago during her first term at St. Ursula's.

There were other similarities to boarding-school life. Because she worked shifts, in Kent she and the other RT operators had been given rooms that were shared by only one other girl. Here at Bothley she slept in the WAAF equivalent of a dormitory, with two long rows of iron beds, shifts or no shifts.

She found, despite those initial, infuriating, despicable tears, she could endure the communal life and the tighter discipline more easily than most. She put it down as much to her boarding-school education as to the new, hard, protective shell she had grown.

She discovered in herself a new, subversive attitude towards authority which amused the other girls, who seemed to turn naturally to her as a leader. If requests or complaints needed to be made, she it was who made them. She gained a stripe, then lost it again when she was discovered climbing in a window long after she should have returned to camp.

She it was who let the air out of the tyre of the car which was bringing some visiting top brass to inspect the WAAFery, thus gaining invaluable time for clutter to be thrown into lockers, papers tidied, lines of washing taken down. And it was she who was responsible for the libretto of the Christmas revue which poked dangerously anarchic fun at the top brass.

"You don't give a damn, do you?" said Penny, the girl who had become her closest companion.

Rachel smiled at that, and raised her newly-plucked eyebrows. She spent a lot of time on her appearance these days, and never lacked escorts for dances or the cinema. Her job meant that she was in constant contact with men of all ranks, and she treated them all with camaraderie and a mild form of flirtatiousness.

"She's a funny kind of Sheila," Dave Seldon complained to Penny. He was an Australian pilot with a handsome, open-air, guileless face. "I don't know what to make of her."

"Nobody knows what to make of her," said Penny. "She's nice, though. A good friend."

"Yeah," Dave agreed, but moodily. He wanted more than a friend.

It was, in fact, to Dave that she lost her virginity—a happening that would have astounded the entire station, had any but Dave known about it. It was generally assumed, from her air of sophistication, that she knew her way around; it was, however, an entirely false impression. Despite the friendliness and the flirting, she kept all men at arm's length.

It happened after her twenty-first birthday party in the January of 1942, for which Dave had commandeered an unused kitchen

at the back of his billet, sufficiently far from the WAAF ad-
mininstrative headquarters to avoid objections regarding noise,
the lateness of the hour, or anything else that could be dreamed
up by what they all, universally, regarded as the kill-joy au-
thorities.

It was a bitterly cold night, but Dave had lit the ancient boiler
for the occasion. There were streamers and balloons strung from
the cobwebbed ceiling, and a borrowed card table covered with
the contents of assorted food parcels, including a fruit cake from
Australia which he had decorated with twenty-one candles.
There was a little wine, too, but only enough for one glass each
with which to drink Rachel's health. After that it was beer or
orange squash.

There was dancing to a gramophone, with everyone roaring
out the words of the songs, and Paddy O'Toole doing his one-
legged-Irishman-dancing-a-jig act without which no party was
complete, and Jerry Wolstenholme reciting ''Napoleon's Farewell to Wigan'' and Dave and two fellow Australians perform-
ing an Aboriginal War Dance.

''Enjoying it?'' Dave asked Rachel, sitting beside her on a
broken-down bed that had been dragged in as extra seating.

''It's a wonderful party, Dave. Thank you.''

''You look gorgeous. Did you really like your present?''

''I loved it.'' He had given her a thin gold bracelet, delicately
chased. ''You were much too generous, though.''

''Nothing's too good for you, you know that.''

''You're sweet, Dave.''

She smiled at him, wishing she loved him. He was so much
in love with her, so eager to please, so handsome, so *nice*!

The music had changed to something slow and smoochy.
Someone put the light out and there were whistles and catcalls
until the door was opened to allow the muted light from the
passage to filter in.

Dave pulled her to her feet, and holding her close they joined
the other couples who were swaying, closely entwined, in the
small space that was all that was available. She could feel his
lips caressing her brow, feel the warmth of his breath. He smelt
wholesome, she thought, like fields and open places. The great
outdoors.

The party was thinning out as people went on duty, or to bed.

His lips moved to the vicinity of her ear.

"Jim's on ops. tonight," he said.

She drew her head back a little to look up at him. His face seemed the face of someone who had never entertained a base thought in his life. He was, she thought, a thoroughly good person—a little diffident and unsure of himself, perhaps, at least where she was concerned, but that was something in his favour. If there was one kind of man she couldn't abide, it was the handsome, swaggering, Lord-of-Creation type of man. Jim Hubbard was rather like that. He was an Australian, too, who shared a room with Dave.

"I hope it keeps fine for him," she said, knowing exactly what Dave had in mind.

"We could slope off," he said quietly. "No one would miss us."

For a moment she danced without speaking, her head turned away from him. Then she looked up at him once more.

"All right," she said coolly; and turning, walked rapidly to the door.

She had to turn to allow him to catch her up out in the passage, for she had no idea where his room was. She saw, by the greater light, that he looked dazed, almost disbelieving. She knew that he was several years older than she was, but suddenly she felt immeasurably older and wiser.

"Upstairs," he said. "There, to the right."

The house was an ex-married quarter, now occupied by six pilots, half of whom were on duty. No one was about. Only Dave, breathing a little heavily, biting his lips, anxious now; and Rachel, walking ahead of him, her head high like a Ziegfeld girl, her emotions in some kind of limbo, her footsteps in time with the thump, thump, thump of the beat from downstairs.

Dave could barely wait to kiss her, taking her in his arms the moment the door closed behind them. She had discarded her tunic long ago, down in the heat of the kitchen. Now he reached to unknot her tie. He was trembling.

"I'll do it," she whispered, laughing; and he laughed, too, and attended to his own tie and shirt buttons, drawing her down on the bed.

"God, you're lovely," he said thickly, kissing her face and neck and breasts. "I love you, Rachel. I'm crazy about you."

In reply she stroked his face and his hair and returned his kisses, hoping, hoping that desire would sweep her away, that this cold, detached creature that she seemed to have become would disappear for ever.

Dave's passion mounted. She gasped as he entered her, but with pain, not with delight. She found the whole process uncomfortable and messy, and really rather puzzling. Why did people make such a song and dance about it? There must be more to it! Maybe she just wasn't very good at it. Maybe Dave wasn't very good at it. Suddenly she wanted to giggle. Mrs. Marryat, where are you when I need you? she thought.

The almost maternal tenderness she felt for Dave, who afterwards lay as if exhausted in her arms, took her by surprise. Was this what it was all about?

"Darling!" Dave propped himself up on one elbow, pushing her hair away from her face. "Was it good? Oh God, I love you so! Was it good?"

And she smiled at him and lifted her hand to his cheek.

"Yes, it was good," she lied.

"Then tell me you love me. Let me have it in words, Rachel."

She hesitated for less than a second.

"I love you, Dave," she said softly.

There seemed, quite simply, nothing else she could say, nothing else remotely appropriate.

Back in her own bed she stared sleepless into the darkness and asked herself how on earth it had all happened. She could give no sensible answer. Why had she said that? Why had she *done* it, for heaven's sake?

Sheer curiosity? Perhaps. Because she was a twenty-one-year-old virgin, and it was high time? Well, that had something to do with it, too. But most of all it was in the hope that only in this way would she be able to feel again—be like other people, warm and responsive and properly alive; a real person, instead of this automaton who seemed always to be an onlooker, always on the sidelines.

The very real danger that she might have become pregnant didn't hit her until the following day, but somehow she knew that she had no cause to worry. And indeed, all, later, proved well.

The next time they met, Dave asked her to marry him, sketching out the future he saw for them as they sat in the Golden Lion, side by side with their hands joined.

"I'm going to carry on flying after the war," he said. "There'll be a great demand for it in Australia, the distances are so huge. You'll love it in Perth. It's a beaut place. Whaddya say, Ray?" His grip tightened. "Are you going to make me the happiest man in the world?"

"Dave, I don't know!"

"But you said you loved me."

"So I do." In a way, she wanted to add, but managed to restrain herself. "Look, we can't talk in here—"

"Where, then? It's bloody freezing outside. Look, all you've got to say is yes or no!"

"No, it's not!" Sadly she turned and looked into his eyes, wanting to be the girl for him—tempted, almost. He'd never treat her badly. He'd be kind, devoted, the best of husbands and fathers. And, she added to herself as she continued to look at his broad, handsome, guileless face, she would be bored in a week. "I'm not ready, Dave. The time's not right."

He looked at her, sighed, gave a short, mirthless laugh.

"No, well, guess you could be right, at that. I could be history by tomorrow night."

"I didn't mean that."

"True, though. OK, let's leave it for the moment—but let's plan a forty-eight together, shall we? I'm due for one. I want to go to London, see some of the sights. We could book into a hotel, get tickets for a show."

"I'm not sure," Rachel said; and felt like a murderess when the light went out of his eyes. "I promised I'd spend my next leave with my friend Alice," she explained.

"What's Alice got that I haven't?"

"I was at school with her. We've been friends for ever."

"Where does she live? London? Well, that's no problem. You could see her. We could take her out for a meal, or something."

Rachel gave her enigmatic smile, but said nothing. She knew that the Rachel who was Alice's friend was in no way like the Rachel who had become Dave's lover, and that inviting her to meet him, laying herself open to Alice's bewildered scorn, was out of the question.

"I'll have to think about it," she said.

*   *   *

They lost another plane and its entire crew that night. Jim Hubbard, Dave's room-mate, failed to return and later his Lancaster was reported shot down over the North Sea.

Losing Jim was a terrible blow to Dave, Rachel knew. Aircrew always put on a show of calm, philosophical acceptance, but Jim was a friend and a fellow Australian. He and Dave had been together a long time. And Dave could be the next. He didn't need any diagrams drawn to show him that.

The next night at the Golden Lion, Dave talked about Jim, on and on; about their exploits when training, the near-misses, the jokes. The time when he lost his way over France and surrendered to a gendarme, thinking he was in Germany. The time when they double-dated and Jim walked off with his girl, leaving him with the bespectacled, buck-toothed, earnest prude who had to be home by nine thirty.

"I'll go to London with you, Dave," she said, when at last he fell silent.

Jim was, momentarily, forgotten.

"You will?" Dave seized both her hands. "That's terrific! I'll find a really beaut hotel, wait and see—private bathroom, the lot. Nothing but the best for you, Ray."

"Well, don't break the bank."

"I don't care if I do."

He looked, she thought, as if she had just presented him with the keys of the kingdom and was conscious, not for the first time, of a feeling of panic. She didn't, for some reason, feel wise any more.

They went on leave on Saturday 14th February of the coldest year anyone could remember. It had snowed all the previous day, and the fields on each side of the railway track were the purest, unbroken white. Rachel had civilian clothes in her case and intended to change into them at Charing Cross, before arriving at the hotel. Dave had, with considerable difficulty and only after phoning six hotels, managed to book a room in the name of FO and Mrs. David Selden, a deception which Rachel accepted as inevitable but tried not to think about.

Increasingly, as the time approached, she found that she was having to gear herself up, persuade herself that she was doing the right thing.

It had seemed right at the time, that night when he was so low in spirits. She had managed, then, to persuade herself that she had only to act as if she loved him to make it come true.

All that had happened was this increasing unease, the feeling that she was being unfair to him and untrue to herself. But it would be even more unfair, she told herself, to duck out of it now, with everything booked and his excitement running high.

"You're very quiet," he said to her as they sat side by side on the train. "You're not having doubts, are you?"

"Don't be silly," she said. "It's going to be a super weekend. I'm looking forward to showing you London."

It was mid-afternoon when they arrived, already growing dark; but not too dark for Rachel to stare in astonishment at an almost life-sized poster that confronted her the moment she stepped out of the train. There, before her, was a picture of Diana Rossiter dressed in the uniform of an officer in the WRNS, hand lifted gracefully to shade her eyes as she gazed out to sea, lovely face glowing with dedication. Beneath her was the legend: "Answer the Nation's Call: Join the WRNS."

"Good Lord," Rachel said, standing and staring. "I know that girl."

Dave whistled. "She's a corker," he said in awed tones.

"I didn't even know she was in the WRNS."

"Maybe she isn't. She's probably a model or an actress."

"The last I heard she was lecturing on Minoan Culture at Cambridge."

"On *what*? Wow! she doesn't look like an egghead."

Rachel smiled as she turned away from the poster. Girls, to Dave, came in two distinct categories, eggheads or dolly-birds. She, she was aware, was a dolly-bird, and he would be put out if she attempted to be anything else. Quote poetry at your peril, my girl, she said to herself.

For that reason she had pressed to see *Blithe Spirit* at the Piccadilly, and kept quiet about *The Merry Wives of Windsor* at the Strand, which would have been her first choice.

The newspaper placards were shrieking the news about Japanese advances in the Far East as, having settled into their hotel and eaten at the Coventry Street Corner House, they walked up Shaftesbury Avenue.

"Dave, I must buy a paper—"

"Come off it, Ray! We don't want any bad news now."

"My friend's parents are there."

"Missing the beginning of the show isn't going to help them, is it?"

He was right, of course. Rachel turned her back on the headlines and tried to forget them, at least temporarily. It proved an easy thing to do, since she adored the show, even if it had been her second choice. The wit and the laughter made her forget not only Singapore but her own personal unease.

"Enjoying it?" Dave asked her as the curtain came down for the interval.

"Very much," she said. "Isn't Margaret Rutherford wonderful? I loved that bit—oh, my heavens!"

Her hand flew to her mouth and her eyes were the size of saucers.

"What is it?" Dave looked over his shoulder, following the direction of her eyes. "Someone you know?"

Laughing, Rachel ducked her head in an attempt to make herself invisible.

"I've just seen my uncle," she said. "Look, that rather portly chap making his way up the centre aisle with the blonde."

"Your uncle? Well, I'm damned! Don't you want to go and speak to him?"

"Not in the least. I never knew what to say to him at the best of times. I shall look the other way and pretend I never saw him."

"Good. I don't want to share you with anyone."

She didn't know why this statement should irritate her so much. The unease, dormant for a while, flared into near panic. She pretended absorption in the programme, fighting down the mad desire to run.

What was wrong with her? Dave was sweet, and very handsome, and he never stopped telling her how marvellous she was, how much he loved her. No one had ever loved her as much as he did. She ought to be grateful.

He didn't know her, of course. The Rachel he thought he loved didn't really exist, had never existed. He loved the smooth and soignée face she saw in the mirror, not the girl inside.

For who could possibly love that girl? She was cold, dead, without feeling. She neither deserved it, nor could she return it.

She was glad when the curtain went up again and once more she was amused and distracted, with all such questions buried deep. It was, after all, only for two nights. She'd cope with that, then try to extricate herself, with as little hurt to Dave as possible.

Maybe this calm and philosophical mood would have continued if Dave hadn't occupied himself during her absence in the bathroom at the hotel by turning on the radio, so thoughtfully provided.

"This place has got everything," he said happily. "I reckon I struck lucky when I found it, don't you? You know who recommended it to me? It was the old dragon that works in the Admin—"

"Shut up a minute," Rachel said, her face expressionless.

It was the calm, measured tones of the BBC late news bulletin that had caught her attention. Lazily Dave reached out a hand and switched it off.

"You look gorgeous, Ray," he said. "Come on to bed. We don't want the news—"

But she had leapt to switch it on again.

"Leave it," she snapped. "I want to listen."

Singapore, said the disembodied voice, was about to fall, and the Japanese were now in virtual control. Many British nationals were known to be captured, their fate unknown.

"And Australians," Dave said, a touch of belligerence in his voice. "They've got thousands of Australian troops out there. Typical Pom attitude—"

"I must go to Alice," Rachel said. "Her parents are there. She'll be distraught!"

"Aw, come on, Ray!" Dave propped himself up on one elbow. "Have a heart! It's late! You can't go anywhere now."

"I could phone her."

Defeated, Dave lay back on the pillows once more.

"Sure, why not? Help yourself."

Alice answered the phone on the second ring. Rachel knew immediately, from the sound of her voice, exactly how her face would look, how her delicate, childish mouth would be trembling.

"Alice, it's me, Rachel. I've just heard the news."

"Oh!" Alice drew a long, shuddering breath. "Oh Rachel, it's awful, isn't it? And there's nothing anyone can do—nothing. Only wait and hope. They say one ship got away last week with a lot of British nationals on board."

"Then they might be safe."

"They might. But—" she paused and Rachel heard the sob in her voice. "Dad wouldn't leave, not until everyone else had gone. And Mummy wouldn't leave without him. I can't feel hopeful."

"Is Susan with you?"

"No, she had to go to Bristol."

"You're on your own?"

"Well—Captain Blackwell was here earlier. He's the War Office man who's taken the two rooms at the top of the house. I told you about him—"

"Is he with you now?"

"No. He had to meet someone and take them somewhere. I don't know where. I didn't take it in. He's not coming back tonight, anyway." She sounded frightened, and very lonely.

"Where's Keith?"

"At sea. Somewhere in the mid-Atlantic by now, I expect. Rachel—" Her voice strengthened a little. "We're engaged. He bought me a ring last week, when he was home."

"Alice, that's marvellous news. Keep thinking about that! Don't let yourself get down."

"But—but—" Rachel heard an unmistakable sob. "He's in danger, too. I can't stop worrying about all of them. Oh Rachel, I wish you weren't so many miles away."

"I'm not," Rachel said. "I'm in London. Alice, don't cry! Listen, do you want me to come over?"

"Oh, *would* you? That would be wonderful! But it's awfully late—"

"Not that late. There are still cabs about the place."

"You're an answer to prayer!"

"See you soon."

Rachel put the phone down, turning to look uncertainly at

Dave, who was staring at her as if he could hardly believe his ears.

"What the hell—?" he began.

"Dave, I'm sorry, but you heard all that, didn't you? I must go."

"*Now*? For God's sake, Ray!"

"I'm sorry," she said. "Really sorry. Look—try to understand. Alice and I have comforted each other ever since we were little kids at school, both with parents overseas. And later, she was marvellous to me when I needed her. Now she needs me. She's worried to death, and all on her own. I must go to her."

"Dammit, *I* need you," he said, suddenly savage. He swung his legs over the bed and stood up, reaching out for her. "You can't do this, Ray—"

"I'm sorry!"

"What's the good of being sorry? Don't you know how I've looked forward to this?"

"Yes, I do know—and I don't want to hurt you, honestly, but I have to go."

"Why can't it wait until tomorrow?"

"It can't, that's all." She evaded his clutching arms and began snatching up the clothes she had discarded only a few minutes before. "She's got no one else at the moment. I'm going, Dave."

"Go, then." This was a harsh, ferocious Dave she had not seen before. "Get the hell out of it—"

He threw himself into the satin-covered armchair and watched her pack her case with a stony expression, his mouth distorted, his breathing heavy. He was smoking, taking short sharp drags at his cigarette, saying nothing.

"When she was ready to leave she went over to him.

"Shall I phone you tomorrow?" she asked him.

He stared at her, his expression unaltered.

"I shouldn't bother," he said. "I know now how much I mean to you, and that's bugger-all. If you go now, you go for good."

She returned his look, but sadly. She sighed, then gave a small, hopeless shrug.

"Goodbye, then," she said; but hesitated a moment even as

she turned to leave. "I really am sorry, Dave," she added softly. "I didn't mean to hurt you."

"Just get out," he said wearily.

It occurred to her as she walked down the thickly-carpeted corridor towards the lifts that the porters and the receptionists, if any were still on duty, would think she was doing a moonlight flit. She would have to plead a sudden call to a bed of sickness, say her husband was still in the room and would be staying on—

Husband! Oh, thank God, she thought, a sudden breathless joy sweeping through her. For the moment Alice was forgotten. Thank God, thank God, thank God—she was out of it! Maybe not with honour, but out of it. She should not, she admitted humbly, ever have got into it in the first place.

She need not have worried about questions being asked, for the lobby was still busy. A small crowd of American army officers were occupying the receptionists, and the uniformed porter was out on the street trying to whistle up a cab for an elderly Frenchman. Seeing his lack of success, Rachel decided to begin walking. There was muddy, city-streaked slush still covering the pavement and banked up by the side of the road, but the night was clear and bright and she knew the way like the back of her hand. She could cut down to the Kings Road through Wilton Place and Belgrave Square—she'd walked it a hundred times.

It seemed longer than she remembered, and the case became heavier with every step. It was after half past one when she turned at last into Shawcross Street; but she knew, the moment she saw Alice, that she'd done the right thing.

"I just can't believe this," Alice said, when they had hugged in greeting. "Tonight, before you rang, I was wishing you were here—and suddenly, there you were. It was just like a miracle. What on earth are you doing in London?"

Rachel looked at her and saw the strain that the bad news and the loneliness had had on her. Her face had lost its look of childish innocence. Alice, she could see, had grown up.

"It's a long story," she said. "I'll tell you some time."

"Come into the kitchen. It's warm in there and I'll make some tea. You don't mind sharing my bed, do you? I'll make up another if you like—"

"No, no, that's fine. I could sleep anywhere, I'm so tired."

"You don't look tired. You look marvellous! Honestly, Rachel, you're so—so *groomed* these days. Like a film star, or a model or something."

"It's still scruffy old me underneath, I assure you. But talking of models—have you seen that new recruitment poster for the WRNS? It's all over the place."

"Mm." Alice was busy lighting the gas, putting on the kettle, already looking better. "Why?"

"It's Diana Rossiter—"

"*No!* Is it? I didn't know. I never met her. Gosh, you always said she was gorgeous—"

"I stepped out of the train, and there she was! I had the shock of my life."

Alice pulled a face.

"You should have thrown a rotten tomato at it, or drawn on a moustache, or something. I knew she was in the WRNS—something very high up at the Admiralty, but—" she stopped in mid-sentence, her face reddening.

"How did you know that?" Rachel asked curiously. Alice bit her lip.

"Oh gosh, I'm such a fool," she said miserably. "I asked Susan if she thought I ought to mention it in my letter to you, and she said better not. She thought it would just upset you all over again." She groaned. "I'm such an idiot, Rachel, so scatty. Trust me to let it drop!"

"Let what drop, for heaven's sake? Come on, Alice, you might as well spill all the beans now you've started."

"Yes, I suppose I might." Alice sighed penitently. "It's nothing important, really. It happened when Keith was home. We were sitting here quite late one night with Susan, drinking cocoa, when Captain Blackwell put his head round the door and said did Susan mind, he'd bought a colleague back with him to sleep on his settee. They'd tried several hotels, he said, and couldn't find a bed for love or money. So of course, you know Susan—she invited them into the kitchen for cocoa too, and said what nonsense, they mustn't think of using the settee, and rushed around making up a bed for him in one of the spare rooms."

"And that was Mr. Rossiter?"

"Yes—well, Captain Rossiter, actually! Wasn't it amazing? He's working at the War Office now, something to do with requisitioning buildings, the same section as Captain Blackwell. We didn't know who it was at first, of course—didn't even catch the name, but gradually it came out that he was an architect, and came from Warnfield and had four children, so it didn't take much to put two and two together.''

"Did he know about me? I mean, that I'd lived here and that you were my friend?''

"Well, I told him, of course. He knew you had lived here, in Shawcross Street, but didn't know the number. I suppose I was a bit—well, hostile, at first, but he was awfully sweet about you, Rachel. Awfully sorry it happened. I couldn't help feeling— well, nothing was his fault, was it?''

Rachel gave a brief laugh at that.

"Maybe not,'' she said. "On the other hand, he was all part of the Rossiter conspiracy—the 'Aren't We Wonderful, Nobody's Like Us' conspiracy. It contributed, I imagine. Tell me, what's Gavin doing now? Did he say?''

"Only that he was flying Lancs. Alannah's with ENSA. She's been touring Scotland with a company, doing lots of different plays in repertory. Marvellous experience, he says—''

"Of course,'' Rachel murmured.

"Barney's in the Middle East.''

"I know. He wrote to me at Christmas.''

"You know, Rachel—'' Alice poured the tea and pushed a cup towards her. "I can't help thinking it was an awful shame you didn't stick with Barney. I always liked him.''

Rachel sipped her tea, looking at Alice over the top of her cup.

"So did I,'' she said. "But it was Gavin I loved.'' She put her cup down. "What are we doing talking about me? You haven't shown me your ring yet, or told me anything about Keith.''

"There!'' Alice displayed her left hand. "Isn't it gorgeous? I always loved sapphires. Keith is so sweet! He writes the most wonderful letters, and I write to him, every single day. We're going to get married on his next leave.''

"I knew he was right for you.''

"We went to see his parents in Winchester—my uncle and aunt. I thought they'd disapprove because we're related, but they didn't. They seemed really glad he'd chosen me. And

Rachel—'' Alice lowered her eyes, fidgeted with her teaspoon as if unsure how she should continue. "Rachel, I must tell you." Still she hesitated, biting her lip. "On the way back we stayed the night at a lovely little Wiltshire pub. Do you think that was awful of us?''

She looked up appealingly, her eyes wide and questioning, as if she really wanted to know. Rachel laughed. Alice was such an *infant*, she thought.

"Of course I don't!''

"As husband and wife, I mean,'' Alice went on, as if Rachel hadn't quite got the point.

"Alice, you love each other, you intend to get married. Where's the harm?''

"Well—'' she looked down again. "It's not the way we've been brought up, is it? I mean, I never thought I would. I never intended to.''

"Did you enjoy it?'' Rachel asked lightly. "That's the main thing.''

"Oh, Rachel!'' Alice was glowing now, her eyes bright. She reached across and clasped Rachel's hand. "Oh, Rachel, it was wonderful! Wonderful! If we never have anything else, we'll have had that night.''

"You'll have lots more,'' Rachel said softly, aware, suddenly, of wanting to cry and despising the cheap sentimentality that prompted such a desire. She got up from the table, took her cup to the sink. "You know, Alice my love,'' she said. "I'm dead on my feet. Is there any chance of bed in the near future?''

"Of course, of course! I'm a selfish wretch, keeping you talking like this.''

"But you do feel a bit better?''

"Lots, thanks to you.'' Alice came close and hugged her. "God knows what news tomorrow will bring, but at least I'll have you to share it with. Thanks for coming.''

"I wouldn't be anywhere else,'' Rachel said. "Now, bed.''

But once there, she found to her annoyance that she was unable to sleep.

She thought of Dave. She'd behaved badly from beginning to end, she could see that now. Poor Dave.

She thought of Barney. Was Alice right? Should she have stuck with him? How could she have done, when she loved

Gavin so? Liking might be important, but it wasn't enough.

And, with a small twisted smile, she thought of Alice. Little did she think she could ever be envious of Alice.

But that's just what I am, she thought forlornly. That's just what I am.

❧ FIFTEEN ❧

It was mid-November when Stefan called with his floral peace offering, but the end of the month before Rachel saw him again.

The book was running away with her, wanting to get itself written. Any moment she could spare away from Tess, she rushed to her typewriter, often working far into the night. She knew she was pale, short of exercise, short of sleep; but a kind of exaltation had her in its grip, interspersed with agonising periods of sheer panic when she felt certain that what she had written was without interest, totally worthless, and that no one, ever, would want to read it.

"You must let up a little," Emma urged. "Make more use of Marlene. She's only too happy to have Tess on Saturdays or in the evenings."

"I just can't wait for her to start work properly after Christmas," Rachel said. "It's going to revolutionise my life."

She took note of what Emma said, however, and one Saturday in early December—a day so clear and bright that it seemed to have been borrowed from spring—she decided to explore the countryside that had tempted and intrigued her from the beginning but had so far been inaccessible in the company of Tess and the inevitable pram.

Marlene came soon after lunch, and Rachel quickly made her escape, heading a little way up the hill, then turning to where steps rose steeply between the cottages, first this way and then that. There were children playing, two women talking at a front door, stocky men in caps and sweaters and seaboots clumping down towards the ferry. There was, she gathered, a football match in Polvear. They smiled and wished her good day, not so reserved now as they had been at first. They were beginning to accept her, in spite of the disgrace of her unmarried state. She'd been right to think that time would help. St. Bethan felt like home now.

Or was that merely an illusion? Maybe the people greeted her because they were kind. To them she was, and perhaps always would be, a "furriner," and a sinful one at that. But *oh!*—she stopped and gasped as she reached the end of the steps and came out on to the path that ran high up above the river—how could anyone not wish to be at home in this place?

It was, of course, the same river that she could see from her windows, but viewed from this angle and in this light it looked unfamiliar—wider, more serene, its surface smooth as satin.

The sight of it was a piercing happiness made suddenly sweeter by the appearance of three swans flying up-river, the beating of their wings as perfectly synchronized as any *corps de ballet*. This is *it*, she thought—not analysing her meaning, not attempting to put it into words, merely recognising that this was perfection.

She savoured it a little longer, then continued on her way. For a few yards she was hemmed in; to her right a stone wall, green with moss and ivies and springing ferns, and to her left the thick band of woodland that lay between her and the river, shimmering between the trees in a series of blinding silver flashes. There were holly bushes thick with berries, and blackthorn, and the lichen-clad trunks of oak and beech, the odd shrivelled leaf still clinging stubbornly to their branches. The path here was wide but muddy. Head down, she picked her way cautiously, so that when, suddenly, the way opened out once more, she was taken by surprise by the sight of Stefan Wisniowiecki standing as transfixed by the view as she had been a moment earlier.

Still dazed by so much beauty, she greeted him, looked, and marvelled and turned to smile at him.

"What can one say?"

He smiled, too, and shook his head as if he, too, were lost for words, and it struck her how much better he looked than when she had last seen him. He seemed younger and happier. Was all this heavenly beauty responsible for that, too, she wondered? For it was not merely that there was more flesh on him, the deeply scored lines from nose to mouth less apparent; he looked less hag-ridden, less likely to give the jerky, disconcerting bows that accentuated his foreignness. One could even imagine a dawning air of serenity.

His smile grew more mischievous.

"Where is baby?" he asked. "In river perhaps?"

"Ouch! That's unkind!" But a good sign, surely, that he could joke like this? "I'm playing hookey—truant," she added, seeing his look of perplexity. "I've run away from my duties and left Tess with a friend. On a day like this, I just had to walk."

"I, too." He looked at her hesitantly. "You go down to creek, I think? Is it, perhaps, that you want to be alone?"

"Not at all." Rachel wondered, even as she spoke, what on earth had got into her. She *did* want to be alone! She wanted time and space to enjoy the sights all around her; and time to think, too. Time to work out that conversation between David and Catherine that was so crucial but was proving difficult. Oh, well—nothing to do now but make the best of it. "Why don't we walk together, if you're going that way?"

"You are most kind," he said; and for the first few minutes conversation between them proceeded on this formal level. Was he enjoying St. Bethan? Yes, indeed, everyone was most kind. And she—did her work progress satisfactorily? Yes, thank you—at the moment it was going well.

It was impossible, afterwards, to remember quite how or when it all changed, at what precise moment the conversation between them became urgent and absorbing, and far more fundamental, causing them to stop in their tracks as they pursued an argument. She forgot David and Catherine and every other character in the novel and was glad—glad to an astonishing degree—that she was walking with Stefan Wisniowiecki.

The sky paled, and the air grew colder, but unaware they stood at the creek's edge and talked of life and love and war. He had lived in Warsaw, he told her, but his family had owned a cabin in Mikolajki, to the north of Warsaw, close to the Mazurian Lakes.

"That's where my heart was," he said. "I could never wait for school to be finished, so that we could pack up and go there for our holidays. It is more lovely than I can tell you—and not

so different from this. There was creek like this . . ." His voice
trailed away, then turning, he bent to pick up a stone that he
sent skimming across the water. "So much is like, Rachel. I
may say 'Rachel?' There were cormorants and herons there, just
as here, and boys who make rafts and boats just like boys of
St. Bethan." He laughed as if the thought of them made him
happy. "And they annoy mothers by forgetting mealtimes and
fathers by growing up and rebelling, I think, yes?"

"Is that what you did?"

"Not so much. I struggle a little, but at finish, I do what they
wish." His twisted, inward smile seemed, she thought, a little
rueful.

"You regret that now?" she asked.

He shook his head.

"No, no, not at all. I wish it, too. I study chemistry at Warsaw
Polytechnic and for few years afterwards we work together, my
father and I. It was good. We came to understand each other,
to be friends, and for that I am thankful now for after early
weeks of 1940, we never saw each other again."

Rachel hesitated for a moment. Did he want to talk? Would
it seem like prying?

"What happened?" she said at last, shyly, not pressing. For
a moment he was silent. He stared out over the creek, but she
knew it was not this stretch of water and these seabirds he could
see.

"My father had factory in Warsaw," he said at last. "It man-
ufactured small things. Light-fittings. Ashtrays. Tubing. Things
that screwed into other things. Things that could be made from
synthetic resins. He was chemist—a clever, inventive man, always experimenting. We had comfortable life. My mother was—
was lady." His face lit up with amused affection as with a
gesture he contrived to illustrate the refined elegance of his
mother. "Her father was high Government official. Important
man! She was cultured, spoke good French, played piano. She
dress me in velvet suits, but other boys laugh and my father
plead for me. We were not really grand, you understand, but
comfortable. It was natural for my father to want his only son
to go into business."

"But you had other ideas?"

"I was boy who live and dream boats. I long to build them

and sail them and spend all my life close to lakes. My mother and sister and I stay at cabin for all of summer, with my father coming from time to time. Later, as I grew older, I spend holidays there working in small boatyard, much like Joe Carthew's. It belonged to old man called Jan.'' He paused for a moment, smiling, remembering Jan. "An old, wise man, he was.'' He hunched his shoulders. "Stooped, like this. Eyes no good. But great craftsman. He tell me—told me?—''I have no son. Come and work with me here and learn craft well, and when I go this yard will be yours.' ''

"It must have been a hard choice.''

He nodded, slowly and thoughtfully. "At home there was much argument. At last I agree to study and give factory trial. All the time I was student, I still returned to Jan and yard whenever I could. But before end of my studies, I met Irina.'' He had only to speak of her, Rachel noted, for his voice to change. He seemed to catch his breath before continuing. "She was music student in Warsaw—''

"So you decided to stay?''

"Boats were my life; music was hers. She could not have lived in Mikolajki, away from music. Besides, she was offered place in orchestra. Violin, she played . . .'' his voice trailed away before picking up again. "But we still kept cabin and sailed each summer . . .'' This time his silence left a sense of almost unbearable desolation.

Rachel was aware suddenly of the chill striking through boots and gloves. The sun had gone altogether now. She shivered and hunched her shoulders.

"Oh, you are cold,'' Stefan said, coming back to the present. "You should not let me talk so much. We must go.''

Not unwillingly, she began retracing the steps they had taken down to the creek, up the steep and narrow track that led to the path above the river. They climbed for a while, in single file and in silence.

"You didn't say what happened afterwards,'' she said when he came alongside her as the path widened at the top. "Do you want to talk about it? Or does it hurt too much?''

His face, half turned from her, was a series of harsh, downward curves.

"I was rounded up and sent to Germany as slave labourer in

1940," he said at last. "My sister Bronia married Jewish doctor just before war. Joseph, his name. He was good, kind man. We liked him very much, though he was of different race. At first he could continue work, but things grew worse and worse. All Jews were ordered to ghetto—my sister too, of course."

He paused again and drew a long breath, but before she could speak, he had taken up the story again.

"By that time I was in Germany, working like slave. Like dog. All this I hear after, from friend who was sent to same camp. My sister was expecting baby. My parents would not let her go to ghetto, so they hide them, Bronia and Joseph. For many months, they hide them in storeroom of factory. But they were betrayed."

"Who would betray them, Stefan? Who could do such a thing?" At Rachel's horrified question, he gave a short, mirthless laugh.

"Who knows? Someone, perhaps, with grudge against my father. Every man in authority who employs and fires labour must have enemies, I think. Or perhaps it was someone who hated Jews. Oh yes, there were many in Poland who did so. Or perhaps it was someone who wanted to gain favour with Germans. Who can tell? All that is certain is that they were found and arrested. All died in Treblinka—my mother, father, my sister and her husband."

Instinctively, she took his arm.

"Stefan, I'm so sorry."

For a moment he stared bleakly at the wide sweep of the glassy river and all the heartbreaking beauty that was spread before them.

"It meant that Irina and Nadya, our little girl, were alone in Warsaw. Her parents were dead and she had no one in the city. I got word to her to go to relatives in mountains, close to Russian border. I thought it would be safer and more comfortable." He paused again. "It was not," he said flatly. "They, too—"

"Don't talk about it now," Rachel said gently. "Later, perhaps."

Slowly he nodded. "Perhaps," he said after a moment. "Is still too near, I think. Some things I am able to speak of with sadness but without—without anguish? Yes? Anguish is word?"

"That, I think, might begin to describe it," Rachel said dryly.

"Other things—" he hesitated. "Of other things I cannot speak." He looked at her and managed to smile. "Don't look so sad, Rachel. So many suffered, but life goes on and must be lived. Soon I will feel this, perhaps. After all, I came through. I survived—oh, perhaps not as man I was, but I am here, yes? Already I have plans."

"That's good," Rachel said.

They walked for a while in silence and when he spoke again it was if he had deliberately moved into another gear, forcing his mind away from past tragedies. His voice sounded stronger and more vibrant.

"I tell no one," he said at last. "But I tell you, today. I say to you, I think, that factory worked with synthetic resins? That I wrote book? There are many different kinds. My poor, boring book concerned possible use of six, and there are more."

"You mean—like Bakelite?"

"Bakelite, yes, is one kind of plastic. There is future for boats in such material, Rachel."

"Bakelite boats? You mean, like ash-trays, only bigger?"

"Now you make fun—but you are not so wrong. Ash-trays are made from moulded resin. Make resin that is harder and stronger material—resin that will not melt in hot sun, or break easily in pieces, and make moulds that are bigger and of different shape, and you have boat. Not big boats perhaps. Not ocean-going yachts—though who is to say what future will bring? But small pleasure boats, almost certainly. Boats that little boys can save money to buy, and families, and old men who want to go fishing."

His dark eyes were alive again, the sadness banished for the moment.

"It sounds wonderful! Not," Rachel added hastily, "that I know the first thing about it."

"I try to tell Joe Carthew that such scheme is possible, but he laughs and thinks I am madman. I understand him. He is a man who loves building in wood, as I do myself. There is nothing like it. Of course I agree that wood is best. For this other I must go back to chemistry."

"Well, good for you!" Fired by his enthusiasm, Rachel turned and smiled at him. "You'll do it, I'm sure."

It was his turn to catch her arm and pull her to a halt.

"Thank you. Thank you," he said.

"For what?" she asked, but he did not answer. For a moment they were still, standing and looking at each other as if for the first time; and for the first time she felt a stirring of sexual interest, an awareness of tension. Was she, she wondered, like Desdemona, loving him for the dangers he had passed through? It was possible.

But she had no wish to fall in love. Nor was she doing so, she assured herself. Not now, not ever. This threatened awakening of emotions long dead, this ridiculous fluttering of the nerves, must be subdued at all costs. It was enough to note with clinical interest that the arrangement of eyes and nose was rather striking, now that he had a bit more flesh on his bones. His eyebrows, she saw, grew in a rather spectacular way, like two dark wings, and his mouth—

Her thoughts shied like a nervous horse at the thought of his mouth, but still she could not look away from him. It was a strong face, she thought, intelligent and humorous and alive— the face of a man who would survive and triumph. A man a woman could be proud to love.

"My goodness, it's awfully cold," she said, digging her hands in her pockets and setting off once more at a brisk pace.

"Please," he said after they had gone a short way. "Do not speak of plan to anyone, Rachel. It is too—" Vaguely he waved his hand in a circular motion above his head. "Too much in air. I tell you so you will see I do not live in past. Others would think me mad, I think, not just Joe."

"Well, I don't," Rachel said, composed once more. "I'm sure you know what you're talking about—and how well you say it, too! Your English is wonderful."

"No, no, not good! I learn at school, long ago, and afterwards meet others in same business, English and American. Now I read to improve my language. Trollope, Dickens, Jane Austen. These were always in our house, in translation of course, thanks to my mother. As a race, we love books, but so little I know of modern writers. You will advise me, yes? Which modern writers should I read?"

The subject of books and writers happily occupied them all the way home; and afterwards, long after they had parted, Rachel was conscious of a feeling of—what? Excitement?

Forget it, she told herself. Concentrate on other things. She had found his company mentally stimulating; that was enough. Falling in love was dangerous and in this case could bring her nothing but more heartache, since it was abundantly clear that he was still mourning his wife. It was too great a risk. Anyway, she didn't have the time or the energy left over from her writing; and it was the writing that was the important thing, now that she had Tess to provide for.

Still the thought of him recurred at intervals during the rest of the day.

"We shall meet and talk again—yes?" he had said as they parted.

"I hope so. Anyway, there are the books you're going to borrow. You must call to collect them. I wonder—" she hesitated for a moment, then made up her mind. "I've a friend, Emma Laity, coming to supper on Wednesday. She's the school-teacher here. Won't you come too? I think you'll enjoy meeting her."

"Thank you. I would like to come."

Mentally she revised the menu. Omelettes wouldn't do, she thought. Not for a man. Fish pie would be better. She'd try to get a nice piece of fish. Maybe go over to Polvear . . .

The evening went well, as she had somehow known it would. Stefan's presence provided a stimulus to conversation, a focal point.

We two women are both on top form, Rachel thought, half-way through the evening; and was wryly amused by the reflection, thinking it cast an illuminating and none too flattering light on their manless state—though Emma, to be fair, was not as manless as all that. She had many friends, many interests. That particular evening she was fired with enthusiasm about a CEMA sponsored play that was being staged in Truro the following week.

"What's 'CEMA'?" Rachel asked. "I've never heard of it."

"That, my dear, is because you've lived until now in the metropolis where you have theatres to right and left. CEMA is Council for the Encouragement of Music and the Arts. It's a sort of peacetime ENSA, sent out to the poor deprived peasantry. We've had some good companies down here. This time they're doing *Arms and the Man*. Why don't you come?''

"We could go together, yes?" Stefan said, smiling at Rachel.

He, too, seemed in the best of spirits, his lively face with its dark deep-set eyes full of warmth and humour. On the walk he had proved himself a good conversationalist, but somehow she had not imagined he could be so amusingly entertaining as he had been that evening.

"Why not?" she replied, getting up to clear away the plates. She paused for a moment as she put them down in the kitchen. Careful, she warned herself. Watch yourself. Don't be disarmed by an attractive smile and a pair of sparkling eyes.

She had to admit to herself, however, that the prospect of this outing pleased her out of all proportion to its importance, and it proved, in the event, as enjoyable as she had hoped. Stefan was as friendly as ever and came back to the cottage for coffee. They did not touch on personal matters, talking mainly of Poland's history, but somehow, as they said good night and he left the warmth of her home to return to the yard where he lived in a bare, converted room that had once been a store, she knew that intangibly their friendship had advanced.

She felt surprised and thankful that here, in this unlikely place, she had met such a friend—and it was, she assured herself, only as a friend that she regretted the comfortlessness of his present quarters. She found herself brooding about it, long after the time when she should have gone to sleep. She couldn't let him spend Christmas there, she thought.

With the approach of Christmas, Izzy Pollard grew ever more self-important, dispensing jars of mincemeat and boxes of biscuits and tins of sliced peaches to her favourites as if no one need imagine that the mere possession of sufficient points in a ration book entitled them to any such favours. Emma, who had made arrangements to spend the holiday with her late husband's parents, pressed on Rachel a chicken which had been given to her by her tame farmer.

"Cook a super Christmas dinner for Stefan," she said. "The poor man's as thin as two boards."

"How did you know I'd invited him?" Rachel asked indignantly. "Honestly, this place is the end! I suppose he told Mrs. Carthew, who told you."

"Not at all," Emma said. "He told Mrs. Carthew, who told Mrs. Hambly, who happened to mention it to Betty Pearce when she came to the school to collect her grandson, who of course, aware of my friendship with you, passed it on at the earliest opportunity. Simple. You realise, of course, that you have the entire village agog."

"Oh, really!" Rachel hardly knew whether to laugh or to be angry. "Well, they can gog all they like! For heaven's sake, one trip to the theatre, one fish supper, a couple of walks—what does it add up to? We're friends, that's all."

And friends, Rachel told herself, were all they were likely to be. He spoke of his wife from time to time, briefly and in passing; but she was not deceived. He still felt her loss and grieved for her constantly. He had no photograph of her, but had mentioned, once, that she had been dark and slightly built.

He had given no other details, and Rachel had asked him for none, but there were times when she felt Irina was present with them—a small, delicate ghost with a cloud of dark hair, full of grace as she lifted her violin and tucked it under her chin. It was Stefan's unswerving love that conjured her up, she felt certain. And she, who had surely made enough mistakes regarding men, was not going to be fool enough to fall in love with this particular one.

She continued to enjoy his company, however; and so did Tess, for he had endless patience with her and appeared to like nothing more than to play the repetitive games she enjoyed so much. He was good-humoured, undismayed by the tears or the temperament without which no child would be human.

"Where is father?" he asked her once. "Does he see her?"

"No," she answered briefly, in a voice that brooked no further questions.

"That is sad," he said after a moment. "If I were her father—"

"Well, you're not, are you?" she snapped; and half humorously, half taken aback, he had sucked in his cheeks, raised his eyebrows and said no more.

Easygoing though he was, Rachel had clear evidence that the angry man of their first meeting was not so very far below the surface. Soon after the walk to the creek, they had met by arrangement to explore the cliff path, and had scrambled down to a rocky cove where they had found two small boys tormenting a gull with a broken wing. Stefan had shouted at them, and raised an arm as if he would strike them, so threatening that they had taken to their heels and fled. He was shaking, Rachel saw as he passed a hand over his face when they were gone, muttering to himself in Polish.

"Unforgivable," he said to her after a few moments. "Unforgivable. They were children, only. I cannot stand seeing any helpless creature hurt, but this loss of control I thought in past. It is not—not *I*, Rachel! What must you think of me?"

"What do I think of you?" Rachel had laughed as she looked at him. "Well, I can hardly be under any illusions, can I? I thought you were going to give me a fourpenny one that first time we met."

"Fourpenny one?" He frowned, not understanding. She had hoped to make him smile, but saw she had failed.

"Hit me, I mean. Stefan, don't be daft," she went on. "If I didn't like you, I wouldn't be here, would I?"

He smiled at that as if with relief. He looked younger all the time, she thought. How old was he? Thirty-five, maybe? She found herself unable to guess, and admitted to herself that she was curious. Only because he was something of an enigma, she thought hastily; not for any other reason. Sometimes he seemed to possess the wisdom of the ages, as if he were a whole generation removed from her. This loss of control that he deplored so much was almost a relief. At least it proved that he was human.

Enduring such spartan living accommodation as he did, he was appreciative of the efforts she made to produce a Christmas dinner. He came bearing bottles of wine, and small presents— a book for her, a doll for Tess.

"Is so beautiful!" he said, looking round the room at the tree she had decorated, and the streamers and swags of holly and cards above the fireplace. So few cards to show for twenty-five years on this planet, she had thought as she set them out. There was one from her mother and father; one from Sylvia and Rex, with a scrawled message below the names to say they hoped she was keeping warm and enjoying the cottage. One from Alice and Keith, now married and living in Edinburgh. One from Susan, sent from Germany where she had a job with UNRRA, working with Displaced Persons. One from Nancy and George, and another from Emma. One from her editor, one from her agent, one from Beattie.

Only to someone like Stefan, she thought, would this seem like abundance.

When Tess was in bed, worn out by the excitement of her first Christmas, they sat down to the meal that Rachel had prepared. All, to her relief, had turned out well. The chicken was succulent, the potatoes crisply roasted, the brussel sprouts still had a bite to them. She'd been worried about the stuffing, that the herb content was too much, but it had been all right. Better than all right. Conversation was easy and unforced. It was, after all, turning out a far better Christmas than she might have expected.

"More wine?" He leant towards her to refill her glass. "That was delicious, Rachel. I have not had such a meal since—oh, I can't remember!"

"The chicken was courtesy of Emma."

"But you stuffed it and cooked it, and did all the rest. And as for the pudding—! Well, I have made a mutton of myself."

Rachel giggled, feeling slightly light-headed.

"Glutton, I think you mean. Unless my cooking has made you feel like a dead sheep."

"Dead—?" He clapped a hand to his head. "Such a fool! Glutton I meant."

"I think coffee might be a good idea, don't you? Why don't you sit by the fire, and I'll bring some in?"

He insisted on helping her to clear the table, but she refused all offers of help with the washing up. When she returned to the sitting room, she found him sitting by the fire, apparently lost in thought. Silently he watched her as she put the tray down and poured the coffee.

"So little I know of your life," he said as she handed him his cup. "I see cards and I know you have friends and family, but you do not speak much of them."

"Well, there's not much family to speak of," she replied lightly. "I've told you about my parents in Uganda. The aunt and uncle who own this cottage are in America—and that's it. Tess is my family now."

He seemed to brood on this a little, but there was something in the quality of his silence that made her aware that questions were on the tip of his tongue.

"If you are thinking about her father—" she began defensively.

"No, no!" Hastily he denied such a thing; then he shrugged his shoulders. "Well, perhaps. But I think only that it is sad for you to be alone. But soon your parents come home, yes?"

"Yes." There was a note of hesitancy in Rachel's voice as if she were, after all, less than overjoyed at this prospect, and he looked at her narrowly.

"What is wrong? You do not wish to see them?"

She gave a brief, unhappy laugh.

"The question is, will they wish to see me, once they know about Tess?"

"You mean they know nothing? You have not told them? But why, Rachel?"

"Haven't the guts," she said, adopting a flippant note. "That's the long and the short of it. Oh, they'll have to know eventually, of course, but sufficient unto the day. Now you see me for what I am," she went on, as he continued to look at her, frowning, not saying a word. "Lily-livered and pusillanimous."

"I don't know those words—"

"I'm a coward, Stefan. I lack courage. I'm scared. No doubt there are other ways of saying it, but that's the essence."

"No! Is nonsense!" He laughed disbelievingly. "Is not easy for woman on her own with baby. You manage well. You are brave."

Rachel sighed and sipped her coffee in silence for a moment.

"Some things I am brave about," she said. "Other things scare me to death. Things like—will my parents ever forgive me for doing this to them? They'll be hurt and humiliated and angry."

He leaned towards her, his dark face intense.

"You are wrong, Rachel." She could see he was having difficulty in finding the right words to express himself. He knocked his head in frustration. "How shall I say? You must be—more fair to them. They, perhaps, are not so small as you think. Yes, perhaps, they will be upset. But can't you trust their—their—" he paused, struggling. " 'Compassion' is word, yes?"

"Maybe," she said.

"If they love you—and I am sure they love you, they will not make this a reason to stop. This is meaning of family."

"Mm." Rachel looked sceptical. His concept was too simplistic. Losing his own family had made him over-sentimental, that's what it was. As far as her family was concerned, hadn't Alannah always said—?

Damn Alannah! She didn't want to think what Alannah had always said. The evening had taken a wrong turn, with all this talk of families. It was dangerous territory for both of them.

"Emma's planning an enormous New Year's Party," she said brightly. "I do hope Marlene's going to be able to sit in for me. Have you been invited yet? I know you will be. Emma's talking about making it fancy dress, and I've been racking my brains about what to wear. Have you got any good ideas?"

Stefan had bought some small cigars with him and thoughtfully he lit one, drawing on it with his eyes still fixed on her. He blew out the smoke so that it wreathed around him, hiding his expression.

"No," he said. "Rachel—" The smoke cleared and she could see his eyes, dark and intense and troubled. "Is not my business to advise—"

She abandoned the bright conversational manner and gave him a small, twisted smile.

"But you're going to do it anyway?"

"Rachel," he said again. His voice was gentle, and he hesitated a little. "Your parents will, I think, be more hurt the longer you keep this secret. And for your own sake, too, you should tell them, not allow them to come and be confronted by grandchild they know nothing about."

"Perhaps you are right," she said at last. "I'm sure you are right. But for God's sake, let's talk about something else. Would you like more coffee?"

"Thank you. Is good. You buy here in St. Bethan?"

"Good Lord, no! There's a little shop near the church in Polvear . . ."

The conversation drifted to other things and did not return to that particular subject; but as if it had cast a shadow, there was no sparkle in the evening now.

They spoke of Emma's party, but without a great deal of interest. They compared Christmas traditions, English and Polish. Stefan described ice-sailing one year on the Mazurian Lakes; she told him about the Rossiter's parties and pantomimes.

They were like two old pensioners talking about the good old days, she thought, and suddenly she found herself deeply depressed as if the day should have built up to a climax more exciting than this.

What the hell did I expect? she demanded of herself.

She didn't know. Not bed, that was certain, or any kind of commitment. She wasn't ready, and clearly nor was he. Perhaps he never would be.

He rose to go, and she made no protest. He had done his best, no doubt; but she had the distinct feeling that, as the evening progressed, he had become increasingly weighed down by memories of other times, other Christmasses.

"I thank you so much," he said when he was about to leave. "It would not have been good to be alone. Not for you, I think, nor for me. We are both Displaced Persons—yes?"

"Perhaps," she said, conscious suddenly of the prick of tears behind her eyes. Damn it, what was wrong with her? It must be the wine. She'd had too much and it had made her over-emotional.

"But you have parents still," he said, taking her two hands to give added emphasis to his words. "That is big thing, Rachel. Please don't hurt them more than you have to."

"All *right*!" She snatched her hands away, her impatience real enough even though she laughed at him and attempted to turn it into a joke. "Point taken!"

After he had gone, she went into the kitchen and with a sinking heart surveyed the sink full of dishes, gearing herself up to tackle them, knowing that the next day would bring its own quota of chores. She picked up an encrusted saucepan that ought to have been put to soak, looked at it with hatred, and crashed it down on the draining board.

"*Bloody* Christmas," she said, the tears that had been threatening for the last few minutes suddenly spilling over.

She turned her back on the mess and returned to the sitting room where she found there was still half an inch of wine in one of the bottles. Sniffing, wiping away the tears with her fingers, she poured the remains into her glass and sat down with it on a footstool close to the dying fire.

"Fool," she said bitterly to herself. "Bloody idiot. For God's sake, pull yourself together."

She sniffed some more, and fumbled in her pocket for a handkerchief. She had Tess, hadn't she? And the book was progressing, wasn't it? She had friends, enough to live on—she was *lucky*, for heaven's sake!

It wasn't as if she wanted that sort of here-we-go-round-the-mulberry-bush, Rossiter-ish Christmas, that suddenly seemed to bloom in her memory as if it had been nothing but fun and good cheer. It hadn't been like that at all.

It had been an illusion, a lie. Without substance. As so much had been. Including Alannah's cruel and frequent remarks about the Bonds' lack of family feeling. That wasn't true either. They did care for each other, even if it were in a different way from the Rossiters. It was crazy to play Alannah's words over and over in her head like an old record.

All, all was a lie. But, in a strange and perverse way, the Rossiters had set a standard. Impossible not to think that this was the way a family ought to be. That somehow she had missed out.

Rachel stared into the fire and seemed to see them all, closely linked, laughing, admiring each other, forgiving each other. Would her parents forgive so easily?

She yawned, tired now. Bed, she thought; and to hell with the washing up. And to hell with the Rossiters.

And to hell with Christmas, she thought as, a little unsteadily, she climbed the stairs. Next year she'd abolish it altogether. But then she remembered Tess, and knew that she wouldn't.

Emma's New Year's party went ahead as planned, but the weather was bad and roads were icy, so that many of her guests failed to make the journey to St. Bethan and no one was anxious to make it a late night.

From the beginning it was clear that Stefan had shaken off the sub-fusc mood of Christmas, as indeed she had herself.

"Did I nag?" he asked Rachel as they walked up the hill to the schoolhouse, her arm through his.

"A bit," she admitted.

"Oh, well." He smiled down at her. "I cannot help being so right, I think. Is my wonderful nature."

"So wise, and modest with it," Rachel mocked him.

Emma had decided not to make the party fancy dress after all. Stefan wore grey flannels and a tweed sports coat, newly bought, and succeeded in looking both more English and more foreign than usual. Rachel noted that women who would not have given him a second glance had they seen him in his donkey jacket and seaman's cap were hanging on his every word; but he looked across at one point and winked at her as if to say— just look at me, don't you find this amusing? And she had grinned back. For once, there seemed no sign of Irina anywhere. There was dancing to records collected from Emma's friends and acquaintances, the dining room cleared for the purpose.

"Embrace me, you sweet embraceable you," crooned Frank Sinatra; and looking up at Stefan, feeling his arm around her waist, finding him looking at her with a softness of expression she had not seen before, Rachel was conscious of a twist of excitement and longing. Was love possible, then? Was it at all possible? She felt breathless at the very thought of it. It frightened her to death, yet sent a shiver of delight through her body.

Oh, the potency of cheap music, she thought, forcing herself down to earth. Noel Coward certainly knew a thing or two.

There were the usual screams of excitement and kisses as 1947 came into being and the chimes of Big Ben were relayed over the radio. Stefan, being the darkest man present, was detailed to do the first-footing.

"Isn't he gorgeous?" said a young, redheaded woman, a schoolteacher from Falmouth. "Such a fascinating accent! I could listen to him all night."

When, later, Stefan deposited her at her door, Rachel reached up to kiss him lightly on the cheek.

"I shan't ask you in," she said. "It's much too late, for one thing; and for another, I have every intention of writing a letter before I go to sleep tonight. A letter to my parents. *The* letter! It's my New Year's Resolution."

By the porch light she could see his smile, the upward slant of his cheeks, the dark bright eyes. He bent his head and kissed her. A reward for being good, she thought. But then his arms tightened around her and he kissed her again, and this time there was hunger in it, and passion, and delight; and for a moment she lost herself in it, drowning in sweetness and joy, all fears swept away, sure that the waiting was at an end. And then, as suddenly, he drew away, his expression unreadable.

Irina, she thought, with a sinking of the heart. Always there. Why can't she see that I'd never come between them, never want to?

"You do good thing, Rachel," he said softly. "I am pleased with you."

She gave a small, trembling laugh.

"You sound like a schoolmaster talking to a promising pupil," she said. "Or a vicar, maybe."

His smile seemed both gentle and regretful as he lightly stroked her face. She was pleased to notice that his breathing was uneven.

"I do not feel like vicar," he said. "No, not at all like vicar." He was silent for a moment, not smiling now, and his hand was cold against her cheek. "Happy New Year, Rachel."

"Happy New Year, Stefan."

For a long moment they looked at each other in a silence that seemed to vibrate with words trembling on the brink of expression. He said no more, however, but turned and left her. For a second or two she stood looking after him. She gave a breath of laughter that ended in a sigh, then she shook her head and sighed again.

She would try to put him out of her mind for the moment. She had to. The most difficult composition of her life lay ahead.

ৈ SIXTEEN ৈ

Winter clamped down on the entire country, bitter and remorseless, made even harder by shortages. The long-suffering British public was exhorted by the Government to save electricity, heat only one room, cut down on the bath water. Meantime bread rationing was introduced, the meat ration cut. Austerity was the word on everyone's lips.

The weeks passed without a letter from Uganda. Sometimes Rachel was quite sure that this was because her parents had cut her off completely; at others, she knew it might well be because the mail was delayed. It happened all too frequently.

It was hard not to succumb to depression, not to fear the worst, even though good things were happening. *With This Ring* was to be published in March, and already seemed to be generating a certain amount of interest. The present book was developing well. Marlene was proving a great success. Tess was healthy, happy, almost walking. Why didn't she, then, feel more at peace with herself?

That was an easy one to answer. Until now she had, in a strange way, taken pleasure in the slow growth of her relationship with Stefan and their dawning dependence on each other. There had seemed no urgency in it. They were loving friends, good companions, and if there were times when a word or gesture had made her suddenly hungry for more, times when she had begged the frail, dark ghost to disappear once and for all, for the most part the relationship had suited her pace as much as his. It was as if she knew a long-sought treat was waiting for her at the end of the road, but recognised that she was not yet ready to savour it. She, too, had been through a period of mourning, after all.

Time, she had felt, was on her side. Sometimes she could swear that he was on the point of losing his icy control, as on New Year's Eve. Sometimes he seemed almost luminous with wanting. Soon, soon—oh, surely soon, the memory of Irina would become bearable and he would be able to love again without fear of faithlessness? She sensed it coming; had even thought, that night when he told her about Anna, that there was an air of excitement about him that signalled the waiting was at an end.

What a poor, deluded fool she had been, imagining her only rival to be a ghost! Anna was beautiful, he had told her—as fair as Irina was dark. He had smiled when he spoke of her.

"She was—*is*, I hope, like quicksilver, all movement and gaiety," he said. "And so talented! She sang like an angel. Back in the old days in Warsaw, she had only to walk into a restaurant for all heads to turn. Irina used to tease her—say that no other woman could be noticed when Anna was there, but they were good friends, with much in common. I hope the war did not touch her too badly."

"I hope so too," Rachel had responded; but she was unable to control an instinctive tremor of unease as she made the required response. Did he realise, she wondered, how his voice had changed and lightened as he spoke of her? How foreign he seemed, suddenly? How full of joy, that this Krasinski family he had known in Warsaw had turned up in London—mother, father, and beautiful blonde daughter?

"I shall see them when I am there next week, of course," he said. "We shall have so much to talk about."

And Rachel had smiled and agreed and wished to die. A ghost was enough to contend with. A live blonde with shared memories was too much.

It was a bitterly cold day towards the end of February that Emma called in for a friendly chat, having battled down the hill in the teeth of wind and icy rain.

"I sometimes think," she said, unwinding a long woollen scarf, "that life is rapidly becoming insupportable. However, I suppose it's marginally less insupportable today than it was yesterday. At least the school is closed and the poor little mites don't have to sit in their coats and hoods attempting to work. All the outside WCs are frozen solid and we've no heating at all. I must say it's blissfully warm in here,'' she finished, subsiding gratefully at the kitchen table.

''It's the only room that is. Coffee?''

''Lovely. Thanks.''

''I have to keep the boiler on because it heats the water, so here is where Tess and I live and move and have our being. Sorry about the festooned laundry. At least Stefan has made me this super pulley thing so I can hoist it all up above our heads.''

''Useful fellow,'' Emma said dryly.

''Mm.'' Rachel was giving nothing away. ''He's in London at the moment, lucky chap.''

She felt a pang of longing as she spoke, not only for Stefan. Even the most ardent fan could not say that St. Bethan was at its best in February; and though she knew quite well that the temperature in London was even lower, still there was something appealing about lights and shops and theatres and libraries.

''Oh?'' Emma looked alertly interested. ''Why?''

In spite of low spirits, Rachel felt amused. Emma was both kind and intelligent, but she was undoubtedly as bad as the rest when it came to gossip. She was utterly well-intentioned, quite without malice, but she did love to *know*—and to pass it on. If Rachel let slip the information that Stefan was seeing a man about plastic boats, it would be all over St. Bethan in no time flat, one more piece of evidence that, say what you will, ''furriners'' were all mad as hatters. Still less could she bring herself to speak of Anna. The village would either pity her, or say it was no more than she deserved, neither of which could she bear.

''Oh, it's just some business,'' she said vaguely. ''He's going to the Embassy. Something to do with his residency. And then he's going to look up some Polish friends.''

She saw Emma's quick probing glance and wondered if her voice had betrayed her feelings.

''When's he coming back?'' Emma asked.

Rachel did her best to shake off her fears.

''He wasn't entirely sure. Sunday, maybe. It depended on his friends.''

''You must miss him. Cheer yourself up by coming to the play on Saturday.''

"Which play?"

"Oh Rachel, I told you—*Pygmalion*! It's another CEMA thing. Why don't you come? There'll be plenty of tickets this weather."

Rachel considered the matter, but declined with thanks. Tess was teething again and had had a few bad nights recently. And the book was so close to being finished now, she really wanted to work flat out. And the weather was so appalling—

"Well, another time," Emma said. "The weather's a killer, I agree. I don't suppose many will turn up at all."

"Now you make me feel guilty!"

"Not at all. Stay and get the book finished. Then you'll be able to kick up your heels a bit."

By seeing *Pygmalion* in a draughty hall? Rachel smiled grimly, but made no comment. Think of the glories of the river, she urged herself; and the coming of spring. Winter wouldn't go on for ever—even this one, which was beginning to seem endless, and which, undoubtedly, was the cause of the feeling of depression that she seemed powerless to dismiss. Even if Stefan chose to stay with Anna, she still had Tess, still had her writing. Her life wouldn't be over. It would just seem like it for a little while. She would recover, bounce back. Oh God, she thought, I am so sick of bouncing back!

When she went to collect her Sunday paper the following morning, she ran into Emma on her way to church. She hadn't missed much, Emma said. The play hadn't seemed quite up to the standard of previous productions. To her mind, the actress who played Eliza had missed the whole essence of the thing and had played her strictly for laughs.

"Not what I would call a very intelligent performance," Emma said. "And the hall was only half full. Oh Lord—it's raining again!"

Rachel dashed home through the icy sleet, pushing the pram before her. Both Marlene and Mrs. Hoskings had flu and had failed to report for duty that week. Perhaps she was going down with it. Maybe that was the reason she felt so dispirited.

She was struck, on her return, by the general awfulness of the cottage. She'd been too busy writing to do household chores, but she couldn't escape them for ever. Dusters would have to be wielded, carpets hoovered. Tess, safe in the large playpen that Stefan had made for her, played with her toys and sang to herself, content for a while to be left to her own devices as Rachel went rather grimly about her work.

Where was Stefan now? He would almost certainly be with the Krasinski family this Sunday morning. Later, they would probably go out for a meal, to some restaurant where all eyes would follow Anna—

"And how do you feel about that, Irina?" she asked, directing her question to the far corner of the sitting-room ceiling. "Would you give him up more easily to your friend Anna?"

Probably not; but he might give himself up. He was better now, on an even keel, not the nervous, hag-ridden man she had first known. Had she been merely an instrument in his recovery, no more important than his work at the boatyard and the peace of St. Bethan? Would he now move up to the next rung in the ladder of his rehabilitation, leaving her behind?

She paused, duster in hand, conscious of rising panic. He wouldn't—surely he wouldn't? She'd been too patient, that was the trouble. Oh, why hadn't she flaunted herself a bit more, played the sex card? She'd wanted to, often enough, but she felt he'd needed time.

And she'd needed time, too. She couldn't deny that. Seeing Barney again had stirred up all kinds of emotions and memories she had thought long dead. They were quite a pair, she and Stefan, when one considered the matter, with enough complexes between them to keep an analyst occupied for years. She resumed polishing the table, forcing down the panic. She was an idiot to worry. Naturally he had been excited about seeing old friends. Who wouldn't be? But still he would come back from London and would rush round to see her, bubbling over with news of all his doings.

"Because he does tell me things," she said to the hovering Irina. "I am important to him. I'd be much better for him than Anna—can't you see that? She's the past. I'm the future."

There, she said to herself as she progressed with her duster to the mantelpiece. Totally mad. That proves it. Imagine talking to a Polish ghost in a Cornish cottage!

She was going stir-crazy, that was the trouble. She'd spent too many days confined to the kitchen. Well, to hell with government directives! She was going to light the fire in the sitting room today whatever They said. There were logs and driftwood in the fuel store and soon she and Stefan could go and beach-comb to get some more. Maybe. Again she fought down panic. Oh, it couldn't all be over, could it?

Tess was getting fed up with the playpen and was demanding more attention. Rachel looked at her watch. A few minutes play, she thought, then lunch, then bed. Then, with any luck, she could count on a couple of hours at the typewriter. She might even finish today—now that would be something to tell Stefan on his return!

The programme proceded as planned; but as she played with Tess, prepared lunch, fed them both, Stefan still dominated her thoughts. Setting all her more personal concerns to one side, this trip of his had enormous implications. He was meeting a boat designer who had shown interest in his radical new ideas, and all depended on Stefan's ability to persuade him that they did, indeed, have possibilities.

And if they did, who knew what would happen? Anna or no Anna, his interlude at Carthew's Boat Yard would be over. A new life would await him somewhere else.

Lost in thought, she held a spoonful of strained beef and carrot just out of Tess's reach, resulting in vociferous complaints which recalled her to her maternal duties with a jolt.

"Sorry, darling," she said humbly, in the face of Tess's blue, accusing stare.

She had just finished mashing a banana for the second course when the doorbell rang. She caught her breath, unable to move for a moment, transfixed by joy. *Stefan!* Who else would it be? It had to be him, come home early after all. Oh, what a fool she'd been ever to doubt him! He'd seen Anna, and still come home to her. Joyfully she rushed to the door.

"Surprise, surprise! Look who's here!"

It wasn't Stefan. For a moment Rachel stared without recognition at the girl with the Veronica Lake hairstyle and the scarlet lips who stood on the step. Slowly her smile died.

"Alannah!" she said faintly.

"In the flesh! Darling, it's pouring with rain, in case you hadn't noticed! Are you going to leave me outside to get soaked through?"

"No, no of course not . . ."

Helplessly Rachel's voice trailed away. Alannah was already inside, looking round the room, exclaiming, admiring.

"What a marvellous room! Such a divine view! Darling, how clever of you to have found it. How *are* you? You look—" she hesitated. "Marvellous," she finished, unconvincingly.

Rachel, clad in the corduroy trousers and thick, baggy sweater that she had almost thrown out the previous winter, swore inwardly. Alannah looked aggressively fashionable in a long, tightwaisted black coat with a little black bowler hat with a veil.

"Alannah, how in the world—" she began, then stopped as she realised the truth. "Of course! You were in the play," she said. "*Pygmalion.* In Truro. My friend saw it last night."

"Really? Darling, why didn't you come too? The place was half empty—pearls before swine simply wasn't in it!"

"But how did you get *here*?" Rachel asked dazedly. "Surely not by bus and ferry—"

"No, no! Oh darling, no, of course not. Someone else in the company was going to stay with his aunt in St. Austell for the night, so he kindly offered to drop me off. Barney got your address from the woman who's living in your house in London."

She was about to continue, but Tess forstalled her. She, it seemed, had decided that enough was enough, and that now was the time to complain bitterly at her mother's desertion.

The roars of rage caused Alannah's pencil-thin brows to shoot upwards.

"What on earth—"

"That's Tess," Rachel said. "Excuse me."

She went through to the kitchen where Tess, in her high chair, had succeeded in smearing herself and much of her surroundings with mashed banana. Alannah, framed in the doorway, dainty and detached, surveyed the scene with ill-concealed horror.

"My God, what's this?" she asked. "Are you in the baby-farming business?"

"Tess is mine. And no," she went on, anticipating the next question. "I'm not married."

Rachel didn't look to see the result of her announcement, but lifted Tess from the chair and set about wiping her hands and face. "She's due for a sleep," she said. "If you'd like to go in and sit by the fire, I'll get her settled. Do take your hat and coat off,'' she added politely, as Alannah continued to stare at her, apparently bereft of words.

With Tess tucked up in her cot, she returned downstairs to find that Alannah had accepted the invitation to take off her outer garments and was looking at herself in the mirror over the fireplace with every evidence of satisfaction. She turned as Rachel came into the room, her expression changing to one of compassion. With arms outstretched she moved gracefully towards her and embraced her closely.

"Oh, you poor darling, I'm so terribly sorry," she said, her voice throbbing with sincerity. "I had no idea! How absolutely frightful for you! How on earth do you cope? Now listen to me!" She took hold of Rachel's shoulders and gazed earnestly into her eyes. "I want you to know that it won't make the slightest bit of difference."

"Difference to what?" Rachel asked.

"Why, to *us*, of course. To being friends!"

Rachel stared at her for a moment with dawning amusement.

"That's a great relief."

"I mean, what are friends for?"

"You tell me," Rachel said. "Would you like some coffee? Have you had lunch?"

She went into the kitchen and Alannah drifted after her hovering in the doorway once more.

"We stopped at an hotel on the way. Darling, it is all right if I stay the night, isn't it? I mean, you can give me a doss-down somewhere? I've brought my jim-jams and my toothbrush in my little bag. You see Terry—that's the man who gave me the lift—he's staying the night at his aunt's house and can't pick me up until tomorrow."

Rachel, setting out cups and saucers and teaspoons, froze for a moment before continuing the task.

"I see," she said.

"Darling, you should see the ghastly little guesthouse where they've put us in Truro! I absolutely jumped at the chance of getting away. I would have phoned, but Barney didn't get the number and you're not in the book."

"It's under 'Courtney.' The cottage belongs to my Aunt Sylvia."

"Oh, I see. That explains it. I wondered why you'd come to such a godforsaken neck of the woods."

"I like it," Rachel said, forgetting the nostalgic dreams of urban delights that had taunted her recently. "This is ready now. I'll bring it through."

"It smells wonderful, darling."

"What's all this 'darling' business?" Rachel asked with some amusement as they settled themselves in front of the fire.

"Oh, everyone's 'darling' in the theatre."

"So it's all going well, is it?"

"Oh yes, I adore it! Of course, this CEMA business isn't exactly the West End, but it's wonderful experience. I'm sure it will lead to something."

"I hope so." Rachel poured the coffee and handed a cup to Alannah. "What part are you playing?"

"In *Pygmalion*? Eliza, of course. In Falmouth we're doing *The Devil's Disciple*. I'm Judith in that. Eliza is more fun. You should have come to see us."

"Well, it's a bit awkward—"

"Oh, yes." Alannah gave a small, embarrassed laugh. "I suppose it must be."

"Well," Rachel said after a short silence. "Tell all! How's everyone?"

"Tell all! I like that! You're the one with things to tell." Putting the cup down on a table by her chair, Alannah leaned forward. "You know, darling, you can confide in me. Why didn't Barney tell me about this baby of yours?"

"Barney didn't know anything to tell."

"But he came to your house—"

"He didn't see her."

"And you didn't say a word! You always were a secretive little thing. Who's the father?"

"No one of any importance."

"Oh, poor Rachel. I really am sorry!"

"So you've said before. You needn't be, honestly."

"But it's every girl's nightmare, isn't it, getting caught like that, finding yourself pregnant? Why on earth didn't you have it adopted?"

Rachel looked at her without answering, a faint smile on her face. I could have written the script, she thought.

"Believe it or not, I wanted to keep her," she said.

"I suppose you were madly in love with the father?"

"Not in the slightest. But I still wanted her. I wanted someone to love, someone that was a part of me." She got up and put more wood on the fire. "Maybe that was selfish," she said as she came back to her chair. "I don't know. I just know that I couldn't give her up."

Alannah still gazed at her, frowning. She shook her head as if she found the whole thing totally incomprehensible.

"What a dreadful tragedy," she said. "I mean—" She shrugged her shoulders. "You can't get away from the fact, darling. You've ruined your life." She shook her head sadly as she turned to pick up her cup. "And it absolutely knocks Ma's little plan on the head," she added, incomprehensibly.

Rachel frowned. "And what little plan might your mother be hatching?" she asked.

Alannah gave her embarrassed laugh again.

"Oh, it was nothing, honestly," she said. "It was just that— well, Ma's worried, and she thought you might help. Not that it's at all possible now."

"Oh?" Rachel's voice was cold.

"Well—" Alannah laughed awkwardly. "It's Barney, you see. We're worried about him. I mean, *really* worried!"

"Why?"

Alannah chewed her lip in indecision.

"It's sort of telling tales out of school," she said at last, "but you are almost family, aren't you?"

"Not that I'm aware," Rachel said.

"Oh, you know what I mean!"

"What's wrong with Barney?"

"Well—" still Alannah hesitated, then took the plunge. "He's been sort of odd since he left the Army. Unsettled. Disorientated. Didn't you think so, when you saw him?"

Rachel considered the matter.

"I thought he seemed—nervous," she said. "Did he go into the antiques business? He was talking about it when I saw him and seemed enthusiastic—"

"God, no! Ma managed to talk him out of that. I mean, imagine going into business with Guy Seamark! He's a frightful drip. Do you remember how he used to moon over Di? And then he

married a common little creature you'd expect to find serving
in Woolworths!''

"But he knows his antiques, Barney said.''

"It would have been an awful risk. The parents advised
against it, quite rightly in my view, so Barney took a job in a
shipping firm. An awfully good job, actually, but he never really
settled in it. It only lasted a couple of months and then he
handed in his notice. Then he tried being an estate agent, but
that was even worse. *Then* he put every penny he possessed into
some doubtful property deal with Reggie Baker. Remember
him? Daphne Baker's brother? We thought the Bakers were all
right, but they weren't at all and poor Barney lost all his savings,
such as they were. Now he doesn't seem to know what to do.
He's—well, we're kind of worried that he's drinking too much.
He's got in with a really fast set.''

"That doesn't sound like Barney,'' Rachel said, astonished.

"It doesn't, does it? Reggie was such a bad influence. Ma
blames him for everything.''

You don't say? Rachel thought, but manfully contrived to
leave the words unspoken.

"Where am I supposed to come in?'' she asked instead, totally bewildered.

"Well, we thought you might help,'' Alannah said. "But of
course, that's out of the question now. The baby's rather put
you out of court.''

Rachel put a hand to her head and closed her eyes.

"Forgive me,'' she said, "but I seem to be missing some
vital piece of the argument here. What the hell has Tess got to
do with anything?''

"Oh Rachel, don't pretend you don't know! I'm talking about
you and Barney. You know perfectly well he's always been in
love with you.''

"Well, maybe once, when we were very young, but not now.
Not since—since Gavin.''

There. She'd spoken the name. Alannah remained unmoved.

"You're wrong. He told Ma he was in love with you. He
said he always had been and that there'd never be anyone else.
He'd tried going out with other girls—God, Daphne Baker never
leaves him alone!—but it's no good. It's you he wants.''

"Really,'' Rachel said, without expression.

"He said that it wasn't any good, that you wouldn't look at him after what had happened with Gavin, and that anyway you were all fired up about your writing career."

"Go on," said Rachel.

"Well, that's it, really. I wasn't there myself, but apparently he managed to convince Ma that you were the only girl he'd ever wanted. We talked it over just before I came on this West Country trip. She feels that in spite of everything, you're the only person who can straighten him out, so she suggested that I should come and invite you back. For Barney's sake."

Rachel stared at her.

"Does he know about this suggestion?"

"He knew I intended to see you. I had to get your address from him. But for the rest—well, Ma said we'd better leave that until I'd sounded you out."

Still Rachel stared at her, shaking her head in disbelief.

"I just don't believe I'm hearing this!" she said. "Your mother is actually asking me back—"

"Well, I don't suppose she'd be so keen on it now," Alannah said. The look on Rachel's face seemed to disconcert her and she seemed to be floundering. "Surely you understand? Having the baby alters everything."

"Why?" Rachel asked coldly after a moment.

"Why? How can you ask that? Surely you must see that you've totally ruined any chance you might have of marriage and a normal sort of life? What man wants to take on somebody else's child?"

"Widows marry," Rachel pointed out.

"*Illegitimate* child, I meant. It's different. It's such a disgrace. I don't know how you can look the world in the face! My God, I'd want to shoot myself! Not that I'd have to. My mother would do it for me. As for Daddy—well, he'd go after the man with a horsewhip."

Rachel's mouth was twisted in a small tight smile.

"Nonsense! Your father would wash his hands of the matter and your mother would assume it was an immaculate conception and apply to have you beatified. Your mother cannot admit that any of you are to blame for anything."

Alannah's pale face grew pink.

"If you're talking about Gavin—"

"And Diana," Rachel pointed out. "Gavin and Diana. Yes, I suppose that's what I'm talking about." Until that moment she had held herself in check, forced herself to see the funny side; said to herself that really, only a Rossiter could possibly behave in this way. Now the bitterness flooded over.

"Leave Tess out of it for the moment," she said. "How your mother has the—the *gall* to send you here with this kind of half-baked proposal, I really can't imagine." She was aware that her voice was trembling. "Can either of you believe that I want anything more to do with any of you after what happened? Did I have one word of sympathy from her when I was in the very depths of despair? Like hell! It was all my fault for making mountains out of molehills!"

"Well, if you're going to rake up the past—"

"Did you come anywhere near me? Not a bit of it! If ever there was a fair-weather friend—"

"I was busy. I'd just been called up into ENSA."

"Rubbish! You could have written. Phoned. *Anything!*"

"I'm going!" Alannah jumped to her feet. "I came here with the best of intentions. You're still bitter about Gavin, that's the truth of it. I'm right, aren't I? You've never got over him."

"Oh yes, I have, Lannie. Believe me. It took me a long time, admittedly, and I made a number of mistakes along the way, but I'm over him now. I don't go for weak men any more. That's why, Tess or no Tess, Barney is not for me. I like him. I wish him well. But no power on earth would make me get involved with a Rossiter, ever again."

"There's no need to be so offensive." Alannah was shaking with rage as she made a grab for her coat. "I wouldn't dream of staying here now."

Without moving, Rachel watched her as she pulled on the coat and began to do up the many buttons that ran from neck to hem. Outside the winter afternoon was darkening and the rain lashed against the window.

Rachel felt the anger drain out of her. Alannah couldn't help being a fool, she thought. Emma was right when she had said that she was unintelligent. Add insensitive and overweeningly self-satisfied and you got somewhere near describing her.

And yet—how potent the past was, after all! Could one ever totally dismiss it? Pretend there had never been affection, or warmth or goodwill or shared laughter? She sighed.

"Where are you going, Lannie?" she said.

"I've no idea! I'll get back to Truro somehow."

"I don't think the ferry will run in this weather."

"Then I'll have to go by road. Call me a taxi."

"You're a taxi."

It was an old Rossiter joke, never very funny, but now it stopped them both in their tracks. For a while they stared at each other then, gently, almost wearily, Rachel laughed, shaking her head.

"Maybe you ought to go outside and we'll start all over again," she said.

ᔦ SEVENTEEN ᔧ

What else could she have done, in view of the appalling weather? It was only for one night, Rachel said to herself as as she went upstairs to get Tess, now awake after her short sleep. Just one night. That was all. It wouldn't really hurt, would it? There was no reason, really, for this feeling in the pit of the stomach that no good would come of it. After all, Alannah had clearly demonstrated her total lack of interest in Tess as a person. Babies were outside her experience—nasty, dirty things to be disregarded whenever possible.

However, the banana-smeared Tess who was borne off so unceremoniously to her cot after lunch bore little resemblance to the clean, brushed, golden-curled infant who was brought down again clad in a pink woollen dress lovingly knitted by Mrs. Hoskings.

"She's really rather cute," Alannah said with some surprise, watching Tess's efforts to haul herself upright by holding on to the arm of a chair. "Poor child! I hope she won't suffer too much."

"Because of me?" Rachel raised her eyebrows in polite enquiry.

"Well, of course because of you! There's bound to be a stigma."

How unfailingly did Alannah go for the jugular, Rachel thought, the familiar feeling of inadequacy creeping over her like frostbite.

"I shall do what I can to guard against it, of course," she said stiffly.

"One would have thought you might have considered it at the time."

"I did," Rachel said, her jaw clenched.

Alannah, supremely unaware of any offence, leaned towards Tess and waggled a long manicured finger, scarlet-tipped.

"Who's a little cutesy-wutesy, then? Come and see your auntie," she cooed; adding, in Rachel's direction and in a totally different voice as Tess gazed at her in smiling indifference, "With those eyes, she could almost be a Rossiter, couldn't she?"

"There are other blue-eyed men in the world, you know."

"I realise that! It's interesting, isn't it, how some women always fall for the same physical type?" Alannah abandoned her efforts to woo the unresponsive Tess who was enthusiastically rooting in a box of toys, and instead reached out towards Rachel and squeezed her arm. "Poor Rachel!" she said. "Honestly, I can't tell you how sorry I am that everything turned out this way. You must believe me."

Tess had managed to totter the few steps necessary to bring her mother the pink rabbit. Rachel swept her up in her arms and buried her face for a moment in her daughter's soft, sweet-smelling curls.

"It's turned out a lot better than anyone expected," she said. "Including me. But what about you, Lannie? Is there a man in your life?"

Alannah sat back and sighed, her compassionate expression giving way to one of acute misery.

"Oh, Rachel, it's so awfully complicated," she said. "Terry—that's the man who gave me the lift—he absolutely adores me. Idolises me, one could say. He begged me to go to St. Austell with him, but I said no, I had to come and see my old friend. After all, friendship is friendship when all is said and done, and of course there was the matter of you and Barney—" She halted at the sight of Rachel's warning expression. "All *right*," she said defensively. "I won't go into that any more, I promise."

"What about you?" Rachel asked, putting Tess down on the carpet and building a tower of large, soft bricks so that they could be knocked down and built again. "Do you idolise him in equal measure?"

Alannah's face twisted with the agony of it all.

"That's what I keep asking myself, darling," she said. "I mean, he's frightfully handsome in a *louche* sort of way and the women in the audience go simply wild about him, but I don't think he'd go down at all well with the family. He's just the sort of man that Ma loathes."

"What sort is that?" Rachel asked politely.

"Oh—" Alannah shrugged. "You know. He's a bit of a non-conformist. He hardly ever wears a tie, and he *will* wear a suit jacket with corduroy trousers. And he always insists on bringing a huge tankard of beer to the table because he hates wine. And, to be honest, he does swear rather a lot. And smoke," she added. "Ma's really turned against smoking. Honestly, Rachel, how could I ever take him home?"

"I do see the problem." Rachel bent to build up the brick tower again, hiding her smile. "On the other hand, your mother was never exactly conventional when it came to dress—"

"She has her standards. This aunt he's gone to see in St. Austell—you'll never believe it, but she used to be in a circus, on the high wire. Can you imagine?"

"They sound a colourful family."

"But just imagine allying oneself—oh, stop it, Rachel! It's not funny."

"I know," Rachel said penitently. "I do understand how you feel—but it does seem to me that if it weighs so heavily, it must mean you don't really love him."

"Oh but darling, I do!" Alannah wailed. "At least, some-times I think I do. But then at others—you see, I couldn't ever marry anyone who didn't fit in, could I? Not like Di."

"I thought Diana had made a brilliant marriage."

"Well—" Alannah made a dismissive kind of gesture. "At least Tom is a gentleman and went to public school and all that. Terry is, well, different. Wonderful in many, many ways—all credit to him for making something of himself—but I just can't imagine him at Kimberley Lodge. The family *matters* so much to me," she went on earnestly. "To all of us, really. I do realise it's hard for you to understand, because the relationship between you and your parents is so very different—"

"So you've always been at pains to remind me," Rachel said,

an acid note creeping back into her voice. "Time for tea, I think, don't you?"

She picked Tess up and took her through to the kitchen, putting her in the high chair. She tied a bib around her neck and swathed her lower half in a Harrington square before giving her a biscuit.

Alannah, who had followed her and now stood in the doorway once more, watched this ritual with fascination tinged with horror.

"Heavens, it's awfully *constant*, isn't it, darling?" she remarked. "I don't know how you cope."

"One learns," Rachel said.

"I'm not sure that I want to. Di doesn't."

"What about her husband?"

"Oh, he wants kids of course. It would be a different story if he had to have them."

"Do you really not like him?"

"Well, we all thought he was marvellous at first, but he's changed. He's frightfully selfish. He insisted on spending Christmas with his family in some godforsaken part of Yorkshire and we didn't see Di at all."

"But don't Diana and—what's his name? Tom?—live locally? You must see a lot of them all the year. Maybe he thought—"

"We know perfectly well what he thought! He told Ma in no uncertain terms and now he doesn't let Di come round at all."

Rachel looked astonished. "I find that hard to believe, knowing Diana."

"Well, she hasn't been home for ages, Ma says. She'd never stay away off her own bat, so it has to be Tom's fault. I'm sure she's utterly miserable."

"She needed someone strong," Rachel said. "It sounds as if she's got it."

"Ma's frightfully upset."

"I can imagine." How upset? Rachel wondered as the kettle shrilled and she went to lift it off the stove. Red-eyed, streaming-haired upset? Writing-of-vitriolic-letter upset? It seemed very likely. Her heart went out to Tom.

Alannah was silent. Rachel filled the teapot, and turning with it in her hand, saw she was contemplating Tess once more, frowning slightly.

"It really is an extraordinary thing," she said. "It's just struck me—Tess looks exactly like Di in that photograph on the little table in the corner of the dining room. You remember it, surely—the one where she and Gavin are sitting together in a big wicker chair. She's holding a teddy bear."

Rachel's hesitation was almost imperceptible.

"I vaguely remember it, now you've reminded me," she said.

"She was about two, I think," Alannah went on.

"Why don't you take the tray through and see if the fire needs another log?" Rachel said, ignoring the matter of the photograph. "I'll just give Tess her juice and be with you in two shakes."

She continued to ignore it when she joined Alannah, resolutely talking of sleeping arrangements.

"I'll put my sheets on the bed in Tess's room, and put clean sheets on my bed for you," she said.

"That's sweet of you, darling," Alannah said; and, to Rachel's relief, appeared to forget Tess's appearance, preferring instead to enlarge on her brother-in-law's shortcomings.

She continued to regard Rachel's efforts to entertain Tess with a wary and astonished eye. Prolonged discussion of any topic was difficult, even impossible, which did not prevent Alannah expatiating at length on the problem of Terry, various rivalries in the Company, and the tedium of having to play Shaw all the time—why not a Restoration comedy, for goodness sake? Or even a modern farce? She adored playing farce. Rachel would hardly believe, she said, how people who had seen her in farce during the war had come up to her in High Streets all over the country to thank her for making life bearable during the dark days of the war. "Miss Ross," they said, "we don't know how we could have carried on without you."

"So really Churchill—indeed, the entire country—has much to thank you for," Rachel commented.

"Well, in all modesty, I think you could be right," Alannah said. "I do wish you could have seen me in *Rookery Nook*, Rachel. I really brought the house down—and you know what they say! Laughter is the best medicine."

"Perhaps," Rachel ventured innocently, "too good a medicine for unmarried mothers?" Alannah pondered the question for a few seconds before smiling thinly.

"I suppose that's meant to be funny," she said.

"Only mildly," Rachel assured her.

"I hope you won't get bitter, Rachel. That would be the worst thing in the world for little Tess."

"I'll bear that in mind," Rachel said gravely.

Inevitably Alannah returned to the problem of Terry; should she or shouldn't she take the plunge and invite him to Kimberley Lodge? Rachel did her utmost to show interest while continuing to build more towers, point out pictures in a book which involved the singing of a number of nursery rhymes, tuck up a fluffy dog in a cot which Tess rocked happily for at least three minutes before climbing on to her mother's lap and demanding a see-saw.

"Don't despair," Rachel said with genuine sympathy, appreciating how tedious her divided attention must be as Alannah looked at her watch for the umpteenth time. "It'll soon be time for bath and bed."

"Is it always like this?" Alannah asked.

Rachel laughed.

"This is a good day! Now admit it—she hasn't grizzled once."

"I'd hate to be here on a bad one, darling," Alannah said.

Inevitably, bedtime eventually came and silence fell on the house. Rachel came downstairs, conscious, as she cleared away the toys that still littered the floor, that Alannah had moved to the mantelpiece again and was now studying a photograph of Tess, taken by Stefan.

"You know, it is remarkable," she said. "She really is the image of Di."

"You're imagining things," Rachel said briskly. "I've fixed the beds. If you need another blanket, there's one in the cupboard, but I think you should be all right. Now, would you care for a drink? I can offer you a glass of white wine. There's nothing else, I'm afraid."

"I'd love some wine," Alannah said. "We have rather earned it, haven't we?"

Rachel was aware, as she poured the drinks, that she was the subject of a long and speculative glance, but she made no acknowledgement of it.

"There you are," she said, handing Alannah a glass. "An unobtrusive, shy little wine with an understated bouquet."

"Cheers," Alannah said absently. She sat down on one of the chintz armchairs and took a sip, her eyes still fixed on Rachel.

"Do you like liver and bacon?" Rachel asked. "I've got enough for two. Or there's eggs and cheese, if you'd rather—"

"Rachel," Alannah said abruptly. "Are you being straight with me? *Is* Tess a Rossiter?"

Rachel gave an exasperated laugh.

"Honestly, Lannie, you're paranoid!" she said. "Just because she's got blue eyes!"

"But it's such an unusual sort of blue. And it's not just that." Putting her drink down, she got up and took the picture off the mantelpiece. "Look at this. See the chin? It's exactly like that photograph of Di!"

"I thought all babies were supposed to look like Winston Churchill," Rachel said lightly. "Maybe they come in two varieties: those who look like Winston Churchill and those who look like Diana Rossiter."

"You're being absurd!"

"No, Alannah. It's you who are being absurd. Just a little bit of elementary arithmetic will tell you that what you're thinking is impossible. Tess is thirteen months old."

"I can't work that out." Alannah sounded cross, as if it were an outrage to imagine that she could.

"Well, add nine to thirteen," Rachel said, with exaggerated patience. "That makes twenty-two. Now count back twenty-two months, and you'll have a rough idea when she was conceived."

"That's no proof of anything. Some babies are premature, some are late. Or so I'm led to believe."

"Not that premature or that late."

"If Ma knew that Gavin had had a child—"

"Stop it, Alannah! I swear I never saw Gavin after the summer of 1940. I couldn't have borne to. Look, I don't want to talk about this."

"Barney, then." Alannah had returned to her chair and lifted her glass to take a sip, but now lowered it to regard Rachel suspiciously over the top. "*Was* it Barney?"

"How could it have been? Barney was in the Middle East."

"He came home early in 1946."

"A year ago!" Rachel's voice was taut with anger. "I've already told you Tess was born in January, 1946. She was conceived—not that it's any business of yours—on VE day, which was the 8th May, 1945. I came up to town with a friend and we joined in the celebrations—a little too enthusiastically, you might think. We'd all drunk far too much, and I'd had practically nothing to eat all day. It was sordid and horrible and I couldn't be more ashamed—but, miraculously, Tess was the result. Okay? Satisfied? Inquisition over? Now I'm going to see about supper. In the absence of any other directives, I propose to cook liver and bacon."

She was upset, and didn't care if she showed it. She had a right to be, she told herself, venting her anger on the potatoes she was peeling at the sink. She should have let Alannah walk out into the wind and the rain when she threatened to. Who but she would go on and on like that? And why the hell couldn't she try to be helpful for a change? She hadn't lifted a finger to help pick the toys up, or offered to peel the spuds or set the table or *anything*!

"Rachel—" Alannah had followed her out to the kitchen. "I didn't mean to make you cross, honestly. Goodness, you are a prickly sort of person these days."

Rachel said nothing, but threw a peeled potato in a pot of water with unnecessary force before picking up the next one.

"Look, I'm sorry," Alannah said. "It was just that—well, it seemed so strange, that's all. You can't blame me for being curious, can you?"

"It's none of your business," Rachel said tightly.

"No—no, I see that now. Honestly. I am sorry, Rachel. Don't go on being cross, *please*!"

Rachel sighed and leant an elbow on the draining board for a moment, a half-peeled potato in her hand.

"You're impossible, Lannie, d'you know that?" she asked, in a voice that had more or less returned to normal. "You've always been impossible! You don't give a damn about other people, do you? You just ride roughshod over everyone."

"I've said I'm sorry," Alannah said.

"So you have." This, in itself, was something of an achievement, Rachel thought as she continued peeling the potato. In fact, now she considered the matter, she couldn't ever remember such a thing happening before. She glanced round at Alannah, rather expecting her to look offended, but instead was surprised by the expression of unhappiness which she could see on her face.

"Forget it, Lannie," she said, more gently than might have been expected only a few moments before. "Just keep off the grass, that's all. It really is none of your business."

"I know. Sorry."

Rachel continued to peel in silence for a few moments. Why wasn't Alannah happy? Terry, perhaps. And, reading between the lines, it seemed that she wasn't making a spectacular success of her role in this particular play. And then there was Diana's defection, and Barney's problems. It could be any or all of those things.

Or perhaps none. Perhaps it was nothing but her imagination. Briskly, she finished with the potatoes and turned her attention to a cauliflower.

"You'll never guess what I found the other day," she said. "There's a trunk of old books and papers dating from schooldays upstairs. I never unpacked it properly, but I was looking for a book of essays I thought might be there, and what should I find lurking at the bottom but *Hurrah for Dymphna*."

Dissension and apologies alike were forgotten as Alannah clasped her hands and shrieked with joy.

"I don't believe it!"

"I'll rake it out after we've eaten. I couldn't resist reading it right through, and d'you know, some of it isn't bad at all. I laughed like anything at that Prizegiving chapter where Miss Whetton-Wyndham gets caught up in the mayoral chain and has to be cut loose by the evil handyman with his hacksaw."

"Oh, I remember it! And what about the fathers' race incident on Sports Day—"

"And the time when Ethel Craddock won the cross-country by hiding behind a cowshed and popping out just yards from the finishing line!"

"And that dreadful head girl's little homily when she discovered the itching powder in her knicker-linings. What was her name? Helen something, wasn't it? Helena, that was it.'' Alannah adopted a solemn and self-righteous tone. '' 'Now remember, girls, never *ever* in the knickers!' Oh, we did laugh, didn't we?'' Equanimity restored, Alannah leaned against the doorjamb and laughed again. ''And now you're a proper writer, just like you said you'd be.''

''You didn't think I could do it,'' Rachel said dryly.

''Oh, I did! Really, I did. You were going to write and I was going to act.''

''And Barney was going to paint. Remember that picture he gave me? That's in the trunk too.''

She hadn't laughed when she'd seen that, Rachel remembered. It had made her sad, reminding her as it did of lost innocence, and a time when Kimberley Lodge seemed a wonderful place full of wonderful people.

''Oh, I'm so awfully glad I came,'' Alannah said. ''We did have some good times, didn't we?''

And some bad, Rachel reflected; but we won't talk about them. She was surprised to find herself feeling a little sorry for Alannah, conscious that somehow the pendulum had swung for the first time, putting her in the ascendancy. Why hadn't she registered before, she wondered, how really *dim* Alannah was beneath all her surface self-assurance? But at least she'd proved a distraction from dark thoughts about Stefan, which could only be a good thing.

The level of the wine bottle went down as they ate their supper and reminisced. Recklessly Rachel stoked the fire up. They could hear the wind whistling around the house. It sent gusts of smoke down the chimney and caused the rain to batter against the windowpane. It was a night when it was good to be indoors.

The phone shrilled, startling them both.

''Rachel?'' It was Stefan. Suddenly it was hard to breathe and her heart was pounding. She angled herself away from Alannah so that her expression would give nothing away.

''Stefan? How are you?''

''Missing you.'' Who could imagine that two simple words could give such joy?

''Me, too,'' she said. She would have said more if she had

been alone. "I have a friend staying tonight," she added, to explain her guarded response.

"That is good. Rachel—" his voice strengthened, full of excitement. "I have such wonderful news. Wonderful! Everything has gone well."

"With Marine Engineering?"

"Of course. What else?"

What else? Didn't he know? Couldn't he imagine? She hadn't invented Anna, had she?

"That's marvellous, Stefan. Congratulations. And what—what about your friends? Have you seen them?"

"Oh, yes. We have meal together last night. It was good to meet with them again and talk of old times. It was—I think, cathartic is word, yes?"

"It could be."

"Seeing them again made me understand, somehow, how far I have come. You understand me?"

"Yes, yes." Oh, how she hoped she did!

"I am so glad I made effort to see them, for soon they go to Canada. They are so excited! New job, new life—"

"You didn't wish you were going too?"

For a moment he was silent, and when he spoke again he sounded puzzled.

"You cannot think that! You must know that all I care for now is here, in England. Rachel—?" He sounded anxious as she made no reply. "Rachel, you are there?"

"Yes," she said softly. "Yes, I'm here."

"We talk tomorrow. I shall be home then. Maybe not until evening, but as early as possible. I come to see you then, yes?"

"Yes," Rachel said, forgetting to be guarded. "Oh, yes, Stefan. Come as soon as you can."

"I have so much to say, so much to ask you." He seemed to catch his breath a little and his voice quickened, became urgent. "Oh, Rachel! So much I want to say that is too important for telephone."

"Then, tomorrow," she said, and did not care that her voice betrayed her feelings. Home, he had said. He was coming home.

"Who was that?" Alannah asked curiously as Rachel retook her seat. "And why are you grinning like a Cheshire cat?" She didn't wait for a reply. "I was telling you about Terry," she went on. "You see, darling, the problem is—"

On and on she talked—what Ma might say, what Daddy might think. Rachel put on a listening expression and thought of Stefan.

Tomorrow. He would be here tomorrow. Oh, she wanted him so; wanted him, mind and body—all of him, all of her, for ever and ever. Was it possible?

Yes, she thought. It was possible. It was more than possible. There was, it seemed, a future for him in this strange business of molded resin boats, something for him to offer a woman. He was the kind of man who would need that.

As for Anna—it seemed she was no threat. Perhaps she never had been. Please, please Lannie, stop talking, she thought, hiding a yawn. She longed to go to bed, longed for tomorrow to come quickly, longed for the waiting to be over, to be done with all pretence of patience.

"What happened to your friend Alice?" Alannah asked, just when Rachel thought she was winding down.

"She worked at the Ministry of Information all through the war, and married Keith in—oh, the summer of 1943, it must have been. You met him," Rachel went on, suddenly remembering. "That night—you remember it, Lannie—that night you bunked off college and came up to town looking for a job with ENSA."

"And we sat outside and talked about the Home Guard. Yes, I remember! He was in the Navy. Rather smashing, as I recall. Well, lucky old Alice! Who'd have thought she had it in her."

"They're living in Edinburgh now. Keith's gone back to University. They're supposed to be coming down here at Easter."

"There was a funny old man there that night—remember him? He wanted to falsify his age so that he could join the Home Guard and drill with broom handles."

"He was killed. His house got a direct hit."

"Oh Lord, how frightful! Was there much damage in that part of London?"

"A fair bit. The church at the corner has gone, and that block of flats in the next road. And remember that terrace of shops just before you turn into Shawcross Street? They were hit by a V2 and totally flattened. God, how I hated those things! They were so silent and so deadly. Much worse than the bombs.''

"But the house itself escaped, did it? Yes, of course it did!'' Alannah gave her knee a small, annoyed slap. "How could I have forgotten? Daddy lived there right at the end of the war, just for a week or so. Wasn't that a fantastic coincidence? He had a friend who worked with Alice's aunt. What was her name? Groves? Graves? *Greaves*, that was it! It's all coming back to me now. Dad had to move out of his flat because of a fire— nothing to do with the doodlebugs, it was after they'd finished. He was about to leave the Army anyway. Well, his friend asked Miss Greaves if Dad could have a room there until his demob, and she said yes.''

"She was always kind," Rachel murmured vaguely; and saying something about putting the kettle on for hot-water bottles, she got to her feet and went to the kitchen.

She filled the kettle and put it on the stove and went to the cupboard where two hot-water bottles dangled by a string from a hook on the inside of the door.

"There's a metal one, if you'd like an extra," she called to Alannah, raising her voice so that it would reach the sitting room. "I can't abide it, myself. It's a vicious thing that burns you as soon as look at you, but you're more than welcome. It's certainly cold enough. I do hope the weather's better tomorrow. It's such a nuisance when we're confined to the house all day. Tell me, what time is Terry coming for you?''

There came no reply from the living room. Rachel stood still for a moment or two, listening to the silence, her imagination running riot. What was Alannah doing? Sitting staring into space? Adding up, speculating, remembering? She went to the door of the kitchen to see for herself and slowly let out a long, relieved breath.

She had taken up *Hurrah for Dymphna* once more, and was leafing through it. Conscious of Rachel's presence, she looked up, smiling.

"D'you remember Daddy laughing at this?" she said. "He was lying in a deckchair in his panama hat, and we sat on the grass and read to him, and he laughed and laughed. I can see him now, can't you?''

The kettle shrilled, and swiftly Rachel went to deal with it, saying nothing.

⧼ EIGHTEEN ⧽

Rachel had felt it an answer to prayer when she'd got back from her abortive trip to London with Dave to find that she was to be sent to Morecombe on a course to update her skills. Dave, not surprisingly, was avoiding her, but it was impossible not to bump into him sometimes and the sight of him made her feel embarrassed and ashamed.

"You used him as a plaything," said Penny, to whom she had confided everything. "You toyed with his emotions." At which they both collapsed in giggles, which made her feel a great deal better. Dave would get over it; and at least, she thought, it redressed the balance a little. When it came to toying with emotions, Air Crew were past masters.

While she was in Morecombe, her grandfather died. It was not entirely unexpected as he had been ill for several months, but she wept for him, remembering the many times when only his affectionate kindnesses had made life at The Laurels worth living.

No leave could be granted, she was told, while the course was in progress, and she had been unable to get away to the funeral, a dereliction of duty which her grandmother never wholly forgave. Even so, Rachel went to Warnfield from time to time out of a sense of duty, always afraid that she would encounter one or other of the Rossiters. She never did.

"Mr. Rossiter—*Captain* Rossiter, I suppose I should say—is in London," Grandma said on an early visit, in tones of great scorn. "What he imagines he is doing to help the war effort I cannot imagine, sitting behind his desk in the War Office. And Alannah, they say, is entertaining the troops. I ask you!"

"She's only acting in plays, Grandma," Rachel felt it fair t point out.

"That's as may be. Mrs. Rossiter, of course, is floating abou the place in some uniform or other, too. WVS, I think, whateve that might mean. Something to do with canteens, I believe. never see her."

"Have you—have you heard anything about Gavin?" Rache asked at last, with great diffidence.

"Not a word. Still in the land of the living as far as I'n aware. You're not still hankering—?"

"No, no, of course not."

"I should hope not, indeed!"

The fact of his continued existence was as much as Rache ever heard about him—but this, she told herself, was all sh wanted to know. The childish obsession was over. She ha grown up, moved on. And moved on from ridiculous experi ments like Dave, too. One day there would be someone. For th moment, she'd wait.

She'd been posted to Scotland after the course, to a bleak remote airfield scoured by winds blowing direct from the Pola cap—a period which she had enjoyed nevertheless, entirely du to the congenial company she found there. She found hersel writing plays and skits, making people laugh, relishing the ap plause. She gained a certain amount of fame, as opposed to th notoriety she had attracted at Bothley. With the CO's encour agement she applied for a commission, but later had second thoughts and withdrew the application. She was happy as sh was, she said.

Her grandmother died suddenly at the beginning of 1945 This time Rachel went to the funeral and was surprised at the regret she felt for an era ending, as well as for a life that had known little joy. If ever it could be said of anyone that she was her own worst enemy then Grandma was the one.

This, she thought as she stood in the bitter wind by her grand mother's grave, was really the end. No more Rossiters, and no more Warnfield, ever again.

Her grandmother's will decreed that her estate was to be di vided between her two children, Ivor and Sylvia, but a small legacy had been left to Rachel, which both surprised and touched her. It was no fortune, but at least she had the means now to buy somewhere to live after the war. After the war! The phrase seemed to conjure up some sunlit, verdant dream world full of smiling men and women at peace with each other and themselves. Victory had been an impossibly distant goal for so long, it was hard to imagine it achieved and accepted.

Sylvia didn't come to her mother's funeral. She had flu, she told Rachel on the phone; was absolutely knocked out by it, quite incapable of travelling so far, but proposed writing to Mrs. Rossiter to ask her to keep various items from The Laurels until she felt able to collect them.

"I don't suppose she'd mind doing that for me, would she?" Sylvia said. "Bearing in mind all the years she and mother were neighbours. Do give her my best wishes when you see her."

"I doubt that I will," Rachel said; and indeed, there were no Rossiter representatives at the funeral.

She travelled back to Scotland, only to find that she had been promoted to sergeant and posted to West Greely in Berkshire.

"The Transport Section!" she said disgustedly to Nancy, the girl who had become her closest friend. "What do I know about bloody transport? I've never been on a non-operational station in my life! I wouldn't have withdrawn my application for the commission if I'd known they were going to muck me about like this."

"Cheer up," Nancy said philosophically. "It can't be for long, can it? Demob must surely be just around the corner. It's all over bar the shouting."

She was right, of course. Though bitter fighting was continuing, it was all swinging the Allies' way now. By mid-March they had crossed the Rhine and were storming eastwards, the German army crumbling before them.

At home, the black-out was lifted, the Home Guard disbanded, and the minds of members of the forces turned to demobilisation. Rachel knew exactly what she was going to do once she was free of the Air Force. She was going to go to London and establish herself as a freelance journalist. Already she had written a few articles and short stories for women's magazines which had been accepted. She felt strong and confident and full of hope. If she bought a house with Grandma's money, she thought, she could let a couple of rooms to ensure a small income and then she wouldn't need to get some boring nine to five job to tide her over the lean times, but could devote her time to writing.

"You're looking extraordinarily gruntled today, sweetie," said Ronnie, AC1 Ronald Havering, sashaying through the door of her office and arranging himself on the edge of her desk. "What's tickling you, may I ask?"

"Lovely after-the-war thoughts," Rachel said. She leaned her elbow on the desk, cupped her chin in her hand, and beamed at him. "What are you going to do, Ronnie?"

Ronnie rolled his eyes heavenwards.

"Don't ask. Go back to designing sets at Covent Garden, one *hopes*, but have the old hands lost their cunning, one asks oneself?"

"Of course they haven't." Rachel gave him a shove. "Go on, get off my desk and let me get to work. God, this is boring! Roll on demob."

"You ain't just whistling Dixie, sweetheart," Ronnie said in an atrocious American accent, as he sashayed out again.

Rachel laughed as she watched him go.

"I don't think he's at all funny," said Cynthia Brocklebank, the girl at the next desk who had been ostentatiously immersed in typing a report throughout this exchange, lips pressed tightly together. "I think he's disgusting."

"Really?" Rachel affected polite surprise. "What makes you say that?"

"You know perfectly well what I mean. He's one of *them*."

"Well, at least you needn't worry lest your irresistible charms send him wild with desire, need you?" she said sweetly.

Cynthia went scarlet, a shade which clashed painfully with her carrotty hair and purple lipstick. Seeing it, Rachel wrestled with her conscience for a moment, then sighed resignedly.

"Look, I'm sorry, Cynthia," she said. "I shouldn't have said that. Ronnie does camp it up, I know, but there's no harm in him. He's a good friend."

"Well, you've got a very funny taste in friends, I must say," said Cynthia, feeding more paper into her machine as if it were an offensive weapon being primed for the kill. "Very funny indeed."

In fact, coming to West Greely so late in the day as far as the war was concerned, Rachel had found it more difficult to make friends than she had done elsewhere. It was hard to rouse herself to make the effort to socialise since no kindred spirit was immediately obvious; and anyway, there was her writing. It was taking up more and more of her free time.

The lack of friends didn't bother her. Peace was coming, even if it seemed sometimes to approach at a snail's pace. By mid-April, the extent of the Nazi atrocities began to emerge as first Belsen and Buchenwald were liberated, and then, later in the month, Dachau. Newspapers were full of the horrors encountered by Allied servicemen entering the camps, and though everyone in the civilised world was aware of the details and had been sickened and revolted by the reports, Cynthia insisted on reading each one aloud at every available opportunity.

"Can't you just shut up about it for one minute," Rachel finally grated through clenched teeth, unable to get the reports and pictures out of her mind, night or day.

"Well, really!" Cynthia, once more, had taken offence. "You can't close your mind to these things."

"But you can stop behaving like a ghoul. Think of some good news. Think of the Russians capturing Berlin. The end can only be a matter of days now."

Even in the Pacific, things were looking up. At the beginning of May, Rangoon fell to the British. Rachel talked to Alice on the phone and found her in good spirits, certain that her parents would soon be leaving the camps where, separated from each other, they had been imprisoned by the Japanese. And Keith, too, now in the North Atlantic, was expected home shortly.

"Isn't it wonderful?" Alice said. "To think of the danger being over! I've never been so happy, Rachel."

The shops had been selling victory flags and bunting since the beginning of April, but it was the fifth of May before the Germans finally surrendered, and the evening of the seventh before it was officially announced that the following day would be designated Victory in Europe day.

On the morning of the seventh, Cynthia crashed into the office waving a miniature Union Jack.

"It's ever so exciting," she said. "People think it's going to be tomorrow, but nobody's certain. Whenever it is, there's going to be a bonfire in the Parade Ground and a dance at the NAAFI. They're putting out the flags now."

"Let joy be unconfined," said Ronnie, who happened to be in the office before her. His voice was flat and expressionless. Cynthia bridled. There was, Rachel thought, looking at her with interest, no other way of describing it.

"Well, you might not be glad the war's over, but others are," she said.

"Of course I'm glad, you silly mare," Ronnie said irritably, adding, in Rachel's direction: "Gordon Bennett, how can you stand it? Let's go to London to celebrate, shall we, you and me? There'll be great goings-on up there." He lowered his voice. "I'll nick one of the staff cars—"

"Ronnie, you can't!"

"Rachel, I can! There's that one that's just been repaired. It's not officially back on strength yet. Go on—be a devil, just for once. Where's the harm?"

Rachel thought about it for a moment. "Okay," she said. "Why not? I could do with a bit of excitement. I've had enough of West Greely to last a lifetime, and that's the truth."

Meeting her in the village the next morning, Ronnie waved away her persistent fears regarding the car.

"Don't give it a thought, sweetie," he said. "We're entitled to the odd perk. By the way, you won't mind if we pop in to see an old friend of mine before we join in the celebrations, will you? She was an opera singer, a fascinating old girl, loves nothing better than a party. Everyone goes there—you never know who you'll meet. She lives quite close to Covent Garden. Vida, her name is. Vida Morell. If you haven't heard of her, your parents would have done. We'll have to try and get some bottles from somewhere."

"Just so long as we don't miss the high-jinks at the Palace—"

"Lord, no, dearie. There'll be bags of time."

Traffic was light until they approached London, with no indication that this day was in any way different from any other. It was not until they approached central London that the crowds appeared, heading in the direction of Whitehall. People looked happy but dazed, as if they hardly dared believe that the fighting was over and the victory theirs. Street traders were selling flags and Churchill buttons and rosettes, and all the shopfronts were decorated with a mass of red, white and blue.

The crowds grew thicker as they drove down Piccadilly and

the Circus itself was alive with flags and bunting and the sound of a piper, dressed in his full regalia. Excitement was building. Rachel could feel it—outside, in streets, and within herself, too.

"You're quite sure we're not going to miss anything—?" Rachel asked anxiously.

"No, no! Calm yourself, sweetie. Winnie's not going to the Palace until this afternoon. Time for a few jars first."

"Your friend won't mind us just dropping in?"

"Mind? Vida mind? Of course not! I told you, she loves a party. I must get a bottle, though."

It wasn't easy. All the provision shops were temporarily open but were packed to the doors, and any form of alcohol, it appeared, was like gold dust. Ronnie finally paid the exorbitant sum of £5 for a bottle of gin ('Don't worry about it, dear," he said to Rachel. "Easy come, easy go. I had a nice little flutter on the gee-gees last week.')

Vida greeted him with rapture when finally they arrived at her dusty, velvet-draped, over-furnished flat in Floral Street. They weren't the first guests to present themselves. Already there was a large red-faced man with side-whiskers and a gin-soaked, wheezy laugh; a baby-faced sailor who greeted Ronnie with even more rapture than Vida had shown; and a Brylcreem-ed Air Force officer attached to a platinum blonde who had the largest eyes Rachel had ever seen.

The bottle of gin was welcomed as warmly as Ronnie had been, and drinks urged upon them immediately.

"No, no, it's not a *bit* too early," Vida assured Rachel, surging up to her in a flurry of black velvet and face powder. "You've a fair bit of catching up to do, my dear. Let me give you some of my fruit cup. You'll love it, I promise you."

Rachel accepted a glass with thanks, thinking that she had never seen such an odd-looking woman in her entire life. She was dressed entirely in black, and her hair, too, was dense ebony, quite straight on either side of her chalk-white face, and cut squarely in a fringe across a bony forehead. It was impossible to hazard a guess at her age, but, Rachel thought, she must be well over sixty—perhaps over seventy. Her dress had the dropped waist fashionable in the twenties, and her shoes were pointed, with fancy buckles. Her mouth was a slash of vermilion, the lipstick applied with, apparently, no reference to the actual shape of her lips.

All those present were in some way connected with the theatre, past or present—and presumably future, too, in the case of Ronnie and the sailor, introduced as Binky, and the airman and his girlfriend.

Rachel stood and sipped her drink, on the sidelines, as it were, listening to the shrieks and the gossip and the speculation; thinking how much she would prefer to be outside with the crowds, knowing what was going on, being part of the celebrations instead of shut away with this collection of oddities.

"This must be awfully boring for you," said the airman, strolling languidly across to join her. "Let me top you up."

"No, I really think—oh," she realised it was too late for protests. "Thank you. What's in this, do you know?"

The airman winked. He had a long face with delicately modelled lips that twitched with amusement.

"Vida's secret recipe. Goes down a treat, doesn't it? Cheers."

"Cheers. I always feel a bit wary about these mixed-up things—"

"I always thought WAAFS were a tough breed. Don't disappoint me, I beg you." He extended a limp hand. "Neil's the name, by the way. Neil Faraday. Remember it, won't you? It'll be up in lights before too long."

He smiled at her, holding her hand overlong, and she smiled back at him, recognising the tactics as those of a professional charmer. But at least he was talking to her. Another couple had arrived—a short, Italian-looking man with his plump wife—to be greeted by screams of welcome from Vida and warm embraces all round.

"Recognise him?" Neil asked, with a jerk of his head towards the short, dark man. "That's Enrico Rinaldi—"

"The tenor? Goodness me." In some surprise, Rachel saw Rinaldi throw his arms around Ronnie. How, she wondered, did a set designer come to be on these sort of terms with an operatic star of such magnitude?

She voiced her astonishment to Neil, who winked.

"Our Ronnie has friends in high places," he said. "Never underestimate Ronnie. How do you come to know him, by the way?"

"We work together. We're both at West Greely, in the Transport Section. What about you?"

"Oh, I'm on Lancs. Chilbury. Hey, you're empty again. Let me give you a refill."

This time she made no protest. Chilbury. Dared she ask? Just how he was—that's all she wanted to know. Stupid, really—Gavin must surely have moved from Chilbury years ago. The chances of this man knowing him were negligible.

She took a sip of her new drink, giving herself courage.

"I don't suppose," she said after a moment, "that you came across a friend of mine? Gavin Rossiter?"

His response was immediate.

"I should say I did!" He shook his head. "Poor old Gav—yes, I knew him well. It was a damned shame—"

Rachel stared at him. Her face felt strangely stiff.

"He—he's dead?"

"Didn't you know? It must have been about—ooh, three or four months ago, I suppose. He'd actually left Chilbury. He was training, not flying ops. any more. Some bloody incompetent fool wrote him off—and himself too, of course. Damn shame, when you think of all the missions he did over Germany—here, are you all right? D'you want to sit down? Drink up, and I'll get you another."

"No, really—you're very kind. I'm all right. It was a shock, that's all. I thought—I thought he'd come through."

The dull morning had given way now to sunshine. Dust motes danced in the shaft of light that filtered between the looped velvet curtains. Rachel looked around the room, at the faded striped wallpaper and the gilt-framed pictures and the heavy mahogany furniture, all dulled with dust and hazy with cigarette smoke. More people were arriving, shrieking, embracing. None of it seemed real. Perhaps it was a dream, she thought. Perhaps this wasn't happening. Perhaps all these strident, gesticulating people and the white-faced witch were figments of her imagination.

Time seemed to contract and expand. How long had they been there? How many of these deceptively harmless drinks had she downed? She found herself unable to guess.

Neil was talking, bringing the girl with the eyes across to meet her. Pamela, her name was. She was a dancer, he said.

"Chorus," Pamela elaborated. "Back row, more's the pity."

"Not for long, darling," Neil assured her, and put another drink in Rachel's hand. "Pam's terrific," he said. "Absolutely terrific. I'm willing to bet any money—"

"I must go," Rachel said, interrupting him. "I must get out of here—get some air."

She found herself out on the street, heard someone call her name, and saw Ronnie hurrying after her.

"What's up, sweetie?" he asked. "You look like death."

"I needed some air."

"And something to eat, I should think. It's well past anybody's lunch time. Let's see if we can get something."

But it was so far past lunch time that they walked all the way to Trafalgar Square without finding anywhere still open, even going as far as the Coventry Street Corner House. That had such a long queue it seemed unlikely that anyone joining it at that late stage would ever gain entry.

They bought packets of crisps and sat on the steps of the National Gallery to eat them, looking down on the milling crowds in Trafalgar Square—at the lions, draped with revellers, and the hurdy-gurdy that played on, at roistering servicemen and women, at all the old and young, rich and poor, who had come to celebrate.

Rachel felt detached from it all. Poor Ronnie, she thought. She ought to give him some explanation. But somehow the words wouldn't allow themselves to be spoken.

"We ought to get up to the Palace," Ronnie said. "There's bound to be a terrific crowd there. About four, they say they'll come out on the balcony."

In the distance, the chimes of Big Ben could be heard, striking three. There was a crackling and a strange whistling sound from a loudspeaker somewhere out of sight towards St. Martin-in-the-Fields, and then Churchill's unmistakable voice could be heard.

"Yesterday at 2:41 a.m. the representative of the German High Command and Government, General Jodl, signed the act of unconditional surrender of all German land, sea and air forces. Hostilities will end at one minute past midnight tonight—"

For Rachel, the rest passed unheeded as silent tears streamed unchecked down her face.

"Hey!" Ronnie put his arm round her. "Brace up, sweetie. We all feel like shedding a little tear, you know. Patriotism *does* that, don't you find? I've only got to hear the distant strains of 'Land of Hope and Glory' to utterly dissolve, but *utterly*!" Tenderly he wiped her eyes with his handkerchief—fine linen, Rachel noticed despite her tears, and exquisitely laundered. "Time to foot it featly down the Mall and cheer the great man in the flesh, not to mention Kingy and Queeny and the adorable princesses. Tell you what—" He reached into his pocket and pulled out a hip-flask. "I was keeping this for emergencies. Have a swig, sweetie. It'll work wonders."

"Will it?" Rachel felt doubtful. She also felt that she had consumed quite enough alcohol—but maybe Ronnie was right. Anything was worth trying. His day would be ruined as well as hers, if she didn't pull herself together pretty rapidly.

She did, indeed, feel better after the prescribed swig; better, but strange, as if she were walking several inches off the ground. Things were slightly out of focus, softened round the edges— and that seemed to include the news about Gavin, too, for suddenly the sadness was cushioned. It was only what he had expected, she thought. Looking back, it seemed as if he had always known it would end like this.

They were so far to the back of the crowd outside the palace that the figures of those on the balcony were like manikins— recognisable as the King and Queen and Winston Churchill, with Princess Elizabeth in ATS uniform, and Princess Margaret dressed in blue, but so distant as to appear unreal.

Rachel and Ronnie were standing among a group of sailors, who were loud and bawdy and very funny. Rachel found herself laughing as helplessly as she had cried not long before.

But this isn't *me*, she found herself thinking. Where am I? What am I doing?

After a while, they moved off to Whitehall in answer to the rumour which said that Churchill would appear on the balcony of one of the Government office buildings to address the crowd. The sailors came too, joining them in a long, linked, unruly line to dance the Palais Glide, all the way across the park to Horse Guards.

Whitehall was already packed, but somehow they managed to sidle through the crowd to get close to the Ministry of Health, said to be the chosen building and now surrounded on two sides by a dense crowd. One of the sailors—the tallest and the brawniest, whose name, he told her, was Fred—grabbed Rachel's arm and pulled her over to the pavement directly opposite the building.

"Come on, boys—lift her up on my shoulders," he shouted to the others.

"No—I can't—oh!—" She was up there, swaying a little as Fred adjusted to her weight, and laughing wildly at the precariousness of her position.

The view was wonderful from this vantage point. She could see the balcony opposite, and crowds stretching all along Whitehall from Trafalgar Square at one end to Parliament Square at the other. The noise was unbelievable, like nothing she had ever heard before—a kind of soughing susurration as of a great wind, sweeping from one end of the thoroughfare to the other and erupting into a giant roar as Churchill and a group of other dignitaries came out on to the balcony.

Everyone was cheering as they recognised the face of the man who had for so long been the inspiration of the entire nation; the noise so great that it seemed the whole of London must be uniting in this one, overwhelming outburst of adulation.

The sudden silence that followed was equally stunning as the crowd waited to hear his words. I must remember this, Rachel thought to herself, owlishly wise. This is important. This is history. If only she didn't feel as if her head belonged to someone else! It seemed such a waste of a wonderful occasion.

"This is *your* victory—" Churchill began, in those gravelly, unmistakable tones, the rest of the sentence lost as the roar erupted again.

The crowd loved him and interrupted him constantly with cheers, but at last, with a final "God bless you all," he was gone.

Rachel was gently lowered to the ground.

"Thanks, Fred," she said, clutching at him, feeling her head swim. "I reckon I had the best view in London."

It was then that she looked around for Ronnie, only to discover that he was nowhere in sight.

"He was next to me coming through the park," one of the

sailors said. "Reckon he got detached in the crowd, some-where."

They looked for him for a few moments, but it was clearly hopeless; in any case, Rachel wasn't at all sure that she wanted to find him. He'd said earlier that he intended going back to Vida's flat later on, which was a prospect that filled her with horror. She thought longingly of Alice and the house in Shaw-cross Street, and of the feeling of sanctuary she knew she would find there. She'd take a taxi—

"You'll never get one, love," Fred said. "Stick with us! We're going to look for some fish and chips."

Her stomach churned with hunger at the thought of it. But they didn't find a fish shop. They didn't even look for one until they had made several attempts to climb Nelson's column.

By this time an hysterical gaiety had them all in its grip. Fred persuaded Rachel that it would be a criminal act to leave the festivities now—what would she tell her grandchildren when they asked what she'd done to celebrate the end of the war, and she said she went home and had an early night?

So she stayed, and was hoisted to sit on one of the lions, from where she conducted a spirited rendition of "There'll Always be an England"; and once back on the ground, she sang and she danced. All the way down the Strand she danced, three sailors to her left, and three to her right, all arm-in-arm; but then, suddenly, they too were gone and she was dancing with two American GIs, one of which she recognised as having perched next to her on Nelson's lion.

"Say, baby," he said. "You're great! You should be in pic-tures, you know that? D'you want a drink?"

"I want some *food*," Rachel said; and was grateful for the chocolate bar he produced.

He produced beer, too, which they shared around sitting on some office steps close to where a huge bonfire was blazing in the middle of the road, its sparks flying heavenwards.

"Gee, I'm glad I'm here, gee I'm glad I'm here," his friend kept repeating like a mantra, a wide, blissful smile on his face.

"Gee, he's glad he's here," the other said to Rachel. He moved a little closer. "Say, you're cute, d'you know that? My name's Chuck. What's yours, baby?"

"I don't think I can remember." Unsteadily, Rachel got to

her feet and pointed dramatically. "Is that a taxi I see before me, handle towards my hand?"

"Come again?"

"I want a taxi. Please, please Chuck, get me that taxi!"

"No, gee, don't leave us—"

She ran towards the taxi, but was beaten at the last minute by a city gentleman in striped trousers and bowler hat who was driven off in triumph in the direction of Leicester Square. She turned, despairing, to find that Chuck had followed her.

"I must go," she said. "I must find a taxi." And to her intense shame, she found she was crying again.

"Aw, come on, honey—" Chuck was embarrassed by her tears.

"I'm sorry, I'm sorry." Rachel delved into her pockets and found her handkerchief. "Don't worry about me. I must get a taxi—"

"There's one!"

Anxious now to speed her on her way, Chuck lunged across the street and hung on to the door of a cab which was just being paid off, turning to snarl threats at yet another GI who was attempting to wrest it from him.

"It's for the lady," he shouted. "C'mon, baby—get in."

Thankfully, Rachel did so and gave the Shawcross Street address. The cabby was talkative. What a day! he said over and over. What a day! She wouldn't believe some of the sights he'd seen.

Rachel could see two of him. She closed her eyes, then opened them again quickly, putting out a hand to steady herself as the whole world seemed to rock sideways. She'd never felt like this before—never so out of control, so helpless and miserable.

"The world is dark," she found herself saying in sepulchral tones, at which the cabby turned round and looked at her anxiously.

"We'll soon get you home, love," he said. "Nearly there. Look, this is Sloane Square. Nearly there."

She was drunk. Pressed into the corner of the cab she faced the fact, and was ashamed. What on earth would Susan think of her? And Alice? VE day was no excuse, nor was the news about Gavin. She had seen this coming, felt herself slipping away from reality, and had done nothing. The day had somehow gathered momentum, run away with her. It seemed to pass before her eyes in a series of pictures: Vida's flat, sitting on the steps with Ronnie, meeting the sailors outside the Palace, dancing across the park. Had any of it happened?

"Here we are, love," the cabby said, in the rallying tone used exclusively for drunkards or the mentally unstable. "That'll be five-and-six."

She gave him a pound note and turned towards the house, collecting herself for the walk across the pavement, ignoring the cabbie's attempt, admittedly halfhearted, to present her with the change. She took a breath. Perhaps, she thought, if she exercised great care, they wouldn't know—

Slowly and deliberately she walked towards the house and rang the bell. Alice would be glad to see her, she told herself, as she waited for an answer to her ring. Alice would welcome her, in spite of her shameful condition. Alice was a good friend. An old friend. Old friends forgave things.

But it was not Alice who opened the door; nor Susan. She stood transfixed, sure she must be hallucinating, that this was just one more surreal happening in a totally surreal day.

"Mr. Rossiter!" she said faintly.

"Rachel, my dear!" He reached out both arms to welcome her inside. "What a wonderful surprise—and just when I was feeling so lonely, too!"

"Alice—?" began Rachel.

"Alice has rushed down to Southampton. She had a phone call from Keith this morning to say he'd just put into port. And Susan's in France—"

She put a hand to her head and swayed a little.

"I was hoping to stay the night. I'd better go."

"Nonsense, nonsense!" He was all kindness, all benevolence. "Susan would never forgive me. The room next to mine is always known as Rachel's room. Besides—" He gave a low, indulgent chuckle. "It doesn't look to me, my dear, as if you're in any fit state to go anywhere."

"I didn't expect—what are you *doing* here, Mr. Rossiter?"

"Living here, pro tem. Come into the kitchen. I'm just getting myself some food—nothing much, just bread and cheese, but I've a bottle of champagne to wash it down. I was going out after I'd had a bite, just to find a bit of life in town, but how much better to share an evening like this with an old friend."

When she made no reply, he took her by the shoulders and laughed again, looking into her face.

"How you've changed," he said. "You're quite the little glamourpuss, aren't you? But what have you been up to, you bad girl?" Humorously he chided her. "Just as well your sainted grandmother can't see you now—"

Her only reply was a sob.

"Hey, come on! It's not as bad as that. You can be forgiven! It is VE Day, after all—"

"Oh, Mr. Rossiter!"

Her head dropped to his shoulder as the tears overwhelmed her, sobs coming from deep within her, racking and painful. She was a child again, helpless in her grief, all her defences stripped away. He held her even closer, stroked her hair, lifted her chin.

"Darling child, what is it?" he asked her, his voice caressing. He sounded so kind, so concerned. He kissed her gently. "There, there, nothing can be as bad as this."

"It's Gavin," she managed to say at last. "I've only just heard."

﹛ NINETEEN ﹜

Rachel, in the unfamiliar, narrow bed in Tess's room, lay sleepless, remembering.

She had put the past behind her, built a new life. Brooding and blaming seemed an unproductive exercise, destructive both to herself and to Tess; but this night, with Alannah's words ringing in her ears, the memories came whether she wanted them or not.

They were dim and fragmented. She could remember sobbing on Hugh Rossiter's shoulder, and the warmth of his arms around her. He hadn't kissed her again. Not then. For a while he had held her and stroked her hair; but then, all at once, his paternal tenderness had turned into something else—and she had responded. She had to admit that.

She had responded!

She had opened her mouth to him, wound her arms around him, strained close to him. Why? Why?

That memory faded, and another emerged. The bedroom. Walls tilting, advancing, receding. Hands—experienced hands—taking off her clothes; and a voice, full of tenderness, soothing, reassuring, laughing a little at her helplessness.

She had protested then. She was sure, afterwards, that she had protested, and remained sure. The voice went on.

"So lovely! Darling child, you've become a beauty! How can I resist you? Don't blame me for wanting you. Let me love you, let me kiss you—here, and here. You want it too! Darling child, you know you do."

And the panic, and the weight of him, and the sinking into nothingness. And the waking next day to a hammering head and a dry, foul-tasting mouth and the rush of horrified remembrance.

She'd taken a bath—had scrubbed herself as if she never could get clean; had drunk coffee and eaten cornflakes; and all the time there was this sick weight in her stomach compounded of shame and anger and fear. Slumped at the kitchen table, unable to rouse herself to move, her eye had fallen on an envelope on which her name was written. She picked it up and studied it. She had never seen his writing before. It was graceful, artistic; an architect's hand, of course.

"Darling little Rachel," he had written.

"I have to be off to Warnfield at the crack of dawn this morning, so am writing to say bless you, sweet child. You made a tired, lonely old desk-warrior very happy!

"Last night was a wonderful experience that must remain our secret. I know you will understand, and hope that you will sometimes think of me with affection."

Affection! Almost two years later the bitterness was as great as it had ever been; and the shame. How could she? she thought now as she had thought then. After all, she had been no child, whatever Hugh Rossiter had chosen to call her. Who would have thought that a twenty-four-year-old WAAF sergeant could have been so stupid?

She forced herself to breathe deeply and slowly. It was pointless to dwell on it, all over again—but how right she was to want to keep clear of all Rossiters, when only a few hours in the company of one of their number made her feel like this!

Think of something else, she urged herself. Think of Stefan; increasingly, it was hard to imagine how any other man could ever have attracted her. Think of the book, now forging ahead satisfactorily. Think of Tess, so bright and pretty and happy. Like Diana? Oh, God, no! She'd never grow up like Diana. Rachel herself would see that she didn't. What about heredity, then?

To hell with heredity, Rachel thought as she had thought so many times before. Tess wouldn't have a mother like Mrs. Rossiter, would she? A mother who would take every opportunity of underlining at all times her superiority over lesser mortals.

The urge to smash that superiority was as strong as ever. How sweet revenge would be! Imagine admitting the truth to Alannah—showing her, once and for all, what a sham it was, this ideal, loving family façade that she had always flaunted.

It wouldn't be difficult. She was halfway there already; could even, possibly, have worked it out for herself in the still watches of the night. She might be unintelligent, but she wasn't *that* unintelligent.

Oh yes, Rachel thought. Revenge would be sweet. The truth would wipe the smug, self-satisfied smiles from their faces for ever. In particular, Mrs. Rossiter's face.

Carina Rossiter. Rachel said the name over to herself. Hers was the blame. She it was who had encouraged the narcissism that had resulted in the unnatural love between Gavin and Diana. She had forced Barney into art college, saddling him with her own ambitions which he was incapable of achieving. She had made Alannah into the self-regarding creature she was.

As for her own life, there was no end to the misery Carina Rossiter had caused. And now, with the supreme egotism of which only a Rossiter was capable, she had invited Rachel back into the fold; until, of course, the next time she offended. Then, no doubt, there would be another withdrawal of approval, another tirade of abuse.

How sadly, Rachel thought, would Carina Rossiter shake her head when told by Alannah that she had an illegitimate child, that she was a Fallen Woman, a suitable subject for charity and pained regret. Would she say that it was inevitable, given her insecure background? Given *that* kind of mother? Thank God her sons had escaped marriage to such a creature, she would say.

Oh yes, Rachel thought. There was no doubt about it. Revenge would be sweet indeed.

She slept at last and woke to the sound of Tess singing to the pink rabbit and making all the unselfconscious Tess-noises that her mother delighted to hear. The wind had lessened and although it was not fully light, it was possible to see that the clouds were much higher and lighter. It was still very cold.

Shivering, she gathered up her clothes and Tess's, and took her downstairs so that they could wash and dress in the warmth of the kitchen.

It was many months since she had relived that night in Shawcross Street. She'd had the sense to see that bitterness was destructive, that she had to turn her face to the future, and she had done so. Now, however, the disgust and panic had come flooding back; and much as she tried to concentrate on Tess's needs, the past had her in its grip and refused to let go.

Rachel remembered the revulsion; the panic when she realised she was pregnant, the fluttering disbelief. She had drunk gin, jumped down steps, taken hot baths—had even contemplated abortion, but was frightened by the tales she had heard and unsure how to go about it.

So the baby had stayed. She had left the WAAF, bought her house in London, and with Nancy's help had coped with the sneering looks of other women at the antenatal clinic, and the cold, brisk patronage of medical staff. There was one nurse in particular—

Oh, why remember? She had Tess.

"You have a lovely little girl, Mrs. Bond," they said—for all mothers were given the courtesy title of Mrs., with or without a ring—and Tess had been wrapped in a blanket and given to her then and there, still unwashed. And Rachel had looked at her and loved her, and wept with joy at her perfection and with relief that the ordeal was over, and she had vowed then and there that nothing and nobody would take this child away from her.

Lost in her thoughts, absentmindedly feeding Tess, it dawned on her that the sound she had heard and disregarded a few moments before was probably the sound of the mail arriving. She left it until Tess had finished the last spoonful, then went to investigate. Unhurriedly, still lost in the past.

And there it was. The long-awaited air-letter from Uganda—and in her father's hand. Her heart sank a little. Her father had only ever written on important occasions; stilted, pedantic little notes to congratulate her on passing an exam, or perhaps to accompany a birthday cheque. It was her mother who had fired off the chatty, inconsequential letters that had kept her in touch over the years. This, she knew before she had touched it, was written because this was an important occasion and he had something momentous to say.

She could hardly bring herself to open it. She brought it through to the kitchen and put it down on the table while she peeled and cut up an apple for Tess, just as if the letter had no significance. Her heart was racing, high up in her breast, almost in her throat. Suppose—suppose—

She snatched at it, possessed suddenly of an impatience to know the worst, and tore it open, holding her breath. Then, slowly, as she read, she gave a long, relieved sigh.

"My dearest Rachel,

"We have only just returned from a month's safari to find your letter waiting for us. By mistake it came by sea-mail, which explains the long delay.

"I cannot pretend that your news was not the greatest shock to us—but oh, my poor child, our hearts go out to you! You may have acted unwisely, but in our view you have paid the price and both your mother and I are sad-dened by the thought of all you must have been through, all without the support of your family.

"Whether you were wise to elect to bring Tess up on your own rather than agree to adoption may be debatable but I cannot do other than say it shows a degree of courage which I find admirable. Why, I wonder, did you not find the courage to tell us at the time? I suppose I can under-stand your trepidation, but surely you know that though we may not approve of everything you do, and though due to circumstances we have been unable to be as close over the years as we may have wished, you are our much-loved daughter and will never be any other.

Oh, dear of him, dear of him, Rachel thought in the Cornish vernacular. A little pompous, a little pedantic, but loving too, his heart in the right place. How could she have doubted him?

"Your mother, is writing to you at greater length. There are so many questions she wants to ask and comments to make, but I thought, in view of the long delay in response to your letter, that I must get this off at once.

"Today we received notification that we have confirmed passages on the *Dunottar Castle*, sailing on 3rd March via the Cape, arriving Tilbury on 5th April. We shall indeed look forward to seeing spring in Cornwall, as well as meet-ing our granddaughter. And of course, our excitement at the thought of seeing you again after so long cannot be expressed.

He signed it "Your always affectionate father," and added a P.S.

"Be prepared for some criticism of your choice of name. Your mother apparently was taught by a nun called Sister Theresa long years ago, and has hated the name ever since! I cannot help but disagree. I consider the diminutive, Tess, quite charming."

Rachel leaned back and laughed at this. Of course there would be criticism, she thought; and questions and comments. There was not the smallest doubt that there would be arguments, too, that she and her mother wouldn't always see eye to eye. But it really didn't matter. That was the most important thing of all. It didn't matter. It didn't alter anything. None of them were perfect, but it didn't stop them being a family, and a loving one at that. Stefan hadn't been impossibly idealistic after all.

"You look as if you're in good spirits," Alannah said, coming in at that moment.

"Yes. I've just had a letter from my father. They're coming home very soon."

"They can't be too pleased about your current situation."

"They're living with it," Rachel said. She got up, folded the letter and stuck it behind a plate on the dresser. "What can I get you for breakfast? I've plenty of eggs. I get them from a farm at the top of the hill."

"God no! I couldn't face eggs. Just coffee, please." Alannah sat down heavily. "I had a simply frightful night," she said.

Rachel looked at her. She had no makeup on, and looked pale and plain, with dark circles under her eyes.

"Was it the wind?" she asked. "We get an awful lot, I'm afraid."

"No," Alannah said heavily. "It wasn't the wind. Not altogether, anyway. I was doing some thinking. Putting two and two together. Rachel, you've got to be honest with me."

"Hang on—I'll give Tess her drink. Here you are, sweetie— yum-yum-yum."

"Will you *please* stop the baby-talk and pay attention to me for once? Rachel, listen! I've got to know! Just as I was going to sleep, it suddenly came to me. Dad spent VE day in Shawcross Street. He told us. I was at home the day after when he came back to Warnfield. He said that there were things to clear up at the office in the morning, so he thought he might as well stay in London and see what was going on, but it was all such a scrum that he went back to Shawcross Street and listened to it all on the wireless.''

"Very sensible," Rachel said, still attending to Tess, her face hidden.

"But was he with you? That's what I want to know. Turn round and look at me, Rachel. Was he with you?"

Sweet, sweet revenge, Rachel thought. With one word, it could be mine. She's handed it to me on a plate.

She thought of her misery and bewilderment when she was made an outcast, blamed for Gavin's decision to go to Spain. The constant belittlement, the remarks that suggested that she was unloved, the lack of support in the greatest crisis of her life.

And she thought of Hugh Rossiter. Of how she had turned to him for comfort and he had taken advantage of her helpless, drunken misery.

Words, she thought, couldn't begin to describe what she thought of Hugh Rossiter.

She took a deep breath.

"No, Alannah," she said. "I spent VE night with a group of sailors and two GIs. So there you have my sordid story."

"Oh!" Alannah drew the exclamation out, as if now she understood, all questions answered. "So that's it! An American!"

Sorry, Chuck, Rachel said to herself. It's a far, far, better thing you do—

"An American with blue eyes," Rachel lied. What did one more lie matter? Or perhaps it wasn't a lie. She couldn't remember noticing Chuck's eyes. "So could we leave this entire subject, please?"

"Well, I knew it couldn't be Daddy, really," Alannah went on. "I mean, he wouldn't, would he? You're younger than his own daughter. And anyway—well, when you think how devoted he and Ma have always been it simply wouldn't make sense for him to look at another woman, particularly at—well, I mean to say, he just wouldn't, would he? Put everything in danger, I mean. Because it would absolutely kill Ma if she thought he'd been unfaithful. Not that he would be."

"Of course not," Rachel agreed.

Suddenly she felt radiant with happiness, as if a weight had been lifted from her, as if all the anger and bitterness and fear and regret had rolled away. And the envy, she reminded herself. That had gone, too—gone for ever. Why should she envy anyone? It was her own imperfect family that had stood the test, wasn't it?

"The wind has dropped. I think it's going to be a nice day," she said; and at that moment the front doorbell rang.

"Oh, my God!" Alannah crashed her cup down in its saucer. "That'll be Terry, and I haven't got my face on yet. Stall him for me, there's an angel." She fled upstairs, leaving Rachel to answer the door. But it wasn't Terry. It was Stefan, and he was smiling.

"I could not wait to see you," he said simply. "I caught night train."

"Oh, Stefan!" It seemed only natural that she should reach out to greet him, and in a moment he was over the threshold and in her arms. "It's so good to have you back," she said as they hugged each other. "But I'm not ready—I'm a mess—"

He drew away a little and looked at her, then bent his head and kissed her cheeks and lips and the tip of her nose.

"You are not mess, you are beautiful!" His expression was tender, full of love. "I changed my mind. Second thoughts, yes? I was impatient. There seemed no point to sleep in hotel, so I sleep on train—arrived at six this morning. I stop off at apartment for wash and shave. Joe is thinking I come tomorrow for work, not today, so I come straight to see you. Is so much to tell you. And to ask you."

Smiling he looked into her eyes; then bit his lip and shook his head, as if in doubt.

"Oh, Rachel. I hope, I hope. Please may I hope?"

Yes, yes, *yes*, she longed to shout, but unaccountably she felt close to tears—she, who hadn't cried for so long, who was too strong for tears, who despised them. Yet she could feel them now, swelling her throat, filling her eyes.

"You weep?" Stefan asked, surprised and dismayed. He held her close then and she could feel his lips on her hair.

"With happiness," she said, luxuriating in it for a moment.

"Then I may hope?"

"It depends what you're hoping for," she said softly, looking up into his eyes, reaching to lay her hand against his face. "I hope, too—but Stefan—" she pulled away from him, sniffed a little and wiped her eyes, smiling at him, at her own foolishness. "Alannah's upstairs, that friend I told you about. She'll be going in a minute."

"Then all can wait until then. So much I have to tell you! And all so good."

"Me, too. Stefan, my father wrote. It's just as you said. They forgive me."

He tightened his arms round her and held her close once more.

"Didn't I say? They love you. I love you. You are much loved.'

"And you," she whispered, as he bent to kiss her. There were no tears now; just a blissful sense of homecoming and rightness, and a silent but soaring trumpet-song of joy.

"Where's my Tess?" he said at last.

"In the kitchen, in her chair."

He went through, and plucked Tess out of the high chair, holding her aloft at arms' length while she squealed with delight.

"She's missed you, Stefan." Rachel said.

"Ah!" He lowered Tess and held her in his arms, ducking his head as she made a grab for his hair. "I, too, have missed her. But no more. No more partings, yes?"

Alannah came back into the room at this point, hair shining and her makeup freshly applied. Rachel introduced her to Stefan who, despite holding Tess, managed to acknowledge the introduction by one of his exotic, courteous bows.

"Miss Rossiter," he said. "I am honoured."

He had bought himself a new coat in London, a fawn-coloured, military-type mackintosh, and he wore it with great style over a dark-blue high-necked sweater. He looked, Rachel thought, rather dashing, a touch piratical. Alannah clearly was impressed and could barely conceal her astonishment that Rachel—poor, poor Rachel, always such an object of compassion—should attract a man such as this. It was, Rachel thought, one of the more satisfactory moments of her entire life.

Alannah flashed her best smile, fluttered her lashes.

"I'm so glad to have had the chance to meet you," she said.

"You know, Rachel and I have been friends for a long, long time—how long is it, Rachel?"

"Ages," Rachel said.

The doorbell rang once more, and she went to answer it. This time it was Terry, who was much as she had imagined from Alannah's description. He was untidily dressed, with thinning hair straggling over his collar, but might, she thought, have been quite good-looking in a raffish kind of way were it not for the bad-tempered scowl on his face.

"Is Alannah ready?" he asked peremptorily, not wasting time on polite greetings. His voice was attractive, she had to admit that. Probably behind footlights, made-up, playing a part someone else had written for him, he would have a certain charm. Right now, however, the charm was somewhat difficult to discern.

He was annoyed and impatient, and didn't mind showing it, acknowledging Alannah's introduction with an ungracious nod, hardly bothering to speak to Rachel at all but addressing all his remarks to Alannah.

"These bloody lanes! I've been stuck behind a farm tractor for miles. Couldn't pass anywhere. I could have been back in Truro an hour ago if I hadn't had to make this detour."

"Rachel." Alannah embraced her and held her for a moment. "It's been wonderful to see you, and your lovely, lovely baby. Thanks for putting me up."

"I'm glad you came," Rachel said; finding, rather to her astonishment, that she meant it. Stefan, it seemed, wasn't the only one who had been engaged in exorcism. "I hope that everything works out all right with Barney."

"Come *on*, Alannah," Terry called, down in the street now and waiting impatiently beside the car.

"I must go. Thanks again."

"Goodbye."

They watched her go, Rachel with Stefan beside her, and Tess in his arms. They waved. Then, when the car was gone, they closed the door and went back to the kitchen.

Like a family, Rachel thought.